About Cathryn Hein

Cathryn Hein is a popular author of rural romance and romantic adventure novels, a Romance Writers of Australia Romantic Book of the Year finalist, and a regular Australian Romance Reader Awards finalist. A South Australian country girl by birth, Cathryn loves nothing more than a rugged rural hero who's as good with his heart as he is with his hands, which is probably why she writes them! Her romances are warm and emotional, and feature themes that don't flinch from the tougher side of life but are often happily tempered by the antics of naughty animals. Her aim is to make you smile, sigh, and perhaps sniffle a little, but most of all feel wonderful. Cathryn lives in Newcastle, Australia with her partner of many years, Jim. When she's not writing, she plays golf (ineptly), cooks (well), and in football season barracks (rowdily) for her beloved Sydney Swans AFL team. Sign up to Cathryn's newsletter at cathrynhein.com for exclusive access to her collection of free short stories, plus all the news on upcoming book releases, exclusive content, giveaways and more. You can also connect via Facebook and Instagram.

Also by Cathryn Hein

The Country Girl
Wayward Heart
The French Prize

The
GRAZIER'S
SON

Cathryn
Hein

FICTION
HQ

The Grazier's Son
© 2024 by Cathryn Hein
ISBN 9781867299363

First published on Gadigal Country in Australia in 2024
by HQ Fiction
an imprint of HQBooks (ABN 47 001 180 918), a subsidiary of HarperCollins
Publishers Australia Pty Limited (ABN 36 009 913 517)

HarperCollins acknowledges the Traditional Custodians of the lands upon which
we live and work, and pays respect to Elders past and present.

A catalogue record for this book is available from the National Library of Australia
www.librariesaustralia.nla.gov.au

Printed and bound in Australia by McPherson's Printing Group

MIX
Paper | Supporting
responsible forestry
FSC
www.fsc.org FSC® C001695

For Jim

Chapter One

In the end, the grave wasn't hard to find. It lay in the shadow of the tallest, most ostentatious monument in the cemetery, as dark, plain and flat as its neighbour was lofty, light and gaudy. The slab sported a single ugly embellishment—a coarse brown block erupting from its polished granite surface. Where the epitaph should have read 'Rest in Peace' someone had stuck a clumsily engraved hunk of brick over 'Peace' to make the epitaph read 'Rest in Hell'.

Shoulders hunched against the early morning cold and fists deep into the pockets of his leathers, Stirling brooded over it for a moment. Then, using the heel of his boot, he hacked at the block. The jarring impact travelled up his right leg and across and shot pain down his left hip. Yet another reminder.

He grunted and scratched his jaw. Whoever had put the block in place meant business. A chisel and hammer and a bit of oomph should do it. Next time.

If there was a next time.

He looked east, to where the fiery tip of the rising sun was creeping over the horizon and slinking rays across the cemetery.

Thick cobwebs of fog hung sluggish in the hollows. Here and there, a few surviving manna gums were glazed in crowns of orange, while further afield, the grey-white fleeces of grazing sheep glowed like ghosts.

It was weird how beautiful he found this place of the dead. But in his experience, the most breathtaking lands were often the most haunted.

Stirling regarded the slab once more. Dougal Benjamin Kildare, a man he'd never met.

A man who was also his father.

He supposed he should feel something, except what? Sorrow? Anger? Regret? How could you feel anything for someone you never knew? And if the allegations were true, someone he wouldn't want to know.

Except he did. Faults and all, Stirling wanted to know this man. Because maybe, just maybe, doing so might help him find himself.

⁂

To his bemusement, there were quite a few cars about in Grassmoor, then Stirling remembered that this was the country. Most people weren't like him, driven out of bed by pain or a churning mind. They rose early as a matter of course. He found a park in the main street near the same cafe where he'd scored an early dinner the evening before and reversed his road bike in. He swung his leg carefully over the seat, plucked off his helmet and headed inside.

Joanne, the proprietor, greeted him with warmth and a little surprise, while the pretty younger girl—Milly? Ellie?—eyed him beneath lowered lashes from behind the espresso machine.

He ordered the 'big breakfast' and asked for a pot of English breakfast tea instead of coffee. Milly-Ellie might be pretty, but he'd learned last night that she wasn't much of a barista.

'Back again,' said Joanne, sliding the payment terminal towards him. 'You must like it here.'

Stirling made a throaty noise that could have been interpreted as anything. He didn't know what to make of Grassmoor yet, except that it was proudly tidy, had a few historic buildings, and so far seemed friendly enough. If you didn't count the 'Hell' brick.

'How was the motel?'

'Fine.'

'Busy day ahead?'

'Probably.'

Joanne twitched with frustration at his blunt answers. Curiosity burned behind her eyes. Grassmoor was a small town tucked into the far western corner of Victoria. Everyone was interested in a stranger.

Stirling thought again about the 'Hell' brick and wondered which camp Joanne stood in. What did it matter? She could think what she liked. Stirling would make up his own mind about Dougal Kildare.

He waved off the receipt and headed for the same seat next to the front window that he'd chosen yesterday. He busied himself with his phone, checking emails and the news, his posture not inviting conversation. Not that he was likely to get any. Only two other tables were occupied. A couple in their thirties sat stiffly at one, gazes flinty as they tried to keep their argument hushed. An elderly man wearing a tweed coat and matching cap sat at another, making no pretence to hide his interest in Stirling.

Stirling smiled as he spotted a message from Olympia. He left it unopened, saving it for when he'd need cheering up later. There were others from friends, a couple more from acquaintances, asking how he was doing. A few tentative inquiries about when he might come back to work, and even more tentatively, if he *would* come back. His mum had sent an email too. Another for later.

Stirling rubbed at his hip, wishing he had a few painkillers to ease the ache.

Milly-Ellie arrived with his tea. 'Ready for a big day in Grassmoor?'

'Something like that.'

'At least the weather's nice.' She laid out the pot, a cup and saucer and a mini stainless-steel jug of milk. 'Are you here for business or pleasure?'

'Business.'

'Oh yeah? Who with?'

'It's a what, not a who.' He watched Milly-Ellie closely. 'Westwind.'

'Is that a farm?'

He nodded. She mustn't be a born and bred local. Or maybe she didn't care.

Stirling returned to his phone, deliberately tapping and swiping. The girl lingered a few seconds longer and took the hint.

His breakfast arrived ten minutes later. No smiles this time as Joanne hovered at the table with his plate. 'Tilly said you're visiting Westwind.' She made it sound distasteful, like he was visiting an abattoir or a murder site.

'That's right.'

'What's Westwind to do with you?'

'Everything.' Stirling held her gaze steadily. 'It's mine.'

'Yours?' Her brows were so furrowed they almost joined. 'How?'

'I inherited it.'

His breakfast tipped precariously. A few mushrooms tumbled off. 'But how?' Joanne laughed, a brittle, forced sound. 'Unless you're Dougal's ...' She trailed off as she registered Stirling's expression.

'Unless I'm Dougal Kildare's son. Which I am.'

The man in the tweed coat and cap scraped his chair back.

'Son,' Joanne repeated. She looked at his face then at the plate and practically slammed it down. Sauce from the baked beans splattered his jacket. His sausages tumbled into the fried eggs, bursting the yolks. Yellow bled across the plate.

She said nothing, any word tightly shuttered by puckered white lips. Her breath whistled as it rushed through her nose. Stirling supposed asking for salt was out of the question.

'Thanks,' he said, using his paper napkin to wipe his front before opening it out and draping it over his lap. Only when he began chewing did she finally stomp off. The old man's stare was like flint.

Stirling ate as he continued to read the news and toss occasional glances at the world outside. The rising sun mottled golden light over the town's historic buildings. It was going to be a fine late winter's day.

He finished his meal and pushed the plate away.

Tilly approached. No flirty friendliness, simply wide-eyed worry. She gathered his plate in silence, then glanced back at the counter and swallowed. 'Joanne, um, she said not to come back again.' She winced. 'Sorry.'

Stirling nodded. He'd expected as much.

He rode to the motel and parked near the reception door. Shaun, the previously affable proprietor, stood rigid behind the counter, wearing an expression like a constipated cat.

'I'd like to book another night,' said Stirling, pulling his wallet from his jacket pocket.

'No vacancy.'

Stirling cast a pointed look over the man's shoulder to where the empty carpark could be seen through the window. Grassmoor had a population of around seven hundred, no tourism industry that Stirling knew of and, being miles from any major highways, little through traffic. The motel was tiny, ten rooms at most, and there'd been few cars the previous night. Stirling could see no reason why the proprietor would turn away good money.

But that was before he'd revealed his identity at the cafe.

He eyed the man. 'Not one single room, you say?'

'Nope.' Shaun bared his teeth in what Stirling supposed was meant to be a smile. 'Sorry.'

'News travels fast,' said Stirling. Joanne must have phoned immediately after their little confrontation. He repocketed his wallet. 'I'll drop the key in the box on the way out.'

Cleaning out his room took minutes. The Ducati came with everything a road bike needed and then some, but its paniers still had limited capacity. Stirling wasn't bothered. He was a man of few possessions and used to travelling light. Besides the occasional painkiller, all he needed was some clean clothes, his laptop, toiletries and not much else.

He eased onto the bike and guided it out of the motel, pausing only to dump the key. Shaun stood in stony-faced sentry at the reception door. Stirling bet he'd watch for as long as he could, just to make sure he was truly gone.

A few turns later and he was on the road heading south to Westwind. Three kilometres out, Stirling checked his mirrors and the way ahead, and gunned it.

Controlled. Skilled. Fearless. That was him. His mettle forged from a career flying Blackhawk helicopters in the army along with five years choppering medical staff in and out of war and disaster zones for German-founded aid organisation *Medizin in Krise*. And the example of a socially minded mother whose favourite saying was 'evil triumphs when good men and women do nothing'.

Or that was what he used to be. What he was now, Stirling didn't know. Maybe today he'd find out.

The road twisted through spectacular countryside. A land of crumples and corrugations, like a Scottish landscape painting that had been balled up then half-heartedly flattened again, leaving gentler peaks and troughs than the Highlands but with views no less stunning.

Each bend brought more beauty. Ancient, hugely girthed trees, bubbling creeks, verdant paddocks grazed by glossy cattle and bright, newly shorn sheep. Through his helmet filtered the sweet scents of an approaching spring. Of lush grass and growth and fertility, and nature shaking off the cold. With the passing panorama, the sourness of his morning faded.

The odometer clocked over another kilometre. Stirling slowed the bike, his heart thudding from the adrenaline rush of the winding ride and the first glimpse of the high stone wings that formed part of Westwind's imposing entrance. A pair of double iron gates appeared. The word 'WEST' crafted in a self-important font was welded into the centre of the left gate, 'WIND' into the other.

The gates had been padlocked when he'd ridden out for a snoop the day before. He'd arrived late afternoon when the shadows were dark and stringy and the air cooling rapidly. His body ached from the long ride and Stirling had been looking forward to spending the night in the house. The solicitor taking care of the estate had organised a cleaner to tidy and air the interior and turn on the fridge. A couple of beers and a defrosting ready meal that he'd picked up from Hamilton on the way through had rattled in his paniers. Hardly a feast but enough.

His keenness had been short-lived. Though William Stoddart, the solicitor, had warned of the vandalism, the smashed finials on the villa's welcoming staircase and graffiti splattered like blood across the pink-tinted stone came as a shock. Stirling's fists had drawn tight around the handlebars, his anger throbbing more powerfully than the Ducati's engine. William had called it 'unfortunate'. For Stirling it was an outrage.

After a quick circle of the property, he'd sat on his bike staring at the silent house and surrounds and feeling like a trespasser, until finally, he'd wheeled the bike around and left. Westwind would still be there tomorrow when he wasn't so fatigued and sore from the road. A proper meal and a good night's sleep in a pub or motel would leave him less prone to the ghosts of his imagination, more able to fight if vandals revisited.

After this morning's hostilities, he was definitely up for one.

Stirling dismounted and dragged the right gate open. Its hinges squealed their protest through the quiet morning and sent a couple of topknot pigeons flapping. He'd need to sort that out if he planned to stay for a while.

He grimaced at the stone wings, both pitted and pocked where some bastard had blasted them with a shotgun. He'd seen plenty of walls like that in his life, just not in sleepy rural Australia.

Stirling remounted and steered his bike through the gate. He rode carefully, dodging potholes and avoiding the thick grass sprouting high along the drive's centre strip. The Ducati weighed over two hundred kilos and his damaged body wasn't up to righting the bike if he accidentally dropped it.

Two stands of messy pines—that would probably go up like Roman candles if they were ever caught in a fire—lined either side of the avenue. Stirling liked them though. He liked the way they formed a secret tunnel, keeping the villa concealed behind a curtain of thick green and brown until the last moment.

He eased the bike to its slowest pace and crept round the final turn with his breath held.

The avenue split, the tree line spreading either side of the homestead to form a pine perimeter, and the drive rounded into a large carriageway with an ornate stone fountain in the centre.

Stirling circled once, twice, then once more for the hell of it. In the daylight, devoid of shadows and foreboding, Westwind glowed.

The thrill of it filled Stirling's chest. His ribs pressed tight against his bike jacket, his heart thudding. How was it possible to feel such pride, such ownership, of something he'd never known existed? Yet here he was, doing laps like a teenager.

And all the time a stray soft wind kept whispering in his ears words which seemed, in his wanting, overwhelmed heart, to sound a lot like *welcome home*.

Chapter Two

Stirling brought the bike to a stop near the fountain. He dragged off his helmet and rested it in front of him, drinking in his good fortune.

Westwind.

The photos he'd googled in the weeks leading up to this trip hadn't done the property justice. Westwind stood as a stone and timber emblem of the huge profits made by the district's nineteenth-century pioneers and pastoralists. Wealth and prestige oozed from every pink sandstone pore.

As did something else. Something that had drawn Stirling here with a longing to find his place in the world now that his previous life had been stripped bare.

From what he'd read, the style was classed as formal Italianate. Decorative, yet classy, with two ground-floor windows shaded by a timber scallop-edged verandah and two upper-floor balconies enclosed with lacy wrought iron. Westwind's locally quarried pink sandstone only added to the air of welcome. If you didn't count the graffiti.

Though hidden in the verandah shadows, he could feel the scream of those blood-red words. A demand his father had taken to heart. DIE SCUM!

The remains of the finials were scattered like exploded eggshells near the front stairs. The wide dispersal of shards indicated the use of a decent sledgehammer and lot of anger. Stirling's gaze hardened. Whoever did it had better have it out of their system because there wouldn't be a repeat. Not while he was in charge.

Stirling rubbed his cheek and sighed. Sitting on his bum wasn't getting anything done. He had things to learn and exploring to do.

Although there would have been symbolism in entering through the front door, Stirling circled the house until he found the rear entrance. The property was his, he didn't need to claim it, and the rear courtyard was flanked by a small cobbled porch where he could park his bike.

The back door opened onto a mudroom, perfect for stowing his helmet and riding gear. A door to the right led to a laundry with a loo and a shower, which at first seemed unusual until he figured that it was probably handy for rinsing off after a muddy day on the farm. Despite its grandeur, Westwind had been a working homestead all its life.

He hooked his coat on the rack and used a nearby jack to pull off his motorcycle boots. Set in racks under the long bench were his father's shoes—a polished fine-grained leather pair with elastic sides, steel-capped worker's boots, long rubber wellingtons and a pair of heavy calf-length roper-style boots, like cowboy boots but plain. Stirling picked up one and checked the size. The same as his.

The realisation had him reaching for the bench. He sat and stared at the wall opposite, wondering what else he and his father shared. Stirling knew from photos that they had features in common—the same dark hair and facial structure, the same mottled khaki eyes.

A picture of Dougal wearing the country gent uniform of pale moleskin jeans and a checked shirt with the sleeves rolled up had shown him to be tall and well built. Stirling was built the same, although his muscle tone wasn't what it once was, and his traumatised left leg looked positively withered.

He tapped the boot against his knee. Country air and work would help that. And time, and these days he had plenty, now he was on leave of absence from *Medizin in Krise*. Stirling tapped again and set the boot down alongside its partner. He'd decide what to do with them later.

The mudroom led into the kitchen, a big comforting space with a central timber table that bore the scratches and dents of its long life and was surrounded by mismatched chairs with worn cushions on the seats. The floor was a dark reddish timber, the cupboards and benchtops in contrasting glossy white. A band of windows over the sink and bench brought in welcome daylight. Where the old hearth would have once had a blazing fire, now an old-fashioned enamel range dominated, a basket full of paper and a stack of logs alongside. Another more modern upright cooker was set into the bench nearby, while an enormous walk-in pantry completed the impression that this was a kitchen made for family.

Its domesticity made Stirling feel like an intruder. He was a helicopter pilot whose skills had taken him all over the world, some jobs benign, some highly dangerous, but all easy to move on from. This wasn't his world. This wasn't even his heritage.

Except it was.

With every tread, Stirling's disquiet grew. The house was silent bar its creaks and cracks, yet the air felt weighted, suspended and expectant, as if any moment Dougal Kildare would step from a room and demand to know what the hell he was doing there.

Evidence of his father lay everywhere. The half-read book on the coffee table. An auctioneer's award on a sideboard. Clothes hanging ready to wear in the bedroom robe. The comb on the ensuite sink, whisps of dark hair caught in its teeth, an old-fashioned silver razor dangling from a stand nearby. A leather-banded watch, the hands stopped at seven forty and *Meliora sequimur*—whatever that meant—engraved on the back.

Abandoning his father's bedroom, Stirling threw his gear into an upstairs spare room, changed out of his leathers into jeans and pulled on a jumper. He headed back downstairs, resisting the urge to slide down the polished timber banister like a boy. He'd only do himself an injury and Stirling had had enough of those for one lifetime.

He spent the next hour making lists and wasting time. The shopping list should have taken a few minutes, but Stirling found himself constantly distracted by small things—paperwork on the kitchen sideboard, postcards, flyers and other ephemera pinned to the fridge, a handwritten recipe book on a pantry shelf, a doorjamb marked with heights and dates. The little stories of his father's— and his family's—outwardly happy life. Stories incongruous to a man who, thirty-four years ago and despite being married with a baby, had met Stirling's mother Amanda at a fundraising dinner in Melbourne and enjoyed a brief affair.

Stirling kept picking up items, hungry for information, only to slap them down with frustration. The names meant nothing. The faces and places. Even some of the paperwork left him flummoxed. Invoices for goods he'd never heard of, services he didn't understand. Farm things.

A timber key rack was set on the wall next to the mudroom door. Stirling contemplated its contents. Work vehicles, he supposed.

What he was meant to do with them, he wasn't sure. Except for maybe a ute and a quad bike, the rest were superfluous. His American-based half-sister Melody had inherited the estate's residual farmland and promptly put it up for sale. The remaining homestead and two hundred acres were Stirling's, along with the house and outbuilding contents.

In their short video call, Stirling had offered that Melody take whatever personal and meaningful items from the house she wanted. An offer that had earned him a sneer in return. She and her mother Brigitte had already done so during the divorce. Melody's tone made it clear both women had washed their hands of Dougal and his Kildare heritage, and that sure as hell included the bastard son no one had heard of until now.

Stirling wished he'd known about the property earlier and tried to preserve some of the integrity of Westwind's original holdings, but he'd been too busy fighting for his life in a German hospital. Stirling had money—dangerous jobs paid well and his expenses were few—but not that kind of money. Nor was there any way he could have known the impact the property would have on him. The visceral pull of it.

He scanned the rack again and selected a couple of likely looking keys. A vehicle would be handy for grabbing supplies, and the cannelloni and beer he'd shoved in the fridge wouldn't last the day.

The morning was glorious though chilly. Stirling hesitated over the roper boots for a few seconds then sat and pulled them on. They moulded to his feet as though they belonged to him. The fleece-lined oilskin vest he shrugged on felt the same. Shoving the keys and his phone into a pocket, he headed outside. Two empty dog bowls sat at the side of the door. He wondered where the animals had gone.

Westwind had several outbuildings in varying states of repair. The closest was the main shed—a modern, three-sided construction diagonally across from the rear courtyard and down a gravel slope from the house.

The shed where Dougal had died.

A shiver shot up Stirling's spine and disappeared. Just a brief frisson, a 'there but for the grace of God' moment, then nothing but a mild sorrow for the father he wished he'd met at least once, and now never would.

He walked on. Another man might have been bothered, perhaps wary of disturbing ghosts. Stirling had seen too much death to fear anything it might leave behind. The living were the ones be wary of.

Stirling zapped the modern-ish remote key as he strode towards the shed and its Toyota four-wheel drive, frowning when it gave no response. Further investigation found the car dead, the battered old tray-top ute parked alongside the same. Brilliant. He'd have to get a battery delivered.

The hope of a spare battery led him to search the other outbuildings. Behind the shed were the old stables, built in the same pink stone as the villa and also heritage listed, and housing farm equipment and a derelict tractor that could probably do with heritage listing itself. But it was the crumbling stone shed a little further away that roused Stirling's curiosity. Like the stables, it had an open centre bay and two wings, each with a large arched doorway that had been sealed with corrugated iron. Where the stables were relatively neat, this was full of junk. Bits of ancient machinery he had no idea the uses of, old tins and metal scraps, tarpaulins and drums.

An interior doorway led to the left wing. A dust and cobweb–encrusted window in the side let in feeble light, barely enough to see by. Stirling rubbed his chin as he considered returning to the house for a proper torch, but even as he thought it, his eyes were adjusting, revealing a shape that had his back and neck prickling and his pulse beating a rapid tattoo.

The floor creaked and groaned as he crossed to investigate. The iron roof pinged a discordant tune as it warmed in the sun. Something scuttled in a corner and disappeared. With so many trip hazards, Stirling concentrated on threading his way towards the dust and tarpaulin–covered form.

He found the corner of the tarp and hoisted it up, coughing when what felt like a hundred years of dust and bird and mouse shit flew into the air.

'Jesus,' he said, staring slack-jawed at his find.

A fender, lusciously curved like the most beautiful of women. His heart pounding, Stirling pulled the tarp back further, exposing the leaf-spring front suspension.

Laughing, he stripped the tarp to the motorbike's rear wheel and caressed the fuel tank, the handlebars, the antiquated gear lever. Once the motorbike would have been a lustrous red, but age and neglect had faded its paintwork to a dull grey-pink. The chrome parts hadn't fared much better, pitted and flaking rust, and cracks hashed the leather seat. Even so, it was magnificent.

'Please be what I think you are,' he murmured, crouching to inspect the engine, an inline four-cylinder F-head with overhead intake valves.

A classic Indian Chief from the 1940s. Unbelievable. Restored, it'd be worth close to a hundred grand.

Grinning, Stirling gathered up the entire tarp. An old pallet loaded with boxes lay behind the bike. He'd dump the tarp on top and clear a path to wheel the bike out into the sunshine for a closer look.

The tarp landed with a whump and a bloom of dust, followed by a gunshot snap. Stirling ducked, reflexes kicking in. Hunched, he scanned his surrounds, his ears tuned in to his environment. Creaks—a lot of creaks and cracks—and dust, rubbish and a decaying outbuilding. The motorbike of his boyhood dreams. No sniper. No war.

He shook his head at his stupidity. He was in quiet country Victoria; no one was shooting at him. He reached for the precious Indian.

Only for his right leg to cave through the crumbling floorboards.

He lunged for the Indian's rear tyre, but that only brought the bike tipping dangerously towards him. With a roar, he shoved it away. The bike smashed into the wall, the impact vibrating the shed. More dust and muck rained down from the rafters but Stirling barely registered it. Something sharp and jagged had torn into a point just above his right knee and ripped upward, hooking him deeper and deeper until it snagged mid-thigh. He was suspended over the broken floor, weight half in, half out of the hole. A hooked fish.

The pain was unbelievable, threatening to cleave in him two. His vision rippled. Nausea threatened, rising on the tide of his fear. Why did it have to be his good right leg?

Stirling braced his arms, breathing hard, sweat beading hot and cold on his brow. This was not the first time he'd been injured. He'd made it through then and he'd make it through now.

Blood—lots of it—was sheeting down his right leg, flooding his boot and soaking his sock. His weak left leg was bent awkwardly sideways and the splintering floor was crackling like fire, threatening to collapse. His heart trammelled as full-blown panic loomed.

Think. *Think*.

Pulling would only rip him open further. He needed to either break whatever had his leg hooked, or lever off it, preferably without further damage.

He assessed the hole his leg had gone through. The poor light and his dribbling sweat made it hard to see but he could make out where the timber floorboards had snapped away from the supporting joists. Despite the unstable noises, the heavier joists looked fairly intact.

Darkness prevented him from seeing what he was hooked on. Stirling reached into the hole and felt around. The back of his hand scraped against something hard and cold. A stone wall, perhaps. Or stacked bricks. He stretched downward, grunting as the twist of his body ignited old pains.

His hand closed around the protrusion. Some sort of sharp-edged metal bracket. Not wide—maybe the width of his thumb—but high gauge and fastened tight to the wall.

'Oh, Jesus.'

To get loose, he'd have to shift up and out at the same time. It would mean pressure on his bad leg—a lot of pressure—and it wasn't ready. But what choice did he have?

Not giving himself time to dwell, he pushed up on his left knee. A different pain rattled through him as his old injury protested the burden. He could take that. By now it was a familiar foe. The other was a different matter. His wound radiated pain in currents. More blood swept his leg.

He kept going, breath hissing as he eased this way and that. If the bracket was straight, it would have pulled right out but it was clear from the tugging and tearing inside his leg that it ended in some kind of hook. He prayed it wasn't barbed.

Sweat stung his eyes as Stirling used his hands to work his leg. The pain was unbelievable. Violent surges that warped his vision and stole his breath. He raged against the weakness stealing into his limbs. This was not his time. It couldn't be. There was too much to learn. Too much to unpuzzle.

Suddenly, Stirling's leg made a wet, sucking sound and something popped. He was free.

He collapsed backward and scrambled on his elbows away from the hole and the rotten boards. His shoulders crashed into a

44-gallon drum. It rocked, its contents sloshing, but stayed upright. Stirling braced against it and jammed one hand on his gushing thigh while he used the other to grapple with his belt buckle.

After a few false starts and some choice language, Stirling dragged the belt from its loops, circled it around his upper thigh and cinched it tight. Holding the end taut, he fumbled for his phone and dialled triple zero.

'Ambulance,' he panted, as he lurched his way upright.

The operator calmly took his details. Though his head was fogging from blood loss and the pain of both legs, Stirling relayed the facts as he staggered his way forward, one agonising step after the other. His work for *Medizin in Krise* had taught him the importance of clarity.

Farm junk pitched around Stirling as he braced against whatever was at hand. Blood continued to leak from his leg. Every moment counted. He couldn't afford to have the paramedics hunting all over Westwind for him. He needed to get outside.

The breeze was delicious on his sweat-streaked face. He stumbled on, trying to talk sensibly as the worker kept him on the line, offering encouragement and the promise an ambulance was on its way. But as Stirling reached the stables, he knew he wouldn't make it any further. The weakness in his legs was too great. His body was leaden, collapsing under its own weight. His head fluttery.

He found a spot facing Westwind and slid down the wall. The pink-stoned villa glowed in the midmorning sun. The home that had lured him here with promises of knowledge and identity he was now close to losing.

Stirling gave a vague kind of chuckle.

On a positive note, at least it was a better view than the barren shithole where he last sat slumped and dying.

And this time, the only person he'd lose would be himself.

Chapter Three

Darcy Sloane carefully wrapped the cherry-print halter-neck swing dress in red tissue paper and tied it with a black satin bow. She plucked a thank-you card from its box and used a red marker to ink her gratitude next to the cartoon image of a dark-haired girl in a red dress. The girl was leaning forward in a pin-up pose, hands on her upper thighs and bright red lips puckered, her skirt billowing up behind to expose a hint of suspender. It was cute and sexy and very VaVoom.

She slid the card into an envelope with a copy of her returns policy and a discount voucher for the client's next order, then secured the envelope to the ribbon using a sticker stamped with the same cartoon figure.

Satisfied all was in order, Darcy lifted the dress into its already labelled post pack and sealed the edge. Pressing her hands to the small of her back, she arched, stretching her tired and aching muscles, and breathed out slowly. After a late night followed by an early morning, Darcy had finally caught up on her orders.

For now. It was only Wednesday, and the start of the week was always quiet. Thursday and Friday would likely bring another flurry and the grind would begin again. Plus she had ready-to-wear stocks to refill.

Not that she was complaining. She had her health, friends, family, a successful fashion business in VaVoom, and dawn had brought a glorious late winter morning of the sort that didn't allow for lolling about, no matter how deserved.

As her gran always said, a busy girl was a happy girl, and Darcy delighted in being both.

She gathered up the other parcels, placed them in a red patent tote and swept her gaze around the workroom. Her eyes narrowed. A tape measure was snagged around the wheels of her sewing chair. Darcy strode over, snatched it up and spooled it neatly before setting the tape in its drawer.

She paused to stroke her beloved sewing machine. A semi-industrial Janome with a maximum speed of twelve hundred stitches per minute, nine one-step buttonholes, two hundred built-in stitches, and a sensor that adjusted feeding speed depending on the fabric. The machine had had a workout this week and hadn't missed a stitch.

With a quick check in the mirror to top up her signature siren-red lipstick and ensure her victory roll hairstyle remained perfectly coiffed, Darcy gathered her tote and headed for the post office.

'One for Perth,' said Lisette Learmonth, peering at the top post-pack's address. 'You *are* getting around, Princess.'

Darcy grinned. 'Wait until you see where the next one's for.'

Lisette's blue eyes widened as she flipped to the second pack. 'Alice Springs!'

'Uh huh. VaVoom is going outback.'

Lisette cast a dry look towards Ridgeview Road, Grassmoor's main street. It was the lull between school drop-off and lunchtime when people were knuckling down to work or catching up over morning tea, and the town was quiet. 'Some would call *this* the outback. God knows we're far enough from civilisation.'

She brightened and began scanning the parcel codes, her daisy-shaped crystal nose-stud flashing as she worked. Like Darcy, Lisette was an eternal optimist, one of the reasons they'd been friends since childhood.

'Although if you keep this up, maybe civilisation will come to us.' She stopped scanning and held up her hands, her head tilted ceilingward, expression dreamy. 'I can see the new town sign now. Grassmoor, Greaser Fashion Capital of Australia.'

'VaVoom is more than greaser fashion,' reminded Darcy a little sniffily. Her designs covered all the fifties fashion trends. If it celebrated femininity, Darcy was into it.

'I know, I know. But it does sound cool. Greaser ... So naughty. So *greasy*.'

Not the image Darcy wanted to project but Lisette did enjoy a tease. Darcy forgave her bohemian friend because it came from love. Others were given short shrift.

She glanced at the clock on the wall behind the counter. Still only nine thirty. Plenty of time to get to the farm to pick up her mum and drive to Hamilton, seventy kilometres away. Lisette might pine for civilisation to arrive in Grassmoor, but Darcy would have been content with a simple nursing centre and physio access.

'Thanks,' she said, taking the lodgement receipt from Lisette and securing it in her tote. She'd email the tracking codes to her clients later, while waiting for her mum. 'Meet you at the ground on Saturday?'

'If I don't get a better offer.'

Laughing, Darcy waved her off and strode for the door.

'Don't you dare turn up in that yellow outfit again, Princess,' Lisette yelled. 'We can't have you putting all the players off like last year.'

Darcy shook her head and kept going. The daffodil-coloured gingham trousers and fine-wool forest-green twinset she'd worn to last season's semifinal had had nothing to do with Grassmoor football team's performance. Besides, if the forecast remained as fine as the Bureau predicted, she'd be wearing something far prettier—and patriotic—than yellow gingham. Word around town was the Grasshoppers—or Hoppers as they were more commonly known—were a chance to go all the way this year. They deserved something special.

Waving at a few main street strollers as she passed, Darcy steered her Mini towards the main road and sped out of town, turning up the stereo to blast the interior with fifties rock and roller Johnny Carroll singing 'Wild Wild Women'.

It might not pay its way like her Janome, but the second-hand Mini was an indulgence she could never regret. The car was slung so low to the ground it was like driving a go-cart. Even at moderate speeds, Darcy felt like she was tearing along, and with its red duco, white racing stripes and VAV00M numberplate, the Mini stood out, reminding people there was a talented and savvy businesswoman in their midst. That Darcy Sloane was not the fashion joke they sometimes mistook her for.

She was closing in on Roseneath when her head jerked to the side in a double-take. Darcy jammed her foot on the brake, veering towards the verge. Long grass made whump-whump sounds as it battered the undercarriage of her little car. Checking the road behind, she shunted into reverse and backed up. With a spin of the wheel, she whizzed the car around in a spray of dirt until it faced Westwind's gates.

Westwind's *open* gates.

Darcy drummed her fingers on the steering wheel. Maybe a real estate agent was checking it out. Maybe Mal McKenzie, Dougal

Kildare's lifelong friend and Grassmoor's only solicitor, was sorting something.

Maybe someone was up to no good.

It was none of her business. Darcy had a hundred better things to do, and an appointment to shuttle her mum to. And truly, why should she care about Westwind? It was just a pretty house.

A pretty house with a tragic history.

Darcy drummed her fingers again. 'Wild Wild Women' gave way to Buddy Holly and the Crickets singing 'That'll Be the Day'.

With a loud huff, she headed up the drive.

Dougal had been dead seven months and the lack of love showed in every pothole and corrugation. The once meticulous landscaping of the front garden was in ruin. Fed by winter rains, weeds had run rampant through what was once a tranquil oasis, inundating flowerbeds and creeping over low shrubs. Branches downed in the last storm lay cast about like broken bones on the ragged lawns. Even the drive's stately pines had lost their grandeur, lower boughs flagging as though weighed down with sadness.

To be fair, the property had been going downhill well before Dougal's demise, an event that had confounded Darcy and most of the district. The Kildares had always been proud of Westwind and to let it falter seemed an anathema. In hindsight the reason was obvious, yet no one realised at the time. No one recognised the signs. Then it was too late.

Too late for so many things.

The carriage circle was empty. Darcy parked near the fountain and regarded the front of the house. Her lips thinned at the DIE SCUM! bleeding across its lovely facade, the smashed stonework. Westwind didn't deserve this. It wasn't the house's fault its owner was a thieving rat, but she could understand how fury and anguish could make some lash out.

Nearly a million dollars stolen from the community. Money belonging to farmers and families and businesses from the sale of livestock and clearing-sale effects that had been held in trust. Money her own family was owed. At first, Dougal had simply been slow paying out. That kind of thing happened sometimes, when meat companies turned tricky or terms weren't fulfilled, or some other issue affected settlement. Nobody liked it, but that was business.

Then the transfers stopped altogether, and the excuses started. As did the anger.

This was Dougal Kildare though. A man who had been agenting for local farmers and businesses without a hitch for years. It wasn't until after Dougal's death that everyone realised the trust accounts were empty and the money was truly gone. Most were lucky and indemnity insurance covered the debt, but for those who were owed for clearing sales, there was no such safety net. They had to wait for money from Dougal's estate, which took time.

Such an awful, wasteful thing. Of property. Of trust. Of life.

Nothing moved behind the windows. Darcy scanned to the sides of the villa. No one. Which didn't mean that nobody was here. They could easily be out the back, lurking in one of the many outbuildings. In the paddocks. Trailing the creek line.

This was none of her business. Truly, it wasn't. A neighbour couldn't be held responsible for another landholder's lack of vigilance. And since her permanent move into town, Darcy wasn't even a true neighbour anymore.

Her focus returned to the graffiti. Five minutes, that's all she'd give it. Five minutes, just to be sure.

She shoved the driver's door open and stepped out, wishing she'd replaced her red patent Mary Jane heels for ballet flats. They were Darcy's favourite pair though, matched her tote and the Mini, and added a much-needed splash of colour to her black and white polka dot wiggle dress with three-quarter-length cuffed sleeves and belt and collar. Image mattered when you were in the fashion game.

Darcy stood for a moment, listening. Bird calls. The distant low of a cow. The rumble of a truck passing. No sounds of destruction, yet something was making the back of her neck tingle, as though a ghostly finger had trailed across her skin.

She shook off the idea and crossed the drive, keeping to her toes to avoid damaging her heels, and trotted up the front steps. She lifted her hand to bang on the heavy timber front door and dropped it. Never, in all her visits to Westwind, had she entered through the front door. But for all she knew, the property could have been sold and the new owners had arrived to take possession. Although surely if Westwind had changed hands, she would have heard. Lisette, bless her, knew everyone's business. It was a perk of her post office position.

Still, it was better to be polite.

She knocked and stood back. When there was no response, she moved to the lounge window and cupped her hands against the glass. It looked the same as it always had—masculine leather couches and chairs, heavy antique furniture. Red and gold rug in front of the fireplace.

She scanned further but couldn't see any movement in the hall.

'Leave it,' she muttered, click-clacking down the stairs to her car, determined to ignore her feelings of unease. But two steps onto the gravel and her hips were pivoting sideways towards the back of the villa.

A sleek road bike bearing a Victorian registration was parked under the porch. Darcy approached it with caution, flicking glances from the Ducati's shiny livery to Westwind's rear entrance. The door was wide open, only a screen protecting the interior.

She moved closer. The tap of her heels on the paving sounded indecently loud in the country quiet. 'Hello?'

Silence greeted her. She knocked on the jamb. 'Anyone home? It's Darcy Sloane. My family own Roseneath, the property next door.'

Still nothing. Whoever owned the bike must be busy elsewhere.

She walked back to the side of the house, mind skipping to the day's chores. Take her mum to physio, email out the tracking numbers and check for new orders, grab some groceries and pick up whatever supplies her dad might need in Hamilton, then home to give him and her older sister Shiloh a hand. They were marking lambs this week. If it weren't for her mum's appointment and her VaVoom commitments, Darcy would be helping them now.

A noise brought her up short. It sounded like a call, as if someone had yelled a weak 'hey'. She turned and swept her gaze across the rear gardens and on to the sheds. Something near the old stables caught Darcy's eye.

She narrowed her gaze and took a few steps forward. Then a few more. Each step lengthening as the form gained shape. A slumped man. Ashen-faced and—

'Oh my God.'

Darcy ran, cursing her heels, fear burgeoning with every stride, the horror growing worse as she neared. Blood, so much blood. Soaking his jeans, the ground around him.

She threw herself down at his side and hovered her hands over his leg, scared to touch in case she hurt him. His eyelids were drooped, his shoulders sagging, hands open by his sides. Sweat beaded his brow and upper lip. His skin had a frightening grey tinge. His breath was so shallow he seemed to be sipping air. She lowered her gaze to his injury, the coppery scent of his blood filling her nostrils.

Dark wings batted the edges of Darcy's vision. She forced a
swallow and breathed long breaths. The man was hurt. Badly hurt.
He needed her brave and active, not falling in a faint.

She scrambled for the basic first-aid training she'd learned at
school, sixteen years ago. 'Can you hear me?'

A slow flicker, then his focus shifted weakly to her. An even
weaker smile followed. His voice was faint and dry. 'Hi.'

'Hi to you too.' She willed calm into her voice. 'I'm Darcy.'

'Stirling.'

'Truly? I had a great, great uncle called Stirling. Terrific name.
Very masculine.' She indicated his leg and noticed the belt around
his upper thigh. 'Looks like you've done yourself a major injury
there, Stirling. I'll need to call an ambulance and do something to
stop the bleeding.'

'Done it.'

'The ambulance? Excellent to hear, because I left my phone
in the car and running in these heels is hell. Now, this bleeding
business. Please don't be alarmed, but I'm going to strip off my
dress.' Maintaining her chatty tone, she unbuckled her belt and
tugged it free, then reached for the back zipper and began pulling it
down. 'Don't worry, I'm wearing a slip.'

She shimmied out of the dress, bundled the fabric, pressed it to
his wound and tightened the belt around her makeshift dressing,
wincing at his wheeze of pain.

'Sorry.'

He managed a shake of his head.

Blood seeped quickly through the dress, although not fast enough
for it to be arterial, she guessed. Even so, the wound was horrific
and Stirling had clearly lost a lot of blood.

She cocked her ear towards the road. Nothing. 'Can you
remember how long ago you called the ambulance?'

'Fair while.'

Darcy had been here several minutes at least. Where were the sirens?

Stirling regarded his hand vaguely, then the blood trail in the gravel and grass, and frowned. 'My phone ...'

'Don't worry about that. I'll look for it later.' She shifted her knees from where a stone dug painfully through her stockings. 'What happened?'

It took Stirling a moment to find his voice. 'Fell through floorboards.' He sipped a few breaths. 'Leg got hooked.'

Hooked was an understatement. What Darcy had glimpsed through the tear in his jeans seemed more akin to being gored by a bull.

She glanced at the stables' arched entrance. The floor inside was cobbled brick, no floorboards to fall through. She scanned the blood trail. It led towards the next old shed, fifty metres away. How he managed to make it this far with his leg torn open was a miracle.

When she looked back, Stirling was studying her beneath hooded lids. She smiled in what she hoped was a reassuring way.

'You're calm,' he said.

That made her laugh. If only he knew of the sweat dampening her armpits and the quake in her belly.

'I'm a born and bred farm girl. Farm girls don't faint at a bit of blood.'

His mouth twitched. Possibly a try for a smile, more likely a wince of pain.

She watched him as she maintained pressure on the wound, scared he'd stop breathing if she didn't. If not for his pasty complexion, Stirling would be a handsome man. His jaw was angular and strong, his nose straight and well proportioned. Dark eyelashes fringed greeny hazel eyes. His mouth, though crimped with pain, was generous. Even through the hunch of his body Darcy could see he was robustly built. A manual labourer perhaps, or a man who worked out.

A builder maybe, come to do work on Westwind. No. A builder would arrive in a work vehicle, not a road bike. A trendy architect type then, here to gather ideas for a renovation. For who though? Rumours about Dougal's will had been ping-ponging around the district for months and no one—except probably Mal McKenzie— knew the facts, and Mal was keeping a low profile these days, the gossip being he'd been devastated by his best friend's betrayal and suicide.

Darcy lifted her head and pursed her lips. Where on god's green earth was that ambulance? Her eyes narrowed. They had better not have the go-slows because of the address.

'So, Stirling, tell me,' she said, hiding her anxiety with feigned cheer. 'What brings you to Westwind?'

He shook his head and stared at a weed near his hand.

'It's a secret? Fair enough. As for me, I saw the open gates and was worried someone was up to no good. Please tell me you weren't here stealing or vandalising things. It'd truly ruin my faith in humanity.'

Again, that twitch of the mouth but his eyes remained deeply hooded.

'You aren't going to sleep there, are you? Because I'm a woman who prides herself on her charm and to have a handsome man fall asleep on me when I'm wearing nothing but a pink silk slip …' She faked a huff. 'That would be quite upsetting.'

His eyelids flickered. 'Handsome, huh?'

'The blood's a bit of a turn-off, but yes. Oh,' she said, finally catching wind of a siren. 'Sounds like the cavalry are nearly here.

Uh-uh.' She waggled a finger she wasn't sure he could see as he released a long, exhausted-sounding breath. 'No passing out.'

'I'll try.' He swallowed. 'For you.' A tinge of amusement entered his voice. 'Woman in a pink slip.'

'Thank you. Your consideration is much appreciated.'

The minutes passed slowly. Darcy tried to keep Stirling's attention with babble but he was drifting, his lassitude frightening her into talking even more nonsense. At the ambulance's appearance in the drive, she uttered a quiet 'Thank god' and sniffed back tears.

She stood well aside as they tended Stirling, answering the few questions she could and grateful for the reassuring smiles thrown by the female paramedic, who Darcy knew a little from town and who had been one of the first responders when her mum collapsed.

Gradually the tension that had gripped Darcy since discovering Stirling began to ease. He was in good hands, the paramedics' arrival delayed not by the name Westwind but another call-out. The pair worked efficiently, unfazed by the gravity of his wound and condition. Only when the trolley was wheeled away, leaving behind her dress in a circle of dirt thick and dark with Stirling's blood, did Darcy's anxiety return.

She spun from the sight. The head of the trolley was almost behind the ambulance doors. Stirling had turned his face towards Darcy. His eyes were open, his pain-wracked gaze fixed on hers.

Darcy lifted a hand, her fingers curling slowly in farewell.

He lifted his slightly in return.

Minutes later, Darcy stood alone in her slip and heels, arms crossed and rubbing herself against the cold and her fear for this unknown man.

Chapter Four

Stirling was in that half-land of sleep where the mind recognises it's time to wake but the body doesn't. He was a candle melted into the mattress, heavy and burned out.

It was the painkillers. To the consternation of the nurses, he'd been refusing them. They'd help him sleep, they said. Stirling knew that, but he'd been down the opiate rabbit hole after the chopper crash and was determined not to return. Except last night his need for sleep had won out. The nurse had been right. His body needed to heal, and it couldn't do that properly if he was exhausted.

He'd swallowed the drugs and let them take him away to wonderful, beautiful unconsciousness. Now the pain was rousing, familiar and almost comforting in the way it reminded Stirling that he was still alive. That it wasn't his time for the great nothing.

It had been close run though. Not as dramatic as having his aircraft shot down and caught in a firefight, but a near enough brush with death. Even before this latest screw-up, his best mate Toby had been calling him 'Felix' for the cat-like nine lives he seemed to possess. Stirling had to be getting down on them. Not that it mattered. All he needed was one.

He kept his eyes closed and listened to the noises of the ward. The nurses talking. Curtains being drawn. Patients easing their creaking bodies out of bed. Visitors greeting loved ones.

His eyes snapped open. Visitors? How long had he slept for? There'd been the usual disturbances in the night as the nurses checked on him, took his blood pressure, temperature and oxygen levels. Activities so routine, that had formed such a part of his life for so long, they'd blurred into one other, and he'd slumped straight back to sleep each time.

He eased his head up, blinking at the light and the crustiness of his eyes, and met the scarlet beam of a woman standing at the end of the bed.

'Hello,' she said.

'Hi.' His greeting came out dry. Stirling cleared his throat as he pushed his fists into the bed beside his hips and carefully eased himself up, hissing as pain flared through his leg.

'Do you need help?' she asked, her brown eyes wide. 'I can call for someone.'

Stirling shook his head for 'no' and to try and clear his brain. She was the woman from Westwind. The woman who'd crouched beside him talking funny nonsense while wearing nothing but a pink silky petticoat, blood staining her lap and hands. His blood. What was her name? Marcy? No. Something else. Something cute, like her.

'I'm good.' Though Stirling knew the grunt in his voice said otherwise.

The overbed table had been swung to the side. His breakfast was on a tray on top. He reached for the juice but the tug on his leg had him collapsing back, breath coming short.

'You could have asked,' the woman tutted. She swung the table around until his breakfast was in front of him and returned to the end of the bed, high heels clicking on the lino.

Stirling studied her over the rim of his plastic juice tub. She was heavily made up. Glossy lips, smoky eyeshadow, dark hair styled into some elaborate scroll thing. Her outfit would have been as sexy as hell if it weren't so ridiculous—tight blue top with a square white collar and tie, and a dark blue skirt that tapered from her hips to her knees and made Stirling wonder how she walked in it.

It was like looking at Marilyn Monroe in a sailor suit.

'You took off your dress and used it as a compress for me. Thank you.'

'I did indeed and you're welcome. Although I'm sure I'm not the first to do that in your presence. Take off her dress, I mean.' She sighed, eyes lowering and luscious red lips pouting. 'Sadly, it's unsalvageable. My favourite wiggle dress too.' She brightened. 'Not to worry. I can always make another. How are you feeling?'

'Okay, considering.' What he was feeling was overwhelmed and more than a bit self-conscious. Stirling knew enough of trauma to realise he'd likely be whey-faced and weak, smelling of hospital and looking stupid in his flimsy gown. All while a glamorous, sparkle-eyed woman stood at the end of his bed, seemingly delighted to see him.

Stirling tried to ease up further. 'Sorry, I've forgotten your name.'

'Darcy. Darcy Sloane.' She moved to his uninjured side and held out her hand. Stirling took it. Her hand was soft and warm, her grip firm. 'My parents own Roseneath.' At Stirling's blank look, she went on. 'The property to the south of Westwind.'

'Right.'

She lifted her bag and balanced it on the side of his bed. 'I found your phone.'

Stirling had asked about his phone and there were mumbles of someone chasing it up with the paramedics, but he doubted that would happen. It didn't matter now. Darcy had beaten them to it.

'I brought a charger too.' She plugged it into the socket above his bedside cupboard and hung the cord over the edge within Stirling's reach. 'Your phone's fully charged so you can start calling people straightaway, which I'm sure you're keen to do. I also locked up the house.' She passed over the keys William Stoddart had given him, and which Stirling had left on the kitchen table.

'Thanks.'

A cheery woman in a pink uniform came in, wheeling a trolley.

'Hello there, young Darcy.'

'Michelle! Hello, you.' Darcy greeted her with a hug. Stirling couldn't help admiring Darcy's figure from behind. Weird the outfit might be, but it did her all kinds of justice. 'How are you?'

'Oh, I can't complain. Nobody listens anyway. How's your mum?'

'She's going well. Still weak and she tires easily, but in good spirits and that's the main thing.'

'But she's walking now?'

'She is. Not far but it's progress.' Darcy smiled. 'You should have heard us cheer the day she took her first steps. Even Shiloh got teary and she never cries.'

'Well, I'm glad to hear she's doing so well.' Michelle stepped back and gave Darcy a once-over. 'You know, my mother used to wear an outfit just like that. Red, it was. Still in the cupboard when she passed.' Michelle tutted. 'No idea why. Wasn't as if she could fit into it. You, though, fit it perfectly. Like a pin-up. But that's what you get when you make your own clothes, isn't it, love? Perfect fit. Not like these sacks.' She plucked at the baggy belly of her uniform.

'I could adjust it for you, if you like. Make that waistline sing.' Darcy winked and dropped her voice to a whisper, her sparkling eyes sliding towards Stirling. 'Who knows what handsome men you could meet on your rounds.'

'Get away with you,' chided Michelle. 'I'm beyond that now.'

'No one's beyond it, Michelle.'

Shaking her head, Michelle reached for Stirling's tray and frowned. 'Not hungry, love?'

He smiled at her. He knew from experience who to butter up. 'Slept in. I'll tuck in now, if that's okay.'

'You do that.' She patted his arm. 'Your coffee will be cold, but we'll be round with another shortly. And some fruitcake.'

'Thanks.' Stirling lifted the lid on his breakfast. Scrambled eggs on toast. He sampled some, grateful to find them at least lukewarm.

Michelle glanced at Darcy then back at Stirling, nose lifting like a bloodhound sniffing prey.

Darcy remained expressionless, which was impressive given her natural brightness. She flipped the white tie at the neck of her sailor collar, pursed her lips then retied the bow. Stirling scooped up another serve of egg and feigned nonchalance. He wasn't going to explain Darcy's presence if she wasn't.

'Well then,' said Michelle a bit tetchily. 'Standing around won't get anything done. You take care, young Darcy. Give my regards to Rachel.'

'Will do.'

The trolley wheels squeaked as she pushed it on.

Stirling sipped some juice and cut an edge of his toast, unsure what to say. A visitor was the last thing he'd expected. No one knew he was here. His next of kin was his mum, and the hospital had been unable to contact her. Stirling told them to leave it be. Amanda Hawley was currently working in a mobile medical team in the Central African Republic and didn't need the worry. He'd shoot her an email now he had his phone.

'Your mum's been sick?' he asked.

'Yes. Guillain-Barre syndrome.'

Between his mum's work for *Medecins sans Frontieres* and his career with *Medizin in Krise*, Stirling had absorbed a lot of medical information but he'd never heard of that particular affliction.

Darcy caught his confusion. 'It's very rare. One morning about ten months ago, she woke up feeling unwell and complaining of pins and needles in her toes and fingertips. The next day Mum was in here, suffering almost full paralysis. She could hardly breathe. It was awful.' Her plump bottom lip dropped at the memory. 'We thought we were going to lose her.'

'But you didn't.'

'No.' Darcy's smile was immediate. 'No, we were lucky. Doctor Majid, one of the emergency doctors, had seen Guillain-Barre before and suspected it as a cause. He did a lumbar puncture and when it came back positive for GBS, he put her straight on to immunoglobulin.' She glanced around the room. 'I'm quite familiar with this place. Mum was here for seven weeks, then another four in rehab. She still visits three times a week for physio. Which is how I come to be here, checking on you.'

'Your mum, will she make a full recovery?'

'She should. It'll just take time.' Darcy gestured at his leg. 'A bit like yourself. Have they said how long you'll be in for?'

Stirling shrugged. 'A few more days.' He hoped. He'd ripped muscle in the fall, torn veins, spilled a bucketload of blood, but compared to his last injury, it was straightforward. No multiple fractures. No dislocated hip. No ruptured spleen.

No grieving for lost friends. Lost loves.

'Can I fetch you anything?' She spread a hand, long-fingered and smooth, the nails short and plainly varnished. No rings. 'Clothes from the house. Grapes? Hospital patients need grapes. It's a given.'

He gave a half-laugh. She was a funny one, this newly met neighbour of his. 'Grapes won't be necessary.'

'Good, because they're out of season and I would have had to buy raisins instead. And raisins are not something a person relying on a bedpan should be eating.' Darcy brandished a finger at his gown. 'You'll need clothes. You can't wear *that* in public.'

She was right. If nothing else he'd need trunks, socks, a shirt. As for his legs, it'd be a while before he'd be able to get into a pair of jeans. It'd have to be trackpants, baggy ones, and those he didn't have.

It was a three-quarter-hour drive to the hospital from Grassmoor, an hour and a half round trip—too much to ask for someone he'd just met. He'd work it out. The hospital would have something. He could always ask someone to buy him clothes.

Stirling set down his fork and rubbed his brow. His wallet was at Westwind. Then he remembered he had his phone and could always transfer money. Thanks to Darcy. He'd have to repay her kindness when he was better.

'It's okay. I'll manage.'

She must have heard his uncertainty. 'It's not a problem, if that's what you're thinking. Like I said, I'm here a lot with Mum. I can easily drop by Westwind and grab whatever you need.'

He'd be mad not to take up the offer. Toby was in Melbourne, a four-hour drive away, and Stirling didn't know anyone closer. And as she said, Darcy would be coming here anyway. 'Okay. There's a travel bag on one of the spare beds upstairs. If you could bring that in …'

'Of course.'

'Thanks, Darcy. I appreciate it.' He lifted his phone from where he'd placed it on the bed. 'For finding my phone too.'

'Speaking of which, what's your number so I can text you when I'm at the house? In case you think of something else.'

Stirling hesitated, then couldn't see what the harm would be and recited his number.

Darcy showed her screen for him to check and hit save, then a few more buttons. Within seconds, his mobile flashed. A return text with her name and number.

'Now you have mine.' She winked cheekily.

Suddenly a breathy woman's voice broke the quiet. 'Vavoom,' she sing-songed. 'Vavoom. Vavoom.'

Darcy checked her screen and blinked. 'Oh dear. I'm sorry, Stirling, I truly must dash.' She shoved her phone away and hooked her bag over her shoulder. 'Call me if you need anything, otherwise I'll see you the day after tomorrow.'

He watched her go, hips swaying, high heels clacking. Marilyn Monroe in a sailor suit sashaying through the halls of a hospital in the far reaches of rural Victoria. If it weren't for his aching body, Stirling might imagine he was dreaming.

'Hang on,' he called.

Darcy pivoted, one hand on her hip, tote held out in her other hand, so that for a moment Stirling forgot what he was going to say. 'I ...'

Her perfectly sculpted eyebrows arched.

'You'll need keys.'

Her mouth opened on the cusp of words and closed. 'Of course. Silly me.'

Stirling handed them back over. This time when Darcy left, it wasn't her figure he was contemplating. It was the words she'd clearly wanted to say yet had failed to voice.

And why she'd neglected to ask who he was and what he was doing at Westwind.

Chapter Five

Darcy glanced at her mum and back at the road. Fatigue lined Rachel Sloane's eyes and mouth. Learning to walk again, retraining nerves and muscles that had forgotten a lifetime's activity, was tough going. Sessions often left her exhausted. On bad days, they also left her deeply depressed.

She tended to nod off during their trips home, but today Rachel had a vacant stare that made Darcy's skin prickle. The session hadn't gone well. Rachel's legs were weak and disobedient, her energy low. The physio promised this was normal but that didn't stop Darcy from worrying, or her mum despairing.

Rachel had once been so strong. This person was a stranger.

Darcy took her hand off the wheel to squeeze her mum's. The past year had been hellish for the Sloanes. Crisis, heartbreak and hardship had chased each other's tails until Roseneath was a whirlpool of anxiety. Rachel's sudden illness had been the rotten cherry on top.

There was hope though. Rachel's recovery, while at a snail's pace, was progressing as expected. Now that the stock and station agents indemnity insurance from the Kildare fraud had come through, the farm was back on track and with time, Shiloh's heart would also mend. Nothing would give them back the year they'd lost to anguish, but Darcy had faith that joy would return. And if joy refused to play, she'd drag it into their lives kicking and screaming if necessary.

'I had three new orders come in while I was waiting,' she said, giving her mum's hand a last squeeze and returning hers to the wheel. 'Two fit and flare dresses and a pair of corset-fronted pants. Repeat customers too.'

'That's excellent, honey,' said Rachel and Darcy was relieved to hear pride in her voice. Running a close second to her gran, who claimed all rights to Darcy's sewing talents, her mum was her greatest supporter.

'The website shop upgrade is certainly paying for itself. My only regret is that I didn't do it earlier, but I'm not going to mope over it. VaVoom is moving forward and that's the important thing.' Darcy formed her next words carefully. 'I visited Stirling too.'

The pride vanished from Rachel's face. Darcy wanted to sigh. Her mum never used to be so judgemental, but she'd become brittle this past year, less forgiving. Part of it was her illness, the rest was fury and hurt. Dougal Kildare hadn't just been their stock agent, he'd been a family friend. A trusted friend. Even a loved one. To have Dougal betray them the way he did had broken something inside Rachel.

Inside all of them.

'He was a bit out of it,' Darcy continued. 'I imagine they've got him on quite strong painkillers.'

She'd related the story of Stirling's misadventure to her family the day it happened. There'd been a great deal of curiosity around the Sloane dinner table that night about who he might be. A caretaker had been the consensus, probably hired by Mal McKenzie to maintain the property and prevent further vandalism.

Then a phone call from an overexcited Lisette put paid to that. Grassmoor was agog with the news that Stirling was Dougal Kildare's son. A son no one knew existed and who had, astonishingly, inherited Westwind. Lisette had been madly googling Stirling Kildare but what little there was online appeared to be for a different person. Figuring if he was some sort of secret baby then his name was unlikely to be Kildare, Lisette called in a favour and scrounged his surname from a friend at the hospital.

Of Stirling Hawley there was even less. No social media accounts, no news reports, no job history. Either he was a very private person or a man who covered his tracks.

Which, for the cynically minded, suggested Stirling might also be a man with something to hide.

'Do you think he'll know where the money went?' Rachel asked now.

'I don't know, Mum. I'd say it was unlikely.'

The last thing Darcy wanted was her mum getting her hopes up. If Stirling had been involved in Dougal's scheme, he wouldn't be about to share the news anyway.

It was fanciful—she'd only met the man twice after all, and their first encounter could hardly count—but Darcy found it difficult to believe Stirling had been a part of the fraud that had caused their family, and other local families, so much stress and had ultimately led Dougal to suicide. Stirling seemed nice, his caution natural for a man who found himself in an alien situation, and he'd laughed at her teasing.

Then again, scam artists were renowned for being charmers.

Still, instinct had Darcy giving Stirling the benefit of the doubt. Something about him warmed her. His attractiveness probably had a lot to do with it, though she suspected it was also his stoicism. It was quite a thing to see a man endure so much and maintain a little humour. Not sexy—blood and near death could never be sexy—but impressive. Stirling was a man of inner strength.

The sort of man Darcy wanted to learn more about.

Saturday rose clear as forecast but with a nasty south-westerly wind bulldozing its way across the landscape. Darcy's plans for her football finals outfit were blown away the moment she stepped outside. She stood in the little courtyard behind her workshop—or atelier, as she preferred to call it—and frowned at the contorted treetops and whoosh of battered countryside.

Not to worry. Another ensemble awaited. Not as delightful as the green fit and flare dress with white and gold spotted inserts and collar that she'd planned, but there'd be no mistaking which team Darcy championed.

It was important to show support. Country sports clubs were like schools. If they withered, the community withered right alongside them. Anything that brought people together, gave them a feeling of belonging and pride, helped keep the district vibrant and alive. Weathering the freezing cold at the Hoppers home ground was a small price to pay. Besides, Darcy rather enjoyed watching fit men coated in mud and sweat pummel one another.

She crinkled her nose again at the sky and ducked back inside. The game didn't start until 2 pm. Darcy had enough time to cut out her latest orders and still have time to spare for glamorising.

At least she would have, had Lisette not come pounding on VaVoom's front door, arms loaded with lattes and vanilla custard slices from Joanne Pascoe's cafe, and a truly hideous grey slouch beanie half-covering her ice-blonde razor-cut hair. Lisette, bless her, was not a fashionista. Though she had swapped her daisy nose stud for an enamelled green and gold four-leafed clover.

'Made by Joanne herself,' said Lisette, thrusting a large disposable cup at Darcy. Everyone knew Joanne's assistant Tilly was a dreadful barista, but she was such a sweet girl no one wanted to hurt her feelings by saying so. Scoring decent coffee was a matter of timing orders for when Joanne was manning the machine.

'I thought we were meeting at the ground?' said Darcy, taking the cup and paper bags and heading for the kitchen, her heels clacking on the polished concrete floor.

The former workshop that had become her home as well as VaVoom's shopfront and atelier had been built in the sixties, with the no-frills architecture typical of the era. Set two blocks from Grassmoor's small business and administrative strip, the building had stood unloved for years. When it went up for sale cheap, Darcy couldn't believe her luck. The workshop might have been bedraggled, but it was nearly a hundred and fifty square metres in size, structurally sound, and as a workshop and home, its potential was enormous.

The moment settlement went through, she'd set to work, painting and decorating with the help of family and friends until uninhabitable industrial drab was transformed into comfortable vintage chic.

'I couldn't wait that long for gossip,' said Lisette, following her. 'And I figured I may as well walk down with you.'

Darcy passed through the doorway that separated the atelier from her open-plan living quarters, and a set of stairs that led to a mezzanine floor and her bedroom and bathroom. The concrete floor had been replaced with softer—and warmer—timber joinery and furniture, and colourful wall art. Darcy had spent months scouring clearing sales for furniture, coming across extraordinary period pieces that were either going for a song or being given away. Every element was well made and stylish. All she'd done was clean and polish, and occasionally paint or stain.

Darcy set down her cup on an artfully distressed, open-shelved island bench and reached below for a couple of plates. 'What gossip?'

'Don't you play coy with me, Princess. You know exactly what gossip.' Lisette settled on a stool opposite and pointed a finger. 'I *know* you saw him at the hospital. So, spill.'

'How do you know that?'

Lisette rolled her eyes.

Darcy suppressed a sigh. She placed the vanilla slices on the plates and turned to the cutlery drawer for some forks.

'There's not a lot to say,' she said, sliding a fork over to Lisette and perching on a stool. 'He's recovering.' She toyed with an edge of slice. 'He looked tired and a bit out of it, poor thing.'

'Probably loaded up on drugs.' Lisette removed the top layer of pastry from her slice and dug into the custard. 'I don't s'pose he mentioned his dodgy daddy?'

'The topic never came up.'

Lisette's eyes narrowed as she sucked custard off her fork. 'What did you talk about then?'

Darcy took a long sip of coffee and wondered why she felt so protective towards Stirling. 'Nothing, really. Michelle Delaney came to pick up his breakfast tray and we got chatting about Mum. I ran out of time after that.'

'That was it?'

'Pretty much, other than asking if he wanted anything from Westwind.'

Lisette's blue eyes turned even brighter. 'So you're seeing him again?'

'If you count dropping off his travel bag as seeing him, then yes. But I don't expect to have any more conversation than my previous visit.'

Lisette pointed her custard-coated fork at Darcy. 'You are *such* a disappointment.'

'What have I done?'

'Nothing. That's the problem. You had him doped up and captive in a hospital bed, and all you can offer me is that you asked if he needed anything. Where's the gossip in that?'

'Lissy.'

'I know, I know. Gossip is the root of all evil. Blah, blah. But I have to live my life vicariously through someone.' Lisette jabbed at her slice. 'Mine's so boring it even puts me to sleep.'

Darcy's heart squeezed for her darling friend. 'Chin up. Today's only young. For all you know, your dream man could be waiting for you at the football.' Preferably someone not named Charlie Shanahan, the local man-tart Lisette had a bad habit of hooking up with.

'Yeah, and next minute you'll be telling me custard's not fattening.'

'It's not. Everyone knows that. It's full of dairy, which does wonders for your bones and skin. Now stop picking at your food and help me cut out these orders. Then, if you're good, I'll do your makeup so you can look even more beautiful for the game than you already are.'

They spent the morning in the atelier with the stereo blasting noughties hits from their teenage years—Lisette refused to listen to Darcy's fifties collection—allowing Darcy to get her patterns cut out with plenty of time to spare.

With the fabric set aside with matching cottons, zips and fastenings, ready for sewing, Darcy perched Lisette on a stool in her kitchen, tossed the abominable slouch beanie aside and went to work on her face.

Twenty minutes later, Darcy plopped a green velvet baker boy hat from her personal collection on Lisette's head and stood back to admire her efforts. 'Truly gorgeous.'

Lisette bounced over to the hammered copper wall mirror to peer at herself. She tipped her head left and right, admiring her glittery gold eyeshadow and the green grasshopper stencils on her cheeks, then grinned and blew Darcy a kiss. 'Thank you. You're a doll.'

'My pleasure. Right,' said Darcy, heading for her bedroom. 'My turn.'

'I'll see you in a couple of hours then, Princess.'

Darcy flicked her a very unladylike finger that only made Lisette laugh.

'That's not very princessy.'

'That's because I'm not a princess, Mistress Lissy.'

'Is that so?'

'It is indeed.'

'You mean you're a bog-standard bogan like the rest of us?'

'Hardly. I,' announced Darcy, raising her middle finger even higher and wiggling her hips, 'am a queen.'

'A queen,' spluttered Lisette. 'Of what?'

'The Queen of Seam! What else?'

Chapter Six

Darcy and Lisette arrived at Goodwin Oval to find Hoppers and Magpie supporters huddled around a series of blazing fire drums on the concrete steps in front of the canteen, sipping beers and hot drinks, and scoffing pies and barbecued sausage and onion sandwiches.

If the morning's wind had been bad, the afternoon's southerly was even more brutal, rattling wires and gutters, and tossing rubbish and poor-fitting hats. To foil the wind, Darcy had wrapped her head in a green and gold rockabilly hair tie with a wired bow that stuck up like hare's ears, but even that was threatening to launch.

Greetings followed them as they wandered, along with several startled looks at Darcy's outfit and more than the occasional titter. The fashion philistines could laugh all they liked. She felt amazing.

'It's days like today I wish I hated football,' said Lisette, scrubbing her mittened hands together. 'Beer? I need alcohol to warm me up.'

Darcy considered a moment, then shrugged. 'Why not?'

'Why not indeed.' Lisette nodded towards the boundary fence. 'Shiloh's here.'

Darcy whipped around. Shiloh had her bum perched on the wire fence, her arms folded and her mouth grim. She wore her usual jeans, leather boots and fleece-lined coat, and a green and gold Hoppers woollen beanie on her head, but she may as well have had a sign on top saying 'Don't come near me', such was the unfriendliness she oozed.

Darcy perched alongside her. Though they shared similar facial features and the rich dark hair common to their mother's side, that's where the sisterly similarity ended. Both were tall women—five feet nine—yet where Shiloh was long and rangy, Darcy was all womanly curves.

Shiloh's skin also bore the wear of her outdoor life. Darcy ached to transform her sister into the beauty she truly was, but the days when Shiloh would let Darcy do her up had long passed. And their mum was right. Shiloh didn't need fuss to make her gorgeous. What she needed was to smile.

'I didn't know you were coming.'

'I wasn't going to.' Shiloh lifted a chapped hand and flopped it down again. 'But it'd be just my luck that the Hoppers would win and then I'd feel like crap for missing out.'

'Nothing to do with Leo playing?'

'Hardly, though I wouldn't say no to watching his head get mashed into the ground.'

Darcy pushed her shoulder against her sister's. 'You don't mean that.' Although Leo did play for the opposition, and while Shiloh's ex might be a darling, the Sloane girls were Grassmoor-born and bred.

'Trust me, I do.' Shiloh looked her up and down. 'You're almost normal today. If you don't count looking like a radioactive duckling.'

'Don't you start.' She smoothed an arm of her neon-yellow, faux fur cropped jacket, admiring the way the pile fluffed and shone.

An online special rather than a VaVoom original, but a style Darcy adored to the point she was contemplating a future faux fur line of her own. She'd teamed it with a green plaid pencil skirt with a fine yellow stripe, tights to battle the cold, and heels. 'How was Mum this morning?'

Shiloh rocked her hand in a so-so gesture. 'A bit better mood-wise than last night but still not great.'

'I'm worried about her, Loh.'

'Yeah. Me too.'

Out on the oval, the players had begun their warm-up. Darcy turned to face them, Shiloh following suit. The Hoppers were at the far end of the ground, running drills in their green and gold guernseys and snowy white shorts.

'She'll be all right,' said Shiloh.

'Of course she will. She just needs something good to happen, that's all. We all do.' Darcy chose her words carefully. 'If you need me at home more ...'

'Don't even think it, Darce. We're fine and you do enough.'

'I can do more.'

'No, you can't. You've got a business to run, a life to live.'

'So do you, Loh.'

Shiloh shook her head and stared fixedly at the players. At the other end of the field, the Magpies were practising shots at goal. Leo kicked and missed to the right. He jogged to collect another ball, his step faltering when he spotted Shiloh, then picking up again. Darcy lifted her hand in greeting. He waved back, though his attention was on his ex-fiancée. Shiloh kept her gaze elsewhere. Darcy had an overwhelming urge to bang their stubborn heads together.

Leo and Shiloh had loved each other since their first meeting, four years ago at a field day when Leo was introduced as the region's new land health officer for Agriculture Victoria. This coming

November sixth should have been their wedding day, but Shiloh got it into her head that Leo had a drunken one-night stand while at a conference and Leo was incensed that Shiloh could believe that of him. Having been cheated on in a previous relationship, Shiloh was hypersensitive to betrayal and the argument had escalated into a stand-off from which neither would budge.

Darcy didn't care what the truth was. All she knew was that these two darling, obstinate people loved one another and were hurting badly.

'Beer time,' called Lisette, walking towards them with three cans in her hands. She shoved one at Shiloh, who regarded it with confusion. 'You looked like you needed it.' Lisette handed the other to Darcy and took a long guzzle of her own. 'Ah, now that's better. So ... any excitement yet?'

'Only Darcy's neon fur blinding everyone,' said Shiloh.

Unperturbed, Darcy gave her sleeve another proud pat. It truly was a lovely jacket. She'd have to make one in leopard print, with a matching beret.

'I hope we win the toss,' said Lisette, looking up at the Hoppers flag snapping in the wind atop the tiny clubhouse. 'We don't want the boys kicking into the breeze in the final quarter.'

They chatted football and watched the warm-ups until the five-minute siren sounded. Spectators began to filter from the sanctuary of the fire drums to the oval fence. The players went into their huddles, arms draped across each other's backs, heads up and attention on their coaches. Darcy found herself admiring taut legs and bums. There was nothing like a nicely fitted pair of shorts to show off a man's assets. She wondered what Stirling's were like. Not very pretty at the moment.

Poor man, he was probably bored silly in the hospital. At least now he had his phone to play with and could call people.

The game began to loud cheers and whoops from the crowd. The Hoppers scored first but the Magpies quickly responded with a goal and followed that with a point. Fired up from their beers, Darcy and Lisette bellowed encouragement from the sidelines, while Shiloh remained her usual cool self. Only when Leo was driven to the ground in a ferocious tackle did she react—her hand jamming over her mouth and eyes wide with alarm.

For a horrible moment it seemed as though Leo would stay down, then he rolled onto his hands and knees, back heaving as he sucked in breaths, and pushed himself up. A few sore steps to test his legs and he was jogging back into the fray.

Darcy and Lisette gave Shiloh the side-eye.

She lifted her chin. 'I wasn't worried.'

'Of course you weren't,' replied Darcy before she and Lisette broke into giggles, which only made Shiloh hold her nose even higher.

Having learned from experience that the quarter-time canteen queue would be frightful, Darcy ducked away early to fetch more drinks.

'Three mid-strength beers, thanks, Carla,' she said. The canteen was run by volunteers, most of whom Darcy knew.

Carla placed the beers on the table and began popping the tops. 'I hear you have a new neighbour.'

That Darcy hadn't lived with her parents for over three years didn't count. She was a Roseneath girl and that was that.

'We do indeed.'

'Is it true he's Dougal's son?'

'So I believe.'

'But you met him, didn't you?'

'I did. At Westwind, but we didn't really get a chance to talk. Too busy trying to stop him bleeding to death.' The quarter-time siren blasted. Darcy snatched up the beers before Carla could probe any further. 'Look out, the hordes are coming. Best get out of the way.'

The hordes were indeed coming. Watching football was thirsty work at the best of times, even more so when it was a final and the Hoppers were trailing by fifteen points. Darcy lowered her head and made a beeline for their spot against the fence but it was impossible to keep a low profile in a fluffy neon-yellow jacket.

'Well, if it isn't Darcy Sloane. Nice to see you out supporting our boys.'

Darcy groaned. Michael Byrne had been friends with her mum and dad since before she was born, which made him difficult to avoid. 'How could I do anything else? How are you, Michael?'

'I'm good, lass. Always good.'

'That's great to hear. How's Samantha?'

'Aw, not bad.' He jerked his thumb behind him. 'Over there with Cait and the kids. Now tell me, this Stirling fellow that turned up, what do you know about him?'

'Not a thing,' she said cheerfully.

'But I heard you saved his life.'

'Not me. That was the paramedics.' She made to move away but Michael blocked her with a nifty sidestep.

'Didn't you visit him in hospital?'

Darcy's smile threatened to become a rictus. *This town.* 'A five-minute courtesy call. I was there with Mum anyway. It seemed the polite thing to do.' She raised the beers. 'Must get back. Lisette will start frothing at the mouth if I don't.'

Twice more Darcy was stopped and asked about Stirling. Twice more she gritted her teeth and replied that she had nothing to offer beyond what everyone already seemed to know.

The pattern continued at half-time, then at three-quarter-time. Fearing what more alcohol might do to her temper, Darcy refused more beer, swapping to hot chocolate and letting Lisette and Shiloh do the canteen run. Still people sidled up to her, their small talk quickly turning to Stirling.

'I don't know why you think I should know anything about Dougal's son,' said Darcy, finally cracking at the persistent prying from an elderly gentleman she barely knew. 'All I did was take my dress off for him. Now if you'll excuse me, I have a football team to support.'

'Helpful,' said Shiloh.

Darcy sniffed. 'Serves him right.'

'You're in for it now.' Lisette eyed her over her beer, her gaze bright with alcohol and mirth. 'Good as saying you were shagging.'

Darcy's shoulders slumped. Didn't she know it? Yet the idea of being associated with Stirling that way didn't bother her as it should. In fact, it rather appealed.

Truly, she could be a silly girl sometimes.

⤜

'Your belongings,' said Darcy, holding up Stirling's travel bag. It was midafternoon on Monday and the ward was quiet, Darcy the only visitor. 'Where would you like it?'

'On the bed's fine.'

She obliged and stood back. Now she'd brought his bag, Darcy had no reason to linger. She should leave, pick up the groceries she needed, grab the books from the library her mum had reserved. Stick to her resolve to keep Stirling Hawley at a polite distance. That she was attracted to him meant nothing. He could be a serial killer for all she knew.

Or a fraudster like his father, as Lisette had reminded her more than once on Sunday when she'd popped over for a debrief.

To many locals' surprise, the Hoppers had won their semifinal by three points and would now take on the Cats in the preliminary final the following week. With Darcy having escaped to Roseneath with Shiloh after the game, Lisette had celebrated the win with more beer but thankfully not another ill-judged liaison with Charlie Shanahan, who was busy sharing his affections elsewhere.

Which had Lisette moaning again about having to live her love life vicariously through Darcy, and that Darcy wasn't helping. Stripping off for Stirling Hawley didn't count. And Darcy would need to be careful there anyway. The old saying of apples not falling far from trees and all that had to come from somewhere.

Advice Darcy reminded herself she should heed.

She trailed her fingertips to and fro over the footboard of his bed. 'How are you feeling?'

Stirling lifted his head from the bag. 'Better, thanks.'

He didn't look as groggy as Friday. His eyes were bright and the skin on his face not covered by stubble was pink and healthy looking. The only indication of his pain was the sharp hiss he'd made when he shuffled up the bed to greet her on arrival.

Darcy indicated a free patch of mattress on his uninjured side. 'May I?'

'Sure.'

She sat and smoothed the front of her skinny denim capris. Normally Darcy adored greaser fashion but today she was feeling less than perfect. The weather had turned awful. The temperature had dropped to the low teens and showers sheeted the countryside. Great for the land, not so great for driving or for carefully styled hair and clothes.

Her red stretch satin bomber jacket had rain spots and the red silk rose she'd pinned in her hair felt heavy and floppy with damp. Worse, with her favourite red Mary Jane heels needing repair after their Westwind adventure, she'd opted for black and they just weren't working.

Not that she'd dressed to impress Stirling, of course.

'Do you have everything you need?' she asked.

'Mostly. A new leg would be good.' Stirling smiled wryly and Darcy noticed he had a faint dimple in his left cheek. 'How was Westwind?'

'The same, if you don't count the bloodstains.'

That earned her a low chuckle. 'No more vandalism?'

'Not that I could see.'

'Good.'

'Oh,' she said, lifting her tote to her knees. 'Your keys.'

She presented them in the flat of her hand. Stirling's fingers tickled her palm as he collected them. Darcy still hadn't figured out why she never admitted on her previous visit to knowing where the spare key was hidden. It wasn't as though she planned to sneak around spying on him. She opened her mouth to tell him, but Stirling got in first.

'Thanks. And thanks again for …' He nodded at his travel bag.

It sounded like a dismissal, or at least a conversation-ender. Darcy jerked upright. She shouldn't have sat on his bed anyway. It was far too intimate. 'You're welcome. If there's anything else you need, let me know.' She dug in her bag for a business card and set it on the blanket. 'This is me, in case you're looking for something to amuse yourself with.'

Stirling studied the card and then her. 'That accounts for it then.'

Darcy stiffened. 'Accounts for what?'

'Your clothes. The retro vibe. Nice branding. I bet you get heaps of people asking where you get your outfits from.'

She hadn't expected the compliment. Often men thought her style of dress a joke. A sexy one, but a joke all the same. Stirling's tone was serious, admiring even, his gaze direct. The stiffness eased.

'I do, although not as often as I once did. People are used to me now. Much of my business is online these days, but it was showcasing my talents locally that got me started.'

'How long has VaVoom been going for?'

'Six years.' Darcy resisted the urge to park her bum back on the bed and tell him all about it. She was sure the question was posed out of politeness. 'Four of them full time.'

'What did you do before that?'

'I was at the Toyota dealership here.'

Interest flickered across his face as though she'd surprised him. 'Doing what?'

'Sales. I was truly excellent at it too.'

He laughed. Not a chuckle but a proper laugh. The sound warmed Darcy's insides.

'Somehow that doesn't surprise me.'

'And you?'

'Me what?'

'What are you excellent at?'

Stirling tipped his head. 'Are we flirting?'

'Of course not.' Although they absolutely were. 'That sort of behaviour could do a man an injury.' She pursed her lips. 'Further injury. I wouldn't want that on my conscience.'

His mouth twisted up in one corner. Not smiling, more thoughtful. He regarded her business card and tapped it against the side of his fist.

Flirting with Dougal Kildare's son. What was she thinking?

That he was gorgeous, that's what. Goodness, now she could add shallow alongside silly to her current list of personality failings.

'Who taught you to sew?'

'My gran.' Darcy smiled at both his continued curiosity and the mention of her beloved grandmother. 'Mum can sew but she doesn't love it. Gran's a gun.'

'You are too. Obviously.'

'Indeed I am.'

The smile was back, complete with dimple. 'No false modesty with you, Darcy Sloane.'

'Not when it comes to sewing, no. It's my passion. I fell head over heels from my first lesson. I can still remember it. Gran helped me make pyjamas for Wilbur—that was my teddy bear. We took him from fuzzy brown obscurity to purple tartan glory in less than an hour, and I was truly gone.' She stroked her shiny sleeve. 'I've been making my own clothes since I was twelve.' Darcy winked. 'Not always to my parents' liking.'

That scored her another laugh, then he sobered. 'It's good to meet someone who's made a life out of their passion.'

She caught the note of chagrin in his tone. 'You haven't?'

'I did,' he said quietly, his eyes lowering. 'It's over now.' For a moment it looked as though he'd say more, then he glanced around the ward and shrugged. 'Shit happens.'

Darcy wanted to probe further. What was over for him? Surely his leg would heal and let him carry on his passion, whatever it was. The injury was serious but not life-changing.

Stirling's expression prevented further inquiry. His gaze continued to sweep the ward like he was assessing a field of play. Darcy slid a look behind her. Two curious faces peered at them from the beds against the other wall. She felt a childish urge to give them a little wave and embarrass them into focusing elsewhere. Except they probably wouldn't. The son of the now notorious Dougal Kildare was too much of a novelty.

She looked back to find him watching her.

'Always an audience around here,' he said and there was no mistaking the bitterness in his tone.

'I know,' said Darcy, trying for humour. 'I do apologise. I tend to have this effect on people and, well ...' She leaned forward and spoke in a conspiratorial whisper. 'I *am* wearing a rather fetching satin bomber jacket.'

He smiled but his amusement was short-lived. He regarded his clenched fists and hauled in a breath, as if the attention exhausted him. Or he was trying to settle burgeoning anger.

'Stirling?'

'It's nothing. Just me. Don't worry about it.'

A lie. Those taut knuckles weren't nothing.

Darcy hesitated then touched his arm. 'It'll pass. Give it time.' Although she couldn't promise that. For some, the damage Dougal had done would rattle through generations. Stirling would always attract their attention.

His head jerked up. His eyes scanned hers, back and forth, back and forth, before resignation turned them dull. 'You know who I am.'

Oh no, Darcy wasn't having any of his self-pity. Nor would she allow him to put her in others' shoes. Darcy Sloane formed her own opinions, thank you very much.

She straightened and regarded him down her nose.

'No, Stirling, I don't. I know who your father is. I know you inherited Westwind. About you?' She hoisted her bag on to her shoulder. 'I know nothing at all.'

Chapter Seven

Stirling shot another disgusted look around the ward before flopping his head on the pillow and staring at the ceiling. Jesus, he hated hospitals. The sooner he escaped the better.

Except that wouldn't be happening for a while yet. He'd had a physio session earlier that morning to assess how mobile he was. Not very, was the conclusion. The injury was healing as well as could be expected—it was the weakness in his left leg that was the problem. It wasn't coping with the extra strain. Even a short trip to the toilet left him sweating and exhausted, his bones throbbing in protest.

He opened his phone to call Toby again then realised he would be at work, and Stirling had caught him up on the news earlier anyway. He tried the novel he'd downloaded instead, but his mind refused to focus. Stirling sighed and lay with his arm draped across his eyes, wishing Darcy would visit again, but he hadn't seen her since Monday and it was now Thursday.

Serves himself right for being a tool.

He'd checked out her website several times since she'd passed him her business card. Once should have been enough to learn all he needed, but after scrolling through her store, Stirling had discovered that not only did Darcy sew all of VaVoom's clothes, she modelled them too. There were images of her wearing all sorts of retro outfits, some of them almost comic in their fifties femininity. Others, like the pin-up range, were far too sexy for a bloke stuck in an open ward with visitors and staff in and out all the time to be looking at. It was hard to stop scrolling though. Darcy had a figure, that's for sure.

'Excuse me?'

Stirling lowered his arm.

A good-looking, if greying, man wearing a tan blazer and navy moleskin jeans stood near the end of his bed. Stirling considered him, thinking how similar he looked to pictures he'd seen of his father, then dismissed the idea. It was the just the clothes and the way he stood, upright and confident. A man who knew his worth. Dougal had the same posture, in the photos. Stirling used to as well.

The man came closer. 'Stirling Hawley, am I right?'

Stirling eyed him warily. 'Yes.'

He nodded. 'I thought so. You have the look of your father.' A slight pucker formed between his brows as his gaze roved over Stirling, then he seemed to shake himself. 'Forgive me,' he said, holding out his hand, his voice deep and cultured. 'Mal McKenzie. I was a close friend of Dougal's. And his solicitor for many years.'

With a quiet grunt, Stirling raised himself a little to shake Mal's hand then rested back. As far as Stirling understood, William Stoddart was Dougal's solicitor. He wondered what that meant.

'I heard about your Westwind misadventure. Thought I'd see how you are.' Anguish darted across his face and was gone. 'Dougal would have expected it.'

'Thanks.' Stirling didn't really know what else to say.

Mal stared around the ward and lifted a hand to the elderly heart attack victim. 'Randall, good to see you. I trust you're being well cared for?'

'Yup, yup. All dandy. They're good here.'

'That they are.' Mal smiled and regarded Stirling once more. 'And you? Are you being well looked after?'

'I am. Just waiting for the okay to get out of here.'

'Not a fan of hospitals, I take it.'

'No.'

Mal raised an eyebrow. 'Do I detect the voice of experience?'

'Something like that.'

Mal rolled his lips together. Stirling knew he was being rude with his abbreviated answers but he didn't know how else to act. He'd always kept himself to himself, and while Mal might have been his father's friend, that didn't automatically make him Stirling's.

'I imagine it was a shock, inheriting Westwind. It was certainly a shock to everyone in Grassmoor.' He shook his head. 'I've been friends with Dougal since primary school, close friends, and even I never knew he had a son.'

'If it's any consolation,' said Stirling, pushing himself up the bed so he could regard Mal more closely, 'I didn't know much about Dougal beyond his name and that he lived in country Victoria.' And that he wasn't a complete deadbeat because he'd helped fund Stirling's boarding school fees.

'Your mother never talked about him?'

'A little.' Stirling avoided Mal's gaze. The subject wasn't a sore point, more an awkward one. Amanda and Dougal had a fling, during which Stirling doubted they'd had the time or inclination to share life stories. One thing he was certain—Amanda hadn't known Dougal was married or had a baby. That knowledge had come too late.

As a little boy, Stirling had often wondered about his father. When asked, his mum described Dougal as a decent man but one who already had a family that didn't need to be hurt. It wasn't until he was older that he read between her words and reached his own conclusion. His father was a cheat and a liar, and as far from decent as you could get. By the time Stirling had matured enough to understand human frailty, that the world wasn't all black and white, his life was elsewhere.

There'd been a letter once, when he was thirteen, sent to him at boarding school. It was short and formal, and gave away nothing more than that Amanda had been sending Dougal copies of Stirling's school reports and that he was pleased at how well Stirling was doing. And that if he would like, perhaps they could meet one day.

Stirling had brooded over it for a week, then thrown the letter in the bin. What did he need a father for?

'I expect you have a lot of questions about him,' said Mal.

'A few.'

'I'm more than happy to answer what I can. When you're ready, of course. As I said, I've known ...' He closed his eyes and took a deep breath before continuing. '*Knew* Dougal since we were boys. I was best man at his wedding. I'm also Melody's godfather, although I can't say I've been very godly.' He laughed softly. 'I was there for the divorce too. We were close.' His voice took on a husky edge. 'I still don't understand why he did what he did. He should have come to me. I would have helped.'

Whether Mal was referring to the fraud or Dougal's suicide, Stirling couldn't tell, and he wasn't about to ask, not with his wardmates listening in.

When Stirling remained quiet, Mal cast around again, his shoulders slumped and his expression slightly lost. 'Well, I won't keep you. I just thought I'd visit. Check if you needed anything and let you know I'm here to help.' He paused. 'Dougal would have done the same for my son.'

Guilt roused Stirling into speech. Mal sounded sincere in both his grief and his offer of assistance. 'Thanks. I appreciate it. And I'll take you up on that offer, to answer questions about Dougal. It's too late to know him personally but I'd like to learn what I can.'

'I look forward to it. Your father was a good man and an even better friend. It'll be a pleasure to tell you about him.' He took a card from his pocket and handed it over.

Stirling nodded his thanks. 'I'll be in touch.' He grimaced and gestured at his leg. 'When I get out of here.'

'Let's hope that's soon. If you do need anything,' Mal indicated the card, 'just call.'

They shook hands. Stirling watched Mal walk away, his head full of thoughts. He'd have to start a list or he'd never remember everything he wanted to know.

Although, given Mal's comments, it seemed that as to why his father committed suicide, there'd never be an answer.

❧

'That's a bloody shame, that is,' said the rideshare driver, tutting as he pulled up. 'Some people, eh?'

Stirling's stomach tightened. He was in the back seat reaching for his crutches and Gavin's statement triggered a spasm of fear. He ducked to stare through the windscreen and breathed out. Westwind's facade hadn't changed. Pink stone, pretty in the afternoon light. Broken finials. Rage-fuelled graffiti.

And the strange sensation of belonging to a place that didn't want him at all.

Stirling grabbed his crutches and pushed open the door.

'Hang on there, mate.' Gavin jumped out and held the door then Stirling's arm as he struggled out, wincing and panting as his stitches pulled and his torn flesh protested the movement. 'You right?'

'I'm good.' He wasn't. Sweat speckled his lip and his heart was hammering. Pain flowed up and down his leg. He should have taken a painkiller. One wouldn't have killed him, yet here he was again, trying to be tough. Letting his fear of addiction override practicality.

'I'll get your bags, help you inside, eh?'

'Thanks, Gavin. Appreciate it.'

He waved him off with a bray of laughter. 'Ah, I'm just angling for a gander at your house.' He kept up his chatter as he collected Stirling's bags. There were only two—his travel bag and a plastic sack containing dressings and drugs. 'Never knew all these old places existed till we moved here. Magnificent, they are. Like being in England.'

Gavin slammed the boot and Stirling began making his slow way to the rear of the house. To his relief, Gavin had been happy to do the conversational heavy lifting for most of the journey from the hospital, distracting Stirling from his aching body with the story of his and his wife Jesinta's 'tree-change' to Hamilton and how it was the best decision they'd ever made. Jesinta had quickly secured a job with the local council but when Gavin lucked out, he decided to give rideshare driving a go, figuring it'd be a good way to meet people and learn his way around. His son, who was some sort of computer expert, designed an app, enabling Gavin to work purely for himself. A few ads in the *Hamilton Spectator* and he was in business. A couple of years on, he couldn't imagine doing anything else.

He'd let on early that he knew exactly who Stirling was. According to Gavin, Dougal was all people had talked about in the district for a while. Now the subject was Stirling himself.

'Jeez, they must have had some money, these old families,' said Gavin, his head swivelling as he admired the house and surrounds. 'Bloody amazing. Talk about riding on sheep's back and all that, eh? I read that some of the houses had proper staff, right down to uniformed chauffeurs for their Rolls Royces. Some even had polo fields and their own racecourse. Imagine that!'

'I don't think Westwind was ever that grand,' Stirling managed to grunt.

'Maybe not. Bloody nice place though. You're a lucky man.'

Despite his struggle, Stirling smiled at the comment. He was a lucky man. Short another of his nine lives but still here, breathing in Westwind's sweet grassy air.

'What I'd do for a place like this. Mind you, Jesinta wouldn't like it.'

'Why not?'

'Too much to clean!' Gavin bellowed with laughter.

Stirling was panting by the time he made it to the back door. He pulled the key from his pocket and tried to insert it in the lock, but his hand was shaking too much. What did he expect? That he'd be fine? The staff had warned him he was in no state to discharge himself, strongly urging he at least wait a few more days. Except Stirling was over the hospital and everything to do with it. Seriously over. And reckless decision or not, he'd walked. Well, hobbled. Now he had to suck it up.

'Here,' said Gavin, taking the keys from him. 'Let me.'

Stirling leaned against the wall as Gavin unlocked the door, grateful for the cold of the stone. His gaze found the Ducati. An enterprising spider had cast a web from one of its handlebars and a light film of dust had settled on the seat and tank. He swallowed and looked away as the pain in his chest threatened to eclipse the pain in his leg.

He'd ride again. He might not feel capable right now, but he would.

'There we go,' said Gavin, holding the door wide.

He helped Stirling settle in the kitchen, then stood in front of the sink chafing his hands as he peered through the far doorway to the rest of the house.

'Help yourself to a nose about,' said Stirling.

Gavin's hands froze mid rub. 'You don't mind?'

He shook his head, smiling at the man's contained stillness, like a wildcat about to pounce. Gavin had gone beyond the call, even picking up some trackpants for him from a discount store. Stirling owed him, and while he'd just met him, he didn't think Gavin would lift anything. And if he did, Stirling wouldn't know anyway.

'I'd give you a tour but …' He shrugged. Not that he'd be much of a guide. Gavin probably knew more about Westwind's history from chatting to locals than him. Stirling's information came from internet searches and consisted mostly of dull facts, devoid of life and colour and narrative. It was people who gave places vitality, who told the stories that mattered and gave context to a heritage he was only now discovering.

Maybe there was a history somewhere in the house. A family Bible with births, deaths and marriage notices glued to the front pages. Maybe even diaries, or old ledgers and the like that detailed Westwind's day-to-day past. He'd have to search. A job for when he was more mobile.

With profuse thanks for his trust and a promise to be quick, Gavin scurried off.

Stirling checked his phone as he waited. A message from his mum, sending her love and hoping he was following doctor's orders, along with a lament that he probably wasn't. Another from Olympia, complaining that he hadn't called. Get-well wishes and jokes from the few mates he'd contacted. Bank and investment statements and other adult stuff. The mess of a normal civilian life that he supposed was his now.

Creaks and groans sounded from overhead, along with the occasional whistle. Gavin was enjoying himself.

Stirling opened an email from Toby. He'd sent a message that morning to let his friend know he was leaving the hospital. Toby had understood even if he hadn't liked it. The email was short, just a few lines, but it didn't need to be more. The attached photo said it all.

Stirling, Toby, Günter and Alina. In a bar in Prague, half-drunk beers on the table, summer sunshine lighting their faces. Stirling had his arm slung around Alina's shoulders. Toby was pointing at them and making his rolly-eyed 'get a room' face. Günter's dimples were pulling double duty as he threw a cheeky wink at someone off camera.

'Good times' was the title of the photo. Stirling's insides squeezed as though gripped by a phantom fist.

They had been. Wonderful times. Times too short and not savoured enough. But they weren't to know the future. They weren't to know that less than three months after that photo was taken, Alina and Günter would be dead, that Toby had lost all faith in MiZ and its cause, and that Stirling would end up so damaged, his chances of flying again were next to nil.

Deep down though, they'd understood the risks, the spectre that hovered dark and sinister over their lives. Which was why they'd partied and loved hard when they could.

He caressed Alina's face for a moment, mentally thanking her, missing her cleverness and compassion and screwed-up bravery, and closed the image.

'Terrific place, Stirling. Amazing. How about that staircase, eh? The workmanship that must have gone into it. They don't make 'em like that anymore. Nope.' Gavin gazed around the kitchen. 'Needs a family, a house like this.' He wiggled his eyebrows at Stirling. 'Won't be a problem for a handsome young gun like you. You wait, the local ladies'll be lining up for the job.'

Stirling laughed but didn't comment. As much as he liked Gavin, he wasn't going anywhere near that can of worms, and he'd already shared too much about himself. Normally he wouldn't be so open, but Gavin was the kind of man who invited camaraderie, and constant pain had made Stirling weak and in need of a friend.

'You know,' said Gavin, frowning, 'it's a strange thing, your old man committing suicide. You remember that case in New South Wales? The woman who stole all those millions?'

Stirling shook his head.

'Last year, it was. Could've been the year before.' He scratched his jaw and waved the problem off. 'Doesn't matter. Anyway, one morning the police raided her house and that afternoon she walked out and vanished off the face of the earth. Everyone was convinced she'd done a runner and was living it up on a yacht somewhere. Then body parts started washing up along the coast. All the experts kept flapping their arms and saying they couldn't believe it. Apparently topping themselves isn't what fraudsters do. They believe in themselves too much. It's the victims who're more likely to jump off a cliff, poor sods.'

'He was probably ashamed. It's a powerful emotion.'

'Maybe.' Gavin's frown deepened. 'Your old man had a lot to live for though. He had a daughter. Grandies to look forward to.' He gestured at Stirling. 'You. Even if he'd gone to jail, he probably wouldn't have been in for long. Two or three years, if that. From what I hear he was well liked. People would have forgiven him.

Not everyone maybe, but enough.' His gaze wandered around the kitchen. 'He had this place. All that land. If he really wanted to get away from here, he could have sold up and gone anywhere.' He shook his head. 'Doesn't make sense.'

It didn't. Not when it was put like that. But who knew what was going through Dougal's mind that day? Stirling couldn't help looking towards the door. The same door his father had walked out of on his journey to the car shed, where he'd thrown a rope around one of the joists, climbed on a drum, set the noose around his neck and stepped off. Mal had found him four days later. Stirling knew only too well what a four-day-old corpse looked and smelled like.

'Suicide never does make sense,' he replied sadly.

'No.' Gavin shook himself. 'Sorry. Shouldn't've brought it up. None of my business.' He slapped his hands together. 'Right then. Anything else I can get you while I'm here?'

'No, I'm good and you need to get back to work.'

'Ah, don't you worry about that. Worth missing a few jobs just to see inside here.' He gazed about again. 'Can't wait to tell the wife. She'll be jealous, all right.' Gavin glanced at the fridge. 'What about food? Milk and the like.'

'The nurses told me the supermarket in Grassmoor delivers.'

Gavin checked his watch. 'You'll have missed today though. I could do a quick run for you.'

'I'm good.'

'You sure?'

'I am.' Stirling stretched out his hand. 'Thanks for your help, Gavin. Appreciate it.'

'Not a problem.' He returned Stirling's shake with warmth. 'You take care now. And like I said, if you need any help getting about, just call my mobile.' He tapped his nose. 'What the taxman don't know won't hurt him and I don't mind a trip around the countryside.'

With a wave and a bang of the door, Gavin was gone.

A hush descended on Westwind. Without Gavin's friendly enthusiasm, the house felt cold, the air stale. Stirling sat at the table, his fingers drumming on the timber tabletop, then with a sigh he opened his phone and googled the supermarket. He could make it through what remained of the day with pantry supplies but tomorrow he'd need fresh food. And he could really go a decent steak. Some fruit too. Vegetables. Bread and cheese and maybe some ham. A chook to roast. Real food.

Moody's Ezymart had no online presence bar a Facebook page advertising the week's specials. Annoying but not insurmountable. Stirling grabbed the shopping list he'd made before the accident, marked the main essentials with an asterisk, and dialled the store.

He was greeted with a no-nonsense-sounding woman's voice.

'I was told you do farm deliveries,' said Stirling.

'We do. Twenty dollars with a minimum hundred-dollar order.'

'I'd like to place an order then.'

'Sure. What property?'

He hesitated. 'Westwind.'

There was a heavy silence. Stirling glanced at his screen to check the connection but it was still open. His jaw flexed.

'Hello?'

'We can't deliver there,' said the woman. 'Westwind's too far out.' She paused. 'Sorry.'

Not a scrap of apology existed in her tone.

Stirling matched it with solid ice. 'It's less than twelve kilometres.'

'Like I said,' she said smugly, 'out of our delivery area.'

'Let me guess, your delivery area is eleven k's and under.'

'Got it in one.'

His fingers drummed as he considered his options. It was the cafe and motel over again. He'd begun to think they'd been anomalies. The nurses hadn't been bothered by him, their care efficient and kind. The wardmates Stirling had suspected of judging him from their beds had wished him well when he'd discharged himself that morning, and Gavin was the personification of amiability.

And Darcy …

'Anything else?' the woman said sweetly.

He laughed at her gall. 'No. Thanks. You go back to enjoying your work.'

Stirling hung up and set the phone down and stared at it. This is what it was going to be like? Fine. He'd faced worse intolerance and fought it. A small town was nothing.

Chapter Eight

Stirling made do with tinned spaghetti for dinner, heated on the upright stove and eaten out of the pot. For dessert he opened a can of pears, spearing the halves with the same fork he'd used for the spaghetti. Preparing the food had been painful enough without worrying about etiquette.

Besides, after the Moody's woman, Stirling wasn't feeling very polite.

The hastiness of his decision to discharge himself from hospital really hit home when he attempted to climb the stairs. Five steps up, the agony in his right leg beat any desire for a proper bed, while his left leg and hip threatened mutiny over the strain. Stirling eased his way back to the landing. He'd make do with the couch and a comforting fire.

Both of which were easier said than done.

Kneeling in front of the hearth was a no-go. Stirling ended up on his bum, sideways to the fireplace, with his legs stretched out. The cleaner had set the space with wood and kindling, and he sent them a silent thanks. Matches proved elusive until, after much grunting and swearing as he hoisted upright again, he found a box in a tin on the mantel. By the time Stirling had eased himself down a second time, he was sweating but that would soon wear off. The house was cold, the encroaching night outside even colder, and the only blanket he'd found was a loosely handknitted wool throw.

When the fire was going, he shuffled to rest his back against the base of the couch and watched the flames.

Through the big bay window, night began to fall in earnest, bringing with it a howl of wind. A south-westerly, from the whip and bend of the treetops. In a few minutes Stirling wouldn't be able to see any of the outside. The loneliness of it sat leaden on his chest.

Why the hell had he forsaken hospital for Westwind? It was an isolated property in a distant part of the state, and he couldn't drive. Nor did he know anyone in Grassmoor and of those he had encountered, half seemed to hate him and the other half it was too soon to tell. As for looking after himself, that was going to be more of a challenge than he imagined.

Stirling gazed around the room, at the high ceilings and ornate plasterwork. At the paintings he knew nothing about. The expensive-looking vases and knick-knacks. The sinuously carved mantel clock claiming it wasn't even seven o'clock. The hardcover books with tatty dustcovers and bookmarks poking out that actually looked like they'd been read.

Shadows flickered in the corners and firelight danced along the heavy furniture. In his efforts to get organised, Stirling had missed turning on the lights. He reached for his crutches then stopped. He'd had enough pain for one night and he'd only have to get up again later to turn them off.

He felt the worn rug beneath his hands and wondered if his father had ever sat like this, contemplating the fire. Contemplating who he was and where he fitted in the world.

He should have arranged a lift to Melbourne. Toby would have put him up for a while. They could have done normal stuff. Talked. Worked out where their lives were going. With plenty of savings, money wasn't a pressing issue. Stirling could afford to take his time.

Instead, he'd come back to Westwind, like it would have answers. Stupid. It was just a grand old house full of memories that weren't his and no one could tell him about, and Stirling was a man with a broken body and a future he didn't know how to plan.

The thought turned his throat thick. He stared at his legs, both now useless, and wanted to punch them.

Stirling tipped his head back, blinking rapidly. It was the pain doing it. Eroding his confidence, honing his fear. He'd been through these emotions before and knew they wouldn't last, but knowing did nothing to blunt his current despair. He had too much piled up.

A new light lit the room, followed quickly by a buzz. His phone, still on silent from the hospital, vibrating like a fly in a death spiral on the couch behind him.

He reached for it and checked the screen and couldn't help smiling. Darcy.

I am very cross with you! read the message. Clearly, word of his hospital escape had got around.

He was debating what to type back when the screen buzzed again.

I would have driven you. All you had to do was ask.

'Not one of my strong points,' he muttered.

Didn't want to bother you, he typed back.

I'm bothered now!

He laughed. Darcy was a funny one. *Sorry.*

No you're not. Are you ok there? Do you need anything?

No. All good.

There was a long pause before he received a reply.

I don't believe you. I will be around in the morning to check.

His heart gave a little skip. 'Tool,' he muttered, shaking his head at his stupidity. It wasn't him. Darcy was the sort of woman who'd check up on anyone.

OK, he typed back and waited to see if she'd respond, but the screen faded and no other message appeared.

With a long breath, Stirling set the phone next to him and resumed his contemplation of the fire while the wind gusted and his legs ached and the rest of his life stretched uncertainly before him.

Stirling woke to shivers and even worse aches than the night before. His injured leg was on fire, his hip throbbed like someone had taken to it with a cricket bat and his neck felt as twisted and stiff as a steel coil.

He blinked into the half-light. It was early, dawn barely creeping in, giving him enough light to see that he'd shucked the blanket to the floor during the night. The fire was down to embers.

With a series of grunts and hisses, he manoeuvred himself to sitting and wearily scrubbed his face with his hands, his stubble making a loud rasp in the morning quiet.

Stirling puffed out a breath and tried to sort his mind. First, he needed the loo. Then he needed warmth and coffee and food. For a moment he harboured a fantasy of toast dripping with butter and Vegemite and realised that wouldn't be happening. Then he remembered spotting an open packet of Vita-Brits on the shelf but without milk they were hard work, and likely riddled with weevils. Which left him with baked beans or spaghetti again.

With a sigh, he reached for his crutches and made the laborious trip to the toilet off the mudroom.

Stirling set a tin of baked beans on to heat and flicked the switch on the electric kettle, staring out the window as he waited for both to do their thing. The ruins of a vegetable patch spread below. It had once been well laid out, with raised beds and stakes and training wires. Now the beds were rampant with weeds and volunteer growth from old crops that had reseeded.

The sight triggered a memory of a village he'd once flown into. Several families of refugees had come across the deserted fertile land and tried to make it home. For a while, Stirling suspected they thought they'd found a kind of peace. Inexorably, inevitably, the war found them. First, the refugees were raided by rebels, stripped of food and supplies in the name of a cause they didn't care about, then abandoned to the advancing forces. By the time Stirling and his team arrived, there was little left except the remains of their painstakingly nurtured gardens. He still remembered the faces of the three hollow-eyed children Toby had found. And the shakes of Alina's head as she went from body to body, hopelessly checking for a life to save. Finding none.

Stirling stared at nothing, lost, before finally jolting himself free. The kettle had clicked off, the beans were beginning to caramelise.

He ate, scrutinising the garden with every mouthful. Structurally, everything looked sound. The raised beds were built with treated timber and galvanised iron. The stakes and trellises were plastic-coated steel, peeling in parts but salvageable. The rest he'd figure out.

He snorted, laughing at himself and nearly choking on his beans. What kind of brain fart was this? Stirling knew as much about gardening as he knew about making a home.

But he could learn. Once he was better.

He set the pot in the sink and poured in water, then snatched up the bag of goodies from the hospital. Screw the fear of opiate addiction. His martyrdom would help no one, least of all himself.

He popped a couple of tabs and swallowed them down with water scooped from his hand. Carrying his coffee to the lounge was an obstacle course of finding a place to set his mug down, then limp-hopping a couple of paces, picking it up and shifting it further along.

An upmarket stereo system sat discreetly on a heavy cabinet and shelves near the door. He studied it a moment and punched the remote. He didn't know what he expected but it wasn't the heavy metal riff of Metallica's 'Enter Sandman' that came blasting through the speakers.

His smile wry, Stirling lowered the volume and checked the CD shelves for something more his flavour. His father's tastes were eclectic—country music, more Metallica along with Guns N' Roses and other big rock bands from the eighties and nineties. There were a few classical albums too, mostly operas, an Elgar collection, Beethoven. A compilation of classic western movie themes. He pulled the disc out and put it on with the sound low.

By the time he had the fire stoked and throwing decent heat again, the drugs were kicking in, along with exhaustion. Unable to cope with anything more taxing, Stirling stretched out on the couch facing the fire and within minutes was asleep.

$\mathscr{F}$

'Now I'm even crosser,' said a voice.

Stirling opened bleary eyes to find Darcy a few feet away, arms folded, red lips pursed.

'Darcy,' he said, his brain not functioning enough to think of a better greeting. He tried to sit up like a normal person and damn near howled at the ripping pain that shot through his thigh and hip.

Darcy grabbed his arm before he tumbled off the couch. 'Truly, Stirling, you are most annoying.' Carefully, she helped ease his legs down, then his body to sitting.

Stirling had to grit his teeth to prevent himself snapping at her. He felt enough like an invalid as it was without Darcy witnessing more of his weaknesses. She was looking gorgeous in a white dress patterned with multicoloured flowers, bright orange cardigan buttoned tight over her breasts, and matching orange headband crowning her shiny up-do. Stirling no doubt looked like a derelict. Probably smelled like one too.

'You let yourself in,' he said instead.

Darcy looked away. For a moment he thought she was going to apologise, then her chin lifted. 'I did warn you I'd be around in the morning.' She indicated the doorway to the kitchen. 'I knocked. Several times. When you didn't answer I worried you might have fallen so I just came in. You look dreadful, by the way.'

He rubbed his face. 'Thanks.'

Darcy tipped her head and regarded him with bird-like curiosity. 'Why on earth did you sleep on the—Ah.' She nodded to herself. 'You couldn't climb the stairs. I knew I should have come over last night.'

'I managed.'

She raised an eyebrow. Darcy had great eyebrows. Dark like her hair and expressive. Sexy. He puffed his cheeks. Never in his life had he thought eyebrows sexy. Must be the drugs.

'It wasn't that bad.'

She laughed then. 'You men,' she said, shaking her head. 'I'll make us a cup of tea.'

She sashayed out and was soon clattering around the kitchen. Stirling thought about following but it was probably safer to stay on the couch. Less painful, at least.

The fire was down again. With an effort, he pushed off the couch, poked the coals and threw another lump of wood on, then hobbled on his crutches to the window. The sky was still dull. A breeze ruffled the trees and threw leaves around the carriageway. A few caught against the back of a bright red Mini with a white racing stripe heading up its back and over the roof, and a personalised numberplate spelling VAVOOM.

'There's no milk.'

Darcy stood in the doorway with her arms crossed.

'It appears there's no food either. What on earth were you thinking?'

'There's tinned food.'

She rolled her eyes. 'I'll start on a list.' She headed off.

'Darcy.'

She must have heard the seriousness in his tone because she turned and regarded him, top teeth pulling on her bottom lip.

'Why are you doing this? I'm no one to you.'

'Someone has to look after you.'

Stirling continued to stare. Silence came naturally to him, but he'd learned long ago it was also a great way to get people to talk.

Finally, she threw up her hands. 'I'm invested.'

'Invested?' The word was like a gut punch. That's what this was about? Darcy wanted *money*? Had his father stolen from her too? His fists tightened around his crutches.

'I found you. You bled all over me. I even took my dress off for you. Call me peculiar, but that makes me feel a little bit invested in your recovery.' She chafed at her arms as though cold. 'We've had an awful year. None of us need any more trauma.'

Stirling's fists relaxed. It wasn't about money. It was about hope and healing and making life better.

'I'd better do my best not to give you any more then.'

She smiled and Stirling felt the warmth of it like sunshine. 'Thank you. That would be very appreciated. Now, I'd better start on this list and phone it through to Moody's. We'll have to set you up an account but that shouldn't be too much of a problem.'

'Ah,' he said, leaning forward on his crutches. 'About that ...'

Chapter Nine

Some days just dawned irritating. Saturdays were normally happy days, but this particular version of Saturday was causing Darcy no end of annoyance.

First, she'd found Stirling on the couch, cold and uncomfortable and not taking proper care of himself. Then she'd discovered he had no food in the house. The fridge contained a single beer and a soggy frozen meal that should have been in the bin a week ago, while the pantry held only dry goods, a few tins of spaghetti, and jams and condiments well past their use-by dates.

The lack of groceries shouldn't have been a problem. Moody's could have delivered, except Katrina Hedditch had decided she didn't want Stirling's custom. The unfairness of the woman's attitude had Darcy stiffening like a starched collar. What did Katrina know of this man? And since when did the sins of the father automatically pass to the son?

Though inside she was seething, Darcy kept her expression pleasant. 'I'm sorry to hear that,' she said to Stirling. They were sitting at the big kitchen table, cups of sugary black tea steaming in front of them. If Darcy had had the ingredients and time, she would have made pikelets or scones, anything to ease the dreadful gloominess of the house. Today she had neither. The Hoppers were playing at Edenhope, a forty-five-minute drive away. She still had to drop into Roseneath, then travel back to Grassmoor and change into her football ensemble, pick up Lisette and drive to the game. Now, added to that, she had to fit in arranging supplies for Stirling. 'That's quite unfair of her.'

He shrugged and blew on his tea.

She picked up the pen she'd found for writing a shopping list and tapped it against the paper. 'I don't wish to defend her, and I loathe gossip, but it might be helpful to know that Dougal's fraud affected her brother Jayden badly. It caused ...' Darcy paused, '... difficulties.'

Stirling set down the mug. 'What kind of difficulties?'

She rotated the pen between her fingers. The 'Kildare Livestock Services' engraving flashed gold on the barrel's black surface. Every local farm probably had several. 'Financial, obviously. When Dougal kept delaying payment for the stock he'd sold, then stopped paying at all, the lack of cashflow caused a great deal of strain. And Jayden has always been a bit hot-headed. It runs in the family.' Darcy smiled weakly. 'There were rumours of—' She shook her head. A rumour like that didn't need passing on. 'Charlene, that's Jayden's wife, took the kids and moved to her parents in Warrnambool.'

'Shit,' he said, rubbing his face. 'I suppose next you're going to tell me he lost the farm.'

'No. Like with all of us, Dougal's insurance eventually covered the debt. Though, if Charlene pushes for divorce ...' Her shoulders drooped. Property settlements were always difficult and there was little chance Jayden had the cash for a payout. Even Dougal had

had to sell off part of Westwind to cover his divorce settlement with Brigitte. Darcy wondered if Stirling realised that.

He was quiet for a while. 'You said us. As in, "like with all of us". By that you mean your family?'

'Yes,' she said, surprised. 'Roseneath was caught up in Dougal's fraud too. I assumed you knew.'

'No.' He regarded the paperwork bundled on the table. When he spoke, it was more to himself than Darcy. 'What sort of man was he?'

A difficult question. A few years ago, it would have been easy to answer. After the fraud and Dougal's suicide, no one was sure anymore.

'A good man. Well liked, admired.' It was Darcy's turn to stare at the paperwork, sadness creeping through her veins. For Stirling, for those affected by Dougal's actions. For Dougal himself, whose shame proved so acute he could no longer live with it. 'For some reason he lost his way.'

Stirling returned his gaze to Darcy's. 'Where did it go, though? The money. That's what I don't get. The where and the why. He must have taken it for something.'

'I don't know. It just disappeared.'

'It's annoying me, not knowing. This man, my father,' he waved at the sideboard where more of Dougal's paraphernalia lay, 'he doesn't make sense.' Stirling frowned and Darcy's heart squeezed at the anguish behind it. 'What was so important he was prepared to steal not only nearly a million dollars of other people's money, but risk everything he was?'

'We've all asked ourselves that. So did the police and insurance investigators, but I don't think we'll ever know. Whatever Dougal was up to, the secret went with him.'

For a long moment, Stirling seemed lost, his gaze a thousand miles away, then he straightened and nodded towards Darcy's pen and paper. 'Are there any other places that deliver?'

'Not to here. Moody's takes care of the local area. But don't worry about that. I can pick up anything you need.' She lifted the pen. 'Milk, I'm guessing. Bread. What about cereal?'

Stirling reached across and curled his hand around her forearm. Warmth spread beneath the wool of her sleeve. 'You don't have to do this.'

'It's no problem. I come past at least every other day on my way to Mum and Dad's.'

'You don't live at Roseneath?'

'No. I live in town. An old workshop I've made into an atelier—a design studio—and home. You'll have to visit when you're better. It's quite marvellous.'

He sat back, chuckling. 'Of course it is. I doubt you do anything by halves.'

His words draped her like a cashmere wrap, cosy and kind and oh so flattering. Darcy was sure her decolletage was turning pinker than the flowers on her dress. 'I try not to. We only get one life. No point in not making the most of it, and I like living brightly. It makes me happy, and the workshop is full of colour and creativity. I miss the farm of course, but I like being in town. It's convenient and people are always popping in to say hello.' She grinned. 'Sometimes too often. I have a "by appointment only" sign but real friends know that as long as they bring cake, they can safely ignore it.'

That deep chuckle came again as Stirling smiled back at her. The cup of tea and chat had revived him. His body had lost its tired slump and the wretched pasty pallor he'd woken with was gone. It made Darcy feel good.

'What really helps is that I can choose my own hours. I can work all night if I want, which was impossible to do at home. Mum and Dad were always lovely and supportive, but Shiloh used to complain that I was ruining her beauty sleep. Shiloh's my sister,' she said. 'She manages the farm with Dad.'

'Older or younger?'

'Older, by nineteen months.'

'So that makes her …?'

'Thirty-two.'

Darcy could see him mentally calculating her age and bit her lip to hide a smile.

'Is she like you?'

Darcy laughed. 'You mean is she a girly-girl? Not in the slightest. Shiloh's a warrior woman.'

'Sounds scary.'

'Oh, she is. But she's a darling too. And very clever.' Darcy remembered Leo and added, 'In most things. In some, she's absolutely hopeless and needs to listen to her sister more.'

Stirling smiled into his mug and took a mouthful of tea. 'Is she married?'

'Sadly, no. She and Leo—her ex-fiancé—were meant to tie the knot this spring but they broke up a few months ago.' She sighed. 'The past twelve months have been truly horrible. There was the business with Dougal, then his awful death. Then Mum got sick, and to top it all off, Shiloh and Leo had a silly argument and parted ways.'

'I'm sorry.'

'Stirling,' she said, touching the back of his hand, 'none of that was your fault.'

'I know. I just …' He knuckled the side of his head. 'I can't help feeling guilty. I've done nothing to earn Westwind except be born, yet here I am walking into a position of privilege when others in the district are suffering.'

'You're wrong.'

He stared at her.

'We're not suffering, Stirling. This is country life. It's a rollercoaster of highs and lows. If it isn't the weather, it's poor commodity markets or plummeting land prices or any number of things. Yes, Dougal's betrayal was a shock, one that hurt a lot of people and caused untold stress, as did his death. But the community is coping, and it'll survive like it always does by putting one foot in front of the other and getting on with things.'

It took him so long to answer, Darcy worried she'd come on too strong. His eyes turned distant, focusing on something she couldn't see. The urge to touch him again made her fingers twitch.

'You mentioned highs and lows,' he said eventually. 'All you described were the lows. What are the highs?'

'The universal things that make people happy—love, friendship, the community coming together. Helping one another and being helped. Our achievements.' She waved towards the window where dust motes danced in a welcome shaft of light. 'A beautiful sunrise. The sound of laughter. Small joys. It's not money, if that's what you think, although no one will ever say no to having more.'

'No.'

'It's relationships. Being involved with others. Oh, and I'll tell you one other thing that makes us Grassmoorians happy. The Hoppers winning, which they won't do if I'm not there to cheer them on.' Darcy pointed the end of the pen at him. 'Shall we get on with our list?'

Chapter Ten

Stirling was tooling around on his laptop when he heard the crunch of tyres on gravel. He checked the time. It was only one thirty and far too early for Darcy's promised return, and unless it was Gavin eager for another nose around, no one else had any reason to visit.

He grabbed his phone and pocketed it, then reached for his crutches and was about to propel his way to the front when a fist pounded on the rear door. Though it didn't help with the draught, Stirling had left the inner kitchen-mudroom door open to ease his access to the laundry loo.

The outside door was pushed ajar. 'Hello?' A female voice.

Stirling manoeuvred his way around the table but whoever it was had no patience. The door opened fully. A tall figure was momentarily silhouetted against the light then strode forward, as though entering Westwind without invitation via the back door was a perfectly reasonable thing to do.

The woman paused to pull off her boots, her face half hidden in the shadows. 'For god's sake, sit down before you do yourself another injury.'

Stirling raised his eyebrows. What was it with bossy women around this place?

Boots placed neatly side by side, his visitor came into the light. Dressed in farm clothes, she was about Darcy's height but with a straighter figure and a walk full of purpose. Her hair was the same rich dark brunette, its length secured in a thick ponytail and exposing a strikingly attractive face devoid of makeup.

'You're Shiloh,' he said.

'Darcy's been gossiping about me, has she?'

She strode to him and held out her hand. Her grip was strong and assured, her hands rough, her gaze keen. Her shake lasted a little longer than necessary, and Stirling had the feeling Shiloh was assessing him closely—his strength as well as looks.

'Let me guess. She called me a warrior woman.' She held up her palm. 'Don't answer. I know my sister.' Fists jammed to her hips, Shiloh scanned the room. 'Feels like forever since I was last here.'

Stirling remained balanced on his crutches, watching her. The familial resemblance was strong. Same brown eyes, same even features, same full mouth.

'I take it you used to visit often.'

'Yeah, when Melody was around. We were friends. Whole family was, although that all kinda ended with the divorce.' Shiloh anchored her gaze directly on Stirling. 'Didn't Darcy tell you?'

'We haven't spoken that much.' He lurched his way back to his chair. 'Was there something you wanted?'

'Other than to check you out?'

Stirling made a noise that was a cross between a grunt and a laugh as he slid onto his seat and rested the crutches against the end of the table. 'And?'

'And what?'

'How am I measuring up?'

For the first time, Shiloh smiled. 'You'll do. For now.'

He supposed that was something.

'I do have another reason for being here. Darcy asked me to drop some food over.' She jerked her thumb towards the door. 'It's in the ute. I'm also under strict orders to make sure you have enough wood, set the fires, and do anything else you ask.'

'That's really not necessary.'

Shiloh harrumphed. 'You don't know my sister. Trust me, it is.' She slapped her hands together. 'I'll bring in the food then get on to the fires.'

She strode out again, snatching up her boots on the way.

Stirling stared at the doorway, feeling like a storm had blown in and out. He regarded the laptop. Darcy had fetched it for him before she left, along with a wool quilt and pillows from the master bedroom in case he wanted to rest, and clean clothes, towels and soap so he could wash himself. She'd tutted over his dwindling supply of logs but hadn't mentioned sending anyone to help. He should have realised she'd do something like this.

Shiloh returned with a cooler and a shopping bag and proceeded to unload both.

'Pumpkin soup,' she said, holding up a container. 'Just zap it in the microwave. Sliced roast lamb. Cheese. Tomato.' Three more containers followed the soup into the fridge. A jar appeared. 'Chutney.' Then another container with butter, what looked like an on old Coke bottle full of milk, and finally, half a loaf of bread that she dumped near the kettle. She reached into the bag and extracted yet another plastic box. 'Muffins—banana, I think. I'm not sure, I just grabbed whatever was at the top of the freezer. They'll still be hard but give them an hour and they'll be right for afternoon tea. Anyway, that lot should keep you going until Darcy returns. Although I suggest you don't stuff yourself too much. She was muttering something about roasting a chook when she took off.'

Stirling's chest felt strange. All this kindness, for him. He wasn't used to it and he certainly hadn't earned it. 'It's more than enough. Thank you.'

'No problem.' Shiloh indicated the enamelled combustion stove. 'Have you lit it yet?'

'No.' Stirling hadn't even considered it. With the kitchen sporting a modern stainless-steel cooker, he'd assumed the old range had been kept just for show.

'Right. Better get it sorted. You'll freeze otherwise.' Shiloh opened one of the lower doors and peered inside. Tutting, she headed for the lounge, returning with a brush, and set to sweeping ash. Stirling began to feel decidedly unmanly parked at the table while Shiloh did all the work.

'You'd think Dougal would have had central heating installed, wouldn't you?' she said. 'Always relied on the range and the fire. I know it's nice but it's a pain in the bum.' She rubbed the tip of her nose on the back of her sleeve and picked up the ash tray. 'How's your leg, by the way?'

'Fine.'

One corner of her mouth tilted. 'Liar.' She marched out.

Shiloh continued in her efficient way, ignoring Stirling's protests that she'd done enough and snorting at his claim of being able to manage. She was bossy and dismissive, but ungrudging. Stirling wondered what had happened between Shiloh and her fiancé.

After setting and lighting both fires, Shiloh washed her hands in the laundry and returned to the kitchen. 'Anything else I can do for you while I'm here?'

There was nothing else left *to* do—except fetch his underwear from the laundry dryer, and Stirling had been emasculated enough for one day.

'No. Thank you. You've done more than enough.'

Her eyes glittered. 'Are you sure? Because I happen to know there's some good wine in the cellar.'

'Cellar?'

'Yeah.' Shiloh tilted her head towards the pantry. 'Under there. You didn't notice the door?'

'No.'

'Dougal liked to keep a good cellar. There'll be Scotch down there too. He was partial to a dram. He and Dad used to get on it sometimes.' She smiled. 'Mum never appreciated those nights.'

'You knew him well.' It wasn't a question, more a statement of envy.

'We were neighbours. Not that old man Kildare was ever happy about that.' At Stirling's confusion, she elaborated. 'Dougal's father, Benjamin. Your grandfather.'

He still didn't get the problem. 'Why wouldn't Benjamin have liked you being neighbours?'

'Because Roseneath was once Kildare land. It was one of the lots acquired under the Soldier Settlement Act. Kildare tried to protest, but he had to shut up in case they decided to take even more. The commission could be catty like that.'

Stirling's tapped a finger against the edge of his laptop and willed himself not to start googling. Shiloh would only think him more ignorant than he already felt.

She gave him a look that revealed she'd already had that thought. 'Come on, the Soldier Settlement Scheme?'

'I've heard of it but that's about it.' Much of Stirling's schooling had taken place overseas. Australian history hadn't been a priority.

Shiloh leaned against the sink with her arms folded. 'So ... Victoria—Australia for that matter—had two soldier settlement schemes. The first implemented after the Great War was mostly a failure. The lots allocated to the returned soldiers were too small and much of the land was poor. Too dry, too stony.' She made a dismissive gesture. 'Land no one else really wanted. Many of the settlers had no farming skills either. The failure rate was ridiculous. There were suicides. Poor bastards had already been through hell and then they were shunted off to the bundu with no support and the expectation they could make a go of it because they were, I dunno, exceptionally brave or something.'

'That was here?' Stirling found it hard to believe this was infertile country.

'Not so much around here. North in the Wimmera, the Mallee, and along the river. There was a bit around Mount Elephant, but here, no. It was a different matter with the second scheme. The government wanted it to work and for that they needed good land.' She gave a grim smile. 'The commission looked at all the old squatter lands with their big houses and oversized estates, and pounced.'

'So, they what, just took it?'

'Pretty much. The commission was powerful and had public opinion on its side. Oh, the landholders got paid, but it was often below value. That left a lot of bitterness, especially when the wool boom hit. Anyway, Kildare had no right to complain. He'd stayed safe at home while men like my great-grandfather got shot at. Westwind was reasonably lucky in that they only took six thousand acres. Other properties had over half their land compulsorily acquired.'

Only six thousand acres? How big had the place been? A hollow feeling overtook Stirling. How little he knew about his history.

'Your great-grandfather got all six thousand acres?'

She laughed. 'I wish. No. Twelve hundred, but we've been lucky enough to add to that over the years. Even with only twelve hundred the timing couldn't have been better. It was the fifties, the Korean war was on and wool was in high demand. Some people made fortunes. Then it all collapsed, of course, but that's farming for you. It either fills your heart or breaks it.'

'Westwind's loss was your gain then.'

'It was. But the Soldier Settlement Scheme also benefitted the district. It brought in new blood. Innovation. Kept the towns alive.' She became subdued. 'For a few decades, at least. Dougal probably has a book on it somewhere. He liked history. Thought it was important to understand the past and learn from it.' She bit her lip, reminding him of Darcy, and regarded the old stove. 'You'd think he ...' Shiloh waved a hand. 'Doesn't matter. You want me to look for some wine?'

'Tempting, but not today. Wouldn't work with the drugs they've got me on.' What he really wanted was to ask Shiloh to stay and share more of her insight, but he didn't know her, and she had a farm to get back to.

'No, I suppose not.' She pushed off from the sink and hoisted the cooler. 'Well, if that's it, I'll be off. Don't,' she said, when Stirling reached for his crutches. 'I found my way in, I can find my way out.'

'I want to. I need the air.'

He followed her through the mudroom and outside. The cooling atmosphere hit Stirling like a slap. As did the sight of his cobwebbed Ducati. He looked to Shiloh's no-frills ute parked at end of the courtyard. A sleek, dark brown dog watched them from the tray.

'Frost tonight,' said Shiloh as she scanned the eastern horizon past the sheds, where the land sloped down towards a creek.

'Good thing I have plenty of wood.'

'It is.' She turned and studied his face. 'There was one other reason I wanted to come over.'

Stirling said nothing, though his fingers tightened on his crutches.

'That land.' Shiloh indicated behind her. 'The flats along the creek.'

'What about it?'

'Do you have plans for it?'

He shook his head. 'Not yet.'

'Would you consider selling?'

No, he wouldn't. Not anytime soon. Stirling had too much to figure out before he could even think of making a move like that. 'Probably not.'

'Right.' She stared eastward again. 'Are you going to stock it, then?'

'I don't know. Should I?'

'Yeah, you should. It's good fat lamb country.'

Stirling regarded the area. Even from this distance he could see the thickness of the grass, its vivid colour contrasting against the afternoon sky. Majestic old trees rimmed the winding creek line. Straight strong fences marked the boundary with the homestead grounds and gardens. She was right. It needed stock, if only to stop it looking lonely.

'I wouldn't know where to start.' Although Stirling supposed he could learn. The question was: did he want to?

'If I were a nicer person, I'd offer to help but I'm not going to. I have enough on my plate. But I will offer to lease it off you. Or we could organise an agistment agreement. That way you retain ownership until you decide what your plans are, and I get access to productive land that would otherwise go to waste.'

It was an idea Stirling might be wise to investigate. Mal McKenzie would be the one to ask. Then again, William Stoddart was the one who'd had charge of the estate. From Stirling's dealings, he'd seemed a competent man.

'I'll think about it.'

'Do that. Although, not to put any pressure, could you do it soon? The season's getting away.'

He nodded and swivelled on his crutches, spying the dog bowls. With all that had happened, Stirling had forgotten about the dogs that must have lived here.

He swivelled back and pointed a crutch at the bowls. 'Do you know where they went?'

'Rascal and Missy? Dougal shot them.'

'Shot them?'

Shiloh nodded. 'Yeah. Poor things. Especially Rascal. He was such a good dog. To be killed like that ...' Her voice took on a husky edge. 'I know he was getting on and would have pined without his master, but still.' She shook her head as she stared at the empty bowls. 'As for shooting Missy, that was stupid and mean. She was a beautiful animal. Full sister to my Lucy.' She indicated the kelpie watching them from the back of the ute. 'Five-thousand-dollar dog. Bang. Gone. Cleaned the rifle and stowed it away all polished like it was more precious than the animals that loved him.' Her mouth went grim. 'I get that Dougal wanted to end his own life, but he didn't have to shoot the dogs. That was a bastard act.'

Stirling swallowed, his own eyes prickling. The callousness of his father's actions was sickening. Stirling had seen plenty of horror between humans but he'd always struggled with animal cruelty.

'Sorry.' Shiloh cleared her throat. 'Probably shouldn't have told you that.'

'No. I needed to know.'

'I'm just so angry with him. Not just for the dogs, but for everything.'

Stirling could imagine. He was angry too. Angry and a bit confused. Why hang yourself when there were guns at hand? Hanging wasn't always an instant death. Or painless. All sorts of things could go wrong. Why risk that when a bullet to the head would have been surer? Dougal had already done the dogs, why not simply turn the gun on himself?

'Anyway,' said Shiloh, her voice back to her no-nonsense tone. 'No point festering over questions that can't be answered. Call if you need anything.'

'Thanks. And thanks again for your help.'

'No problem.' She strode to her ute, arm flicking out in farewell. She ruffled Lucy's ears and planted a kiss on her head as she passed. The dog wriggled with joy.

Stirling watched her reverse, then hobbled around. His gaze landed once more on the dog bowls and he paused, an icy shiver spearing his spine.

He stared at them a moment longer, then shook his head and limped into the house.

Chapter Eleven

Stirling was restless for the remainder of the afternoon. He couldn't get out of his mind the unfathomability of Dougal shooting his dogs.

Questions raged like wasps in his head. Buzzing, persistent. He simmered with worry that something had been overlooked at Westwind. But how could that be? Apart from the enigma of the missing trust money, Dougal's death had been an open-and-shut suicide. Another sad rural statistic.

'Let it go,' he kept muttering. Except Stirling knew he wouldn't. His vexation was too locked in.

At four, still edgy and bothered, Stirling shot Toby a text to let him know he'd be calling. He put on the kettle to boil and stared across the breeze-blown landscape to the ranges. Stirling considered Toby more brother than friend. If anyone could help ease his mind, it'd be Toby.

In his darker moods, Stirling sometimes wondered why Toby stood by him. They'd met in the army—Toby a medic, Stirling a pilot. Something made them click, and in the years since, though they weren't always in the same part of the world, their friendship had endured.

It even survived that last MiZ mission. How, Stirling didn't know. It was Stirling who'd been flying the chopper. Stirling who'd crashed the aircraft, plunging their team into a hot zone. Toby had been unhurt but trapped in his seat. Günter died on impact. Refusing to take shelter and ignoring both Stirling's and Toby's pleas for her to stay put, Alina had first crawled to Günter, then, when she'd realised there was nothing she could do, wriggled noseward to Stirling, snatching supplies along the way. She'd patched him up the best she could, only for a bullet to take her in the arm, then another in her stomach, before the death shot slammed into her chest and threw her down forever.

Stirling still had nightmares about that moment. The way her pretty mouth had parted. The shock in her eyes. Then worse, Alina's blooming knowledge followed by fear and pain and apology.

Toby admitted to nightmares too. Yet he'd never blamed Stirling. Not for Alina's or Günter's deaths. Not for the loss of his faith in MiZ, an organisation he'd joined on Stirling's recommendation. It was the risk of the job. A job Toby had gone into with open eyes and now didn't want any further part of. He'd keep Stirling in his life, however. Friends stuck by each other. That's just how it went.

When his tea was brewed, Stirling set his mug alongside his laptop, along with a muffin, and began the video chat.

Toby's broad, freckled face appeared. From the brightness of his eyes, he'd already indulged in at least one post-shift beer. 'Felix! What's doin', man?'

'Nothing.' Stirling dragged his hand down his cheek. 'Everything. But that can wait. How was your day?'

'The usual. Totally nuts.'

'Oldies misbehaving again?'

Toby gave an exaggerated eye roll that Stirling knew was feigned. Though overqualified and lacking the security and benefits of a permanent employee, Toby enjoyed his job as a casual nursing home care worker. 'You have no idea. I swear the buggers do half the stuff they do for sport.'

'Just keeping the fun in life.'

Which earned Stirling a snort and head shake. 'For them, maybe. But I really don't need to know that kind of detail about their bowel movements.'

Stirling snorted.

Toby took a slug from his beer. 'Anyway …' He focused on his screen. 'I'm more interested in you. Leg playing up?'

'No, it's fine.' And it was. Stirling had subjected the wound to a careful inspection earlier when he'd washed. Yeah, he'd have yet another ugly scar to add to his collection, but he'd live.

Toby leaned closer. 'Something's up though.'

Stirling ground the heel of his palm into the corner of his forehead. The worry wasps were quieter but still there, still insistent. 'Maybe. I don't know.' His hand flopped back to the table, rattling his plate and sloshing his untouched tea. 'This thing with Dougal, I can't get my head around it.'

'Which bit?'

'All of it.' Every time he considered Dougal's last day, he felt sick. 'He shot his dogs. Before he killed himself. Just … shot them.'

Toby blew out a breath. 'That's harsh.'

'Yeah. It is.' He was quiet for a moment as the whys clamoured. 'Why shoot the dogs, then hang yourself? Why not just turn the gun on your own head? Get it over with, fast and clean. Why the change of MO?'

'Maybe he wanted to suffer.'

'Christ.'

'Come on, man. You know this shit rarely makes sense.'

'This just seems to make less sense than normal.' He sighed and stared at his palms. 'Too much thinking time on my hands.'

'Sounds like it.' Toby grimaced. 'Look, I know you don't feel it helps you the way it does me, but have you thought about talking to Eva?'

Eva was the psychologist assigned to them by *Medizin in Krise*. The organisation had been good to them both in the aftermath of their trauma, covering the costs of their mental as well as physical rehabilitations. Toby had found his chats with Eva helpful and had encouraged Stirling to do the same. He had, a couple of times. Probably he should do more of it but the thought of retracing those moments with a stranger left him cold.

Stirling shook his head, strangely shamed and unable to meet Toby's gaze.

'Think about it,' Toby said quietly. 'For me.'

'I will.'

A crackling silence formed between them. Then Toby grinned. 'So, what else has been happening?'

Stirling made a face, hiding his relief at the change of conversation. 'Women.'

Toby did a double take. 'Women? Already? Didn't you just do a runner from hospital?'

Stirling rolled his eyes but was inwardly glad of Toby's wisecrack. Anything was better than that knowing stare. 'Not like that. Remember that girl who found me? Darcy?'

'Marilyn Monroe in a sailor suit? What about her?'

'She called in this morning. Found me asleep on the lounge and proceeded to boss me about because I wasn't taking proper care of myself. Then she went to make tea and cracked a fit because there was no food. Couple of hours later, her sister barges in with an esky full of supplies.' He held up his still uneaten muffin. 'Muffins, roast lamb, soup. You name it.'

Toby laughed. 'Lucky you.'

'Yeah. If you don't count the female bulldozing.'

'I dunno. You always liked them bossy.'

They were quiet a moment, made silent by the ghost of Alina, a woman who'd never held back from ordering men around, especially when it came to anything medical.

Toby was the first to snap out of it. 'What's the sister like?'

'Attractive in a down-to-earth way. Capable. Could probably beat you in an arm wrestle. Runs a farm with her dad.'

'So, nothing like the other.'

'No.' Darcy was one of a kind. 'I also had a bit of a moment on the phone with the lady at Grassmoor's one and only supermarket. They're meant to deliver to local properties but when I told her Westwind, she claimed it was out of their zone. Turns out she's another hater.'

Toby gave him a slack look. 'And you want me to visit this Grassmoor?'

'It's only a few people,' said Stirling. 'Darcy's been good. And Shiloh—that's her sister. Besides bringing food, she set all the fires. Although she was probably only softening me up.' At Toby's frown, Stirling explained. 'She wants to buy one of the paddocks. I think she thinks I'll only ruin it. She's probably right. All I know about grass is that it's green, and sheep and cattle like it. Shiloh's the one who told me about the dogs.' Stirling wrapped his fingers around the mug. 'I can't reconcile it, Tobes. It doesn't fit.'

'How do you know? You never knew him. Just because Dougal's your dad doesn't mean he can't be an arsehole.'

'I know.' Stirling sighed. He hated being injured and helpless. He hated that he was being nagged by something he couldn't nail down or fix. 'There's something else too. Something the rideshare driver said to me, about how it's not typical for fraudsters to commit suicide. They have too much self-belief in getting away with it.'

Toby watched him with a frown.

'It's not like he would have gone to jail for long, either. He had Melody. Friends.' Stirling raised his hand. 'This place.' His voice dropped. 'Me. He must have thought something of me to leave me Westwind.' Stirling checked Toby's expression. 'You think I'm reading too much into it.'

'Maybe. Probably. The thing is, Felix, if your old man didn't kill himself, then that means someone did it for him.'

'Yeah, I know.' Stirling rubbed his hand over his head. The idea that Dougal could have been murdered was ludicrous.

'Have you checked the coroner's report?'

'Not yet.'

Toby shrugged, then emptied the can and crushed it in his fist. 'Then you know what to do.'

Chapter Twelve

Stirling cupped his hands around his mouth and breathed in deeply. On the screen in front of him was the Coroners Court's 'Finding Into Death Without Inquest' for Dougal Benjamin Kildare. A public record, easily downloadable and available to anyone with an internet connection.

He dragged his hands down his jaw and rested his chin on the points of his fingers, the gesture prayer-like. But there was nothing to pray for. Nothing to hope for. The finding was unequivocal: his father had died by his own volition.

Toby had been right yesterday. Stirling was reading too much into it.

Why, then, did he remain so disturbed?

He eased himself upright, wincing at the pull on his wound and aching hip, and put the kettle on. Outside, morning dew coated the ground in a rich blanket of diamond droplets. Stirling wished he felt as sparkly. He'd spent Saturday night on the couch, a little more comfortably thanks to a dose of painkillers and Darcy's exacting care, but his sleep remained troubled.

She'd arrived around seven, flush-cheeked from her afternoon at the football, loaded with groceries and wearing an extraordinary green and gold dress that scooped tight and low over her chest before flaring out from her waist in multiple gathers.

Her lips were siren red, her eyes smoky with shadow, her hair teased into a sixties-style beehive. She looked ridiculous and incredibly sexy at the same time. Stirling had to concentrate to stop himself perving at her luscious curves.

The Hoppers had won their game, to widespread shock, and were through to the grand final. A party was now raging at the Goodwin Oval clubrooms—a party to which Darcy needed to return to keep watch over her friend Lisette in case she did something dumb, like scuttle off home with some bloke called Charlie Shanahan.

'Not that he's awful or anything,' Darcy had said as she unloaded the small cooler she'd set on the kitchen table. 'He's just ...' She tossed Stirling a pained look. 'Not right for her.'

'You think she deserves better.'

Darcy sighed. 'I do, but I hate saying that. Who am I to judge? It's Lisette's life, not mine.'

'You're her friend, you want to look out for her.'

'I do. Still ...' She lifted a whole fresh chicken from the cooler and regarded it wryly. 'I had plans to roast this for you tonight.'

'No need. Shiloh brought plenty of food. Thanks for that, by the way.'

'My pleasure. She wanted to introduce herself anyway.'

'She did that,' said Stirling in a tone that drew a sharp look from Darcy.

Her gaze narrowed. 'Please tell me she didn't offer to buy the flats. She did, didn't she?' Her chest puffed in indignation. 'I *told* her ...'

Stirling kept his focus above her neckline, though it took serious effort. 'I managed.'

'I'm sure you did but she shouldn't have bothered you with it.'

Darcy had unloaded the remaining bags, placing the items he would need most on the bench rather than stowing them in the pantry, to 'save him the walk'. Then she'd fussed around some more, checking the fires, asking if there was anything else she could help with, apparently reluctant to leave. Whether that was because of him or a lack of enthusiasm for dealing with her friend, Stirling didn't know.

He'd asked for an extra blanket for the couch, a request that had brought on a mild scold about him needing proper rest and an offer to return and help him upstairs to bed later. When that was refused, Darcy offered him her old room at Roseneath.

'I'm fine here,' he'd replied.

She planted her fists on her hips. 'Sleeping on a lumpy old couch is not fine.'

Stirling shrugged. 'I've had worse.' And he had. Much, much worse.

'Oh, yes?'

He waved her off. 'Stories for another time.' Probably never. Although if she kept visiting like this, they'd have to find something to talk about. Anything would do as long as it kept him focused on her face.

Darcy eyed him for a long moment, then she'd sighed and stomped off to fetch enough blankets, quilts and pillows to furnish a dormitory.

When his makeshift bed was made, complete with top sheet folded back in a neat triangle and a cloud of pillows for his head, she returned to the kitchen and stared about, rubbing her arms. 'Are you sure you'll be all right?'

'I'm fine, Darcy.' A smile in his voice kept it warm. She was a kind woman. A bit bossy and more than a little quirky, but soft-hearted. Soft in all the other right places too. 'I promise. You don't need to worry.'

'I do, though.' She spread her hands. 'Like I said, I'm invested.'

She'd departed after that, leaving Stirling regarding the door, torn between wishing her back and knowing he shouldn't get involved. What would he do with Darcy anyway? It wasn't as if he was in a fit state to try anything, and a woman like her would probably be repulsed by his scars.

His mind wasn't in a good place either. Talking to Toby had triggered memories of Alina. The plans they'd started to make. Another year with *Medizin in Krise* and then a move to Switzerland to be close to Alina's family, and try for a normal life. A few years later, maybe they'd even start a family of their own.

Their relationship was never meant to go that far. In the beginning it'd been sex without ties, a visceral response to danger and their adrenaline highs. They'd laugh it off afterwards and swear not to do it again. There were work rules. Except it kept happening, and as the months passed the laughter stopped, replaced with talk about what the hell they were doing and what it meant.

Toby had warned him. Had warned Alina too. But they were young, high on hope, and didn't listen.

They should have.

Stirling's guilt was an ache that wouldn't go away. Guilt not only for the crash—even though rationally he knew the fault wasn't his—but for getting involved with Alina in the first place. If he hadn't, maybe she wouldn't have taken the risk of trying to save him. Maybe she'd still be alive.

The bubbling kettle brought Stirling back to the present. He glanced outside. The dew was burning off and the land looked clean and fresh and bright. He could almost see the weeds growing in the warming soil of the messy garden. When his leg was better, he'd get in there and clean it out.

His mouth curved. There he was again, projecting a future when he could barely navigate the present.

He made his coffee and set it next to his laptop, then limped his way back round to his chair and the coroner's report. Apart from mentions of the stress Dougal had been under from clients pressuring him for payment—which must have been, to be fair, extreme—Dougal had seemed fine in the weeks leading up to his death.

Katrina Hedditch, who worked at Moody's and who Stirling suspected was the lady who'd refused his delivery order, noted that Dougal had said he was feeling 'a bit strained' when he shopped at the supermarket a few days before his suicide, but had otherwise appeared normal. Lisette Learmonth claimed Dougal was his usual charming self when he visited the post office earlier in the week. While Mal McKenzie said that though Dougal had seemed anxious when they chatted the day before his death, neither the conversation nor his tone gave any hint of the bleakness of Dougal's soul.

Stirling sipped his coffee and frowned at the screen as he read, again, the pages covering the 'Circumstances in which the death occurred'.

From the coroner's timeline, Dougal had last been seen in person on the Thursday before his death by Katrina at Moody's, where he'd purchased a bag of potatoes, assorted vegetables, a chicken breast, some bacon and a small cut of roasting beef. On Friday morning, he spoke to Mal over the phone but made no mention of the vandalisation of Westwind. Later that evening, a local noticed lights on in Dougal's Grassmoor office, even though it was well after midnight.

It appeared Dougal had worked late at Kildare Livestock Services, then locked up for the weekend and returned to Westwind, at which point it was speculated that he discovered the 'DIE SCUM' graffiti and stonework damage. On Saturday morning around eleven, Mal tried to phone both Dougal's mobile and landline but the calls were unanswered. He hadn't worried though, assuming Dougal was somewhere on the farm where reception was poor.

Sunday came and went with Mal still not having heard from Dougal. He said he was concerned but not greatly so. Dougal had a busy life, and while they were close friends, they didn't live in each other's pockets. It was only on Tuesday morning when he visited the office and found it locked that Mal feared something wasn't right and drove to Westwind. There, he discovered the dogs shot and Dougal hanging in the shed, where he'd likely been since Saturday afternoon.

No suicide note was found.

The tract left Stirling's heart thudding. Strange, the intensity of his reaction. He'd read of more terrible things, had direct experience of death and human suffering, yet the simple language and loneliness of Dougal's last days hit Stirling like a gut punch.

The pathologist's report recorded the cause of death as hanging, with no unexpected signs of trauma. The toxicological analysis was negative for common drugs and poisons. Not even alcohol was found.

The last detail had Stirling fingering his eyebrow. From what he'd learned, Dougal liked a drink, and if Shiloh's claim about the cellar was true, Dougal had plenty on hand. Why not ease the pain of suicide with a drink or ten?

Being drunk would have at least explained the dogs. With his thinking muddied, the idea that they would somehow suffer without their master might have made a kind of sense to Dougal. Yet he was sober.

Maybe he thought he might botch the hanging if he were intoxicated. If so, why not take the less risky option and shoot himself?

Stirling slouched back. The report should have given him closure. It was all there on the screen, a careful and dispassionately written document setting out Dougal's life and untimely death, along with the probable reasons for his suicide.

So what was making Stirling's skin prickle? The dogs? That could be down to his own love for dogs and his disbelief that someone of his blood could shoot a beloved pet.

That Dougal's grocery shop indicated he'd been thinking of future meals, at least for a few days? Hardly conclusive.

The fact and method of Dougal's suicide? Like Stirling had noted to Gavin, shame was a powerful emotion. As for him choosing hanging, who knew? Dougal's mind had to have been a mess, his thinking jumbled and short on reason.

The lack of a suicide note? Perhaps one had been left in the shed and it had blown away, lost to the winds.

No, it was the fraud itself. Stirling might have answers for the rest, unsatisfactory as they were, but the question of the money remained. Why? What was it for?

For a long time, he stared unseeing at a spot above the fridge, his coffee forgotten, turning over why he should care about a man he hadn't known, and who hadn't known him. And whether, in his uncertainty and isolation, Stirling had fixated on a mystery that didn't really exist.

Finally, he dropped his gaze back to the screen and the last few points on the report.

Pursuant to section 67 (1) of the Coroners Act 2008, I find that Dougal Kildare, born 19 May 1957, died on 11 January 2021 at Westwind, Epsom-Grassmoor Road, Grassmoor, Victoria, and the death occurred in the circumstances described above.

I convey my sincere condolences to Mr Kildare's family for their loss.

'Let it go,' Stirling murmured, heavy with sorrow and tired to his bones.

He closed the laptop and gathered his crutches. A rest would do him good. Except his journey didn't take him to the lounge and the warm swaddle of his temporary bed. At the door, Stirling turned, as though unbidden, to the hall and Westwind's grand entrance. He limped past the magnificent staircase and followed the ornate carpet runner to the western side of the house.

And to the dusty silence and stale air of Westwind's library and Dougal's home office.

Chapter Thirteen

Darcy revved the Mini up the drive more recklessly than was wise, given its potholes and washouts, and the long shadows cast by the fast-lowering sun where wallabies could hide. She'd been kept late at Roseneath, first helping Shiloh and her dad with the lambs, then with her mum, who was having a bad afternoon and who Darcy was reluctant to leave on her own.

The rush was unnecessary, of course. Stirling wasn't going anywhere, and it wasn't as if she'd specified a time. She'd simply said she'd check on him on Sunday afternoon, invested as she was in his recovery.

What a laugh. Darcy cared about his recovery, of course she did, but it was more than that. She cared about *him*. He intrigued her with his mystery and quiet fortitude, his anguish over Dougal, as though he bore some sort of blame for his father's deeds. That Stirling was handsome didn't help keep her attraction under control either. Even Shiloh had labelled him 'a bit of a babe', which was high praise indeed. Shiloh wasn't easily moved. Leo had been the exception.

Darcy should not be thinking this way about him. She barely knew the man and she had no idea of his plans. From the little he'd said, she suspected Stirling didn't know either, although he must have a life to return to.

Whatever that life was, he'd likely resume it, leaving Westwind, Grassmoor and her far behind. What else could he do? Westwind's remaining acreage was too small to be anything more than a hobby farm, and historic houses could be money pits. As it was, many of the district's magnificent mansions had been left to crumble because few could afford their upkeep. Darcy supposed Stirling could be independently wealthy, but a man still had to have something to give his life meaning.

Common sense dictated that any feelings Darcy harboured for Stirling were a waste, yet with each encounter they grew. The mere mention of his name had her heart skipping. All Darcy could hope was that it didn't trip over and land her face-first in regret.

She knocked at the back door and turned the handle. The door from the mudroom to the kitchen was also closed but she could hear faint laughter from within. Stirling must be on the phone. There'd been no other vehicle in the drive.

Her knock on the inner door was answered with a 'come in'.

Darcy poked her head inside and then the rest of herself when Stirling beckoned her to enter. He sat at the end of the big kitchen table, near the range, his chair sideways and his legs outstretched. A stack of hardcover books was piled alongside the computer, a notepad and pen close by. The kitchen smelled deliciously of roasting chicken. He'd put it on himself.

'Gotta go, Olympia,' he said.

Darcy's buoyant heart turned leaden. Olympia. A girl's name. Maybe even a girlfriend's name.

She set the container of homemade ginger snaps she'd brought near the kettle and feigned disinterest in his conversation by peeking inside the oven. The trussed chicken lay in a tray surrounded by vegetables. From the aroma and hiss and spit of its skin, she guessed he'd buttered and salted it for crispiness and flavour. Someone had taught him how to cook. She wondered who.

'Why?' The girlish voice sounded tinny through the laptop speakers. 'We haven't spoken for *aaaages*.'

Stirling hesitated for a moment. 'I have a visitor.'

'Is it Darcy?' Olympia asked, her tone rising. 'It's her, isn't it? Call her over. I want to meet her!'

He shook his head. 'Maybe another time.'

'Angel! You introduce me!'

He glanced at Darcy with a lack of enthusiasm.

Darcy wasn't sure she was keen either, but the voice sounded young. Too young for Stirling. Perhaps Olympia was a relative—a sister or a niece.

He breathed in. 'Would you like to meet my friend Olympia?'

'I'd be delighted.' What else could she say?

He shifted his legs under the table to make room for her by his side. Darcy crouched to inspect the screen. A strawberry-blonde teenager grinned out at her. She had bright blue eyes and an adorable sprinkling of freckles across the top of her nose and cheeks.

'Darcy! Hi!' The girl bounced up onto her knees and back again. 'I'm so thrilled to meet you. Angel has just been telling me all about you!' Although loaded with youthful exuberance there was no missing the clipped edges of her British accent.

'Angel?' Darcy looked at Stirling. His face was like stone. She regarded Olympia again.

'My name for him. It's short for Guardian Angel.' Olympia's gaze shifted to Stirling and sharpened. 'You haven't told her, have you?'

He shrugged. 'Nothing to tell.'

Olympia rolled her eyes. 'You're hopeless.' She beamed at Darcy and bounced up and down again. 'Angel saved my life just like you saved his.'

Darcy raised an eyebrow at Stirling, but he was studying the pile of old hardcover books on the table. 'I think he might have overstated my first aid.'

'That's not what he said.'

'Hmm,' replied Darcy. They would have a chat about this later. 'Is that how you met? Stirling being a hero?'

'I'm not a hero,' he muttered.

'No. He was on Andiamo—that's Dad's yacht—when I flipped my jet ski and hit my head. Everyone was too busy watching dopey Isabella parading around in her bikini to notice.' Olympia let out a long sigh. 'Except for Angel. He was watching over me. He dived straight in and kept me above water.'

'Goodness. He really was a hero.'

'Not. A. Hero.' If Stirling's words were any tighter, they'd squeak.

'Yes, you are!' Olympia clapped her hands. 'Have you told her the rest?'

'No. And it's definitely time to go.' He reached for the lid of the laptop.

'Don't you dare!'

'I'm daring, Olympia. Say hi to your dad for me.'

'No! Darcy, tell him not to go! He'll listen to you!'

'I'm happy to keep chatting,' said Darcy cheerfully.

Stirling threw her a look that had 'traitor' written all over it, then returned to the screen. 'Sorry, Olympia. I need to check my roast.'

'Nooo!'

'Bye now. I'll talk to you next week.' Though Olympia was still yelling, Stirling firmly closed the lid. He hoisted himself upright and, using only one crutch, limped to the oven and cracked open the door.

'I can do that,' said Darcy.

'My roast.'

She rolled her eyes even more wildly than Olympia. 'Yes, and well done you. I am suitably impressed but I'd rather not have to tend to the burns you're likely to give yourself.'

He shut the oven door and limped aside. 'The veggies aren't ready for turning anyway.'

Good. It'd give them time for a chat. She had questions.

'A yacht, huh?'

He rested against the wall with his arms folded. 'Mmm.'

'Was this in England? I noticed Olympia's accent.'

He shook his head. 'Corsica.'

'Right.' She rolled her lips together to stop from grinning. 'Sounds like nice work.'

He shrugged. 'It was okay.'

The man was frustration central, but Darcy had no intention of backing down. Her curiosity had been curtailed too long. She leaned against the sink with her arms out either side and hands rested on the bench, her body as open as his was closed.

'Olympia's father must be incredibly grateful to you for rescuing her.'

'He is. There was nothing heroic about it though. Just luck I happened to be watching.'

'You weren't interested in the bikini woman?'

That at least earned her a laugh and caused him to drop his tightly folded arms. 'Isabella's so far out of my league it'd be a waste of time even looking.' He must have seen the disbelief on her face. 'She's a model.'

Darcy screwed up her nose. Surely, he didn't mean who she thought? 'We're not talking Isabella Macedo, are we?'

'We are.'

She blinked as a thousand questions exploded across her mind. How on earth did Stirling find himself in that kind of company? 'This boss of yours ...'

'Alexander Maugham.'

Darcy gave a spluttery laugh and waited for some indication he was teasing. None came. 'You're serious?'

'Yep. I only worked for him a couple of years. Didn't suit me. Would you like a drink?' He indicated the pantry. 'Shiloh said there's a cellar full of wine down there. Feel free to raid it.'

'Ah, no.' She was still recovering from the Alexander Maugham revelation to be more articulate. The online payment process systems entrepreneur was known as much for his patronage of the arts as for his billions, and for the loss of his beloved wife to brain cancer only a few years after their daughter was born. 'Thank you. It's been a long week and I still have to drive home. I can fetch you something if you like?'

'Thanks, but I'd better stick to water.'

Taking the hint, she took a glass from an overhead cupboard, filled it from the tap and handed it to Stirling, then poured one of her own, sipping as she regarded him, desperate to pry but worried he'd clam up.

He eyed her up and down, his cheek dimpling. 'Cute outfit.'

Darcy stroked the bib of her khaki vintage-inspired dungarees that she'd teamed with a green, blue and white checked flannelette shirt. That he noticed filled her with delight, and she was relieved she'd applied pink lip gloss before leaving Roseneath. Unfortunately, she also stank of sheep.

'Thank you. One of my own designs.'

'I thought it might be. You have ones like it on your website.'

'You checked out my website?'

'I did.'

As one of her least popular products, Darcy's line of dungarees were buried deep in the shop. Stirling must have had a good search around to find them. The thought had her body twitching with the urge to perform a skippy dance. She should move away from the range. It was making her hot. Not to mention worsening her sheepy pong.

'I apologise for smelling like sheep. I would have changed only I was in a rush to get over here so I could get your dinner on.'

'But I'd already done it.' Amusement finally sparked in his lovely greeny-hazel eyes—eyes that matched her dungarees, like some sort of karmic wink. 'Despite appearances, I'm not totally useless.'

She returned his smile. 'Apparently not. So ... how did you come to work for Alexander Maugham?'

'I got approached by one of his people.'

Darcy took a deep breath. Back to digging for gems again. 'To do what?'

'Personal pilot.'

'Pilot? As in, private jet?'

'Helicopter.'

Darcy did her best at nonchalance and failed dismally. She could feel the admiration radiating off her, reaching out towards Stirling, wanting to entwine around him the way a cat coils around its owner's legs. A little girl–saving hero *and* a helicopter pilot? The warmth sweeping her body definitely wasn't from the range.

'Goodness,' she said, rather breathlessly.

He huffed a laugh. 'It's not that special.'

'Of course not.' She waved off the idea. 'Everyone pilots around billionaires and supermodels and hangs about on yachts off glamorous places like Corsica.'

'It wasn't all like that. Most of the time it was boring. Lots of sitting around waiting or ferrying people about on short trips. Anyway, enough about me. I haven't asked how last night went with your friend.'

Darcy indicated a kitchen chair. 'May I?'

'Of course.'

She sat. Stirling did the same but sideways, with his legs stretched towards the range as they were when she arrived. Somehow he managed to make loose trackpants look good.

'Last night did not go well, to answer your question. Charlie was being charming and Lisette can be incredibly headstrong when she's had a few.'

'Ah. Sorry.' Slowly, his dimple made an appearance as he regarded her beneath long lashes. 'I have a mate who could take him out, if that would help.'

'Oh, you do, do you?'

'I do. Several, in fact.'

She tilted her head to the side. They were flirting, the delicious buzz of it was cascading tingles down her spine, but there was also something else there. A secret trying to peek around the sides of his natural reticence. 'How intriguing.' She leaned forward and balanced her chin on the edge of her hand. 'Tell me, how does a nice man like you come to have dangerous friends like that?'

He shrugged. 'I was in the army for a while.'

'How sexy.'

He laughed. 'If you think so.'

Oh, she most certainly did. Stirling would look extremely inviting in camouflage gear.

'As a pilot?'

'Yeah. Blackhawks.'

She widened her eyes. 'And that's not sexy?'

He shook his head, but he was smiling, perhaps even a little embarrassed. Darcy liked him even more.

'You went from the army to working for Alexander Maugham?'

'Not quite. I had a stint flying offshore oil and gas operations off West Africa for a while.'

'That sounds dangerous.'

'Only sometimes.'

She was sure he was underplaying it, but Darcy knew nothing about helicopters or the kind of work he'd done. 'And now? Besides being newly minted landed gentry.'

Stirling's amused snort revealed what he thought of the 'gentry' comment. Then his gaze left hers and focused on the laptop, all amusement gone. 'I guess I'm between jobs.'

Darcy frowned as she recalled the moment in the hospital when they'd talked about passions, when he'd said how good it was to meet someone who'd made a life out of their passion, and implied his chance was over. Had he meant his pilot's career?

That didn't seem right though. His injury would heal with no lasting damage. Surely he would fly again?

'Lucky in a way, I guess,' said Stirling.

Darcy's frown deepened. 'How?'

'Gives me time to sort out this place. Find out where I come from.' He hefted one of the hardcover books and studied its faded dust jacket. It was an old tome, well thumbed but in good condition. He looked up. 'I spent the morning checking out Dougal's library.'

'Oh, that's a lovely room.' Even as a child, Darcy had adored it. With its heavy furniture and walls of books, it was old fashioned and deeply masculine, like stepping into a bygone era. She always expected to smell cigars and brandy—instead it smelled of leather and fossilising books. She and Shiloh had spent quite a few wet winter days playing board and card games there with Melody, before the divorce moved her away. Sadly, the friendship never endured. It had been more about proximity than fondness anyway.

'I thought it might tell me more about Dougal. What made him the person he was, that kind of thing, but ...' He dumped the book. It slid across the table close enough for Darcy to read the cover: *Men of Yesterday: A Social History of the Western District of Victoria 1843–1890.* 'Bit early I guess.'

Darcy's heart squeezed. The poor man, longing for a family he was destined never to know.

As if aware of her pity, Stirling straightened. 'I learned a bit about the Kildares though. I had no idea they'd been here so long or that Westwind was so big.'

'It was, in its heyday. As were many pastoral runs in the region.' She smiled, relieved to hear a hint of pride in his voice. 'You have a lot of history behind you.'

'So it seems. Shame the recent part is so tragic.' He let out a long breath and caught her eye. His expression turned sheepish, causing Darcy's belly to flip-flop. 'Don't look at me like that. I'm fine. Just being a misery guts because I'm bored and pissed off and feeling sorry for myself.'

Darcy opened her mouth to tell him that with all that had happened he was allowed to feel miserable, only for his phone to sound a loud cock-a-doodle-do.

'That'll be time to turn the spuds,' he said, swiping the screen and silencing the discordant squawk. He reached for his crutch.

Darcy was up before Stirling could gain his feet. 'Don't you dare.'

'I can do things.' He nodded towards the oven. 'As I've proved.'

'Yes, and now I'm here you don't need to.'

'You're very bossy, you know.'

'I'm taking care of you.' She tugged on oven mitts. 'As I've mentioned, I'm inv—'

'Invested. Yeah, I got it.' Stirling shook his head and grimaced, though his eyes were crinkled at the edges and his little dimple had popped. 'All because of a dress.'

'A truly splendid dress, I'll have you know.' Darcy lifted her chin. 'I loved that dress and miss it dearly.'

She could feel his gaze following her movements as she sat the roasting pan on top of the stove and used tongs to turn over the vegetables. He'd even thought to include two small onions. The sight of them, along with the two pumpkin wedges, warmed her. Last night Darcy hadn't mentioned staying for dinner, only that she'd make the roast, and he hadn't asked. Clearly the expectation was there.

She tilted the pan and used a spoon to draw up the fat over the chicken and when it was nicely basted, she returned it to the oven.

'How long?' he asked, holding up his phone.

'Twenty minutes should do it,' she said, wiping her hands on a towel and thinking some lovely green beans would complement the roast perfectly.

'Do you have a busy week ahead?' he asked.

'I do.' She opened the fridge door and rummaged in the crisper. 'I'm previewing a new summer design as a teaser to the collection's full launch in November. With a bit of luck, it'll bring in a few orders, which means I need to make sure my current ones are up to date. Lots of sewing ahead. Then there's my usual trips to Hamilton for Mum's physio, and whatever help Dad and Shiloh might need at the farm. Speaking of which, you must be due for a check-up?'

'I am. But I'll manage.'

She shut the fridge door. 'How?'

'I have ways.'

Darcy gave him the side-eye as she carried the beans to the chopping board. 'Another of your helpful friends?'

'Something like that.'

'I may be bossy, but you,' she pointed the tip of her knife his direction, 'are frustrating.'

Stirling regarded her calmly. 'If I told you, you'd either tell me off or demand I let you help. I'm just stopping the argument in its tracks.'

'Accepting help isn't illegal, you know.'

'I know.'

Darcy began topping and tailing the beans, tossing them into a copper saucepan.

'I like staying in control,' Stirling admitted when she remained quiet.

Darcy looked over her shoulder. 'And you're feeling out of control right now?'

He made a humphy kind of sound that she took as a yes.

'Is there anything I can do?'

Stirling snapped out of whatever trance he was in. 'You've done enough. And you're busy.'

'I don't mind. Honestly.'

He shook his head again, then levered up on his crutch, headed for the drawer and began taking out cutlery.

Darcy took the hint and chatted about the Hoppers and their chances in the upcoming grand final, only to discover Stirling preferred rugby union.

'Not much choice when you're at an English public school,' he said, which then set off a conversation about his schooling and his mother. Stirling's pride in Amanda and her achievements flowed through every word.

'She sounds amazing,' said Darcy. The chicken was out of the oven and resting along with the vegetables. She'd set the pan on the stove and sprinkled in flour to soak up the juices and brown.

'She is,' said Stirling. 'I worry about her though. I know she's more than capable of looking after herself—she's told me enough times—but still.'

'I can imagine.' He'd mentioned Amanda was in the Central African Republic and while Darcy knew little about the country, she recalled news stories about violence and kidnapping and suffering people. 'She must have worried about you in the army too.'

'Not so much the army, but with MiZ she did.'

'MiZ?' asked Darcy, draining some of the bean water into the roasting tin.

'*Medizin in Krise*—MiZ. That's who I went to work for after Alexander. It's a German-founded aid organisation, a bit like *Medecins sans Frontieres* except that it operates more like a guerrilla operation. We deploy small teams of medics into crisis zones for pure emergency relief, do what we can and get out, then pass on the intelligence to other organisations so they can coordinate more comprehensive aid.'

'Crisis zones?' Darcy stopped stirring. 'Like war zones?'

'Sometimes.'

'That sounds incredibly dangerous.'

'It's the medics who face the real danger. They're the ones on the ground.'

Darcy wasn't sure about that. Aircraft and their pilots always seemed to be the target in movies. 'You did this all over the world?'

'Not all over. Mostly Africa and the Middle East. El Salvador once. That was nuts.'

'You're taking my breath away.' And he was. The risks he must have taken in his life, the dangers he'd faced ... 'You no longer work for MiZ?'

A glance told her the question wasn't welcome. 'Technically I'm on extended leave.'

'But you'll go back?'

He shrugged, his gaze lowered.

Darcy decided not to pry further. She poured the gravy into a glass jug, set it on the table and laid out plates ready for serving.

'Thigh or breast?' she asked, carving knife at the ready.

'Thigh,' he said.

'A man after my own heart. I do love good legs.'

For some reason, that had Stirling's mouth narrowing.

'Here you go,' she said, depositing his laden plate in front of him.

'Thanks.' He leaned forward and took a long sniff. 'Smells great.'

'Your work.' She laid down her own plate and settled into her chair. 'You put the roast on.'

He poured a generous pool of the gravy over his meal and toasted her with the jug. 'Proper gravy though.'

'But of course.' Darcy tutted. 'You're in the country now, Stirling. It's a must.'

They ate in silence, disturbed only by the shift and pop of logs in the range, Stirling occasionally offering compliments and saying he couldn't remember the last time he enjoyed a roast dinner.

When they'd finished, Darcy set the chicken and leftover vegetables aside to cool, stacked the dishwasher and ran water in the sink to wash the copper pan and roasting dish.

A warm hand cupped her shoulder. 'Leave them.'

Stirling was close, wonderfully so. Darcy wanted to turn into his arms, but would it be appreciated? Their friendship was young and she still knew too little—about him, about his future. Her tingling body would have to learn patience.

'They won't take much effort.'

'I know. Which is why they can be left for me to do in the morning.' He indicated his crutches. 'The challenge will do me good.'

Remembering his comment about needing control, she gave in and wiped her hands clean. 'Are you planning to sleep on the couch again?'

'I am.'

She fought the urge to scold. And the desire to offer her bed in town. 'I'll fetch some more logs.' She was out the door before he could argue.

With Stirling's couch remade and a jug of water and a glass placed within reach, there was nothing else to hold her at Westwind.

She clasped her hands in front of her belly. 'I guess I'd better head home.'

Darcy had hoped for at least a small protest. Instead, Stirling smiled. A genuine one that made his dimple dip and her silly heart to butterfly.

'Thanks for everything.'

'I don't mind.' She tilted her head coyly and bit the bottom corner of her lip. 'As I may have mentioned, I'm—'

He laughed and held up a hand. 'Invested. I get it.' He sobered. 'It's a hell of an investment you're making for a dress. Even a dress you loved.'

She met his gaze. 'I think it's worthwhile.'

Neither spoke but the air between them vibrated. Darcy's fingers curled as the hush continued. Was he waiting for her to make the first move? She wasn't normally hesitant. Darcy considered her heart and body precious, things to be cared for and to be careful with, but that never stopped her from going for what she wanted. And right now, she wanted Stirling.

Her lips parted. Stirling's gaze darted to them and back to her eyes. A sad smile tipped his mouth.

'Darcy …'

'Yes?'

He shook his head, slow and regretful. Darcy's butterflying heart sank.

'Don't go thinking I'm something I'm not.'

'How do you know I'm thinking anything?'

'Just don't. I'm not ...' He breathed out hard. 'It doesn't matter. Thanks for all your help.'

It was a dismissal and Darcy took it with her chin held high. But his unfinished sentence stayed with her as she travelled through the darkness to Grassmoor.

I'm not ...

Not worth it? Not who you think I am?

Her hands tightened on the wheel. Whatever Stirling was or wasn't, she was determined to find out.

Chapter Fourteen

Lisette bustled into the atelier just after seven on Monday evening. She held up a shopping bag as she passed Darcy at her cutting table on the way to the kitchen.

'Pizza, red wine, and burnt fig and honeycomb ice cream. All the food groups. And my company, which is far more important than any food.'

Darcy's shoulders eased a little. 'You're a darling, Lissy. Thank you.'

'My pleasure, Princess. I was looking for something to liven up my Monday night.' Lisette dumped their goodies on the bench. 'Of course, you do understand that it'll cost you.'

Darcy smiled and shifted her pattern weights until the fabric was properly secured. A quick double-check, and she began the tense process of wheeling her rotary cutter around the pattern. There was no room for error. She couldn't afford the time or the waste of fabric.

That morning, Darcy had posted photos of her preview dress on her website and her social media accounts, expecting a few inquiries, perhaps an order or two. Instead, the comments and shares began piling up almost immediately, despite the dress's near $500 price tag. At first, Darcy had been delighted, then as the day progressed and demand only increased, mildly panicked. VaVoom was a one-woman show yet, by late afternoon, she had enough business to keep three seamstresses flat out for a week. At 6 pm, shaken and sweating, she labelled the dress 'Sold Out' and phoned Lisette, who immediately went into rescue mode.

'Right,' said Lisette, sauntering across the studio now. 'Pizza's in the oven, ice cream's in the freezer and medicinal wine is,' she held out a glass to Darcy, 'right here.'

'Give me a minute.' Darcy continued to cut as Lisette made a beeline for the tablet that was feeding Darcy's speakers. Seconds later, The Platters' 'Smoke Gets in Your Eyes' gave way to Kylie Minogue's early noughties hit 'Can't Get You out of My Head'.

Lisette shimmied over to Darcy's sofa and perched on the back. She knew not to disturb Darcy when she was busy. Although that didn't extend to not swapping her vintage playlists for the sounds of their teens.

Darcy bit her tongue and kept her focus. Thank goodness she'd ordered extra bolts of cotton. The pink tea-party-patterned ruffle dress took a lot of fabric, and many of the orders had been for plus sizes, which warmed her heart. Everyone deserved to look pretty, and with its shirred bust, slim-fitted inverted 'V' lower bodice and tiered full skirt, the design was wonderfully flattering. A dress made for sunshine, romance and happy days. Darcy couldn't wait for warmer weather to wear her own version. Preferably in front of Stirling.

Stirling … Oh, that moment in the kitchen. Even thinking about it made her forget about her bulging order book and her heart dance like the dress fabric's whimsical flowers, teapots and cups and saucers. The way his eyes had drifted to her mouth and lingered hungrily still gave her flutters. He'd wanted her as much as she wanted him, but they were both held back by fear. His, she had yet to understand. Her own was simple—why risk losing her heart to someone whose future was undecided?

Unless Stirling had already decided that he wouldn't be staying and wanted to spare her that pain? She wouldn't put it past him.

'Well?' said Lisette, the moment Darcy finished her run.

She set down the cutter, pressed her hands to her spine and arched. She'd have a permanent crick after this week if she wasn't careful. 'I could ask you the same thing, person who broke her vow to never again sleep with Charlie Shanahan.'

'I know, I know.' Lisette let out a long sigh. 'It'd be so much easier if he weren't so lush in bed. And don't you dare make that face—you look like your grandmother. Anyway, there's more to the relationship than sex.'

Darcy arched her brows and reached for her wine, making sure to stand well clear of the cutting table as she sipped.

Lisette harrumphed. 'Yeah, okay. There's not. Like you're Miss Goody-Two-Shoes.'

'I'm not the one who slept with Charlie. Again.'

'Oh, and what about our secretive new stranger, hmm?'

'Silly me.' Darcy pressed the back of her wrist to her forehead as though about to collapse on her fainting couch. 'How could I forget the quick frolic I managed with poor injured Stirling between looking out for you Saturday night and working my socks off at Roseneath all Sunday?'

'Sunday night.' Lisette pointed a finger. 'You missed Sunday night.'

Darcy lifted her chin. 'We cooked and ate. That's all.'

'Of course you did.'

'We did.'

Lisette rolled her eyes and shook her head. '*Such* a disappointment.'

Darcy flipped her the bird, which made Lisette laugh. There was something very funny about someone so ladylike giving the finger while dressed in a purple twinset and pearls and iris-patterned capris.

She took another sip of wine and returned to her pattern. Why oh why did she choose to kick off the collection with such a complicated dress? The answer was obvious—because it was gorgeous and showcased her skills in both sewing and patternmaking, and it fitted VaVoom's sexy, figure-celebrating, light-hearted brand to a T. Or tea, as it were, given the fabric motif.

Lisette wandered over to Darcy's design book and flicked through to the back where Darcy logged her ideas-in-progress.

With all she'd had on lately, and the summer collection already underway, there had been few new additions. Except last night, unable to sleep for nerves about her upcoming advertising campaign and the memory of that heated moment with Stirling, Darcy had retreated to the kitchen with her coloured pencils and a mug of hot chocolate. The result was an aviator jacket in black suede with an oversized khaki fleece collar and cuffs and natty zips, teamed with cropped, black and khaki striped jeans with zips up the legs.

'Hey, this is cool.' Lisette held up the sketch. 'The show and shine car crowd will love it.'

'Thanks. One for next winter, I think. If I ever survive these orders.'

'You will. You're the Queen of Seam, remember?'

Lisette flicked through a few more pages then set down the folder to watch Darcy work. The stereo switched to Black Eyed Peas' 'I Gotta Feeling' and Darcy smiled—she had a whole lot of feelings.

'Uh-oh,' said Lisette.

'Uh-oh what?'

'You like him.'

There was no point in making a secret of the fact. It was obvious from the frequency of Darcy's visits to Westwind, and the way she bristled when anyone asked about Stirling. Besides, Lisette had known her since they were children and would call her out on any lie.

'I do.'

'Are we talking "lusty-like" here or "I'm designing my wedding dress" like?'

Darcy completed the final run, set the cutter aside and picked up her scissors. She stared at the fabric and then forlornly at Lisette. 'Quite a bit of both.'

'Woah. That's pretty major.' Her nose screwed up. 'You really feel that way?'

Darcy sighed and pulled her stool from behind the sewing desk. 'I shouldn't, I know I shouldn't. It's silly. *I'm* silly. But …' She breathed out. 'Oh, Lissy, he's so sexy and so brave and so interesting. He's … like no one I've ever met before.'

For a moment Lisette said nothing, just blinked. The admission had obviously left her feeling a little rattled too. Darcy was not one to gush, especially over a man.

Finally Lisette shook herself. 'Okay, spill. I want to know *everything*.'

Darcy swallowed. She adored her friend, but Lisette was a terrible gossip and instinct told her Stirling wouldn't like having his business bandied around town.

'You have to promise to keep it to yourself,' said Darcy. 'I mean it.'

A brief wince crossed Lisette's face, but she nodded. 'Promise.' She held up her little finger. 'Super-pinky promise.'

Darcy breathed in deeply, then returned to her cutting board to share what she'd learned while she worked.

By the time she'd finished, Lisette was sagged against the couch as though overcome by Darcy's revelations. She fanned the front of her neck. 'That is so hot. And he's a honey on top of it all. No wonder you're mad for him.' Her tone turned wondrous. 'God, who'd have guessed?'

'I know. It's extraordinary.'

'You wait till—'

'No!' Darcy rubbed at her chest where a sudden whirlpool of fear swirled. 'You promised.'

'But—'

'No, Lissy. This is between us. I don't think he wants it public knowledge and you promised. The only reason he admitted his past to me was because I interrupted him chatting to a friend who gave him away.' And, she suspected, because Stirling trusted her.

'It'll come out eventually. You know what this place is like.'

'I know it will. And I'm sure Stirling knows that too. But let's give him what peace we can, hey?'

Lisette's shoulders slumped. 'The most exciting thing to happen in Grassmoor for months and you make me keep mum. So not fair.'

Darcy returned to her work. 'I'm sure you'll get over it.'

'This,' said Lisette, wandering towards the kitchen where she'd left the wine bottle, 'I am not sure about.' She returned with her glass refilled and shimmying to Ricky Martin's 'She Bangs'. 'You and him … that would be so cool.'

Though she couldn't agree more, Darcy scoffed. 'I think you're getting just a little ahead of yourself.'

Lisette peered into Darcy's face. 'Am I?'

'Yes!'

'Come on. You were practically planning your wedding dress only a few minutes ago.'

'That was just—' She snapped her mouth shut. Lisette was right, but that didn't mean she should act on her feelings. 'Number one, I'm not sure he's interested in me. And two, there are no guarantees he's going to stay at Westwind. Why take the risk?'

'Fine.' Lisette walked away only to swing back. 'Be hardnosed. Save that fragile heart and play it safe. But while you're wallowing in your safety, how about sparing a thought or two for that underused vagina of yours. Poor thing must be just about rusted over.'

Darcy nearly took a slice out of the fabric she was cutting.

'Admit it,' said Lisette. 'It's been a while. A bit of wild pilot sex might do wonders for your creativity.'

'He's injured!'

'He's a man, I'm sure he'll manage.'

'I'm busy!'

'A girl needs her exercise breaks.' Lisette grinned as Ricky Martin hit his banging crescendo. 'You know what they say, sex is as good as a five-k run.'

Darcy couldn't help but splutter a laugh. Lisette's ability to cheer her up was one of the reasons Darcy adored her. 'Oh, shush with you. It's not going to happen.' Not any time soon, at least. 'Now, come help me lay out the next order.'

They worked until the oven timer went off, then broke for pizza and ice cream, over which Lisette lamented the mistake she'd made again with Charlie.

'I just can't seem to stop. He gives me that smile and I just melt.' She rested her chin on her hand. 'It's pathetic.'

'It's not pathetic.'

'It is, and you know it.' She sighed. 'I know he's using me.'

'As you are him.' This was a conversation they'd had before. Darcy would not condemn Charlie, no matter her own feelings towards the man. Her job was to remind Lisette she was her own woman. 'Women are allowed to like sex, Lissy. And as long as it's consensual, we're allowed to enjoy it whenever, however and with whoever we please.'

'Tell that to Dearest Frances.'

'I shall,' replied Darcy with a regal lift of her chin. Dearest Frances was a local busybody who had been Darcy's nemesis since school. Darcy had no regard and even less patience for the woman, or any others of her ilk. 'If the subject ever comes up.'

'*If* it ever comes up?' Lisette's eyes widened. 'No, Princess. No. There are no ifs about it.'

'Because you horizontal-tangoed with Charlie?' That was old news. Only the diehards bothered to tut over Lisette's behaviour these days.

Lisette cocked her head for a moment. 'Actually, I think it was all vertical. Anyway, I mean you, dopey. You'll be the reason for the knicker-twisting.'

'Me? What have I done?'

'Oh, I don't know … publicly admitted to stripping for Stirling for starters. And you have been spending a lot of time at Westwind.'

'Oh truly,' Darcy scoffed. 'The poor man can barely walk. Besides, who could possibly know I've been calling in to Westwind?'

Lisette gave her a look.

Darcy groaned. Grassmoor, bless its cotton socks, really got her goat sometimes.

'Gird your royal loins, my Queen of Seam,' said Lisette, clearly thrilled the attention wasn't on her for a change, 'because for you, there's no "if" about the subject of inappropriate sex being raised. It's a guaranteed "when".'

Chapter Fifteen

Mal McKenzie had sounded delighted when Stirling phoned on Tuesday morning and asked if Mal had time to chat about Dougal. Now the man was relaxed in a cane chair in the paved sunken garden sculpted into the slope below the derelict vegetable patch on Westwind's north-eastern side. The firepit at the centre flickered orange and yellow, teased by the cool breeze sweeping up from the gully below.

The view was stunning. To the north, the distant ranges carved grey mounds into the vibrant early spring sky, while down the slope, the creek tumbled past before gurgling off into the distance.

Stirling hadn't paid much attention to the area on his first visit. Like the vegetable patch, the sunken garden had seemed cold and lost, the stones covered in moss and the occasional patch of slime, and the firepit filled with murky water. But after ten minutes of Stirling's company in the kitchen, Mal had suggested they sit outside and make the most of the fine afternoon. If Stirling could manage the short walk.

Stirling appreciated the chance to get outdoors. He'd been restless all morning, and not just from being housebound. It was nerves from meeting Mal. This was the man who could add colour to his sketch of Dougal. Who might have explanations for the many questions that tormented him.

Mal's familiarity with Westwind was driven home when he'd fetched a handsome, if dusty, cane table and chairs from a shed, then wood for the pit. Soon the fire was alight. Mal then ordered Stirling to stay put and disappeared into the house, returning a while later with cups and a plunger of coffee and the container of Darcy's biscuits.

'She's a wonderful girl, that Darcy,' Mal remarked when Stirling mentioned the ginger snaps were hers. Mal was relaxed in his chair, moleskin-clad legs and patinaed leather boots at angles to the fire, and a felt fedora shading his face. 'Terrible about her mother. Especially on top of all the other problems. Have you met them, the Sloanes?'

Stirling shook his head and reached for another ginger snap. 'Only Shiloh.'

'Ah, now she's something. If I weren't so old …' Mal chuckled. 'She'd be too much for me anyway.'

Stirling suspected Shiloh would be too much for many.

'They're good people, the Sloanes,' said Mal, picking another biscuit for himself and biting into it.

Stirling didn't comment. He had the peculiar impression the man was fishing.

Mal smiled. 'But you didn't ask me here to talk about the Sloanes. It's Dougal who's on your mind. Where to start?' His gaze turned distant as he stared across the fire to the hills beyond, then he sighed and leaned forward to rest his forearms on his legs. 'Whatever else I say, I want you to know that I considered your father the best of men. We had our ups and downs, I won't lie about that, but that can be said for any friendship. It's not just me, either. Dougal was well respected around the district. Well liked. Admired.' The last word caught, and he cleared his throat. 'A good man, Stirling. The kind of man you should be proud to have as a father.'

Despite Mal's heartfelt sentiments, Stirling wasn't buying. He'd spent too long brooding over the anomalies in Dougal's life and death. What he wanted was answers.

'It doesn't fit though, does it? With what he did. All the people he hurt.' Including the son he'd never met. 'A good man?' Stirling shook his head, the residual sweetness of Darcy's biscuit turning bitter in his mouth.

'You're angry. I understand that. We all are.'

How could Mal understand? Stirling certainly didn't get it. He didn't get any of his feelings—not his anger, not his sorrow, not his hurt.

Yet Dougal was still his father, still his blood.

'We're all fallible, all flawed. Every one of us. Dougal …' Mal's eyes closed briefly. 'He made a mistake, got caught in something he couldn't handle.'

'What, though? Look at all he had.' Stirling gestured at the house, the lush paddocks, the creek and ranges. At the richness surrounding him. The history.

'I know. None of us can make sense of it.'

This wasn't helping. This 'mistake'—like it was petty-cash theft instead of a near million-dollar fraud—Dougal had made was one of the major things Stirling needed to reconcile.

And why the hell had Dougal shot the dogs?

'I miss him,' said Mal, the crack back in his voice. 'I feel like I've lost a brother. The irony is, if old Benjamin had had his way, we wouldn't have been friends at all. Dougal, though, he always did enjoy defying his father.'

Stirling's ears sharpened. 'They didn't get on?'

'Most of the time. Benjamin was old school, straight from the squattocracy. His lot didn't mix with my lot.' The smile he threw Stirling held no humour. 'Workers. Tradesmen. My dad was a diesel mechanic. Mum was a cleaner. She even worked here for a while.' He nodded at Westwind. 'Before she had me.'

'How did you meet? You and Dougal?'

'Primary school. We were little terrors together.' Mal laughed. 'Not terrible little terrors, but still a handful. Benjamin did his best to discourage the friendship. So did my parents, for that matter— Mum especially. I think she thought Dougal would abandon me and I'd get hurt. But Dougal hung strong.'

Stirling stared at the fire, his brow furrowing as he sifted through the facts about his father's life. 'Didn't he go to boarding school?' A particularly prestigious one, if Stirling's memory was correct.

'For secondary school.'

'Yet you remained friends?'

'We did.' Mal gave another one of those throaty chuckles. 'Turned out the local principal thought I was a clever bugger. One day he called me into the office and handed me an application form for Dougal's school. Said there was a scholarship going and I should apply. So I did, and I got it.' Mal used a rusted star picket to poke at the logs. 'Scholarship kids weren't always treated great, but I thrived. Being friends with Dougal made sure of that.'

Stirling nodded, remembering his own boarding school days. He sipped his coffee and watched the sparks drift up and die like fireflies. At least Dougal had been loyal to someone, which was more than could be said for the local businesses and families he ripped off.

'We had quite a few years when we didn't see much of one another.' Mal tossed another lump of wood in the pit and used the picket to manoeuvre it into place. 'He came home to Westwind, and I went on to university then worked for a firm in Geelong for a while. We kept in touch though. It was Dougal who convinced me to set up in Grassmoor.' He smiled wryly. 'Not the smartest move financially but I missed the place, and Mum and Dad weren't getting any younger. I'd met Candice by then and she liked the idea of moving here. Healthy country air and all that. Dougal entrusted me with his business and was good enough to put the word out. I did all right.'

It sounded like Mal owed Dougal a great deal. Stirling wondered what his father had got out of the relationship. Brotherly companionship or something else? Getting one over his snobbish father, perhaps? Maybe Dougal got a kick out of playing lord of the manor and helping someone his family considered inferior.

He shook the thought away. Theirs had been a long friendship and Mal seemed a decent bloke. Dougal had his faults, but Stirling didn't want to believe that of him.

Mal set down the picket and leaned back, his face turned to the sky, and Stirling did the same. Though the sun was still weak, it was pleasant, and the fire took the sharp edges off the cool day. Magpies and other bird life tuned the air. It was a shame the remaining acreage had no livestock. A few sheep or cattle would have filled in the last of the landscape's lonely hollows.

The moment brought Darcy to mind. She'd texted last night to apologise for not calling in and to check if he needed anything, and that she'd ask Shiloh to drop by this afternoon to fetch wood inside. That she was distancing herself should have left him relieved. Instead, Stirling was disappointed.

He felt Mal's gaze on him and realised he'd zoned out for a while. 'Sorry, drifted off.'

'It's a pleasant afternoon for it. What else would you like to know?'

Stirling considered for a moment. What would ease this anxiety he couldn't shed? Should he even raise his list of issues surrounding Dougal's death? 'Did he ever … mention me?'

'No. No one knew you existed until you turned up here.' Mal hefted the picket again and pushed a log further towards the fire's centre. 'I can't tell you how upset I am that Dougal felt the need to keep you secret. He knew I'd never betray a confidence.'

Stirling shrugged. 'I suppose in the beginning he wanted to save his marriage, then the secret kind of went on.'

'Not that much—his marriage, I mean. He barely put up a fight when Brigitte left.' Mal stared at the fire. 'That was costly.'

'The divorce?'

He nodded. 'Not just the land he was forced to sell. Melody sided with her mother and refused to have anything to do with him after that.'

Which helped explain why Melody had washed her hands of Westwind and Stirling. Both were too much of a reminder of her father and his feet of clay.

'Why did they divorce?'

'I guess they grew apart,' said Mal. 'Maybe Brigitte knew about you, although if she did, she kept it to herself.' He paused. 'I wouldn't be surprised if there were others besides your mother. Dougal had always been fond of the ladies and vice versa.'

There probably had been others. If Dougal had an affair with his mum, albeit brief, then Stirling doubted she was the first nor the last.

'Wasn't there gossip?'

'Not really. Dougal was very well liked and if he did have affairs, he was discreet about it.'

Stirling eyed his father's best friend. Best friend and solicitor. Except for that final will.

'You said you looked after Dougal's affairs?'

'I know where you're going with this.' Mal rested the picket against the chair. 'The will.'

Stirling nodded.

Mal stood and paced to the other side of the firepit and stared out. 'I didn't know about it. He never said. That's the worst of it. He never said a thing.' His head bent, his shoulders giving a small shudder.

Stirling waited.

Mal straightened and dragged his palm down his face. 'I can't help thinking that his death was partly my fault.' His voice held a tremor. 'If I'd have been a better friend ...' He shook his head and faced Stirling. His eyes were moist, his mouth downturned. 'I should have realised something was wrong, paid more attention. I should have—' He whirled around.

Stirling allowed the man his grief. He wasn't feeling that stable himself.

'I'm sorry.' Mal managed a weak smile. 'It's the guilt. I don't think I'll ever get over it.'

'Normal with suicides,' said Stirling as he used his crutch to rise. And he knew too. Suicide was too common among Defence Force veterans and serving members. Twelve hundred in the past two decades alone. There were few who missed being touched by it.

'I hope I helped,' said Mal, gathering the coffee cups and plunger.

'You did. Thanks.' A lie. There were still too many holes, and hearing out loud that his father was likely a serial philanderer hadn't helped either. Stirling was a risk-taker but only with his own life. He had never, and never would, cheat on a woman.

Dougal's path had been wrong in so many ways, and it had taken a terrible toll.

Kildare genes or not, that way was not Stirling's.

Chapter Sixteen

'An Indian, you say?' said Gavin.

'Classic 1940s,' said Stirling. 'Inline four-cylinder F-head. Curves like a cresting wave.'

Gavin whistled. 'Well, I'll be blowed.'

They were in Hamilton on their way to see William Stoddart. Stirling had already been to the hospital for his outpatient appointment. His leg was healing well and he'd been given the okay to be more active, along with exercises to help rebuild the muscle. Which meant no excuses not to sleep in a proper bed, even if the thought of climbing Westwind's magnificent staircase made him break out in a sweat.

Last night he'd made it to the second step before canning the idea. Mal's visit followed by Shiloh and her father dropping by had left Stirling drained. His legs were too heavy, his heart even more so. The couch wasn't the best of beds but the lounge was warm, the fire comforting, and he'd made a kind of home downstairs. Upstairs was still Dougal's, and his father's ghost refused to rest, hammering at Stirling's uneasy mind like a vengeful poltergeist.

He'd been glad to meet Peter Sloane though. It had felt wrong not having introduced himself to his nearest neighbour, especially one who hadn't had a great year either. Like his daughters, Darcy and Shiloh's father had been open and welcoming, offering to lend a hand should Stirling need it. Then chuckling, because it seemed the girls already had him sorted. Peter's tone when he mentioned 'the girls' was that of a proud and loving father. Stirling warmed to him even more, to the point he promised to visit Roseneath for dinner when he was up to it.

Not his usual style.

'Who d'you think it belonged to?' asked Gavin. They'd earlier discussed the news about a local farmer putting a Daimler Regency Empress up for auction after dragging it from a shed. The classic car was predicted to be worth a small fortune and had other locals contemplating the forgotten contents of their own sheds.

'I don't know. My grandfather, I guess.'

Gavin shook his head. 'Unreal.' He slapped the steering wheel. 'I bloody love this place. Fascinates me no end.'

Stirling smiled. There was no pretence with Gav and he possessed a generous heart. When Stirling had called to hire him for a morning, Gavin had agreed without hesitation.

'An Indian,' Gav repeated a few turns later, whistling and shaking his head. 'What are you going to do with it?'

If he'd asked Stirling that question a month ago, the answer would have been instant: he would have restored the bike. Escaped into the simple distraction of stripping and cleaning its engine and parts, piece by painstaking piece, leaving his mind to float free. And maybe find somewhere for it to land.

He scanned the scenery. Hamilton was a nice town, tidy and dignified. Though a cutting southerly was blowing, the late morning sun was bright, encouraging locals to hit the streets. People walked dogs, pausing for casual chats at storefronts, comfortable in their environment. Stirling envied their ease.

He'd hoped Westwind would help him find his place in the world, his ease too. Instead, all it had brought was unrest.

'I don't know,' he said finally, struggling to hide the fatigue in his voice.

'You don't want to restore it?'

'I wouldn't mind. Restored, it'd be worth a bucket.'

'But?'

Stirling grimaced. 'Might be a bit beyond me right now.'

'Your leg? I guess that'd make things hard. You wouldn't have to do it on your own though. I could help. Be happy to. I've pulled apart a fair few bikes in my time.' Gavin flapped a hand. 'Maybe not an Indian, but plenty of others.'

Stirling looked at him.

'True. Worked in a service centre as a teenager. Bike-mad, I was. Rode motocross for years. Did most of my own mechanics. So, you know,' he cleared his throat as though suddenly nervous, 'if you're looking for an assistant ...'

Gavin's hope quivered across the car. The man really wanted to help.

'Thanks,' said Stirling. 'I might take you up on that if I go ahead. I'm mechanically minded but I've never tackled a project like this before.'

'Most of the time it's about patience.' Gavin braked in front of William Stoddart's office and reached for his phone. 'I'll check a few things out while I wait.' He grinned. 'Just in case.'

Stirling's smile lasted until he opened the door to William's offices, then he remembered why he was here.

William Stoddart was a trim, silver-haired man who had to be in his seventies but wore his years younger. After the usual handshakes and affable small talk, he settled down to business.

'You wanted to discuss leasing some of Westwind's remaining land?'

'Lease or agistment. I don't know anything about either, but it seems a shame to have good farmland sitting there doing nothing.'

'You haven't considered stocking it yourself?'

'No. I wouldn't have a clue what I was doing and I don't want that kind of commitment right now. Shiloh Sloane from Roseneath is keen to take it on, sooner rather than later. She's only next door, so I guess it makes sense.'

William nodded. 'Fair enough.'

He went on to outline Stirling's options: the need for a detailed description of the exact land involved, any assets that might be included, right of ways, start and conclusion dates, options to extend. It sounded more complex than Stirling imagined but William assured him it could be easily settled.

'Was there anything else?' he asked, when Stirling indicated he'd talk again to Shiloh and take it from there.

'One thing.' Stirling hesitated, wondering how best to put his question. 'Dougal's will.'

William prompted him on.

'He changed it quite close to his death.'

'Yes. The week prior.'

'Did he say why?'

'No, he didn't.'

'Was he ...' Stirling stared at his hands for a moment. 'Did he seem okay to you? Depressed or stressed?'

'Not to me. If anything, he seemed determined. He was adamant that the new will be drawn up quickly.' William held up his palm. 'And no, he didn't give a reason for his haste.'

Stirling drew in a breath. 'I don't get why he suddenly moved from Mal McKenzie to you. They were close friends. Mal had managed Dougal's legal business for years. Why change?'

William's brows wrinkled. 'But it wasn't completely sudden. Dougal came to me several months before to have a new will drawn. I was surprised when he contacted me, to be honest, but it made sense in the end, given the will's contents.'

Stirling sat forward. 'And they were?'

'The same as the last, except that instead of you inheriting Westwind, it was going to Mal.'

Stirling sat back and blew out a breath. Mal was to inherit? Why the hell would Dougal do that? They were friends, close friends, but friendship rarely scored you an historic house. And no matter that they'd never met, Stirling was at least Dougal's blood.

'Did Mal know this?'

'I don't believe so. Unless Dougal made him aware of the fact, there'd be no reason for him to know.'

If Mal had known he was to inherit, then that was a powerful reason for wanting Dougal dead. Except they were friends, like brothers, if Mal was to be believed.

And Dougal had committed suicide. The coroner's report had made that clear.

He rubbed at his forehead as if that would calm his reeling mind.

'Does …' Stirling closed his eyes for a second, unsure how far to go.

'Stirling?'

He lifted his head and flicked his fingers. 'Sorry. Doesn't matter.'

The solicitor's tone softened. 'It's difficult to understand Dougal's mindset, but I think it's clear in hindsight that he was under extreme pressure, and likely deeply depressed.'

'I get that. What I don't get is why he wanted to change his will. Again.' And so close to his suicide.

'I assumed he and Mal had a falling out.'

'You didn't ask?'

'It's not my place to. It's not uncommon for people to change their wills, especially when they involve valuable assets, and to be honest, Dougal was a new and important client. I didn't want to upset him. As I mentioned, he was in a determined mood.'

A falling-out made sense, except Mal had made no mention of one. He'd said they'd had their ups and downs, like most friendships, giving the impression it was business as usual between the two of them in the weeks and days before Dougal's death.

If that were the case, how to explain Dougal changing his will? Not once, but twice, then hiding the fact from the man who had been not only his legal advisor but his best friend.

William's gaze was heavy with sympathy. 'I'm sorry I can't help you further.'

'It's all right.' Stirling propped his single crutch and stood. 'I guess there are some questions that will never be answered.'

William rose to shake Stirling's hand. 'I knew your father, maybe not as well as Mal, but I did know him. His death, all that happened ...' He shook his head. 'It was a shock. To everyone. Dougal was a good man.'

'Yeah,' said Stirling. 'So I keep hearing.'

Dougal Kildare—the good man who'd done bad things, and then died from the shame.

If only Stirling could believe that.

◈

Darcy's description of the library as lovely wasn't how Stirling would describe it. The room was more old-fashioned man-cave than lovely. It was comforting though, radiating geniality and warmth even with the fire unlit. The sort of place where, in the past, he imagined men would have mingled with their post-dinner ports and whiskeys, while the ladies chatted in the sitting room and uniformed staff cleaned up the dinner mess.

Dark timber shelves lined the walls, each thick with books of varying age. There was no order to the collection. Heavy, cloth-bound volumes fought with paperbacks, pamphlets and ledgers, interrupted by the occasional knick-knack or trophy. Of the trophies, most were for clay-pigeon shooting. One was for a hunt-club race. All belonged to his grandfather and made Stirling wonder where Dougal had fitted in this world.

A Persian rug bursting with floral motifs dominated the centre floor. A wingback leather chair occupied one corner, a long wooden desk another, while a low round coffee table with a silver bowl on top—another of Benjamin's prizes—held pride of place in the centre. Below the wide velvet-draped window sat a plush cushioned couch, perfect for relaxing with a book on a bright day.

Stirling wasn't interested in relaxing. He was searching for answers.

It was hours later when he found the box. He was standing on the seat of the wingback chair, his shins and knees braced uncomfortably against it to stop himself tipping as he inspected one of the higher shelves. The box was wedged between a pile of vintage Department of Agriculture journals. Why they still held place in the library was anyone's guess. Collector's items maybe, or perhaps Westwind or Benjamin were featured somewhere between their yellowed pages?

The top layer of magazines had flopped around the box, hiding it from view. Stirling set them on a cleared space of shelf below and lifted down the box. It was a handsome item, rectangular in shape with a parquetry lid edged in brass and sides made of a golden-hued timber. A box for gloves, he wondered, or maybe for handkerchiefs?

Too masculine for jewellery and too narrow for a pistol, even an antique one.

It had a plain brass lock but no cartouche with a name engraved or anything else to reveal ownership. Stirling carefully stepped down to the floor and tipped the box this way and that, checking the underside for any other clues. Its contents slid about with a dry shushing sound, like a snake weaving through hayed-off grass. Whatever was inside was soft and light, most likely papers.

But what kind of papers and who did they belong to? And why did they need to be under lock and key?

He prised at the lid with his fingers but it was tightly fit, the lock secure. He set the box on the desk, and with a grunt of effort, climbed back on the chair and hunted across the shelf with his fingers, feeling for a key. Unsuccessful, he returned to the floor and scrambled through the pile of junk he'd collected on the desk. Bits and bobs from the shelves that he'd set aside to inspect more closely later. Scraps of paper, bookmarks, a small, screwed-together nut, washer and bolt, fine brass keys perhaps for clocks, a long thin silver tool with a hook on the end, a leather-covered notebook.

He tried the clock keys, unsurprised when neither fitted.

Stirling collapsed onto the wingback chair with the box on his lap and stared at the empty fireplace. What right did he—a virtual stranger—have to break into someone's private trove?

Every right. Westwind was his, Dougal was dead, and he needed to know.

The sharp horn-handled letter opener only scratched the lock and dinged the timber. Stirling hoped the box wasn't rare or valuable, then decided he didn't care. Its contents were all that mattered.

Tucking the box under his arm, he snatched up his crutch and limped to the kitchen, flicking on lights as he passed.

It took a narrow screwdriver scavenged from a drawer in the laundry to crack the lock. Unfortunately it also cracked the timber. Stirling tried to feel guilty and couldn't. By the time the lock snapped he'd had enough of the stupid thing. He dragged the box closer and opened the lid.

A strange odour wafted from the contents. Stale paper and something else, like faded lavender. Except the item on top wasn't paper or a flower. It was a cellophane sleeve.

He lifted it out, his frown deepening. Inside the sleeve was a curl of dark hair. He turned it over and back again. That's all it was, just hair.

'Weird,' he muttered, moving on to the next item.

It was a scrap of newsprint, not new but not yellowed enough to be antique. A snipped article and photograph. He studied the boy in the picture. A good-looking lad of about nine or ten with a broad grin, wearing a wide-brimmed hat, what looked to be moleskin jeans, and a tweed jacket over a shirt and tie. Every inch the young country boy.

His eyes skipped downward, widening as they took in the caption, then the article.

He read it twice and set it aside, then leaned his chin on his hands, thinking back over the conversations he'd had, the words and the gaps between.

On its own, the article he could dismiss. With the hair though, that opened a whole new train of thought.

One Stirling wasn't sure he wanted to follow.

Chapter Seventeen

Darcy groaned and stretched her back, then rose from her sewing machine. She carried the dress to the ironing board to press the final seam but as she flattened it, her eyes blurred. They'd been itching and aching for a while, strained by the constant concentration and close work. This was another warning.

She unplugged the iron and wandered to the front window. An indigo twilight covered Ridgeview Road in a velvet blanket. Even as she watched, it was fading. Another day almost gone.

Monday night she'd worked until one in the morning, then risen at five on Tuesday, dragging her sorry body into the shower and forcing herself to dress properly for the day ahead when all she'd wanted to do was laze around in her favourite flannelette pyjamas and a pair of woolly ugg boots.

Wednesday had been even worse, but she'd ploughed on. Darcy prided herself on quick order fulfillment and if keeping that standard meant she missed several hours of beauty sleep, so be it. She had also built VaVoom on quality and meticulous attention to detail throughout the buying, production and delivery process. If she kept going, she'd put that in danger, as well as her physical and mental health.

Darcy looked back at her work area. Neat piles of fabric surrounded her cutting station, each representing a dress to be sewn. To the side of her machines, hangers of garments decorated the racks like floral bunting.

Despite her weariness, Darcy's chest swelled with pride at the sight. The summer preview dress had generated a lot of work but it was excellent for VaVoom's bottom line and boded well for the full collection. If that proved as successful as this first dress, she could start delegating some of the work—tedious chores like packing and postage, loading tracking numbers and filing invoices.

First though, she had to make it through this current challenge.

What she needed was a distraction, and what better diversion than a handsome brave helicopter pilot whose gaze burned with heat and want and turned her insides squishy?

Humming Elvis Presley's 'It's Now or Never', she fetched her phone.

Feeling I have been remiss checking on my investment. Free?

She gripped the phone, jittery for his reply. Seconds passed, then minutes. Darcy's jitters gave way to sagging shoulders. She stared again at the street, now completely dark except for the flashing headlights of an occasional passing car.

On previous evenings when she'd checked in, Stirling had messaged straight back, assuring her he was fine and that Shiloh had arranged plenty of firewood and food. Last night they'd enjoyed a brief conversation about how Darcy was managing, Stirling asking her to take care of herself. The message had left her feeling warm and fuzzy and did far more for her flagging energy than any coffee could have done.

Tonight it seemed he was busy. Or had other plans. Maybe even with Shiloh.

'Oof, you ridiculous girl,' Darcy scolded. Fatigue was making her crazy. Shiloh had no interest in Stirling beyond the creek flats, and she didn't need to worry about those now with the agistment agreement. While her sister was a gorgeous woman, Darcy would bet her beloved Mini that Stirling didn't look at Shiloh the way he'd looked at Darcy on Sunday.

Shiloh would give him short shrift if he did, anyway.

She sighed and wandered back to the window and pressed her forehead against the cool glass. One call and Lisette would be here, ready to offer encouragement, silliness and noughties music, but her friend had done enough through the week, dropping by with treats, wine and good cheer. Besides, tonight Lisette would be at the Hoppers Thursday football training, along with half the district, watching the boys go through their final paces in preparation for Saturday's grand final.

She supposed there was always Roseneath. A cosy dinner with her family, the comforting familiarity of farm talk and local news. Their love and pride at her success. All heartening, all important, but not what she craved.

Darcy stared at her mute phone, and with a resigned grimace, turned back to the ironing board. As she reached to plug in the iron, her phone pinged.

Sure, was the message.

Darcy's heart bounded like a happy puppy. Stirling might be a man of few words but at least he'd typed the right one.

Another ping sounded. *Have you had dinner?*

Not yet.

Good. I've made enough pasta sauce to feed an army. You'd do me a favour by eating some.

I am all for doing favours for brave and noble pilots. Then, before he could reply and tell her off for the brave and noble comment, Darcy typed, *See you soon!*

She dashed to her mirror and checked her outfit: a favourite pair of corset-waisted fitted black jeans teamed with a red and white striped long-sleeved jersey top with ruching around the bustline, and a pair of brilliant white sneakers. More comfortable than her usual VaVoom glamour, but she had no doubt that Stirling would appreciate it, particularly the deeply scooped neckline.

A quick touch-up of scarlet lippy, a rapid donning of her red stretch-satin bomber jacket, a snatch of her keys and patent red tote, and Darcy was out the door, her delighted hum of 'It's Now or Never' giving way to 'Are You Lonesome Tonight?'.

❦

Darcy sashayed into Westwind's kitchen with a joyous smile, a laden tote bag, and a 'Goodness, something smells scrumptious. May I stay for dinner?' that earned her a welcoming grin from Stirling and more happy puppy heart bounds.

'Hi, Darcy.'

He was at the stove, a tea towel thrown over one shoulder and the sleeves of his cotton shirt folded up, stirring the contents of a stockpot. Another large pot on a rear burner clouded water vapour into air already made steamy and redolent with the rich scent of ripe tomatoes. He'd set the table for two.

Casting off her jacket and tote, Darcy sauntered over and balanced on tiptoes to kiss his cheek.

It was hard to tell if Stirling's flush was from the warm stove or her kiss but at least he didn't jerk away. If anything, he looked charmed.

'Sorry,' she said, gently buffing the spot where her lipstick had left a mark, though Darcy wasn't sorry at all.

He rested the spoon on the rim of the pot. 'You're in a good mood.'

'I'm always in a good mood.' She propped her bum against the bench and folded her arms. 'Haven't you realised that by now?'

Stirling adjusted the other burner and faced her, his little dimple hollowing. 'I'm learning.'

His gaze dropped briefly to her neckline and quickly away. He reached behind her, and for a thrilling moment Darcy thought he was homing in for a proper kiss. Instead, he plucked a box of pasta from the bench and was back at the stove, ripping open the box before she could think to trap him in place and leave dinner to boil dry as they indulged in something far, far tastier.

Oblivious, Stirling upended half the pasta into the rear pot and poked down the strands. 'I hope you're hungry. I got a bit carried away.'

Darcy swallowed down her breathlessness and ordered herself to get a grip. 'I am, as a matter of fact. Oh,' she said, heading for her tote and hoping a little distance would restore her frazzled brain. 'I brought wine. Nothing special—a cabernet from the pub. They don't have a wide selection.'

Stirling used his phone to set a timer and nodded towards the pantry. 'You do remember there's a whole cellar down there.'

'I know. But I doubt you could tackle the stairs and I have my pristine sneakers to think of.' She lifted a foot and twisted it left and right. 'Imagine the dust!' She added a theatrical shudder.

Stirling's gaze skipped from Darcy's foot up her leg to her hip and thought better of venturing further. Darcy's skin buzzed as though touched.

'I see your point.' He hobbled to a cupboard and reached inside for some bowls.

'You're not using your crutch,' she said, cracking the bottle's screw-top lid.

'I don't need it when I have plenty to hold on to. The exercises are helping too.'

'But that's wonderful. You'll be out and about in no time.'

'With a bit of luck.' He set the bowls on the bench, then found two wineglasses. 'Only a small one,' he said, when she held up the opened bottle and raised an eyebrow. 'Don't tell my doctor.'

Darcy winked. 'Don't worry, I'll keep it our little secret.' She passed Stirling his glass and pressed her own against his in a 'cheers' gesture. 'To your continued recovery.'

'Thanks. And to VaVoom's ongoing fashion domination.'

She laughed. 'I don't know about domination. As long as I have happy customers who keep coming back, I'll be satisfied.'

'You're not after global fame and fortune?'

'Not really.' Darcy scrunched her nose. 'Maybe a little recognition.' She slid fingertips over the back of a chair as she considered further. 'Not that I'd say no to a million or two.'

'I don't think any of us would say no to that. What would you do with it?'

'Buy a new overlocker.' She thought wistfully of the Janome five-thread overlocker she'd been coveting since purchasing her new sewing machine. While her current overlocker was adequate, the 1200D was a truly professional beast and they'd make a stunning pair. She did like things to match.

His eyes sparkled. 'You really love sewing, don't you?'

'I do. It's creative, practical, and can even be environmentally friendly when you upcycle pre-loved clothes. And there is nothing quite so heartwarming as making a woman—or man, for that matter—feel beautiful.'

'I'll toast to that.'

They shared a lingering smile until Stirling set his glass down to check on his pots.

Darcy took their water glasses and filled them from the tap. The kitchen table was clear of the paraphernalia she'd encountered on other visits. No laptop, notebooks or books, only her mum's biscuit container, sitting washed and gratifyingly empty at the end.

'You enjoyed your biscuits then?'

'They were great. Didn't last long.'

'I'm glad to hear it. I'll get Shiloh to drop you over some more.'

'Thanks, but I have crackers and I don't need the sugar.' Stirling rubbed his lean belly.

'Oh, stop it. You're in terrific condition. Besides, everyone knows homemade biscuits have no calories.'

He swung back to the stove, his tone dry. 'Not that terrific condition.'

'You'll come good. Look at you already, getting around without crutches. You'll be back to normal in no time.' Then what would he do? Darcy shoved the biscuit container in her tote to distract herself from the thought. 'Speaking of which, besides overexciting my sister, what have you been occupying yourself with this week?'

Stirling shrugged. 'Sorting through the library.'

'Find anything interesting?'

He didn't answer for a while, seemingly lost in stirring his pasta sauce. 'A few things.'

Darcy frowned. She wanted to probe but there was something in his voice. A hesitancy, as if he hadn't wanted to give away even that much.

His phone cock-a-doodle-do-ed, breaking the moment. Stirling killed the rooster alarm and donned some mitts.

Darcy watched with trepidation as he hefted the pasta pot from the stove. 'Are you sure you wouldn't prefer me to do that?'

'I'm fine.' Which was not what his grunt said, but if Stirling wanted to play silly strongman, she wouldn't interfere.

And he managed fine, even if Darcy didn't think the moisture on his forehead was due to steam from the pasta water, and he did allow her to place the bowls on the table once he'd served.

'Somebody taught you how to cook,' Darcy remarked after her first mouthful. Where she'd expected garden-variety bolognaise, instead was a luxurious dish of thick tubular spaghetti in a sauce made of spiced tomato, pancetta and a large measure of pecorino. 'This is absolutely delicious. What is it?'

'Bucatini all'Amatriciana. Alexander's personal chef showed me how to make it.'

She laughed and rolled her eyes. '*Of course* he did.'

'She. Paolina liked to baby all her boys.' Stirling caught her look and grinned. 'Not like that. Paolina's older than my mum.'

Darcy hid her relief with a tiny sip of wine.

'I make a mean panna cotta too.'

Was he trying to impress her? Darcy hoped so.

'You do appreciate,' she said as she twirled more bucatini around her fork, 'that I'll be expecting proof of this culinary prowess.'

'That'll teach me to brag.'

The kitchen was warm, the food wonderful, and Stirling ... he made her want to gushy-sigh and swoon like a romance novel heroine. Given Westwind's historic magnificence, the reaction would be quite fitting. Although, perhaps a delightful frock—in lavender or lilac with white flowers and a hint of lace—would be more appropriate for gushy-sighing than stretchy tops and capris. An off-the-shoulder number for maximum heaving bosom.

The thought made Darcy giggle.

'What?' he said.

'Oh, nothing. Just me being silly.'

He raised both eyebrows.

'I was thinking about dresses.' She indicated the rest of the house with her fork. 'I've always found Westwind's architecture inspiring.'

He scanned the room. 'I suppose it would be.' Then he locked his gaze back on hers. 'It'd make a great location for a photo shoot.'

'It would.' Her eyes widened. 'Actually, you're right. It'd be perfect for my summer collection. The new range is full of romantic dresses in pretty colours, the kind you'd wear to garden parties or high teas at grand old houses like this.'

'All yours, whenever you like.'

Darcy's breathlessness returned. Heat flushed her chest and cheeks. 'Thank you. That's very kind.' And an offer she would take up. Throw open the curtains and flood the rooms with light and Westwind would provide the perfect tableau to display her clothes.

Stirling shook his head. 'I'm the one that should be thanking you. You and Shiloh.'

'It's been our pleasure.'

She beamed at him and was rewarded with a smile in return. How delicious it would be to linger with him over the bottle, cosy in the warmth of the kitchen while they shared more about their lives. Their hopes and dreams. Their futures. Together.

Darcy straightened. She really should stop being so foolish.

They continued with their meal, Stirling asking questions about VaVoom and how she planned her collections, and where her inspirations came from, besides Westwind.

She gave her usual answer about her addiction to classic movies, music and magazines. The glamour of the era, with fashion's celebration of the female figure and femininity. Her grandmother's patterns and those she sometimes found at clearing sales and charity shops, along with the vintage pattern books she bought over the internet.

'The trouble is vintage is so popular now that they're getting harder and harder to find. And expensive. It's not a major problem—I can draft my own patterns—but the old patterns can be marvellous creative stimulants.'

Stirling looked thoughtful for a moment, then shook his head.

'What is it?'

'Nothing really. I just had the thought there might be some here.'

It was an idea, but unlikely to have substance. 'I wouldn't have thought so. Westwind women tend to be designer label rather than homemade.'

'Why doesn't that surprise me.'

'Well, you are from landed gentry.'

'Not very landed anymore.'

It was Darcy's turn to laugh. 'No. Shiloh is thrilled by your offer, by the way.'

'She is?' He gave a 'could have fooled me' shake of his head.

'I know. It can be difficult to tell with her. My sister's personality hails from the stoic side of the family.'

'Which makes yours from?'

'Oh,' she said, giving her best coquettish smile, 'definitely the passionate side.'

Stirling reached for his wine and took a gulp. Darcy smiled to herself.

'There's something I wanted to ask you,' he said when they'd both finished eating. He was fiddling with the pecorino packet, refolding the cling film carefully over the open end. 'About Mal. Not so much Mal, but his son.'

'Oh. Yes. Little Xavier. That was awful.'

'You know about it?'

She nodded. 'I was only ten, I think, when it happened.' She tipped her head. 'Maybe eleven. It was so sad. He was our age. All that life ahead of him.' Poor little boy. Darcy had been too young to fully comprehend the tragedy, but she'd felt the horror and anguish of those around her. It had cast a pall over the area for months.

'What happened? I did a search, only the news reports I found were a bit light on details.'

'He tipped his quad bike over riding along a slope above the creek. Broke his neck, I believe. An ambulance was called as soon as they found him, but it was too late. Nothing anyone could do. Mal and Candice were devastated. So were Dougal and Brigitte. I remember Mum bursting into tears when she heard. Shiloh and I were banned from riding the quads for months.'

'What was Xavier doing here?'

'He was here often. Mal and Dougal were best friends and Dougal was Xavier's godfather. Although I think things cooled off for a long time after the accident. Candice refused to set foot on Westwind again. She wouldn't come for the memorial either.' Local lore also had it that she refused to speak to Dougal too, but Darcy didn't know the truth of that. 'She and Mal divorced not long after. Couldn't cope with their grief and blame, I suppose.'

'There's a memorial?'

'Yes. Dougal had it built alongside the creek edge near where he died. It's still there.'

Stirling was staring at her but there was no focus in his gaze. His thoughts were elsewhere.

'Why do you ask?'

He shrugged, his eyes clearing. 'Just something I found.'

'Something about Xavier?'

'Yeah.'

'I imagine Dougal felt terrible guilt about the tragedy, with it happening on Westwind and on one of his quads. He'd want to remember him.'

'Mmm.' Stirling's gaze turned distant once more. Then he shook himself and indicated her dish. 'I'll clean up.'

Darcy snatched his bowl and set it on top of hers. 'You stay right there. It's cook's privilege to relax after a meal.'

Though she tried to keep him seated, Stirling refused to obey orders and together they washed and cleaned, until there was nothing left for Darcy to do except wipe her hands and accept it was time for the evening to end. This pleasant part of it, at least. She still had hours of work ahead.

'Next time I'll bring something for sweets,' she said, folding the tea towel carefully over the back of a chair. 'Speaking of next time, would you like to come to the football on Saturday? I can pick you up and bring you home.' Darcy could ill afford the time but there was no way she'd miss Grassmoor's grand final.

Stirling shook his head. 'I doubt I'd be welcome.'

'Don't be a ninny. Of course you'd be welcome. Besides, everyone will be far too busy worrying about the game to bother with you.' She eyed him. 'You'll have Shiloh and me to run interference if they do. And Lisette. Your very own security detail.'

'You're admitting I need one then?'

Darcy gave him a look. 'Oh, shush. Come on, it'll be fun and Lisette is dying to meet you.'

Still, he hesitated.

'I'll buy you a pie. Maybe even a beer to go with it.'

He considered for a while longer. 'Will Mal be there?'

'I would imagine so.'

He nodded, not to Darcy but to himself, and stared at the doorway to the hall with his lips firmed. 'All right.'

Chapter Eighteen

Goodwin Oval swarmed with people despite the vicious weather. Stirling was wrapped in one of Dougal's tweed coats with a wool jumper and shirt underneath, and a green and gold Hoppers scarf that Darcy had insisted on draping artfully around his neck, and still the freezing south-westerly cut through him with razor efficiency.

Darcy, on the other hand, looked sensational in an eye-burningly bright fluffy yellow jacket and a hip-hugging green and yellow tartan skirt, her hair tied up with a wired bow that whipped and bent in the wind like a donkey twitching its ears. He'd learned in the car on the way to the oval that it was the same get-up she'd worn to the semifinal. Darcy was disappointed that she couldn't create something new, but the canary fluff jacket had proven good luck so why not give it another whirl?

The yellow jacket was driving Stirling nuts. All he wanted to do was stroke it. Stroke *her*. He'd never come across a woman who glowed the way Darcy did. She blazed through the crowd like a sunbeam and made everyone around her seem dull. It wasn't just her clothes, it was her. The brilliance of her smile, the way she walked and talked, proud of her femininity, proud of her dressmaking skills. Proud of herself in a way that held no conceit, just pure confidence.

It was as sexy as all hell.

'Here you go,' said Lisette, shoving a beer at Stirling and beaming. With her sparkly eyes, laughter and cute nose stud to match her green and gold face paint, Darcy's best friend was almost as much a firecracker as Darcy. Lisette was pretty too, in a fun, fresh way. Stirling figured that Charlie bloke had to have rocks in his head.

After doling out the remaining beers to Shiloh and Darcy, Lisette held hers towards the centre of their little group. 'To the Hoppers and victory!'

They'd been the focus of attention since arrival, and not because of Darcy's jacket. Stirling had been given more up and downs than an elevator. Men and women turned to whisper to one another as he passed, speculative gazes switching between Stirling and his dazzling companion.

Darcy smiled and waved and called hellos, sashaying along beside him with supermodel poise. Stirling remained silent, concentrating on his footing. Though he was becoming more mobile by the day and thought he could get away with one crutch, Darcy had insisted he bring both. The crowd was likely to be tight and excited and he could be accidentally jostled. She might be an excellent seamstress, but bending down in a pencil skirt as fitted as the one she wore to help up a fallen Stirling was rife with danger. He was suffering enough attention without attracting even more by tripping over.

They'd found Lisette and Shiloh on a stepped concrete apron not far from the Hoppers changerooms and with a good view of the oval and the coaches boxes. After introductions and small talk, Lisette had skipped off for supplies, while Shiloh and Darcy chatted and Stirling tried to ignore the stares of the people around them.

'Going okay?' asked Darcy, sidling close.

Stirling's nose twitched. She even smelled gorgeous. Not strongly perfumed but a subtle vanilla scent that made him think of licking ice cream. It was going to be a long day.

'I'm good.' He scanned the crowd. No sign of Mal yet. Maybe he wasn't into football. 'You don't have to keep checking on me, you know.'

'Yes, I do. I want you to have a nice time.'

'I'm sure I will.' How could he not with Darcy by his side?

Despite the cruel wind and the locals' cloying curiosity, Stirling was in an upbeat mood. Toby had promised to ride out the following week and stay for a while and Stirling couldn't wait to get him here. He missed his buddy, and there was plenty to keep them busy. Besides all the vehicles' flat batteries, underinflated tyres and general service needs, there was the Indian to muck around with. An eager Gavin had been shooting through parts info all week— 'just in case'—and his enthusiasm was proving infectious.

Most of all, Stirling needed a friend to talk to. Someone impartial, not close to Westwind or Grassmoor, who could help him work through his suspicions and make sense of the strange items he'd found. The secrets he feared lurking beneath the dust of Westwind's past.

A cheer went up as the blue and red Titans ran out on to the ground. A few minutes later, a roar sounded as the Hoppers jogged from the changerooms. Lisette produced an impressive wolf-whistle, while Darcy somehow managed to bounce up and down in her high heels. Even Shiloh whooped and waved an arm.

Stirling effected a precarious clap, balanced on his crutches and tucking his beer against his belly. His experiences of Grassmoor had been far from positive, yet today he couldn't help feeling uplifted by the community solidarity. The Titans had won the premiership for the last three years and were the favourites, but there was a genuine buzz that this could be a green and gold year.

The siren sounded the ten minutes until kick-off warning. Darcy cast a glance at the clubrooms and handed her can to Shiloh. 'Hold this for me? I need to brave the ladies.'

Stirling watched her go over his shoulder, his gaze on her wiggling hips, her slender calves. When he turned back, Shiloh was at his side.

She took a sip of her beer and eyed him. 'You like my sister.'

'I do.'

She nodded, still studying him. 'Huh.'

Whatever that meant, Stirling had no idea.

Shiloh indicated his jacket. 'One of Dougal's.'

'Yeah. I didn't bring a lot of clothes with me. It's freezing cold and they fit.' He shrugged. Truth was, wearing Dougal's clothes gave him the willies but he didn't have a lot of choice. At least the jeans and shirt and underwear were his.

'Suits you,' she said, then grinned and nudged him. 'Careful, people will think you've taken your squattocracy roots to heart.'

Stirling laughed. 'Not this little black duck.'

Shiloh's grin fell as she took in the man edging his way towards them. A good-looking bloke with sandy hair and a jutted jaw as bristly as his mood. There was no mistaking the powerful build of the man. His focus was on Shiloh but he was giving Stirling plenty of attention too. Unfriendly attention.

'Leo,' said Shiloh, without a scrap of welcome.

'Shiloh, good to see you.' He turned to Stirling. 'Leo Brooks.'

They shook hands, Leo's grip firmer than it needed to be. Behind Leo's back, Lisette was observing the encounter with unrestrained glee. Winking at Stirling, she took out her phone and began to tap.

'You're at Westwind,' said Leo, his hands rolled at his side.

Stirling nodded. He wasn't sure what was going on, but Leo was fairly burning with hostility. 'For now.'

'Not planning on hanging around then?'

Stirling glanced at Shiloh. Her arms were folded, the beers dangling by the rims from her fingers, her eyes raised to the sky.

'Maybe,' he said. 'I don't know yet.'

A muscle flexed in Leo's cheek. 'Right.'

'Leo,' said Shiloh on a tired breath.

Suddenly, Stirling got it. Leo was the ex-fiancé and clearly had the wrong end of the stick. He looked at Lisette for help but she was too busy enjoying the encounter.

'What?' said Leo.

'You know what.'

The two stared at each other, a whole lot of hurt on both their faces. Stirling wanted to step back and dissolve into the crowd.

'Leo!' Darcy bustled between them like a happy duckling, snatching her beer back from Shiloh and shooting her sister a wide-eyed glare as she passed. She kissed Leo hello then immediately returned to Stirling's side and looped her arm through his, tucking him as close as his crutches would allow in an overt display of ownership. Leo's clenched fists immediately relaxed. Darcy turned her face up to Stirling's. 'Leo's our local land health officer.' She smiled at Leo. 'An excellent one too. Dad said he might bring Mum down at half-time for a little while. They'll be thrilled to see you.'

'At least someone will be,' muttered Leo, casting a look at Shiloh, who was picking madly at the pull tab on her beer can, looking as though she might cry. He waited for her to glance up and sighed when she refused. 'I'd better go.'

He nodded at the girls then at Stirling, and with his hands deep in his pockets and his shoulders hunched, he turned away, throwing a final glance over his shoulder at his ex-fiancée before disappearing into the crowd.

'Truly, Shiloh,' said Darcy. 'You are the most frustrating woman. That man adores you and all you can do is ignore him.'

'Shut it, Darce.' Shiloh was blinking rapidly.

Darcy opened her mouth to say more then changed her mind and stroked her sister's arm instead. Shiloh jerked it away and focused on the oval.

The encounter cast a brief cloud over the group that was quickly relieved by the siren signalling the game was about to start. Eager fans pushed closer to the boundary. Youngsters leaned over the chainwire fence, waving arms and scarves. Men yelled encouragement, while several young women dressed in grasshopper costumes cheered and hooted from behind the coaches shelter.

In the centre of the ground, the umpire tossed a coin and the two captains inspected the result. The crowd whooped when the Hoppers captain indicated that his team would start off kicking into the wind.

The players took their positions, psyching themselves with a few bumps and scrags on their opponents.

'Oh, I hope they win,' said Darcy, her voice so fearful it had Stirling wishing he could make her hope come true.

He shook his head. He needed to get a grip.

Finally, the umpire held the ball high, then blew his whistle and thumped the ball into the ground. It bounced skyward and the two ruckmen charged, arms lifted in a fight to be the first to tap the ball to their team's advantage.

The game was on.

⁂

At half-time, Shiloh went for pies while Lisette braved the queue for another round of beers. The Hoppers were seventeen points down, the wind having heavily favoured the Titans in the first quarter and forcing the Hoppers to play catch-up in the second.

Stirling used the break to visit the loo. He levered up the concrete steps, using his need to focus on his footing as an excuse to ignore the stares and occasional smiles.

As promised, Darcy, Shiloh and Lisette had run interference whenever they'd been interrupted by locals, changing subjects to the football when conversations turned personal. Not that Stirling was giving much away.

Only a couple of stalwarts made it through his protective posse. The first was a middle-aged couple who introduced themselves as Michael and Samantha Byrne, apparently good friends of the Sloanes. They were polite enough and Stirling did his best to respond in kind for Darcy's sake, explaining that he was born in Melbourne but had lived all over thanks to his mother's job with *Medecins sans Frontieres*—a revelation that elicited impressed coos. Just as it looked as though the conversation would take a darker turn in Dougal's direction, they were interrupted by an elderly, walnut-faced woman wearing a voluminous camel wool coat and a hat that appeared to have been made from an entire fox.

She'd introduced herself as Jayne Bucknall of the 'Aberglynn Bucknalls'. Stirling learned afterwards from Darcy that the Bucknalls were one of the old dynastic families and that Aberglynn was a property even more magnificent and historic than Westwind. Jayne no longer lived in the big house, preferring her modest home in Grassmoor where it was easier to keep tabs on the locals. Shiloh thought there might be some connection by marriage between the Bucknall and Kildare family trees. After his encounter with Jayne, Stirling hoped not.

Stirling had listened politely as Jayne asked Darcy after her mother's health, how Roseneath was faring, and Darcy's business. All the while he sensed the old lady's scrutiny and knew she was only biding her time before she returned to her true purpose.

Finally, Jayne homed in on Stirling with sharp eyes and an even sharper tongue.

'I was unsurprised to learn Dougal had an illegitimate son. His father Benjamin was no different when it came to women.'

Stirling was too gobsmacked to do anything more than stare.

'How did you enjoy the first half, Mrs Bucknall?' Lisette butted in, her voice high and timorous. 'Not the score we wanted but our boys are really putting in.'

'Don't interrupt, Lisette.' Jayne carried on as if Lisette hadn't spoken and flicked a leather-gloved hand. 'Oh, no one ever talked openly about these matters, of course, but we all knew. Not that it ever bothered us. We understood our worth.'

Stirling could only guess at who the 'us' and 'we' were. The landed gentry ladies, he supposed.

'Anyway,' she said, looking Stirling up and down as though he were a prize ram, 'better you at Westwind than that Melody. As spineless as her mother, that one. Married an American.' She gave a disparaging sniff. 'Kildares are better than that. Although,' she focused on Darcy, 'perhaps something to bear in mind, Miss Sloane.'

For a moment, Stirling was too distracted by the spineless comment about his half-sister to untangle her meaning, then his bemusement at Jayne's plain-speaking fled. He stared at her as hard as she'd stared at him. 'I am not my father, nor my grandfather.'

A brief flash of something crossed her face. Approval? Gratification?

'Perhaps not. We shall see, shan't we?'

With that, she strode off, leaving Stirling fuming, Darcy apologetic, Shiloh frowning and Lisette clutching her belly with laughter.

Now, ten minutes later and with his temper controlled, Stirling found himself more interested than angry at Jayne's claims. Dougal was clearly a womaniser—Stirling himself was proof of that—but Benjamin?

What did it matter? As he'd said to Jayne, Stirling wasn't his ancestry. He was his own man.

Which then begged the question, what the hell was he still doing here? He'd arrived in Grassmoor with the hope that by learning about his father he might learn about himself. Yet now it seemed Stirling's journey was not about who he was, but who he wasn't.

Chapter Nineteen

Stirling exited the disabled cubicle, the metallic clang of the door catching the attention of the man soaping his hands at the washbasin.

'Stirling,' said Mal, looking over his shoulder. 'I didn't expect to see you here. Good of you to come and support the local team.' He indicated Stirling's scarf. 'Darcy's doing?'

For a moment Stirling paused, then hobbled on. 'Who else?'

'I should have guessed she'd drag you down here.'

They walked out into the sunshine and despite the surrounding pine trees, were immediately buffeted by the wind.

'It's getting worse,' said Mal, clamping down on his hat and narrowing his eyes at the sky.

It was. The treetops were flicking like whips. Everywhere Stirling looked, people were holding onto hats and coats. The flagpole rope rang a discordant tune as it banged against the steel pole.

Stirling checked to the south. At least they wouldn't have rain anytime soon. Lisette had said rain would put a serious dampener on the Hoppers' chances.

'Not a bad thing for the Hoppers in the final quarter,' he said.

Mal regarded him with interest. 'You're a footballer?'

'Rugby man. Darcy's friend Lisette has been filling me in on the nuances.'

'Ah.' They walked on a little further, Mal nodding at people he knew, which seemed to be everyone. 'Weren't you born in Melbourne?'

Stirling wondered how he knew. He'd given as little away about himself to Mal as he had with everyone else. Except Darcy. 'I was, but most of my schooling was in England.'

Mal nodded to himself. 'Because of your mother's job?'

'Yeah.'

They reached the concrete apron. Ahead, Darcy and Lisette were laughing with one another and once again Stirling was struck by how vibrant and alive Darcy appeared compared to the world around her. His heart squeezed painfully.

By some unspoken message, both Stirling and Mal paused to watch them. Shiloh seemed to have disappeared.

Stirling took the moment to say what had been on his mind. 'I learned about Xavier. I'm sorry.'

Pain wobbled across Mal's face and was quickly suppressed. 'Thank you.'

'Darcy mentioned there's a memorial.'

Mal nodded. 'Your father was generous enough to build it. Candice and I were welcome to visit whenever we wished. Candice never wanted to. Too painful, I suppose. I do though. Did.'

'That welcome still stands. Whenever you want.'

Mal responded with a creased brow, as if surprised by Stirling's offer. 'That's very generous.'

Stirling shrugged. 'It's an important place for you.'

'It is.' He kept up his slight frown. 'You know, you're very like your father. He was a giving man too.'

Perhaps too giving, thought Stirling, thinking of Jayne Bucknall's comments about the Kildares' womanising.

There was more he wanted to mention but now wasn't the time. They had a football team to cheer on and Stirling would have other opportunities to probe about Dougal's strange stash of mementos. Mal pushed out his arm to open a space for them to squeeze through and together they nudged their way to Darcy, who turned and beamed at Stirling with such delight his lungs stopped working.

Lisette passed him a beer. Darcy, he noticed, had a hot drink.

Darcy greeted Mal and commented it was nice to see him out. 'Dad will be sorry to have missed you. He had hoped to bring Mum down but he just messaged that she's not feeling up to it.'

'A shame, but probably for the best with this wind,' said Mal, grabbing his hat as another vicious gust threatened.

The siren sounded the end of half-time. The players returned to the ground to whoops and cheers that were lashed away as fast as they were called. Darcy finished her drink and tossed the cup into a 44-gallon drum that was serving as a bin and moved closer to Stirling. She rubbed the fluffy fabric of her arms.

'Are you cold?'

'Not really. More anxious. It would be such a boost for Grassmoor if we could win. It's been a bad year.'

Stirling stared stonily at the oval, too aware of who'd helped cause the district's bad year.

A warm hand touched his fist where it was tight around the grip of his crutch. He drew in a breath and looked at Darcy.

Her expression was soft and kind and made him want to bury his face into her neck and breathe in her vanilla goodness. Instead, he managed a reassuring smile and focused back on the oval. Her hand remained on his for a little longer, then she gave it a brief squeeze and let go, his skin immediately feeling the cold where hers had been.

The football game ground on. Lisette kept up a constant barrage of whoops, whistles and cheers, speckled with the occasional heckle and boo. Darcy's hand kept flying to her chest as though holding her heart in place. Even Mal, who Stirling had expected to remain stoic, shouted intermittent encouragement.

Stirling found himself caught in the excitement. When the Hoppers managed to score a goal, he cheered with everyone else, hammering a crutch on the concrete and sharing an ecstatic grin with Darcy as she bounced beside him, donkey-ear headband ties flapping.

With two minutes remaining, and the Hoppers holding a shallow three-point lead, supporters for both teams were biting their nails.

'I think we can do it,' Darcy said breathlessly.

'Of course we can,' said Lisette, her face pink and shiny with hope.

The crowd groaned as the Titans were awarded a free kick. They didn't wait around, immediately sending the ball towards the centre, only for it to punched forward by a Hoppers player and scooped up by Charlie Shanahan.

Lisette's voice was hoarse from shouting but that didn't stop her. 'Go, Charlie, go!'

Darcy joined in, Mal adding to the growing roar.

'Kick it, Charlie!'

'Come on,' muttered Stirling, urging Charlie on. If they could kick this goal, it'd be all over.

Charlie bounced the ball. Once, twice. A Titans player swung in for a tackle. With supreme confidence, Charlie palmed him off, sending the player skidding, and pivoted away. Two Titans broke from their men and rushed towards him. The crowd noise turned thunderous.

Charlie lined up the ball, drew back his leg and kicked.

Another hush fell. Like a field of sunflowers tracking the sun, every face on the ground followed the ball as it flew towards goal. Then every Hoppers supporter began to moan as it drifted left. As it was about to cross through for a point, the siren sounded.

For a moment there was nothing, then the ground erupted.

Lisette shot a fist into the air. 'Yes! Yes, yes, yes!' She screeched like a banshee and grabbed hold of Darcy, hopping her around and squealing. She let her go and grabbed Mal and kissed him, then laughed uproariously at his shock.

Darcy looked at Stirling, her face alive, her voice wavery with awe. 'We won.'

Stirling's heart pounded. 'I know.'

She launched herself at him and kissed him right on the mouth.

For half a heartbeat, Stirling was too thrown to react. Her breasts were against his chest, her lips soft, her fluffy neon arms around his neck. Then pure want kicked in and he kissed her just as hard in return.

Darcy stepped back, her eyes wide and her mouth open. Fingers splayed over her chest. Their connection had lasted seconds but Stirling was left as wrecked as if a cyclone had raged through him, his excuses for not wanting her scattered like storm debris.

He wanted—needed—to gather them up, pull himself together. Remember the why nots. Remember to protect her. Protect himself.

Yet in that breath-stolen moment, all he wanted was do it again.

Chapter Twenty

Stirling hobbled another lap of Westwind's front verandah, his gaze on the driveway and his ears alert for vehicles. The only sound was birdsong, the distant rumble of a tractor and the thump of his increasing heartrate.

He stared at the empty drive thinking, for the hundredth time, that he needed to get a load of gravel and a grader in to flatten the potholes. And a slasher to sort out the weed jungle choking the garden that in the early spring flush was growing worse by the day. The fountain could also do with a scrub and the ugly graffiti and broken staircase finials still had to be dealt with.

'Jesus,' he muttered, raking fingers through his hair. He'd done nothing since he arrived except chase ghosts.

Toby would help toe him into line. If he ever arrived.

Road noise had Stirling lifting his head. He knew that sound, the winding down through the gears of a powerful engine, the whirr of deceleration. He hobbled down the steps, his eyes on the driveway.

Finally, the bike appeared.

Toby waved but didn't stop. He did one lap of the fountain, then another and another, his head swivelling like a weathervane with each turn towards Westwind. He braked near the steps, killed the engine and pulled off his helmet. His hair was flat and sweaty from the journey, his freckled face flushed, his grin broad.

'This is *yours*?' he said, gaping at the old house. Toby had seen the photos, but Stirling knew what he meant. The real Westwind was something else.

'Yeah.'

Toby shook his head. *'Maaan.'* He followed that with a half-laugh, half-snort. 'Unbe-freaking-lievable.'

'How was your ride?'

'Unreal.' Toby dismounted and set his helmet on the bike seat. Then he grabbed Stirling's hand and gave it a brief shake before dragging him close for a man-hug.

'Great to see you, Tobes,' said Stirling, his voice hoarse and his chest tight at the fierceness of his friend's embrace.

'And you, Felix.'

They parted, both clearing throats and pretending the hug had been no more than good friends greeting one another.

Toby gawped again at Westwind. 'I can't believe this is yours. I mean, I saw the photos but ... this? It's like a bloody chateau.' He grinned. 'Suits you.'

'Hardly. What's to bring in?'

Toby shooed him away. 'Leave it. There's not much and I'll sort it.' He scanned Stirling up and down. 'You're not as lame as I thought you'd be.'

Stirling shrugged. 'Been a bit better this past week.' Although the truth was, he was putting on a show for Toby and had left his crutch inside. He'd been doing that more and more, and while his leg still pinched like crazy, his bung hip let him know in no uncertain terms when it had had enough of taking the extra weight.

'Good.' Toby switched to eyeing the debris and the graffiti. 'Nice people around here.'

'Some better than others.'

'I'm guessing the "some" includes Marilyn in a sailor suit?'

Stirling laughed. Darcy would be a discussion for later over a few beers and the pizzas he planned to make. 'Come on. I'll show you around.'

They spent the next half-hour wandering Westwind's rooms. Stirling didn't linger in the library, urging Toby out with the promise they'd return later. Like the topic of Darcy, the library's secrets could wait, and Stirling didn't want to spoil the mood. Toby's jokes and laughter made the house feel like a proper home, free of the mutterings of unquiet generations.

With the house tour complete, Stirling led Toby through the mudroom to the rear courtyard.

'Poor thing,' said Toby when he spied Stirling's Ducati. 'When do you think you'll be able to ride again?'

'Not sure. A few weeks, maybe. I'll see what the physio says.'

They crossed the pavers and followed the gravel drive down the slope towards the main shed, where the farm vehicles sat dust smothered and neglected, the final bay empty. Westwind cast a long shadow behind Stirling and Toby, and the breeze, though light, added to the rapidly cooling air. Below, past the thickly grassed slopes and fringe of trees, the creek spilled its way through the countryside before disappearing around a curve.

Stirling's already slow pace slowed even further as he neared the shed and its desolate bay, until finally he stopped, anchored in place by sorrow and regret and the phantoms he couldn't stop chasing.

Dougal wasn't here. Nothing was here. The rope Dougal had used was gone, whatever he'd stood on put back in its place. It was just a shed.

But this place was like the dogs; it bothered him in a way he couldn't identify.

Toby was about to open the door of the Toyota four-wheel drive when he realised Stirling wasn't directly behind him. He looked over his shoulder and frowned. 'What is it?'

Stirling shook off his unease. 'Nothing.' Citing the fading light, he suggested they head back to the house. There was pizza dough to make and fires to sort out, and Toby should probably shift his bike to the back of the house and bring his gear inside. They could check out the cars and other sheds tomorrow.

With Toby to help, Westwind was soon crackling with warmth and old rock music from Dougal's stereo. Toby was propped against the bench with a beer, watching Stirling knead dough.

'Gotta love a bloke who likes to cook.'

'I like to eat. The cooking bit I can give or take.' Stirling formed the dough into a ball, set it in a ceramic bowl and covered it with a damp tea towel to rise. He indicated the lit range. 'Got a good wood oven. May as well make the most of it.'

He pulled out the end chair and turned it to face the range, then eased into it and stretched his legs out. A heavy ache had settled into his hip. Between his preparations, pacing and Toby's tour, he'd made it do too much.

Toby remained standing. 'So ...'

Stirling raised his eyebrows.

'Come on. Marilyn.'

'Her name's Darcy.'

Toby tipped his beer towards Stirling. 'You're the one who called her Marilyn.'

Stirling didn't answer for a while. Darcy's celebratory kiss had been two days ago and he was still processing his feelings. Lust, he got. What bloke wouldn't lust after Darcy? It was the other stuff, the deeper feelings, that bothered him. How lost he felt when he was near her, like he'd forfeited control of his body. That she held the power to mould him to her will like putty and he'd gladly bend and soften to her command.

He'd been so unravelled by her on Saturday that when Mal had offered Stirling a lift home, he'd accepted, then felt like crap when Darcy tried and failed to hide her disappointment. He'd let her down, and Stirling had wanted to punch himself for it ever since.

'I like her.'

'That much I figured.'

Stirling shook his head. 'Really like her.'

'Ah.'

'Yeah, ah.'

'And the problem is?'

He sighed and took a sip of beer. 'I don't want to start something we both end up regretting.'

'Why would you regret getting it on with Marilyn?' Toby held up his palm at Stirling's scowl. 'Yeah, yeah. Darcy.'

'I don't know. She's settled here. I'm ...' He dragged a hand up and down his cheek. 'I don't know what the hell I am anymore.'

Toby didn't laugh. He understood only too well. 'Makes two of us.'

Stirling straightened immediately. He scanned Toby's face. 'You okay?'

'Yeah.' Toby waved him off. 'I'm fine. I wouldn't mind earning a bit more. The pay in aged care is crap.'

'Is that all?'

He didn't say anything for a moment. 'Couple of bad nights, nothing to write home about. I talked to Eva again on Friday. Helped a lot.'

'Good.' Stirling leaned back, the weight in his chest easing. 'Good.'

Toby's tone was quiet and careful. 'She could help you too, you know.'

The words hung heavy in the kitchen, old words, spoken many times before. Stirling sighed quietly. Toby was right. Stirling couldn't keep living his life as though defined by the crash. He wanted to move on. A psych could help with that stuff.

'I'll call and book a session.'

'Soon.'

'Yeah, soon.' Next week. This week was for spending time with Toby.

For a moment, Toby looked like he was going to argue, then kept whatever it was inside.

They drank, soaking in the sounds of the crackling range and Westwind settling its bones for the night.

'I don't know what I've got to offer her,' Stirling said quietly, swallowing down his anxiety at revealing such a deep fear. 'Darcy, I mean. I'm a busted-up ex-pilot who doesn't even know if he'll fly again. And she's ...' Vibrant and beautiful and so alive he wanted to absorb her under his skin. Stirling's shoulders slumped. 'She deserves better.'

'Ugh, man. You're pity-partying on me? Look around you.' Toby threw his arms wide. 'You're living in a frigging chateau!'

'I'm being realistic.'

Toby considered that over a long slug of beer. 'Huh, who'da thunk it.'

'What?'

'You, being a coward.'

Stirling stiffened. He was no hero but he was far from a coward. 'It's not cowardice.'

'You sure about that?'

Only Toby could speak to him this way. There was also the unpleasant possibility that his friend might be right. Again.

Toby regarded him seriously. 'Is it because of Alina? You're scared of losing someone again?'

A good question.

'No.' He huffed. 'I don't know. I can't seem to think straight anymore.' Stirling stood and crossed to the sink, balancing his fists on the steel edge as he faced his reflection in the window. Outside it had grown dark. The wind was up. He could hear the faint bash of it against the thick walls, like a ghoul demanding entry. 'There's something off here, Tobes,' he said quietly. 'Really off.'

'You mean about your old man?'

'I think it might be about more than him.' Stirling faced his friend. 'Come on, I'll show you.'

Toby followed Stirling down the hall, carrying their beers. Away from the warmth and light of the kitchen, Westwind was filled with gloomy corners and seeping cold, yet Toby's company seemed to soften their edges.

The box that Stirling had found the week before was on the library desk where he'd left it. He lifted off the lid and laid out the contents: the newspaper article about Xavier, the lock of hair, several photocopied school reports, photographs of Xavier in sports and school uniforms, baby hand and footprints inked onto a folded piece of card, a photograph of an attractive brunette kissing the cheek of a smiling toddler.

Toby inspected each item, throwing glances at Stirling as he did. His furrowed brow showed Stirling that Toby thought them as odd as he did.

'These are personal, Tobes. More than godfatherly interest. More than guilt. They're ...' He fingered the cellophane packet of hair. 'They're intimate.'

'What are you saying?'

Stirling shook his head. 'I don't know.'

But he did know. The idea was lodged deep in his gut and wouldn't budge.

Toby dragged fingers through his messy hair. 'You think Dougal was Xavier's father? That he had an affair with Mal's wife?' He sounded incredulous. 'They were best mates.'

'Wouldn't be the first time that's happened.'

'Yeah, but ...' Toby dropped his gaze to the desk. Xavier smiled up at them from his picture. Toby touched it, then leaned closer. He looked at Stirling and back at Xavier, then held the picture up next to Stirling's face. 'Oh, man.'

'Tell me about it.' It was Stirling's turn to rub at his head. 'It's not like Dougal doesn't have form. I'm proof of that.' And maybe like father, like son, if what Jayne Bucknall said about Benjamin was true.

'Do you think Mal knows?'

Wasn't that the question.

'I doubt it. From what I can gather, Mal worshipped the boy. If he had any suspicion Xavier was Dougal's, he wouldn't have asked him to be godfather.'

Toby shrugged. 'Could be the reason he was asked.'

'Big call though. You'd hate the man, not make him your son's godfather.' And even in death, Mal had nothing but praise for Dougal.

Except for that one comment, muttered during Saturday's drive from Goodwin Oval to Westwind, when Stirling had mentioned his encounter with Jayne and asked if Mal had heard anything about old Benjamin's affairs. Mal hadn't, but then said the Kildares always did have a habit of coveting what wasn't theirs. At Stirling's stare, Mal had apologised and said he was thinking about Dougal's theft.

Now, with Dougal's treasures laid out, Stirling wondered if that wasn't a lie. And how many more lies Westwind had yet to reveal.

Chapter Twenty-One

Darcy folded the last of her dress orders and smoothed her hand over the fabric, her heart full. She couldn't recall a time when she'd been this exhausted. Or this proud. It had taken ten days of relentless work, too much caffeine and far too little sleep, but every one of her orders was done. If she didn't have to walk these last packages to the post office, she'd crawl into bed and sleep the remainder of the day.

Smiling, she wrapped the dress, taking extra care with the bows. Fatigue pricked at her eyes and made her usually nimble fingers clumsy. It had been worth it. Every stitch, every pressed seam, every facing and buttonhole and zip and gather. She'd shown herself the future, and it was damned fine.

Darcy made herself tidy her hair and apply a layer of scarlet lipstick before she walked out. Dead on her feet she may be, but standards must be upheld and though her teal swing dress was plain by Darcy's standards, it was still stylish and deserved spruced hair and lippy.

She spotted Lisette through the post office's big glass window. Her friend was perched on her swivel stool at the counter, chin on the heel of her hand and a preoccupied stare.

Lisette broke into an excited wave the moment she spotted Darcy. She jumped off her stool and stood quivering at the counter, her fingers tap-dancing over the surface like a pair of lively spiders. Something was up.

'Princess!'

'You are far too perky for this time of day, Mistress Lissy. Have you no compassion?'

Lisette grinned. 'None whatsoever.' She clapped her hands twice and then bobbed them around like a child about to receive a birthday present. 'You'll never guess—'

'Business first,' said Darcy, dumping her pile on the counter.

'Aren't you in a mood?' Lisette sniffed at having her fun spoiled.

'Not in a mood. Just exhausted.' Darcy watched the street through the window as a grumbling Lisette scanned the satchels. Wednesdays were usually busier than this. 'It's a bit dull out there today.'

'Only for those who've been holed up in their sewing castles. For the rest of us …' She gave a little jiggle. Clearly this was big news Lisette was being forced to hold in.

Darcy feigned a long sigh. 'Okay, you're busting to tell me. Give.'

'No, no, Princess.' Lisette gave a butter-wouldn't-melt smile and fluttered her eyelashes. 'Business first.'

If Darcy wasn't so tired, she would have laughed. Instead, she shook her head and checked her phone for emails and orders. Both were quiet. Darcy couldn't help feeling relieved. A few days rest would do her the world of good. She wanted to model and photograph some clothes on Friday and needed to look her best.

'There,' said Lisette, passing Darcy the lodgement receipt and bundling the satchels into the pick-up crate. She settled back on her stool, propped her fists under her chin and wiggled her eyebrows. 'Developments.'

'I'd actually guessed as much.' At least it wouldn't be about Charlie. Lisette had finally washed her hands of him on grand final night, when the Hoppers vice-captain had been caught in the loos being rather naughty with someone who wasn't Lisette. To Darcy's relief, Lisette had been quite sanguine about the affair. She suspected it was the toilet sex.

'So …' Lisette gave another joyful jiggle. 'Sally Monroe was in Moody's this morning grabbing a few things, when she spots this man at the checkout. Dark hair, a few curls, serious freckles. Not overly tall but fit and muscled. About our age and more than a bit babelicious.

'Anyway, Katrina starts chatting away, as she does—the weather, that kind of thing, trying to soften him up so she can get nosy. And the bloke doesn't respond much, but Sally reckons he kept wearing this smart-arsed smile, which had her watching him even more closely. Katrina's just about finished processing the groceries when she finally asks what he's doing in Grassmoor. He replies that he's visiting a friend.'

Suddenly, Darcy began to see where this was going.

'Yeah,' said Lisette, nodding, her eyes flashing. 'So Katrina goes, "Oh yes, which friend?" and the bloke breaks into this huge grin and says, "My good mate Stirling Hawley, out at Westwind. Perhaps you know him?"'

Darcy covered her mouth. It would be mean to laugh, but if anyone deserved a comeuppance it was Katrina Hedditch.

Lisette giggled her way through the rest of the story about how completely thrown Katrina was, torn between outrage and the need to complete the transaction because, as a small-town business, Moody's wasn't in a position to knock back a sale. In the end, she'd taken the money and then closed the checkout and stomped off, even though Sally was still waiting to be served. Stirling's friend then completely charmed Sally by throwing her a cheeky wink and sauntering out the door as pleased as punch.

'Isn't that just delicious?'

'Very,' said Darcy, unable to control her own giggles.

'I bet Stirling got a laugh out of it when he heard. I wonder who his friend is?' Lisette mused. 'Did he mention he was having visitors?'

Darcy shook her head. 'No, but he'd have no reason to tell me if he was.'

'Doesn't give away much, does he?'

'He doesn't know us. And I think he's naturally restrained.'

'But he wants to. Know us, that is. Especially,' Lisette jabbed a finger towards Darcy, 'you.'

Darcy waved her lodgement receipt. She did not wish to discuss her love life in the post office. 'I'd better get these tracking codes uploaded.'

'He does, you know. We all saw the way he looked at you on Saturday. The way he *kissed* you.' Lisette made puckering noises.

'Indeed. And then we all saw the way he scuttled off home with Mal.' That still hurt. Had Stirling thought she'd jump him the moment she got him alone? She had more class than that, even if the idea had crossed her mind more than once.

That kiss... How could there have been so much in something so brief?

Lisette flapped her hand and made a *pfft* noise. 'He's just playing hard to get.'

In Darcy's experience, men did not play hard to get. They either wanted you—mostly for sex and sometimes for more—or they didn't. Stirling wanted her for the former, of that she was sure, and Darcy would be a more than willing participant should the opportunity arise. The latter? She had felt an inkling of more. Had *hoped*. Now, she didn't know.

The thought made her slump. She was too shattered to be thinking about this. It was too disheartening, and Darcy hated being disheartened.

'Hey,' said Lisette.

Darcy returned her gaze to Lisette.

Her expression was pure kindness. 'You're special, you know that. Special, talented and gorgeous. And don't you ever forget it.'

Oh, her friend was such a sweetheart.

Darcy stiffened her spine and set her shoulders. Lisette was quite right. They were special women. Very special, and boo-sucks to anyone who thought otherwise, including Darcy's inner critic.

'You and me both, my darling. You and me both.' She grinned. 'Now, if you'll excuse me, I'm going to make myself even more special and gorgeous by collapsing into bed and sleeping away the bags under my eyes.'

Blowing Lisette a kiss, she strutted out, every inch the Queen of Seam.

⁂

Darcy woke at four and stretched luxuriously. Her limbs were still heavy, but her mind had lost its fuzziness and she felt brighter than she had in days.

She rolled her head to the side. The last of the day was sparkling behind the gaps in her blinds. She should get up, shower and drive to Roseneath. She hadn't seen her mum and dad since Friday and apart from trips to the post office, had been stuck inside since the grand final. The family kitchen would be comforting and cheerful, and if she probed carefully enough, Darcy might even discover where Shiloh had disappeared to on Saturday. She hoped it was somewhere with Leo.

Finally, she released a long breath and forced herself out of bed and into the shower.

The Mini slowed of its own accord as it neared Westwind. Darcy told herself no, that the goal was Roseneath, dinner, some sisterly time with Shiloh, a check on her parents, especially her mum, and home to bed. No Stirling. Yet there was no stopping her indicator flicking on or the wheels turning into the gravel drive.

A blue Subaru sedan was parked at the front of the house. Darcy braked to park alongside then let the Mini crawl onward as she spotted Stirling in the distance, near one of Westwind's many old stone sheds. Two other men were close by, crouched on their haunches, inspecting a ratty old motorbike.

She pulled up several metres away and opened the door. Stirling, who'd been tracking the car for the whole of its approach, hobbled over and rested one hand on the door edge, the other poised to help her out.

'Hi,' he said, and Darcy was thrilled to see his dimple making an appearance.

'Hello, you,' she said, taking his hand. She eased out and before he could escape, kissed a spot on his cheek close to his mouth. Why hold back when Darcy was special, talented and gorgeous? 'How have you been?'

'Good.' His gaze traced her face, before slinging to his companions. 'I have company.'

She grinned. 'So I've heard.'

'How?' Stirling grimaced and shook his head. 'Don't answer that.'

Darcy deliberately looped her arm around his and hugged it. 'You should know you can't keep secrets in Grassmoor.'

His eyes shifted to the house and back to her. 'I wouldn't be too sure about that. Come and meet Toby and Gavin.'

Darcy shook hands with Toby, who regarded her with amused interest. She wished she'd taken more effort with her outfit. The burgundy twinset and pearl necklace, black cigarette pants and matching patent loafers had been fine for a trip to Roseneath. Not so fine for impressing Stirling's friends, or the man himself.

Toby was as dishy as described, although not in Stirling's class. His curly-haired cheeky attractiveness, soft brown eyes and solid handshake made Darcy warm to him immediately.

'Very glad to meet you, Darcy.' Toby bobbed his head at Stirling. 'Felix has mentioned you a lot.'

'Felix?'

'Hasn't he told you? Typical.' Toby made a face at Stirling. 'Nine lives, this bloke. Like a cat. Mind you, after this latest screw-up, he's probably down to one.'

'One's all you need,' said Stirling.

Gavin thrust out his hand for Darcy to shake. 'Gavin Cooke. And you can only be Darcy of VaVoom fame. My wife heard about your shop when we moved here. Thought it was a terrific thing. Recommended it to our daughter, Katie. I think she's bought a few things too.'

'How lovely. I'll have to keep an eye out for her name so I can pop something special into her next order.'

'Katie'd be thrilled, she would.' He beamed at her, another likeable man. Stirling seemed to attract them. 'Come to check on the young fella, eh?'

'Actually, I was on my way to Mum and Dad's. They're on the property next door, Roseneath. But for some strange reason,' she paused to slant a smile at Stirling, 'my Mini seemed to steer itself here. How do you know Stirling?'

'Got a rideshare business based in Hamilton,' said Gavin, his chest puffing out. 'With an app and everything. Stirling booked me to bring him home from hospital. I guess you could say we hit it off.'

'You just wanted me for my house,' said Stirling.

'True.' Gavin looked back up the drive at Westwind and sucked air between his teeth. 'Good blokes are a dime a dozen, but you got to admit, it's a hell of a house.'

When they'd finished laughing, Darcy turned to Toby. 'And you?'

'Army mates.'

'You're a pilot too?'

Toby shook his head. 'Medic.'

'Toby joined MiZ with me,' said Stirling.

'Oh.' Another hero. Lisette would be beside herself when she found out. 'Grassmoor must seem very dull after all that action.'

'Oh, I dunno. I had a fun time at the Ezymart when I called in this morning. I'm sure you've heard.' He ended with a cheeky wink that made Darcy laugh.

She gestured at the old motorbike. 'Please tell me you're not planning to ride that.'

'Not anytime soon,' said Stirling.

'Not until it's restored,' said Gavin, rubbing his hands together. 'Then watch out.' His voice turned wondrous. 'What a project.'

All three men beheld the bike with awe that bordered on the comical. Darcy held back a giggle.

'Where did you find it?' she asked.

'In one of the outbuildings,' said Stirling. 'This was what I was looking at when I fell through the floor.'

'Ah, the fateful day of our meeting.' She moved in for a closer inspection. 'What is it?'

'A 1940 Indian Chief,' said Gavin. 'Inline four-cylinder engine, leaf-spring front suspension, coil-spring rear, closed fenders ...' He whistled out his breath. 'Beautiful machine. Beautiful.'

It didn't look that beautiful to Darcy. The Indian was dusty, rusted and rat-eaten, but each to their own. Although those curvy mudguards did give it a certain style. Womanly, almost. Which probably explained much of the men's bike worship.

'Amazing it's been hiding in that shed all these years,' said Toby. 'You'd think your old man would have done something with it.'

'Probably couldn't fit it into his busy schedule,' said Stirling.

Darcy frowned at the edge in his voice.

Toby grabbed Stirling's shoulder and gave it a companionable shake. Something passed between the two men. Darcy wondered what it was before scolding herself that it was none of her business. Except she wanted everything to do with Stirling to be her business.

'Have you found the Buick?' she asked, making a mental note to find photos of more Indians and add them to her inspiration file.

Three heads swivelled towards her.

'What Buick?' asked Stirling.

'The one in the old slaughterhouse.'

'Slaughterhouse?' asked Toby, then gave an amused snort. 'Man, this place.'

'Not unusual for these old properties,' said Gavin. 'They were like mini villages at their height.' He smiled sheepishly at Darcy. 'I developed a bit of an obsession with all the old properties when we moved here. Got a bit worse since I met Stirling. He's enabling, letting me hang around here.'

Darcy laughed. 'I can see how Westwind would feed an obsession. It's a beautiful property, although it wasn't quite as bustling as some. But yes, there was a slaughterhouse here.' She pointed to an overgrown gravel track. 'It's about five-hundred metres that way, before you get to the fence.'

'There's another car in there?' asked Toby. 'Like, an old one?'

'Yes. A Buick. We sometimes played in it as kids. I only remember the name because Melody called it that. It was a rat-infested wreck back then, so God knows what it's like now. It's old though. Definitely vintage.'

Gavin and Toby exchanged a look, then turned their faces to Stirling like a pair of eager dogs.

'Go on then,' he said.

For a moment, both did nothing, then they were hurrying off, jostling each other like schoolboys.

Stirling watched them with a smile. 'Now look what you've done. They'll be at it for hours.'

'All part of my cunning plan to get you alone.'

'Is that so?'

'Oh, yes.'

'Funny, I was hoping for the same thing.'

'You were?' Darcy blushed at the high ring in her voice. Truly, must she sound so desperate?

'Yes.' He looked at his feet for a second then held her gaze. 'I wanted to apologise for leaving so suddenly on Saturday.'

Not quite what she expected, but it was nice he felt the need apologise. And it was a touch too early in their relationship for declarations of undying love.

'Why did you?'

He rubbed his eyebrow. 'I didn't want to spoil things and Jayne's comments threw me a bit.'

The poor man. A football grand final was hardly the place to learn about your grandfather's moral failings. Stirling had had enough struggle dealing with Dougal's.

'Understandably,' said Darcy. 'It was quite uncalled for.'

'But probably true.'

Darcy didn't know how to answer that. If anyone was in a position to know about Benjamin's alleged philandering, it was Jayne. They were from the same elite circle, where social rules were different and the privileged took their privileges. Especially the men.

'For what it's worth,' said Darcy, 'it's not something I've ever been aware of. There's been no talk from my family. Nor has Lisette ever mentioned it and she tends to hear these things.'

His tone remained sombre. 'No one knew about Dougal either. Yet here I am.'

Darcy shrugged. 'Your mother and Dougal could have been a one-off.'

'I doubt that.' He held her gaze. 'I meant what I said on Saturday. I'm not like them, like Dougal and Benjamin. I'm ...' His face scrunched as if finding the right words hurt.

'Hey.' Darcy placed a hand on his chest. Stirling's heart beat a rapid tattoo against her palm. 'It's okay. You're better than that. I know.'

He searched her face. 'How?'

'I just do. I knew from the moment we met that you were a good man.' She smiled and slipped a little closer. She could smell the dust on him and something else, something lovely. Sandalwood, a fragrance she adored. Its creamy soft scent made Darcy want to press more than her hand against his chest. 'Call it women's intuition. Or maybe I was just dazzled by your handsomeness. I do remember calling you that while you were bleeding all over my dress.' She put a tease into her tone. 'Or perhaps you've forgotten that moment?'

He swallowed, even then his voice had a husky edge. 'Never.'

'Good,' she said, her own voice not quite steady.

Her closeness was having the desired effect. His pupils were wide, his breath shallow, his heart pattering fast. Her own pulse stormed through her arteries as though gathering for a sprint.

'Darcy ...' He slid his hand to her neck, cupping it, thumb gently caressing her jawline.

Desire flared at the want in his voice, at the tenderness of his touch. At the fizz of the air as it heated and vibrated between them. There was no cold, only heat. Heat and want.

Darcy tilted her face further upward. They were going to kiss and it was going to be magic. The buzz in her bones told her so.

A shout went up from the distance. 'Felix, get your arse down here!'

Darcy sucked in air. *No, no, no. Not now.* But Stirling had already stepped back.

He glanced over his shoulder. 'I guess they found the Buick.'

'I guess they did.' And Darcy had no one to blame but herself.

'Felix! Stop canoodling and check this out!'

Stirling closed his eyes. Then he smiled wryly and brushed his knuckles down the side of her cheek. 'Maybe another time.'

'I hope so.'

'Yeah,' he said. 'Me too.'

Chapter Twenty-Two

Toby stood at the door to the library, Dougal's dirt- and grease-stained work clothes too long for his legs and arms, the cuffs rolled up like a kid wearing hand-me-downs.

'I'm heading into Grassmoor. Want to come?'

Stirling eyed the old ledger he'd been scanning in between adolescent daydreams about Darcy. He'd found a series of the ledgers lined up on one of the lower shelves. Heavy, leather-bound tomes with pedantic ink-written columns itemising all the property's income and expenditure going back to the 1800s. Reading them was dry and dull and yet strangely compelling, helping to keep his mind from drifting to places it shouldn't. He'd worked his way into the 1920s and even found the entry for the purchase of the Buick.

'Yeah, all right.' Apart from grand final day and a trip with Toby to show him around and point out Dougal's boarded-up business, Stirling hadn't been into Grassmoor since he'd been booted out by the cafe and motel.

He marked his place with a notebook and closed the ledger. He'd scan the rest later, although why he was bothering he didn't know.

What was there to learn from decades-old accounting, except that Westwind had seen periods of extraordinary prosperity, and that the Kildares had expensive tastes? But he'd promised himself he'd do this properly and if that meant going through dusty old books, then so be it.

Besides, apart from mucking around with the Indian and now the Buick, Stirling didn't have that much else to do. Thanks to Gav delivering batteries and Toby's tinkering, the farm vehicles were back in working order. Stirling had bitten the bullet and moved into the master bedroom, leaving Toby with the room further down the hall, next to the main bathroom. He was gradually working his way through Dougal's belongings and nicking clothes to wear around the farm.

He'd managed a couple of phone calls with his mum and chatted a few times with Olympia, but even that was proving a trial. All the teenager wanted to know was how Stirling's romance with Darcy was progressing. When Stirling muttered about it being early days, Olympia had regarded him with a combination of pity and disbelief that only made him feel more stupid.

He wanted her. She wanted him. Yet taking that step wasn't that easy.

After a bit of research and a check with Gav, Stirling had found a highly regarded stonemason who'd agreed to assess the vandalism. All the paperwork for his agreement with Shiloh was complete and any day she'd be moving in her ewes and lambs. The woodpile was stocked after Toby turned himself into a sweat-stained mess one afternoon chopping a stack of wood for the fires. Though it irritated Stirling no end to stand uselessly by, he wasn't quite mobile enough to do more and Toby promised he'd found it therapeutic.

They headed into Grassmoor in the four-wheel drive. Stirling tried not to miss his Ducati as they swept around the turns. The ache was there though, deep and constant, a throbbing reminder of the speed and control that had been such a major part of his life and now seemed far away. Still, the way he was healing, he'd be on the bike again soon.

He let the scenery go to focus on Toby. His friend had worn a weird, almost sly expression since starting the car, and Toby wasn't sly. Mischievous, but not sly. 'What are we doing in Grassmoor, anyway?'

'Not we,' said Toby and pointed at Stirling. 'You. I'm taking you to see Darcy.'

Stirling's heart gave a mad hiccup. He'd secretly hoped they might spot her in town, strutting the street in one of her enticing outfits, polished and dazzling and untouchable, like a heroine from a classic film, but he hadn't bargained on them meeting person to person. Stirling was unshaven, wearing three-day-old jeans topped with one of his father's wool jumpers, and had hair like a hippy from not having been cut for weeks. What a Romeo. He really needed a barber. Or some clippers.

'You could have mentioned that before we left,' he protested. 'I thought we were picking up food or something.'

'Would you have come?'

Stirling had to think about that. 'Probably not.'

'I don't know what your problem is with her. She's seriously hot. And hot as hell for you. Why hold back?' Toby glanced across the cabin at him. 'And don't give me that crap about her deserving better. She might be hot but you're not a bad catch yourself.' He broke into a grin. 'Big chateau, bit of land.' Toby nudged him. 'Pilot.'

'No job, scarred from arsehole to breakfast time.'

Toby snorted. 'Women love scars. It's manly.'

Stirling shook his head. His scars were ugly, especially the ones on his legs. And Darcy had said she liked good legs.

'Come on, man. Give the girl more credit than that.'

Stirling stared at his friend. Since when could Toby read his mind?

Toby shrugged. 'You're an open book when it comes to her.'

Stirling bloody hoped not. Even he'd been surprised by the intensity of some of his raunchier Darcy thoughts. And they'd been growing worse since nearly kissing her a few days before.

Grassmoor was busier than he remembered it. Moody's carpark was nearly full. A few locals leaned on trolleys near the entrance, passing the time. A group of men in fluoro work gear sat outside the takeaway, scoffing pies and sandwiches at its small kerbside benches, cold drinks at hand. Through the cafe window, Stirling could see Tilly ferrying coffees to a table. As though sensing his scrutiny, she looked up, her smile shy when she recognised him.

Someone else who didn't hate him. Stirling's list of locals was starting to skew in favour of the likers. Any more and he was at risk of feeling welcome.

They passed the boarded-up front of Kildare Livestock Services. At least no one had kicked in the panels. It was a sad sight though, one Stirling felt in his belly. He wished he could rummage inside but, as with assorted other assets, the building had been sold to cover debt and Stirling had no claims on it or its contents. Anything of interest would probably be in the hands of the police, the same as the paperwork and computers from Westwind.

Toby followed the main street further along for a while and did a U-turn, parking in front of a nondescript brick building with a wide front window shielded by interior plantation shutters and a garage door to the side. Its glossy red main door stood out like a clown's nose.

Darcy's atelier.

Toby alighted. Stirling hesitated, wondering why the hell he was so nervous. This was Darcy. Gorgeous Darcy who made no bones about wanting him, and who Stirling desperately feared he'd disappoint.

Toby rapped on his window and gave a 'what the' gesture.

Stirling swallowed and got out, cursing at the pain that shot up and over him as he forgot to take care with his leg and hip. Hiding the worst of it, he headed for the door. A white plaque with Darcy's pouty pin-up girl logo was riveted to the wall alongside. Old rock and roll music filtered from inside.

VaVoom by Darcy. By appointment only.

Stirling gave Toby a look.

'Ignore it,' he said. 'We're good.' At Stirling's expression, Toby shrugged. 'I phoned her. Said we might drop by sometime today.'

'When?'

'I dunno. I didn't give a time.'

'Not that. When did you call her?'

'Earlier this morning.' Toby folded his arms. 'Don't look at me like that. Someone had to do something. You've been looking like your balls are about to explode since her visit.'

Stirling had to breathe through his nose to stop from thumping his mate, even if there was truth in the comment. He hadn't wanted anyone this much since he was a teenager. 'You're a shit.'

'I know. It's why you love me.' Ignoring Stirling's gripe, Toby rapped on the door. When there was no answer, he tried the handle. It opened to a blast of heat and music. Toby peered around the edge then jerked back out again.

'Oh man.'

'What?' Not waiting for an answer and worried for Darcy, Stirling shoved open the door. He scanned the room. It was much larger than he imagined. One side was filled with machines and fabric and giant racks containing rolls of fabric and haberdashery. The other …

Oh man barely covered it.

Darcy was posed in a skimpy red and white halter-neck playsuit on a wooden platform in front of a giant pull-down backdrop of an impossibly blue tropical ocean and sandy beach. She was crouched forward, bottom poked out, shoulders tilted slightly towards the large DSLR camera she'd set up on a tripod several metres away, and had one hand out with a yellow rubber duck balanced on her palm. Her silky dark hair had been left down, except for one side that was pulled back and fixed with a trio of red roses. A pair of dangerously high red heels made her legs look endless.

As for her cleavage ...

Stirling's brain scrambled. Even a hello was beyond him.

'Hi!' she called. 'Won't be a minute.'

She changed poses. Standing erect with her legs close together, shoulders back and the duck held out to the side. She held the pose for three seconds then rotated to kiss the duck on the end of its beak, one leg kicked up behind her. She moved again, cupping the duck in both hands low against her belly, the duck facing the camera. Stirling could have sworn it was wearing a grin. God knows, he would have been.

Three more poses followed, each as demurely provocative as the last. Stirling thanked his lucky stars his jeans were baggy and Dougal's old jumper stretched and long. Toby stood beside him making snuffling noises as he tried and failed to smother his glee.

'You planned this,' muttered Stirling.

'Nope. Innocent. Perfect though.'

It was. Completely and utterly perfect. He couldn't shift his gaze from her. If he'd had any doubt about Darcy's hourglass figure before, it was gone now. She was pure woman—hips, waist, breasts ...

Stirling swallowed as she raised her arms behind her head, one leg forward with the toe pointed. The pose lifted her boobs even higher. He gritted his teeth against the need to slap his hands over Toby's eyes.

'There we go,' she said, stretching her arms upward and giving a little jiggle. A few skippy steps and Darcy was at the camera. She fiddled with a couple of buttons and scrolled back through the images on the screen. 'Not too bad.' She smiled at them. 'Do you want to see?'

'Yeah,' said Toby, elbowing Stirling when he failed to answer.

'Sure,' he said, not meaning it. He was having enough trouble controlling himself without looking at photos of Darcy's cleavage and bum. And it was too bloody hot in here.

Stirling could feel her eyes on him as he flicked through the photos. He tried to keep his expression neutral, but it was impossible. Darcy was amazing.

'They're great,' he said when they reached the end, meaning it.

'Thanks.' She shut down the camera. 'I think I'll try with a different background though. I have a backdrop of an art deco hotel pool that might be more fun. Make it a sort of poolside cocktail-hour theme. I could hold a martini with a little umbrella and glacé cherries. I'll see. Sometimes you have to experiment until you get the right feel.' She beamed at Stirling, then gave a little 'Oh' and clapped her hands. 'How remiss of me. I haven't given you a proper hello.'

Her kiss landed at the very edge of his mouth. Soft and warm and tingling with the promise of more. Stirling's scrambled brains started to leak out of his ears.

She kissed Toby too, although his was far briefer and on his cheek.

Darcy returned to Stirling and took his hand. 'Would you like a tour? Come on.'

'I might go for a wander,' said Toby. 'Leave you two to it. Grab a coffee or something.'

'If you go to the cafe, make sure you get Joanne—she's the older lady—to make your coffee,' warned Darcy. 'Young Tilly's a darling but her coffee is truly awful.'

Toby waved and sauntered off, whistling something that sounded suspiciously like 'Love Is In The Air'. Stirling could have throttled him.

Darcy squeezed his hand. 'I'm so glad you're here. I've been dying to show off my atelier to you.'

She walked Stirling through her work area, explaining the processes from pattern design to cutting to sewing and pressing.

He examined the custom-made racks where her fabric rolls were stored. 'Where do you buy from?'

'Commercial suppliers mostly. Some of the woollens come direct from the mills and I occasionally source specialty fabrics from textile designers. I go on buying trips three or four times a year, although a lot of suppliers have online showrooms now and you can request samples.' She smiled as she regarded the wall of material. 'Buying trips are fun. It's always exciting to see what colours and designs are coming up. They can be great for triggering ideas.'

'What about fashion shows. Do you do those?'

'Not so much. I used to do a lot of rockabilly festivals and the occasional show and shine, but they were too big a time suck. I found I could do just as well and save more money exploiting social media. There's only so much of me to go around.' She spread her arm towards the rear of the room. 'Come see the rest.'

The kitchen was functional, industrial and spotless yet she'd given it personality with knick-knacks and artwork. Stirling accepted Darcy's offer of coffee and wandered back to the lounge, which joined the workspace. The entire layout was open plan, each section zoned by strategically placed rugs or furniture, most of which was fifties style. Chrome and vinyl, minimalist and modernist and borrowing heavily from art deco, but bright and cosy, thanks to Darcy's handmade homewares, quirky art pieces and dozens of decorative photo frames. Stirling liked it. The rooms reflected their owner: stylish and sexy and warm.

He wandered over to a shelf on the wall to study the photo display more closely. Family, friends, birthday parties, dogs, events, her studio. The shelf was crammed with Darcy's loves and memories.

He paused in front of a snap of Darcy and Shiloh as teenage girls, Shiloh perhaps sixteen or so and Darcy around fourteen. Even then she was luminous, her smile and eyes wide and happy. It was Shiloh he found surprising. Though as tall and lean as she was in adulthood, she beamed out of the photograph with the same cheerfulness as her sister.

'She's beautiful, isn't she?' said Darcy from behind. When Stirling turned, she held out a mug.

Stirling took it with a thanks. The coffee smelled delicious and a far cry from the ordinary grind he'd been tolerating at Westwind. 'She is.'

Darcy's gaze turned a little sad. 'I do hope she and Leo can sort themselves out.' She pointed to another photo, a candid shot of the couple with their arms rested on a fence rail, the sun on their faces as they shared a laugh. 'They're meant for each other.'

'What happened?'

'Stubbornness, a refusal to talk, unresolved baggage. The usual relationship killers.'

'You sound like you know from experience.'

'I do, actually.'

Stirling suddenly wished he hadn't commented. That Darcy had past lovers was a given but that didn't mean he wanted to know about them.

Amusement tugged her mouth. 'I am thirty, you know. I have had a life.'

'I never thought you wouldn't have.'

She looked back at the photos. 'It's funny, when I was a teenager I never in my wildest dreams imagined myself single at thirty. It's just not something that happens around here.'

'So why are you?' It was a question Stirling had pondered more than once.

She laughed at that. 'Isn't it obvious?'

Not to Stirling.

She set down her coffee mug, held up her fingers and ticked off her faults. 'I'm too high maintenance, too focused on my business, too provocative, too feminist, too fussy. Oh, and my favourite—a closet lesbian probably in a secret relationship with Lisette.'

Stirling spluttered into his coffee. '*What?*'

'I know. It's ridiculous.' She sighed and picked up her mug and took a sip. 'People are so silly. Although I will concede that I'm fussy and focused on my business—not that I consider either a fault. I've worked jolly hard to make VaVoom what it is and I have too much self-regard to take on any man just because it's the expected thing. I deserve love and respect and orgasmic sex.'

Stirling spluttered a second time. 'Right.'

She smiled at him as though she'd said nothing untoward at all. 'Come see my bedroom,' she said, plucking his mug from his hand and setting it down with her own. 'You'll love it.'

Darcy's bedroom was adorably crazy. The entire far wall was covered by a black and white photographic mural of a crowded cocktail bar, with men in dinner suits and women in elegant gowns. The bed in front was king-sized, with a white quilt and pillows and a red throw to match the red and white floor rug.

The other walls were decorated with fancy mirrors and more silver-framed black and white photos. Stirling peered closer at a series of five, and swallowed hard as he recognised the model. Worse, she was wearing even less than she was now—just a lacy bra and knickers with stockings and stiletto heels.

'They're great, aren't they?' said Darcy. 'A friend of mine who does boudoir photography took them.'

'They are.' Stirling couldn't drag his gaze away. The poses she was pulling earlier had nothing on these. He forced himself to look at her. The real woman was better anyway. 'They're amazing. You're amazing.'

Her expression lit up, lips parting, eyes glittering, colour blushing her cheeks. 'Thank you. That's quite the nicest compliment.'

He stared at her, this vibrant, unique woman who turned his insides out and made his heart stumble. 'I think I'm going to have to kiss you.'

'Then you should do that.' She nodded vigorously. 'Definitely. And soon please. I'm rather keen, if you haven't already guessed.'

Stirling laughed and cupped her face. 'Funny, gorgeous girl.' Then his mouth was on hers and all the uncertainty, all the fear at where his life was headed vanished into nothing, leaving only happiness and the deep, intense need to stay exactly where he was.

With her.

Chapter Twenty-Three

Stirling was braced against the wall, mouth sliding down the silken skin of Darcy's neck, one hand full of pert, peaked breast, the other slipping inside the leg of her playsuit, when the atelier door banged and Toby called out.

Stirling's growl wasn't one of lust.

Reluctantly, he uncoiled Darcy's thigh from his, set her down and rested his hands on her hips. Darcy's arms remained draped around his neck as though unwilling to let him go. Stirling knew the feeling.

For a long, stunned moment they stared at one another, then Stirling grinned and pressed his forehead to hers. Her hair was mussed, tresses tangled around the loosened flowery clip where he'd plunged his fingers into her hair as their kiss deepened. Lipstick smudged the corners of her swollen mouth. A faint trail of redness from his stubble tracked her cheeks and throat. She looked completely wanton, bright eyed and happy. All because of him. Stirling's heart squeezed.

'Well,' she said. 'That got heavy fast.'

'Sorry.'

'Oh, no.' Darcy poked a finger into his sternum. 'Don't you dare be sorry. I was having a wonderful time.'

Stirling was glad to hear it.

'You guys better not be having sex!'

Stirling sighed and kissed her, except what was meant to be a brief kiss had Darcy curling against him again like a cat. Stirling groaned with the effort to pull away then groaned some more when Darcy gave a low whimper and gripped his jumper to keep him close. This girl …

'I'm coming to *fiiiind youuuu*!'

Darcy laughed and shook her head. 'You stay right where you are, mister!' Then to Stirling she said, 'You have lipstick all over you.'

'I figured I might. Your hair's a bit of a mess.'

'Yes.' She pulled out the clip and tossed it on the bed. They both looked at it. Darcy bit her lower lip and Stirling guessed she was thinking the same as him—how close they'd come to ending up in said bed. She sighed, her breath long with disappointment. 'I suppose we'd better tidy ourselves.'

Stirling let out a sigh himself. 'Yeah, although I'd prefer to get messier.'

'So would I.' She poked him in the chest again. 'Your friend.'

'That's borderline right now.'

Toby had made himself at home on the couch when they made it back into the lounge. He set down his phone and eyed them up and down. 'Good.'

That was a matter of opinion. Good would have seen Stirling in bed with Darcy for the rest of the afternoon.

'How was your coffee?' asked Darcy.

'I didn't bother. Went to the pub instead. Publican seemed a decent bloke.'

'He should be,' said Darcy. 'He's my cousin.'

Toby chuckled. 'Figures.' He eyed Stirling. 'Ready?'

To leave Darcy? No, but they couldn't hang around all afternoon. Darcy had work to do and Stirling had … dusty ledgers to read, cupboards to go through and clippers to hunt down. Westwind seemed the kind of place that would have some. A number two all over would do the job.

'I know it's short notice but would you and Lisette like to come over for a barbecue tonight?' he asked.

'Oh, Stirling, we'd love to, but I can't.' She clasped her hands together. 'It's Gran's birthday. She lives in Hamilton. All the family's gathering and taking her out to dinner.'

It was on the tip of Stirling's tongue to ask her to call in on her way home but that would be unfair. Darcy had put in a full week and would likely to be tired.

She touched his hand. 'I'm sure we could manage tomorrow night, if that would work?'

Stirling glanced at Toby, who shrugged. It wasn't his call. 'We can do Saturday night. No problem.'

'Wonderful. Lisette can bring dips and biscuits and I'll sort out dessert. What else would you like?'

'Nothing,' said Stirling, hoping that dessert meant Darcy in a lacy bra and suspender belt. 'Just yourselves.'

'Are you sure? I don't mind doing more.'

'We'll be fine.' He and Toby had an evening and morning to plan. They'd figure it out. Besides, it wasn't food Stirling cared about.

The weather gods were feeling merciful Saturday morning. The day glowed like one of Darcy's smiles. As Stirling cut up chickens to grill, he couldn't help his own smile. Darcy was coming for dinner. Except this would be more than dinner.

Was he ready for her?

A good question. Stirling hoped so. He was mad enough for her. He just had other stuff to sort out.

The mudroom door banged behind Toby as he tromped in, legs confettied with grass clippings from whipper-snipping the neglected lawn around the sunken garden.

He paused to inspect Stirling's marinade ingredients. 'Looks interesting.'

'It will be.'

Stirling would marinate the chicken in black pepper, garlic, chilli flakes and whatever herbs he could scrounge from the garden for a makeshift *pollo alla diavola*, another recipe he'd learned from Paolina. Some halved grilled lemon, potatoes baked in the coals and a simple salad would round off the meal. Nothing fancy and maybe even a bit scant, but from what he knew of Darcy, he had no doubt she'd bring plenty of other food to keep them going.

Then, after dinner …

'You can stop smiling to yourself any time you like,' said Toby.

Stirling hadn't realised he was. 'Can't help it.'

'Yeah, righto. You got the hot girl. No need to rub it in.' Toby eyed the kitchen table and sighed. 'Thank god for your old man's cellar.'

He'd brought up several bottles last night, along with a head full of cobwebs and an expression like he'd found the Holy Grail. The cellar, it seemed, was more well-stocked than Stirling had imagined.

It was on the tip of Stirling's tongue to mention Lisette. The girl was single, attractive and bubbly—a bit like Darcy in ways—but that didn't mean she and Toby would like each other.

Stirling separated a leg from a thigh and dropped it in a bowl with the other cuts, while Toby scooped up an armful of scrap paper from the pile near the wood basket.

'What's that for?'

'Setting the fire.' Toby boggled his eyes. '*Duh.*'

Stirling hit back with a sneer. Then he remembered what he'd been meaning to ask since the night before. 'Hey, you haven't come across any hair clippers while you've been poking around?'

'Nope. But I did find a little brown bottle of malathion mixed with DDT. That made my eyes water, let me tell you.'

Stirling only just missed slicing the top off his index finger. '*What?*'

'DDT.' Toby gave a single nod. 'Serious.'

'Jesus.' Stirling would have to phone the council or ask Shiloh what the disposal protocol for banned pesticides was. Whatever the answer, that bottle wouldn't be staying at Westwind. 'What the hell would they have kept that for?'

'Dunno. Label said it was dog wash. It looked pretty old. Probably forgot they had it.'

Stirling closed his eyes and breathed in deeply as he tried not to imagine what else could be lurking around the farm. It'd been going since the mid-1800s. There could be anything out there.

Toby headed off with his papers. Still in mild shock, Stirling set the bowl of marinating chicken in the fridge and mentally checked off chores as he washed his hands at the sink. Twice. Even the mention of DDT was giving him the willies. There wasn't much more to do really. Plenty of time for a cup of tea. Toby would probably appreciate one too.

After setting out mugs, Stirling returned to his favourite chair, stretched out his legs, and gazed vaguely around the room. Now that he was used to it, he liked the kitchen. It had homeliness and warmth. The kind of place where a family could relax and talk.

His gaze landed on the wastepaper basket. An old copy of the farmer's journal *Stock & Land* sat on top. Curious, he snatched it up, disturbing a scrap of paper beneath that wafted to the floor.

He set the *Stock & Land* aside and, with a mild grunt, leaned down to check what had fallen, surprised to find not newsprint or glossy junk mail but a square of quality cartridge paper, two of its edges torn.

He flipped it over. At first he couldn't comprehend what he was looking at, then his mind began to focus. 'What the ...'

He dug back into the pile. He didn't have to look far to find the remaining three pieces. He laid all four in front of him and matched the torn edges.

His heart began to thud, heavy and loud, as if in warning.

Stirling scanned back and forth, still scrambling to get his brain around what he was seeing. The kettle boiled and clicked off. He ignored it.

It was a building plan. No, that wasn't right. More a concept drawing or artist's impression. A low, simple, rendered block construction with light ochre walls and corrugated iron screens in front of the windows. For privacy, he supposed.

Just a building. Except it wasn't.

What had Stirling's heart thumping was the name emblazoned across the building's portico. A name that shouldn't make sense, yet, for him at least, did.

A name that, should the project eventuate, would turn the district ablaze with questions and gossip and expose a respected man for the cuckold he was.

The Xavier McKenzie-Kildare Nursing Centre.

Forgetting the tea, forgetting his chores, even momentarily forgetting Darcy, Stirling shoved his chair back and hurried out to find Toby.

Chapter Twenty-Four

Darcy flicked the indicator as the turnoff to Westwind neared. She sucked on her lip, suddenly so anxious she didn't care if she ruined her lippy. It was six twenty-seven and they were due at Westwind at six thirty. On time and a perfect start to what she hoped would be a perfect evening.

One that would end even more perfectly in bed with Stirling.

'Do you think I'm being silly, Lissy?' She twisted her hands around the steering wheel. 'Wanting him this badly when he could disappear tomorrow?'

Darcy had spent the trip from Grassmoor getting Lisette up to speed about Stirling's visit to the atelier and how hopeful she was that tonight could be the start of a proper relationship, but now she was here, she couldn't help a twinge of doubt.

Lisette reached across and squeezed her arm. 'I think it's brilliant. It's been too long between drinks. You deserve this.'

'But what—'

'Nuh-uh, Princess,' said Lisette, waggling her index finger. 'Don't think of the end. You know what happens when you start doing

that. Think of the now. The wonderful, beautiful, glorious now.'
Then she laughed and waved her arm towards Westwind's stately
iron gates. 'Think of the sex!'

Darcy had, nearly every waking minute since the hot and
heaviness of Friday. She smiled. Think of the sex indeed. Lisette was
right about what happened if you let 'the end' into your thoughts—
it was like admitting defeat before you'd even started, and Darcy
loathed defeatism.

'You're so lucky,' Lisette said on a sigh then leaned forward as
the mansion came into view, magnificent in its Italianate splendour
though still sadly marred by the vandalism. 'Stirling's a honey.
And that house is fit for a princess, which, of course, you are.'
She grinned at Darcy. 'Imagine. You could be Princess Hawley of
Westwind instead of Princess Darcy of VaVoom.'

'I prefer the Queen of Seam, thank you. And you, Mistress Lissy,
are definitely getting ahead of yourself.' Darcy was perfectly happy
in her atelier. Westwind *was* beautiful though.

The man inside even more so. And she was going to sleep with
him tonight, oh yes, she was. If she weren't driving, Darcy would
have drummed her heels on the Mini's floor.

Half her morning had been taken up baking a pavlova for dessert,
the remaining hours determining the right balance of seduction
versus barbecue attire. In the end, she'd chosen a plum jersey top
with puffed sleeves and a square neckline. Her knee-length, high-
waisted denim skirt was a nice blend of sexy and casual, snug in all
the right places but still allowing movement.

Recalling Stirling's admiration of her fluffy jacket, she'd opted
for a black hand-knitted angora cardigan that practically screamed
'stroke me' and made her feel lovely. A long faux-fur coat was
currently tucked around the pavlova, cream and fruit containers to
keep them from tipping over but could be easily retrieved should
the night air turn chilly.

Darcy parked in the rear courtyard. The back door was shut, then it was suddenly yanked open, and Stirling was limping towards her.

Darcy's stomach swooped at the sight of him. Comfortable jeans, a wool jumper over a lightly checked shirt with the sleeves of both pushed up, plain boots, and eyes that didn't move from her face. The intensity of his gaze launched a crazed rabble of butterflies inside her, their crashing wings driving her heart to match the beat. She felt like a teenager in the grip of a terrible crush. Except this was no crush. This was the blaze of an older, wiser woman in love.

Her mouth parted. *Love?*

Dangerous territory. She hardly knew the man. Yes, Stirling was handsome, courageous, intelligent, kind and respectful—all admirable qualities—but there was still much she didn't know about his past and she certainly didn't know his future.

Lisette had the right attitude. Concentrate on the sex. Love, should it blossom, was another game.

'Are you going to get out or stay here the entire night ogling?' asked Lisette.

'Very funny.' Darcy unclipped her seatbelt and pushed open the door. Stirling was waiting with an outstretched hand, clean-shaven and with a new military-short haircut that further chiselled the edges of his already sublime bone structure. She took his hand, her skin tingling from the touch, and straightened. 'Nice buzzcut.'

'Toby found some clippers.' Stirling rubbed a hand over his head and flicked his friend a look. 'Mistook me for a sheep.'

'You're the one who said you wanted it short,' Toby called over the top of the car.

'I like it,' said Darcy, and to prove it, kissed him square on the mouth. It was meant to be a tease, more than a peck but not a proper kiss, except their bodies had other ideas.

'Oh man, are we going to have to put up with this all night?'

Darcy drew away and glanced around to find Toby shaking his head. He grinned and introduced himself to Lisette. 'Hey, I'm Toby.'

'Lisette. Nice to meet you.'

'Likewise.' He gestured at the Mini. 'What are we bringing in?'

'Pavlova,' said Darcy.

'You made a pav?' Toby looked from Darcy to Stirling and back again.

'I did indeed. With passionfruit.'

'Passionfruit.' Toby rolled the word around his mouth as though savouring it, then blew out his breath. 'Awesome.'

With the meringue safely on the kitchen table and its toppings in the fridge, Stirling and Toby carried Lisette's trays of biscuits, dips and crudites out to the sunken garden, where the fire was already blazing. Cane chairs scattered with cushions and an assortment of wool rugs surrounded the pit. A portable CD player rested on the stone wall feeding music into the air.

The men set the snacks on a cloth-covered table where plates, glasses and cutlery were stacked. A dusty bottle of red wine stood ready for opening next to a pile of fine linen napkins and an empty breadboard.

Stirling had clearly gone to some effort. It seemed they were both out to impress.

Toby dragged a cooler from under the table and opened the lid. 'What's your pleasure, ladies? We have wine, beer and ...' He dug around and drew out a can, screwing his nose up as he read the label. 'Diet lemonade. That stuff'll kill you.' He shoved the can back and dug some more. 'There's water in here somewhere.'

'Beer for me,' said Lisette.

'Actually, I might have a beer too,' said Darcy.

Stirling fitted a neoprene cooler to her bottle and handed it to her, while Toby took care of Lisette's.

'What shall we toast to?' asked Toby when they all had drinks.

'Friendship,' said Darcy.

'Don't be boring,' said Lisette. She winked at Toby and held up her beer. 'We should toast to the only thing that matters.'

'Pavlova?' suggested Toby.

Lisette rolled her eyes at him. 'To love, of course.'

Which made him laugh. 'Yeah, why not? There's enough of it in the air tonight.'

'Give it a rest,' said Stirling, sounding like he'd been ribbed all afternoon.

They toasted one other. Darcy felt Stirling's gaze like a caress. She wished she knew what he was thinking. Such open talk of love would make most men want to run a mile, yet he didn't appear bothered.

As if by mutual agreement, Toby and Lisette wandered over to the edge of the sunken garden where the view was best over the gully and creek, leaving Darcy and Stirling in private. In the distance, the ranges were turning purple as the day bled out. Soon, they'd be in the dark, with only fire glow and a string of candles placed at intervals along the wall for light.

Stirling bent close to her ear. The tickle of his breath coursed electricity down her spine. 'Did you wear that cardigan on purpose?'

'I did, actually. Does it make you want to stroke me?'

His gaze burned. 'You have no idea.'

'Oh, I think I do.'

He ran a finger around the edge of her jaw. 'You must have a hell of an imagination then.'

'Ah, but I'm very creative. I thought you'd have realised that by now.'

He chuckled then turned his attention to the fire when a log shifted and shot up a flurry of sparks. Using a rusty steel picket, he poked the log back towards the centre. The embers pulsed hot and red, like Darcy's desire.

She watched Lisette and Toby. From the drift of conversation, they were enjoying a chat. What interested her more was their body language.

'I think those two are hitting it off,' said Darcy softly.

Stirling glanced at them and frowned. 'You think?'

'Mmm.' Darcy knew her friend. She knew that alert, almost predatory expression of a highly interested Lisette.

'You drove here together.'

Darcy had been waiting for this. They hadn't discussed arrangements and she'd guessed he'd wonder about them. 'We did.'

He nodded and stood with his back to the pit and one fist shoved into his jeans pocket. Darcy joined him, the warmth on her back luscious. Before them, Westwind stood haloed against the sunset, the sky behind busy with birds racing home to roost in the tall driveway trees, their squawks and chatter overlaying the boombox's decidedly seventies soundtrack.

'That doesn't mean I can't stay,' she said, bumping her hip against his. 'The night, that is.'

Stirling took a mouthful of beer. She could see from his little dimple that he was trying to hide a smile. 'What about Lisette?'

'I took liberties.' Darcy regarded the house as though fascinated with its splendour. 'And may have mentioned that your couch is very comfortable. I hope you don't mind.'

He tucked an arm around her shoulders and kissed her temple. 'Funny girl. And no, I don't mind. She doesn't need to spend the night on the couch though. There are plenty of beds.'

'That probably haven't seen a warm body for years.'

'Probably not.' He eyed the house as Darcy had. 'It'll do it good to have people rattling about.'

'Are you suggesting that Westwind has ghosts that need scaring?'

'Not that I've seen.' He kissed her again. 'I'm not scared of ghosts anyway.'

'Of course you aren't. Big brave man like you.'

'Not that brave. If it weren't for Toby, I'd probably be still thinking up excuses why I shouldn't kiss you.'

'I'm delighted you came to your senses.'

'So am I.' He gave her a look that turned her insides to mush, then let his arm drop from her shoulders. 'I'd better get this damper on.'

It was then that she noticed the cast-iron lidded pot on the ground near the table. Stirling carried it to the edge of the fire pit and balanced it on the ring of bricks, then used a spade to carefully scoop coals from the fire and spread them over the lid.

'If you're trying to impress me,' she said, 'I'm impressed.'

'That's the idea.' He swapped the spade for the poker and reorganised the fire. 'You've lived in Grassmoor all your life?'

'Except for a few years in Hamilton.'

'You lived in Hamilton?'

Darcy shrugged. 'I worked there. It was easier and ...' Did she truly want to mention her ex? No. Not tonight. Tonight was about the now, not the past. 'It made me feel like a proper adult.'

His attention returned to the fire. 'One of life's milestones, going it alone.'

'Yes.' Although Darcy hadn't been strictly alone.

He straightened but didn't let go of the picket, balancing it on its tip, his expression unreadable. 'Have you ever heard about a nursing centre being built in Grassmoor?'

'Of course. It's been mooted many times over the years but never seems to get up due to lack of funding. A shame. Grassmoor is crying out for one. They've been hugely successful elsewhere. Real community hubs, and having one would certainly save us a lot of travel and Mum a lot of stress. Why do you ask?'

He shook his head.

'Stirling?'

He opened his mouth then stopped and retrieved his beer. 'It's nothing. I'd better act like a proper host and pass round these nibbles.'

She frowned at him and would have probed further if not for Toby and Lisette rejoining them. Within minutes, Stirling's question was lost in the chatter and laughter of friends getting to know each other, and an evening alive with possibility.

It was after ten thirty and the sky was like stretched velvet, satin-stitched with a silver moon and lustrously sequinned with diamantes. Although the cold was fierce, nipping with icy teeth at any legs and toes that dared creep too far away from the fire, Darcy couldn't have imagined a more splendid evening.

Lisette had turned up the music and the sunken garden was bouncing with T. Rex singing 'Metal Guru'. They'd had plenty of laughs at Dougal's music tastes, but his CD collection had proven highly successful—the perfect combination of old-style rock and roll and sentimental tunes.

Between them, Lisette and Toby had cleaned out the cooler of beer and were now on to red wine. Darcy nursed her own glass, taking care with her sips. Stirling, she noticed, did the same.

'We should take those plates inside,' he said.

Dessert had been a major hit, especially with Toby. He'd had two serves and savoured every bite. Between their intoxication and sugar highs, he and Lisette wouldn't be making it to bed any time soon.

'We should,' replied Darcy, rising immediately to help Stirling with the plates. She'd been wondering when a polite time would be to stir him into action. From the way Toby and Lisette were grinning at each other, they'd be more than happy with a bit of alone time too.

The house was eerily quiet, only the hum of the fridge and the low crackle of the range breaking the hush.

Stirling closed the dishwasher door and smiled at Darcy. 'Here we are.'

She sidled closer, head tilted back and her most teasing smile tipping her mouth as she pressed her palm to his chest. 'And about time too.'

'I was trying to be polite.'

'So was I.' Darcy fingered his jumper. It really was time to get him undressed. 'But it's late and I've had a beer and two glasses of wine and now I'm at the point where I'm over politeness. What I'd like,' she inched even closer, 'is to get very,' she reached her mouth towards his, 'very rude with you.'

If Stirling had any more to say, Darcy didn't give him time. She hooked her arm around his neck and closed her mouth over his, and in that instant their lust, held on simmer all evening, hit boiling point.

Not caring if she got scalded, Darcy dived in, holding nothing back, her kiss hot and bold, heavy with rapid breaths and laden with yearning like she'd never experienced. Every part of her reached for him—skin, muscles, organs—as though pulled by desperate want, powerful and possessive. She could not get enough of this man. Not his lips, not his scent, not his unleashed desire.

And from the intensity of his kiss, Stirling felt the same.

'Oh god,' she breathed, arching as Stirling's lips kissed, nibbled and gently sucked their way across her jaw and down to the now hypersensitive skin of her throat, while his hands caressed her waist.

Stirling worked his mouth back towards hers, pausing to suck on the lobe of her ear and shooting exquisite electric charges straight to her groin. He found her lips, hungry for more. Hungry and delicious with the residue of the night—wine, a hint of cream, and tangy, sexy passionfruit.

His palm found her breast.

'Oh,' she panted again, only this time there was an edge to the plea. If he went there, there was no end to what she'd let him do. Darcy cupped her hand over his, stilling the thumb that brushed back and forth across her nipple. 'No,' she said.

Stirling froze. 'No?'

Darcy quickly clarified. 'No! I mean, yes, please, but …' She waved an arm at the window. 'Not here.' She lifted her brows. 'Upstairs?'

He pressed his forehead against hers, eyes fixed on Darcy's. 'Yeah.'

His grip firm on her hand, Stirling led her to the stairs and paused at the bottom. 'I'm still not great at these.'

'That's perfectly all right. You can lean on me.'

'I'd rather be doing other things with you.'

'All in good time, my gorgeously eager man. All in good time.'

The master bedroom was neat, enormous and very masculine. Darcy wandered over to the king-sized bed and ran her hand over the duvet, then turned to face Stirling. He stood with his back to the door, watching her with a blistering gaze.

Darcy took a step away from the bed and drew one arm and then the other from her cardigan. She held it out to the side and let it plop softly to the floor, her eyes never leaving Stirling's. The denim skirt was next, the sound of the zip going down competing only with their increasingly loud breaths in the silent house.

'Darcy,' rasped Stirling as she stepped out of the skirt, revealing a lacy set of burgundy knickers, suspender belt and stockings. He visibly swallowed.

Her top went next, again dangled from her hand and dropped on top of the cardigan, until she stood proudly in her lacy balconette bra, bikini underpants and Mary Janes, and an inviting smile.

His voice was low and husky. 'You're incredible.'

'I am indeed.' Darcy tipped her palms out. 'I'm also all yours.'

He came closer, his step more like a stalk, the hunger burning off him setting fire to her skin. He placed his hands on her waist, his touch cool. Shivers shot over her heated body. He stared for several thudding heartbeats, eyes tripping over her face, her lips, down to her heaving chest and back up again.

His dimple made another appearance. 'Be gentle with me? I'm an injured man.'

'Not a chance,' she said and launched herself at him.

Chapter Twenty-Five

Darcy woke to a room filled with light. They'd forgotten to close the curtains and now the morning sun was streaming through the east-facing window and throwing kaleidoscope of colours over the floorboards and rugs.

Beside her, Stirling's long, muscled form radiated warmth and, if his night was anything as glorious as hers, satisfaction. Darcy's body was ripe with smugness.

She stared at a beautifully crafted ceiling rose and smiled to herself.

'What are you smiling at?'

Darcy rolled onto her side and tucked her hands under her cheek. Stirling was on his back, his face turned to hers. His gaze was tender and loving and made her heart gambol like a lamb.

'I'm feeling smug,' she said. 'What's your excuse?'

'Same.' He shifted onto his side and stroked a strand of hair from her forehead. 'Good morning, gorgeous girl.'

'Good morning, handsome man.'

Stirling slid his finger slowly downward, tracing her chin and throat, before coasting it back and forth across her upper chest, leaving mini earthquakes of delight in its wake and causing Darcy's nipples to peak. His smile revealed he hadn't missed the reaction. 'Did you sleep well?'

'I don't recall a lot of sleep happening last night.'

'No.' He watched his finger trace upward and drift across to the point of her shoulder and down her upper arm. 'Your skin is so smooth. I want to kiss it all the time.' His gaze went to hers. 'I want to kiss *you* all the time.'

'Feel free. My lips are ready and willing.'

Instead, he continued his teasing caresses, apparently fascinated by the shivers and goosebumps they caused. Darcy's breath turned shallow. A low pulse began to throb between her legs.

'What are your plans for the day?' he asked.

'Besides staying in bed with you?' She placed her hand over Stirling's heart, pleased to find him as affected as her by their caresses. His body hair was the same rich brown as his hair and lightly patterned in a sexy 'T' that spanned his chest and dove down to other delicious locations. 'Drop Lisette home, then head to the farm. Help Mum around the house. Try and get my sister to give up what's going on between her and Leo.'

'Are they together again?'

'I don't know. Shiloh's being very Shiloh about the whole affair. All I know is that she and Leo had a conversation at the grand final. It must have been some conversation. She was missing for an entire quarter.'

Darcy flicked at his left nipple. Stirling sucked in a breath, then responded by tracing his finger further down her arm, shifting the sheet lower until her hip and thigh were exposed.

'What about you?' she asked.

'I have a few things I need to follow up. Other than that, tidy, muck around on the Indian with Toby.'

She tweaked his other nipple. 'Nothing else?'

He grinned and rolled her onto her back, hovering over her with his weight on his arms and his bad leg to one side. Last night's explorations had revealed a heavily scarred but far from unattractive body. In fact, Darcy had found the scars a surprising turn-on, especially when he remained tight-lipped about how they'd come about. From something heroic and danger-filled, she was certain. And painful. Those had been serious injuries.

Stirling's body was like an exquisitely designed clothing pattern, cut and stitched into uniqueness, his past woven into each fabric piece. Darcy loved it.

'I have plenty I'd like to do,' he said, sparks in his gaze.

Darcy tipped her head and bit the corner of her lip as she spread her hands over his belly and slid them lower. 'What's stopping you?'

'Nothing,' he whispered, lowering his mouth towards hers. 'Nothing at all.'

It was midmorning by the time Darcy and Stirling made it downstairs. After a brief check of the house, Darcy found Lisette outside with Toby. She was sitting on the stone wall surrounding the sunken garden, swinging her legs like a little girl as she watched Toby scrape coals from the fire pit into a bucket.

'Don't you look the princess who's found the pea,' said Lisette. 'Not that you're a pea, Stirling. Far from it, if the Princess's satisfied smile is anything to go by.'

'You can stop any time you like,' said Darcy without rancour. Her eyes narrowed as she inspected her friend more closely. For someone who should have been miserable with a hangover, Lisette was looking suspiciously pink-cheeked and relaxed. And was that a love bite on her neck? Darcy eyed Toby, who returned her look with a 'Well?' one of his own.

Well indeed.

Was this a good thing? Darcy didn't know. Toby seemed a nice enough man, and his closeness to Stirling had to be a positive, but his life wasn't here.

She let it go. It was probably just sex.

Unlike what Darcy had shared with Stirling. She hadn't felt this alive, this joyous, this *cherished*, in years.

The day was bright, the air redolent with the scents of spring. Each gentle zephyr brought woody scents from the surrounding trees, reminding Darcy of Stirling's sandalwood bodywash, which they'd had a frolicsome time soaping one another with during their extended soak in the bath.

The thought made her wish they were back there, exploring, sharing touches and smiles, and little anecdotes from their lives. She'd learned more about him in those intimate moments than she had during any of their conversations. Small things, like that he loved dogs but had never owned one, and would covet trips to the country homes of boarding school friends as much for the joy of being near their dogs as their friendships. That he and Toby had hit it off after Toby treated Stirling for a broken nose that he'd suffered during a bush rugby match while on exercise somewhere in the Queensland outback. That it was thanks to Stirling's mother Amanda, and her equally smart and competent friends, that he'd developed his respect and admiration for women and their abilities.

That he hoped Darcy would meet Amanda one day.

A casual comment that had left her breathless. These were not the words of a man who didn't have at least one eye on the future. A future that included Darcy.

'Are you ready for home?' she asked Lisette. 'I have a few things I need to do before I head back to Roseneath.'

'Sure.' Lisette slid off the wall. Instead of heading to Darcy, she stepped close to Toby. 'Thanks.'

He looked down at her with a kind of wonder. 'Any time.'

'Good, because I'm definitely interested in a return round.' She patted his chest and sauntered past Darcy and back towards the house, Toby's avid gaze dogging her every step.

He glanced at Darcy, then at Stirling. He grinned, gave a 'What can I say?' shrug, picked up the bucket and strode off, humming a tune that sounded distinctly similar to '(I've Had) The Time Of My Life'.

Darcy exchanged a wide-eyed look with Stirling. For a moment they could only gape, then Stirling wrapped his arm around Darcy's neck and dragged her to his chest and kissed her hair. His chest was heaving with suppressed laughter.

'This place,' he said.

'Yes,' replied Darcy, hugging him and feeling like a host of benevolent angels had blessed her world overnight.

This place, indeed.

Chapter Twenty-Six

The stonemason was a chunky, wrinkled man named Helmut who kept his long grey hair in a man-bun and wore a pair of drill work shorts despite the late-afternoon cool. He snapped a few more photos with his phone, released another series of tuts, then stood back, rubbing his neck as he surveyed Westwind's graffiti. Stirling girded himself for bad news.

'Shoulda got in touch when it was done,' said Helmut in a tone that suggested the graffiti was Stirling's fault.

Stirling shrugged. 'Wasn't anyone here to care then.'

'Ruddy disgrace.' Helmut surveyed the rest of the front wall. 'One of the few places left built from this sandstone. National treasure, is Westwind.'

'But you can fix it.' A statement, not a question. If Stirling sounded positive, Helmut might feel the same. The stonemason had warned over the phone and again on arrival that he only did graffiti-removal as a sideline, something he fell into simply because he kept getting asked about it. Gav had promised Helmut was well-regarded, and Stirling wanted the graffiti gone. He wanted the finials replaced too. Two birds, one stonemason.

And Westwind back to its full glory.

Helmut rubbed his neck again. 'Lemme talk to my mate in Geelong. He's the real expert. Paint like this is hard to remove at the best of times and this has been allowed to soak in. Best guess is it'll need solvent.' He sucked on his teeth. 'Nasty stuff. Gotta have all the protective gear for that.'

'And the solvent will do what?'

'Draw the paint to the surface.' Helmut patted the wall near the worst patch—the giant letter S of scum. 'It's soaked into the stone now. Right in.'

'You can't blast it off?'

Helmut reeled back as though slapped. 'No! Do that and you won't have any stone left.'

'Right,' said Stirling, only just stopping himself from apologising.

The stonemason gave the wall another caress. 'Gotta be gentle. No abrasives.' He shot a look at Stirling. 'No detergents either. They can leave residue. Won't do anything to the paint anyway. You need to break down its molecular structure and draw it out. A poultice of organic solvent should do it. We'll need to test to work out which one. My mate might have ideas; even then you'll likely be left with ghosting.' He gave Stirling a once over. 'S'going to cost.' He paused. 'A lot.'

Stirling sighed and leaned against a verandah post, one hand in the pocket where he'd shoved Helmut's business card. Despite the chill wind, his leg was good today. Still pulling and occasionally painful but heading towards normal. Well, post-crash normal.

'I was getting that impression. You'd better give me a quote.' Not that it would matter. Stirling would likely give Helmut the business anyway. 'What about the finials?'

Helmut crossed to the front stairs and trailed his hand down the stone balustrade to where the finials had once decorated the ends. 'Easier job. Won't be able to match the sandstone exactly. They don't quarry up there anymore.' He gestured towards the distant range. 'But we should be able to find something that won't look out of place. You have photos?'

Stirling had to think for a moment. Most of the images he had were low-res downloads from the internet that were hard to make out details, but there was a large front-on photograph of Westwind hanging in the library that should work. He could take a snap with his phone and message or email it. Other photographs probably existed somewhere. Funny, he couldn't recall seeing any though. No albums, no boxes of loose snaps. He could only assume Melody had organised them to be sent to her in America, or to her mother.

Mal would likely have some too. It'd give Stirling an excuse to get in touch and dig a bit more. The nursing centre plans were still bugging him, and not just because of Dougal's proposed name. He'd phoned the architects who had drawn the concept and learned it was just that—a concept. They'd been waiting on Dougal to secure the finance to move on when he died.

'Should be able to find something,' said Stirling.

'Good. The heritage people can get their knickers in a twist if you don't replace these things exactly.' Helmut stepped onto the gravel and looked back at the house, admiration smoothing some of his wrinkles. 'Grand old place, Westwind. Done a few jobs here over the years. Repairs mostly. The memorial.'

That had Stirling's ears pricking. 'Xavier McKenzie's memorial?'

'That's the one. Terrible tragedy. Only a little boy.' He shook his head. 'Upset Dougal no end. Upset everyone.'

Stirling nodded. If what he suspected was true about Xavier's parentage, then Dougal would have been more than upset. In fact, now that he thought about it, Dougal's one and only letter to Stirling must have been sent around the same time. Perhaps having lost one son, he'd reached out to another.

And what had Stirling done? Thrown the letter away like a spoiled brat. *God.*

He held out his hand. 'Thanks for coming out, Helmut. Shoot me a quote for both jobs and I'll get back to you.'

'Will do.'

Helmut was about to open his car door when Darcy's red Mini appeared in the drive. She circled the fountain the wrong way around to bring the Mini alongside.

She alighted and beamed a wide, scarlet smile that made Stirling's heart lift. 'Aren't I the lucky lady? Two of my favourite men in one place. How are you, Helmut?' She hugged him with affection and stood back. 'More importantly, how is darling Diane?'

Stirling only just managed not to roll his eyes. Of course she knew Helmut.

'She's good. Keeping busy with the grandies.'

'How many's that now?'

Helmut's chest puffed out. 'Three.'

'Very busy, then.' She laughed and then sobered when her gaze landed on the graffiti. 'Do you think you'll be able to help?'

'Maybe.' Helmut didn't sound confident. 'Even if we get the worst of it off, you'll still see its ghost.'

'That'd be a shame, although anything is better than this ghastly mess.' She crossed to Stirling and held his arm. 'I know you'll do your best, Helmut.'

The stonemason's eyebrows lifted slightly at Darcy's possessive move but he made no comment. Instead, he nodded at Darcy before addressing Stirling. 'Don't forget those photos. Email address is on my card.'

With a final wave, Helmut stepped into his ute.

As soon as it passed into the shade of the driveway trees, Darcy rolled into Stirling's embrace and draped her arms around his neck. 'Hello, handsome man.'

He grinned back at her. 'Hello, gorgeous girl. Nice dress.'

It was too—an outlandish floral number with bright pink lace trim that hugged every curve from knee to neck. Demure, yet provocative as hell. Her hair was soft today, parted on one side with the crown teased up and the remaining tresses hanging loose and lightly spiralled.

'Thank you. It's a couple of seasons old now but it makes me feel bright and sunny. Much like you do.' She kissed him. 'How was your day?'

He rested his hands on her waist, thinking of how they'd rested there only this morning, when she was naked and arched on top of him. They hadn't spent a night apart since Saturday.

'Okay. I suspect your friend Helmut's going to charge me a bomb. Speaking of which, is there anyone you don't know around here?'

'Plenty.'

Stirling wasn't sure he believed that.

Darcy tipped her head sideways to check the house. 'Where's Toby?'

'Cleaning rats' nests out of the Buick.' Despite a few mutterings about work nagging him to come back, Toby had decided to stay on for a few more days.

'Nice. So, we have Westwind to ourselves?'

'For a while.' He slid his hands up and down. 'Were you thinking of something?' He definitely was, although it might have to wait.

Darcy's eyes widened innocently. 'Me?'

Stirling laughed. 'Can you help me with something first?'

It was a steep descent to the creek, but Darcy handled the four-wheel drive like she'd been doing it all her life, which Stirling supposed she had. Though he should have been paying attention to the track and landscape, his focus kept shifting to her thighs and the way her muscles flexed under the tight dress when she changed gear. Darcy knew he was looking too and kept sliding him knowing glances. After insisting that she'd drive, Darcy had changed her heels for a pair of shiny red rubber boots that she kept on hand in the boot. Stirling thought she looked adorable.

The track ran out and they neared the creek. She followed the tree line to the north-west, the ute bouncing on the lumpy ground. Now and then on the far side of the creek, glimpses of an overgrown trail appeared through the vegetation, zigzagging back and forth as it wound up a steep slope. Stirling wondered where it went. He couldn't recall a public road on that side of the waterway. Not one that close to Westwind.

Darcy slowed to a crawl as the creek looped back on itself to form a natural glade carpeted with grass and surrounded by thick-girthed trees growing at angles along the waterline where they'd slumped when the flow undermined the roots. In the centre of the clearing stood a stained stone statue on a plinth—a hunched angel dappled with fading light, her face buried in her hands. Even streaked with moss and dirt, she was heartbreakingly beautiful.

Darcy parked several metres away and alighted. Neither of them said a word.

Stirling walked to Darcy's side and took her outstretched hand. Together, they approached Xavier's memorial. Etched into the stone plinth was a brief epitaph.

In loving memory of Xavier Michael McKenzie.
Let the little children come to me, and do not hinder them,
for the kingdom of heaven belongs to such as these.
Matthew 19:14.

Stirling's throat closed over. Darcy must have sensed it because she squeezed his hand, and he was grateful he'd done this with her and not alone.

He gazed around. Despite its bleak air, it was a pretty spot. Green and lush and peaceful. The shallow creek burbled in the background and birds chirped and chattered. A smooth wide rock had been positioned three or so metres from the statue. A place to sit and remember, Stirling assumed. He traced the path that led to it, where the grass was stumpier from over-trodden soil. Past the rock, the track veered off towards the creek where a lower section of bank appeared to have been gravelled. Odd. He looked back towards Westwind, but the house was hidden from view by the steep slope.

Darcy smiled wanly. 'It's a melancholy place, isn't it?'

'Yeah. Nice though. Peaceful.'

She regarded the angel. 'It was good of Dougal do this for Mal and Candice.'

'It was. But I suspect it was as much for him as them.' Atonement as well as sorrow.

'Yes. As Xav's godfather, Dougal must have been terribly grief-stricken.'

Stirling rubbed his mouth where the words he wanted to say rolled like marbles, hard and cold. What would be the point though? Let Grassmoor continue to believe Mal's truth. There was no harm in it. And if Mal's ex-wife had kept the secret, then why should Stirling reveal it? It wasn't his story to tell.

Besides, he had no proof Xavier was more to Dougal than his godson.

Except for the boy's hair. There was that. A simple comparison between Xavier's DNA and his own would give an answer. But Stirling didn't need it. That Dougal had been given the lock said enough.

'I suppose there'd be a measure of guilt too,' said Darcy. 'His property, his quad bike.'

'It happened right here?'

'Further up the slope, where it's steeper. I guess Dougal chose this spot because of how lovely it is. Where it would be easier to reflect on Xavier's life instead of his death.' She swung a rubber boot though a clump of grass. 'He's a nice man, Mal. Grassmoor has been fortunate to have someone of his calibre. Dad reckons he was a big deal with a financial law practice in Geelong and doing really well for himself before he decided to return home to the quiet life. Pity he and Candice never had any other children.'

'Why didn't they?'

'I don't know. Maybe they tried and it just didn't happen. Then when Xavier died …' She spread her fingers. 'It's not uncommon for couples to break up after the death of a child. The pain is too awful. I can't imagine what it must be like.' She looked at him. 'Have you ever lost anyone you were close to?'

Not trusting his voice, Stirling nodded, his mind filling with Alina.

Darcy's gaze hung on his face and he knew she was waiting for more. He wanted to give it to her. He wanted to give her anything she desired. Yet his natural reticence made it hard to find the words.

'Before I came here ...' He cleared his already thickening throat. 'I was in a crash late last year. We were flying in to help a group of refugees who'd taken shelter in an abandoned village. One of the women had been in labour two days and needed urgent care. It should have been safe but there'd been a screw-up with the intel. We were shot down. Took out the tail rotor. I tried to control the crash but ...' Stirling sucked in a long breath. His failure still ached even though in truth there was nothing he could have done. The terrain, the wind, the attack stole what little control he had left. 'Two of my team were killed. One of them was a medic, a doctor. Her name was Alina. She was Swiss. We'd been ...' He rubbed his mouth. 'We'd been talking about quitting MiZ and moving there, to Lausanne, closer to her family. Maybe starting one of our own.' He stared at the weeping angel, his heart leaden with guilt as it always was when he remembered Alina.

A gentle hand pressed on his upper arm. 'I'm so sorry, Stirling.'

He kept staring, unable to speak. At least the woman and her twin babies had lived. It was some solace that his team's emergency rescue had saved her too. Alina would have felt it was somehow just. Like his mother, she could be fearsome when it came to women's health.

'Is that where your scars are from?'

He nodded. She'd asked before, when they were in bed, another time in the shower. He'd replied that he'd had a few adventures and Darcy had seen through his nonchalance to the sensitivity below and dropped it.

'Saving my life is what got her killed.'

'And you feel guilty because of it.'

He didn't answer for a while. 'I just want to be worth it.'

'You are, Stirling. You are.' And with those words, Darcy wrapped herself around him and held him close.

Stirling remained rigid for a moment, then relaxed into her embrace. She was soft and sweet and smelled of goodness. Of home and compassion and love. Maybe even a way forward.

But to move on to that, he'd need to figure out the past, and he wasn't sure he could.

Or, given the sticky web of lies that lingered there, whether he should.

Chapter Twenty-Seven

'Are you worried he's still in love with her?' asked Shiloh.

'It's the million-dollar question, isn't it?' One Darcy had been pondering since Stirling had revealed that part of himself by the memorial only a few hours earlier. She smoothed the skirt of her dress. 'I don't think so. But it was only late last year he lost her.'

'That's still a lot of months ago. Nearly a year.'

Darcy and Shiloh were perched on a bench in Roseneath's rear garden with rapidly cooling mugs of tea. Their parents were inside, watching the ABC news on television. The faint sound of it drifted on the air along with the zip and whirr of myriad insects as they crazed around the back porch floodlight.

Shiloh sipped her tea. 'Could be that he didn't love her that much.'

'They were thinking of starting a family. I'd say he loved her.'

'So were Leo and me, and look how that ended up.'

'Oh, Shiloh.' Darcy shifted onto her hip to face her sister properly. 'You still don't believe he cheated on you? Please tell me you don't.'

Shiloh sucked on her bottom lip and stared into the darkness.
'No.'

Which was progress. Darcy knew her sister though. 'I'm hearing
a resounding "but" there.'

'How are we meant to move forward after what we did to each
other? Knowing we have that capacity to hurt. Not just the capacity
but the willingness.' She shook her head, eyes glistening. 'The things
we said, Darce. The things *I* said.' She turned away.

'Hey.' Darcy gripped her sister's free hand, demanding her
attention. 'You'll get there. It'll take time, that's all.' She squeezed.
'You still love him, don't you?'

Shiloh nodded, holding in a tsunami of emotion. Darcy's heart
went out to her. Shiloh was the eternal stoic. Strong, and proud
of that strength. Emotion this big was hard for her to process, let
alone express.

'Leo loves you and you love Leo. You have all you need for
forgiveness.'

Shiloh was silent for a while then she sighed and had another
mouthful of tea. 'What about you? Are you in love with Stirling?'

It was Darcy's turn to sigh. She leaned back into the seat and
kicked out her legs. 'Yes. I was rather hoping it was a mild crush but
then Saturday happened.'

'Let me guess. Sex.'

Darcy bumped her shoulder against Shiloh's. 'Truly marvellous
sex, in case you were wondering.'

No,' replied Shiloh, dry as a parched paddock. 'I wasn't.'

'It's more than sex though. It's …' Darcy frowned as she fought
to explain her feelings. Feelings that had suddenly blazed to life in
a rush of heat and longing. 'He's such a decent man, Loh. Kind.
Smart. Brave. Caring. Good-looking. All the things you could want.'

'Does he love you?'

Another million-dollar question. 'I don't know. He likes me. A lot. I sense that much. Love, though?' Darcy held her gaze. 'I guess I'll find out in time.'

'Assuming he sticks around.'

'Why wouldn't he? Westwind is here. I know it's early days, but I think he's developing a real connection with it. Anyway,' she lifted her chin and straightened her shoulders, every inch the Queen of Seam, 'I'm here.'

'Idiot,' said Shiloh. Then she sobered. 'Just be careful, Darce. I know you think you know him, but he's still a stranger. We don't know anything about his life. Not really. I don't want to see you hurt.'

'Stirling wouldn't hurt me. Not deliberately.'

It was the one thing Darcy was sure of. Stirling didn't hurt people, he helped them. That's who he was.

The man she loved.

'Huh,' was all Shiloh said.

Darcy took one look at Lisette's expression and dumped her satchels on the counter with a whump. 'What now?'

'Oh, you know.' Lisette twirled a hand in the air. 'Nothing too terrible. Just that you and I apparently had a weekend orgy out at Westwind.'

The words 'Well, I certainly did' flashed smugly in Darcy's head. Hers was an ongoing sex spree too. She still tingled pleasantly from Stirling's lovemaking earlier that morning. And again last night, when she'd hurried, bright and positive, straight into his arms after leaving Roseneath.

Fortunately, the post office was empty and she could make fun of the gossip. 'An orgy? Is that all? I thought from your expression it was going to be something scandalous.'

'Scandalous enough if Tina Downs' cat's bum mouth was anything to go by.'

'How on earth did she hear that delightful piece of news?' Tina Downs was Darcy's grandmother's age. Although sadly without the same outlook on life.

Lisette peered down her nose. 'Where do you think?'

'Katrina?'

'Uh-uh. Worse.'

'Oh,' said Darcy with disgust. 'Truly?'

Lisette nodded. 'Dearest Frances, bless her rotten cotton socks.'

'That woman.' She shook her head. Some people couldn't help themselves. Often gossip came from jealousy or boredom, or from someone mishearing a piece of innocuous news and turning it into something harmful. When it came to anything Darcy Sloane–related, Frances Green's opinion verged on the malicious, and all because Darcy's ex was Frances's close cousin. Darcy could shrug that rumour off as she'd shrugged off others. It was the inferred slight against Stirling that worried her—the outsider corrupting local women. He had enough against him without that kind of scurrilous gossip.

'What took her so long?' asked Darcy. It wasn't like Frances to be slow on the uptake.

Lisette tapped a finger against her lip. 'I'm not sure. What I'm more interested in is how she learned we were at Westwind. I didn't tell anyone. Unless you did?'

'Only Shiloh. Mum and Dad might have guessed but they wouldn't say anything. Maybe Toby mentioned it in passing when he was out and about.' One thing was certain, Stirling wouldn't have. 'He enjoys a stir.'

'At my expense? Yours?'

'No. You're quite right.' Hurting Darcy would hurt Stirling, and while Toby might be cheeky, she couldn't see him being deliberately mean.

Lisette began scanning satchels. 'It's weird though, don't you think?'

It was, rather. With the front so heavily treed, Westwind wasn't visible from the road and Darcy had parked her Mini in the rear courtyard. Perhaps someone had seen them turn in through the gates, although how that amounted to an orgy was a question only Frances Green could answer.

'Are you going there now?' asked Lisette.

Darcy shook her head. 'No. To Hamilton. Mum has a late physio appointment. Speaking of which, do you need me to grab anything while I'm in town?'

'More condoms?'

Darcy laughed, although Lisette's quip made her realise she needed to do the same. 'Toby was that good?'

Lisette passed the lodgement receipt to Darcy and gathered up the parcels. 'Put it this way, I intend to go back for more.'

'So do I,' said Darcy, fluttering her hand below her throat and feigning breathlessness. 'So do I.'

Lisette laughed. 'Oh, Princess, you've got it *baaad*.'

Darcy lowered her head. 'I know.' She stared at the counter, mouth turned slightly down. Then her eyes slid up to meet Lisette's. For a second, she held them, then her hands flew into the air and she beamed. 'And isn't it just marvellous!'

Chapter Twenty-Eight

Stirling stood in Grassmoor's main street and eyeballed Mal's office. It was a simple brick building wedged between a charity shop and a business called Grassmoor Wool. The glass door had 'Malcolm McKenzie, Solicitor' embossed in gold on the front. Stirling regarded the paper he was holding and wondered again what the hell he was doing.

Besides the questionable wisdom of revealing his discovery to Mal, the drive in had made his leg ache. At Westwind the farm ute had given him no problems. He'd driven a couple of laps around the fountain, then a longer run past the sheds and back to prove he could change gears without trouble, and while he'd experienced a few twinges, Stirling was confident a short trip into Grassmoor would be straightforward. Except there was a big difference between a brief spin around a driveway and cycling up and down gears and parallel parking.

When Stirling had phoned the day before, Mal had warned that Thursday would be busy. A local cattle sale was the reason, apparently. Stirling had silently scoffed at the idea. Grassmoor was a tiny country town, not much more than a village. How could it ever be busy? Yet today it was. Farm vehicles hogged the parking spaces. There were even a couple of trucks with crates on the back. Here and there on the footpath and in the supermarket carpark, small groups of people stood in the morning sunshine, chatting.

He tapped the sticky-taped edge of the sheet against the ball of his fist and stared towards Joanne's cafe. Through the window he could see Tilly wiping down a table. Four doors past the cafe, forlorn and out of place, was Kildare Livestock Services. Its boarded windows staring blankly at the bustle.

The sound of a door opening had him looking up.

'Stirling,' said Mal, pulling the door wider and stepping aside. 'Come on in.'

'Mal.' Stirling paused at the threshold to shake Mal's hand. The other man's eyes shot to the paper Stirling held and his brow furrowed before smoothing. 'Thanks for seeing me at short notice.'

'Always happy to make room for Dougal's son.'

The office was neat and small, the walls a soothing cream, with a light veneer and glass counter at the front where perhaps a receptionist had once sat. As Mal had explained on the phone, he was meant to be retired but when locals kept calling for favours, he'd decided to work a few mornings a week.

'How are things at Westwind?' Mal asked now from behind his desk, picking up a silver fountain pen and rotating it between his fingers.

'Fine.' Stirling, seated opposite, kept the paper in his lap out of sight.

There was something not quite right about the solicitor's pose. A truly relaxed man would be leaned back, his body open. Mal was perched forward, like a hound sensing blood.

'I've had someone come and have look at the graffiti and stonework at last.'

'Good. It was terrible seeing it that way.'

Stirling took the inferred criticism on the chin. Mal was right. He should have dealt with the job earlier, but injury and uncertainty had left him uncharacteristically lax. Not anymore.

'You mentioned you found something?' said Mal.

With a slow exhale, Stirling unfolded the drawing and pushed it across the desk.

Mal's gaze skittered over the paper, then up at Stirling, his expression curiously lacking in surprise. A second scan changed that. He locked hard on the heart of the drawing, where the centre's name emblazoned the building. For a moment, Mal froze. Then his lips drew back, exposing teeth jammed as tightly as his fists. Colour suffused his neck and spread across his cheeks and a breath hissed between his locked jaw. The paper shook.

It was rage. Rage so tightly held it could burst a man.

Stirling tensed and planted his feet square on the floor. Readying himself in case Mal lashed out.

Except he didn't. As suddenly as it had appeared, Mal's rage vanished. Impassiveness returned. He was merely a simple country solicitor regarding a curious document.

He gave a small shrug. 'Interesting. Where did you find it?'

'In a pile of papers destined for the fire. You didn't know about it?'

'No.' Mal's eyes flickered again to the centre of the paper where his son's newly double-barrelled name was written. His gaze bored into Stirling. 'I had no idea.'

'Of Dougal's plan for a bush nursing centre, or the name he wanted to give it?'

Mal was silent for a few seconds, then, with deliberate movements, he began to fold the drawing, closing it down. 'Both. As for the name, I imagine that was an error on the artist's part.' He gestured at the sticky-taped edges. 'Probably why Dougal tore it up.'

Stirling nodded. Maybe that was the truth, maybe it wasn't. Mal's shock and rage at the centre's name was real. That the drawing existed had seemed less of a surprise. His manner now had Stirling's skin prickling.

Or was he reading too much into it?

He ran fingers across his forehead. 'Is it possible that this is what Dougal wanted the money for?'

'Very possible. Grassmoor has been lobbying for a nursing centre for years. Finally getting one up would be a coup.' Mal pressed down the final fold and pushed the plans away from him. He leaned back and hooked one leg over the other. 'Strange thing to do to a community though. Take with one hand and give with another.'

'I thought the same. According to the architects, he was waiting on finance for the centre.' Stirling grimaced. 'I guess the concept drawing was to give people an idea of his vision.'

'He never showed it to me.'

'Perhaps because he knew you'd be angry about the name.'

Mal's smile was as tight as his tone. 'Why would I be angry? He was honouring my son. The McKenzie-Kildare was obviously an error.'

'Maybe.'

Mal stared at him. Stirling held it. Dougal's secret glowing like hot coals between them. 'What are you trying to say, Stirling?'

He spread his hands. 'Look, Mal, I'm not here to cause trouble. I'm just trying to figure out what went wrong for Dougal.'

'He stole a great deal of money from people who trusted him and when he couldn't live with the shame, he killed himself. It's as simple and as tragic as that.'

Stirling shook his head, trying to work out where to go from here.

'You think there's more to it?' Mal prompted.

'I don't know. What I do think is that he wanted to build a nursing centre in Xavier's memory and needed money to do it. But to steal to get it? I'm struggling to reconcile that.'

'As are we all.'

Stirling reached for the paper and slid it towards himself, frowning. 'He must have been confident he could return it.'

'The money?'

'Yeah.' Dougal must have transferred it to some sort of investment. Something hard to trace that he could make a quick buck on and repay the capital back to his trust accounts before anyone noticed. It would have been a hell of a coup if he'd pulled it off, presenting funds to the community for a much-needed facility. He'd be a local hero. The question was, did he have that kind of knowledge? Dougal had some financial acumen—he ran a farm and a business after all—but enough for a no-risk, get-rich-quick scheme that would fly under the regulator's radar? Hard to believe.

Unless someone had done it for him. Someone he trusted implicitly.

Stirling regarded Mal. What had Darcy said about him? Something about him having done well working in finance.

His lungs hollowed out, like he'd been punched in the chest.

Stirling took a few seconds to compose himself then gathered the plans and rose. He needed to get out of here, away from the distrust crawling cockroach-like through his mind. Away from the intensity of Mal's stare.

'I've taken enough of your time,' he said.

Mal rose too. 'It's been no trouble.'

Stirling nodded and went to turn away, then stopped. Across the desk, Mal stiffened. One heartbeat passed. Two. Then three.

The words, when they came, were quiet. 'He must have loved Xavier very much to want to do this. On top of the memorial.'

'He was Xavier's godfather, as close to a son as he was going to get.' Mal smiled, seemingly oblivious to the needle of hurt his comment had thrust into Stirling. 'Thanks for showing me the plans. I'm sorry I couldn't be more help. Don't hesitate to call if you have any other questions.'

They shook hands, Stirling unsurprised to find Mal's grip firmer than on arrival.

'Take care at Westwind, Stirling. I've no doubt you're a capable man but as you've discovered,' he tipped his head to Stirling's leg, 'old farms can be dangerous places.'

The door clicked closed behind Stirling. He didn't need to turn around to know that Mal would be watching him, worrying. Let him worry. If Mal had anything to do with Dougal's death, anything to do with those missing funds, Stirling would dig until he found the truth. Threat or no threat.

Was he reading too much into Mal's parting words though?

What was a threat from a seventy-year-old, anyway? Stirling might not be the man he once was, but he was young, a trained soldier who'd seen more than his fair share of violence. Mal was a desk jockey, a soft-handed white-collar worker. What danger could he present?

Across the street, Joanne worked her cafe. Nearby, two men in wide-brimmed felt hats and checked shirts chatted to each other. A car passed, then a small courier van.

Life went on in Grassmoor. Stirling's remained at a standstill, burdened by the questions he had yet to find answers to.

And a gut-deep suspicion that refused to fade.

He glanced at the sky. The sun hovered directly overhead, the sky a magnificent springtime azure feathered with light cloud. He should drive back to Westwind, do something productive.

Except Darcy was close, and right now he needed the comfort of her glowing optimism.

He climbed into the ute, started the engine and pulled out into the street, unable to stop one last glance through the solicitor's window. Mal was nowhere to be seen.

Darcy's Mini occupied the parking space at the front of her home, as red and glossy as her lipstick. He pulled in behind, his heart already lightening.

He knocked on the door and waited, fists in his pockets. Faint strains of rock and roll filtered from inside, overlaid with a kind of stop-start whirr. One of her machines. A car slowed as it passed, the driver and passenger with their heads turned towards him.

Another half-minute passed. The song changed but the whirr went on. He paused, disappointed and unsure. Darcy was busy being creative. He shouldn't disturb her.

He really shouldn't.

Stirling's second knock silenced the whirr, then the door swung open and Darcy was in front of him, one hand cocked on her hip. For a heartbeat, her face was stern, then recognition brightened it like the sun. He opened his mouth to say 'Hi', only for Darcy to grab a fistful of his jumper. Next moment, she had dragged him inside and up against the wall, her chest pressed against his and one arm hauling his face to hers as she booted the door shut.

Any thought of Mal and threats disappeared, lost inside the passion of Darcy's kiss and the wriggle of her excited body against his.

This. This was why he was here. Why he needed her. The world could be ugly. Ugly, dangerous, vicious. Heavy with hurt and sorrow. But never in Darcy's orbit. She made the world a place where love and passion flourished.

'That was a hell of a welcome,' he said, when they finally came up for air. Stirling's chest pounded from lack of oxygen.

'I missed you. And you surprised me, and I do like a handsome surprise. What are you doing here anyway?' Darcy's eyes widened. 'Oh my goodness. Did I just slam the door in Toby's face? The poor man!'

Stirling laughed. 'No. I drove myself in.'

'Truly? But that's wonderful news.' She clapped and then winked. 'Must be all that sexual healing you've been getting.'

'Must be.' He stroked her face. She was immaculately made-up, except shorter from wearing flats instead of heels. 'I hope I haven't disturbed you.'

'You could never disturb me.' Darcy leaned her head to the side to kiss his hand then grabbed it. 'But I'm very glad you're here. Come on.' She led him towards her cutting table and arranged him nearby. 'Stay there.' A few seconds later, she had a measuring tape wrapped around his shoulders, a pencil tucked in her mouth and a notepad on standby.

'Are you planning on making me something?'

'Indeed I am.'

His gaze followed her every move as she measured and scribbled down numbers. He was stupid in love with this girl. 'I don't need you to sew for me, Darcy.'

'This isn't about need. This is about me wanting to.' She measured his chest, her eyes gleaming as she read the tape. 'Nice, but I already knew that.'

'You're nice.' He reached to drag her close, wanting to kiss her again. And more. A lot more. 'In fact, you're better than nice.'

'No, no.' She batted his hand away. 'Stay still.'

Although it pained him, Stirling obeyed. It was kind of sexy experiencing Darcy's professional attention, like being touched without being touched. Hints of her sweet scent wafted as she moved around his body. Her dress was tight and cut low, giving him a good view each time she leaned near. She was teasing him too. Stirling had been professionally measured before and Darcy seemed to be taking a lot longer than necessary.

'Okay, I'll bite. What are you measuring me for?'

'Nothing major. Just a drill cotton shirt for you to wear around the farm. Don't think you're too special though.' She tapped his nose lightly with her pencil. 'I make them for Shiloh and Dad. I'll embroider Westwind on yours of course, instead of Roseneath. Just so you know where you belong.'

Where he belonged …

Could he really belong at Westwind? Stirling wished he knew. One thing he did know was where he belonged right now, and that was with Darcy.

'Have you finished?' he asked.

'I think so.' She eyed him sideways. 'Why? Did you have something in mind?'

'Yeah,' he said, wishing his leg was strong enough that he could lift her in his arms and carry her to her room. Another time. Instead, he cupped the curve of her face with both hands and drank in her funny uniqueness. 'Only if you're not too busy.'

Her arms hooked around his neck and she leaned her hips into him in that way she had. 'For you, my handsome man? Never.'

Chapter Twenty-Nine

Stirling tossed his phone and the nursing centre drawing on the kitchen sideboard and grabbed a glass of water. He stood at the sink, his gaze out the window across the garden but his mind on Darcy. Her enthusiasm and energy, innate and addictive. Her lack of inhibition; a woman proud of her body and needs, eager to share and give pleasure. The way she looked at him, admiration and desire glittering her gaze, making him feel like the biggest and best of men.

It would be easy to blame his feelings on dopamine and oxytocin, but the way he felt was greater than hormones. This was deep. Soul-deep.

He stayed at the sink, staring towards the ranges to the drone of Toby steering a ride-on mower around the yard. He'd come to Westwind with the idea that by discovering who Dougal was, Stirling would find himself and from that work out his future. He might not yet have succeeded with his father, but a future existed. At Westwind. With Darcy.

Easy.

'Shit,' he said, gripping the sink edge.

He'd need a job. Not straight away. Stirling had enough money to keep himself going for a while and he needed to heal properly, but his joblessness couldn't be ignored.

Except what the hell could he do? Even if he could fly—and there were no guarantees that he'd ever be physically or mentally functional enough, and certainly not in high-risk environments— what pilot jobs existed in this rural corner anyway? Heavy labour was out of the question, at least for the medium term, and he had no other marketable skills. Not civilian ones.

He'd find something. Stirling might not have normal job credentials, but he was intelligent, resourceful, trustworthy, knew how to work in a team and was unafraid of a challenge. And there weren't too many who could name Alexander Maugham as a referee.

With a sigh, he headed out to find Toby.

Stirling found his friend at the far end of the house block, behind the last shed where the neglected yard was thick with spring grass and weeds, and old pines lined the boundary.

'I thought we agreed I'd take care of this,' said Stirling when Toby rode over and killed the mower.

Toby wrenched off his cap and wiped his sleeve across his brow. Dust and grass speckled his face and arms. 'Figured I'd save you the hassle.' He gave Stirling an up and down. 'How'd you go?'

For a moment Stirling thought he was referring to Darcy and was about to tell him to mind his own business, when he realised Toby meant Mal.

'He's involved.'

'How?'

'I wish I knew.' Stirling leaned against a pine tree and crossed his arms. 'My guess is he had something to do with the financials.'

Toby draped his arms over the steering wheel. 'What did he say about the name?'

'Refused to acknowledge it. Claimed it was an error.'

'Don't suppose you can blame him.'

'No. He knows I know about Xavier though.' Stirling picked up a pinecone, inspected its knobbly surface for he didn't know what and dropped it. 'He said something weird when I left.'

'Oh yeah?'

Stirling kicked at some pine mulch. 'It sounded like a threat.'

That had Toby sitting up. 'What sort of threat?'

'Just said for me to be careful around the farm. Accidents happen. As I've already discovered.'

Toby's nose crinkled and Stirling sensed his friend's doubt lingering in the air with the pine scent. 'Sounds more like advice than a threat.'

'Yeah.' Stirling scraped his hand over his head. 'Probably paranoia.' He let his hand fall. 'He showed no surprise about the centre though. That must mean something.'

'Or nothing.'

'Maybe,' said Stirling, then repeated the word on a sigh. He couldn't let go of the idea that there was more to Dougal's misconduct and possibly even his death.

'What are you going to do about it?'

'Keep digging.' What else could he do? If his gut was right and there had been foul play, Stirling could no more abandon seeking justice than he could have abandoned the MiZ mission and left those refugees to their fate.

'I figured as much. Watch your step, though. If you're right, then Mal could be a dangerous man, but if you're wrong ...' Toby gave him a look that suggested there were worse fates than confronting a murderer.

'I'd be making a mess of things in Grassmoor. Yeah, I know. I'll be careful.'

Toby said nothing for a moment then scanned the sky. The sun was heading west, the shadows lengthening. He patted the steering wheel. 'I should get on.'

'Leave it for tomorrow.'

Toby shook his head, his eyes not meeting Stirling's. 'I'm expected back at work Sunday,' he said. 'They're short-staffed and desperate, and I've got rent and a bike to pay for.'

Stirling blew out his breath. He'd known Toby couldn't stay forever but he'd tucked it to the back of his mind.

He gripped Toby's shoulder and gave it a shake. 'You don't have to explain. It was good of you to stay as long as you have.'

He'd liked having Toby around. He kept Westwind's ghosts quiet. Stirling would miss his easy company too. Other than Darcy, and he supposed Shiloh and Lisette, Stirling didn't know anyone else locally. There was Gav of course, but the older man lived seventy kilometres away and had a business to run.

'I can hang maybe an extra day or two if you need me to.'

'No. You get back to your life.' Stirling grinned to hide his disappointment. 'Darcy and I will make good use of the empty house.'

'I bet,' said Toby with a snigger and a glance at Westwind.

Stirling followed his gaze. The sun had fallen far enough to bathe the front in its glow and turn the pink stone to pale apricot. He hadn't asked for or earned Westwind, but it had buried its way into his heart the way Darcy had done with his soul.

He'd make this work. Somehow.

Toby drummed his fingers on the steering wheel, then looked up with his cheeky expression. 'We could arrange another barbecue?'

Stirling laughed and squeezed Toby's shoulder again. 'I'll check with Darcy for when Lisette is free.'

Neither the weather nor Lisette's schedule were on Toby's side. Both women were booked for a doe's night Friday, leaving only Saturday for Toby's barbecue and the forecast was so dismal they'd have to do something inside instead. With time to kill, Stirling spent Friday morning on a video call with his mum. Aware of how tough Stirling's year had been, Amanda's eyes had glistened when he talked about Darcy and his hopes for the future.

He then took a deep breath and did what he should have done a week ago. When he finally managed to speak to the police officer in charge of Dougal's case, it soon became obvious that while the investigation was technically ongoing, solving it was not a priority.

'It's the problem with shell companies set up in tax havens,' said the officer, a woman named Phillipa Tan. 'Secrecy provisions can make it nigh on impossible to crack who the ultimate owner is. In this case it's a chain of companies. Think of it like a stack of matryoshka dolls. You open one, only to find another beneath.'

Apparently, Dougal had been sending money in increments to one of these companies. Smaller amounts at first, then larger, as though he'd been testing the waters before diving right in. From there, the money had come and gone before finally disappearing.

'Wouldn't setting that up take specialist knowledge?' asked Stirling.

'Yes and no. It's a simple process, but you need a legitimate address in the haven of your choice and for that you need a service provider. Which isn't as hard as you think. There's a building in the

Caymans that's the registered address for nearly twenty-thousand shell companies.'

'Sounds expensive.'

'Not really. Maybe a thousand dollars, plus the annual fee to your nominee director.'

Stirling's eyebrows rose. Surely a specialist legal or accounting firm wouldn't be that cheap?

'Dougal's set-up was complex though,' Phillipa continued. 'He's had advice—expert advice—and that always costs. Except we've found no outgoings or receipts for anything like that.'

'So how did it come about then?'

'My gut feeling? He was suckered into a scam and they did the legwork to give credence to the deal. There are plenty about. Schemes offering tenfold returns on an investment, playing on people's greed. Dougal probably thought he could use the trust money to earn hyper profits, return it before anyone realised, and keep the difference.'

'Surely he wasn't that stupid? I mean, I never met the man but from what I can gather he was smart, successful. Seems out of character.'

'It's money,' said Phillipa. 'People can behave in all sorts of uncharacteristic ways when it comes to money. Was there anything else?'

There was plenty: the nursing centre concept and its connection with the missing trust money, Mal and Dougal's fault-filled relationship, Stirling's disquiet over Dougal's death.

'One thing,' he said, frowning at the folded nursing centre design on the sideboard. 'The companies or funds or whatever had to revert to someone on Dougal's death. Who benefits?'

'No one. They're the proceeds of crime.'

'But if they weren't?'

'You tell me.' Phillipa's tone lowered, suspicion creeping through her slow reply. 'Maybe it'd be you.'

'Like I said, I never even met the man.'

'Yet Dougal left his family's historic property to you. A curious thing in itself, don't you think?'

'Yeah, I do. Which is why I'm trying to figure him out.'

He thanked Phillipa for her time, hung up and stared at the screen of his open laptop. Could Mal be the ultimate beneficiary? In which case, what did he plan to do with the money once he liberated it? Not build a nursing centre, that much was obvious.

Stirling rubbed at his forehead, mulling over his next step. Perhaps Alexander could help. He would understand this stuff or know someone who could explain it better, but Alexander had more important things to do than chase riddles based on Stirling's gut feelings.

He let it go and spent a pleasant boys' afternoon with Toby, pulling the Indian to pieces and laying each part out in perfect order on a giant stretch of canvas, while both of them made semi-serious jokes about their ability to put it back together again.

Saturday morning brought the bureau's promised blustery change, with the wind dragging nasty little rain clouds up from the coast that seemed determined to dump their loads right over Westwind.

With an outdoor party off the cards, Stirling and Toby rearranged the lounge, bringing a velvet sofa forward to join its heavy leather mate in front of the fire, and placing a coffee table in the centre. They'd taken an early run to Hamilton for supplies, after which Stirling had amused himself in the kitchen, making a lasagne fit to feed ten that he'd serve with a simple green salad. Dessert was store-bought chocolate mousse. There was a limit to Stirling's enthusiasm for kitchen slavery.

The girls turned up at six thirty, bearing bottles and more food, Darcy resplendent in a pair of ankle-length blue pants and a white shirt tied at the waist. A hint of lacy white bra showed through the shirt. Stirling would bet the Ducati that her knickers matched.

'Hair of the dog,' said Lisette, passing a bottle of sparkling wine to Toby to open and kissing him hello. 'God, I need it too.'

Stirling relieved Darcy of a cane basket loaded with chips, biscuits, cheeses and dips and gave her a lengthy welcome kiss. She tasted of toothpaste and smelled of Darcy-ness. 'What about you? Feeling okay after your doe's night?'

'Now that I'm here, yes.' She linked her arms around his neck, arching into him, and dropped her voice to low huskiness. 'Bed wasn't the same last night without you in it.'

'Same for me.' Stirling pressed his forehead to hers, his gaze gulping her in. 'We'll make up for it tonight.'

Her thumbs caressed the soft spot beneath his ears, eyes twinkling with promise. 'We most certainly will.'

They settled in front of the fire with drinks and Darcy's nibbles, laughing at Lisette's recap of the doe's night misadventures—most of which appeared to be hers. The fire crackled cosily while Dougal's music played in the background. Stirling didn't miss the way Toby kept close to Lisette, or the way he looked at her.

Neither did Darcy. She leaned in close. 'It's a shame Toby has to leave.'

'Yeah. He'll be back though. It's not far and we have a motorbike to finish restoring.'

'Good.' She hesitated a moment, then braced. 'And you? Have you decided what you're doing?'

Stirling stared into his beer then into her hopeful gaze. He wanted to promise her the world but he needed to sort himself out first. Letting her down would be worse. 'I'm working on it.'

'Oh.' Her voice took on a false cheer. 'I'm sure you'll figure it out.'

'I want to.' He felt for her hand. 'There's a lot here I like.'

That made Darcy's tight smile loosen. She touched a finger to his chin, drawing him towards her. 'There's a lot here I like too.'

The kiss had Stirling's heart somersaulting.

'Oh, get a room,' Lisette scolded, as a hunk of something pinged off Stirling's head and bounced onto the floor.

'We just might,' said Darcy, standing and pulling Stirling up with her.

Toby widened his eyes. 'You can't. There's lasagne.' He faced Lisette, panic making his voice high. 'Felix makes awesome lasagne.'

'In that case,' said Stirling, 'we'd better eat so I can take Darcy to bed.'

Which earned him another pock of cheddar to the head and a 'bloody rabbits' sledge from Lisette.

As it turned out, they didn't get to bed until late. There was dancing, sparked by Tina Turner singing 'Nutbush City Limits' and Lisette squealing about how her nanna taught her the dance as a little girl, followed by a demand that everyone join in. A cutthroat game of poker with matchsticks as stakes followed, but at Lisette's suggestion they turn it into strip poker—enthusiastically endorsed by Toby—Darcy announced that if there was any undressing to be done, it would happen in the privacy of Stirling's bedroom, thank you very much.

Leaving Lisette and Toby to their own games, Stirling followed Darcy up the stairs to be happily entertained by Darcy's personal version of strip poker. With matching underwear.

Morning brought a cool but clear day and favourable riding conditions for Toby's journey back to Melbourne. Stirling and

Darcy cooked a late breakfast that everyone enjoyed in the sparkling sunken garden, and at one o'clock, Toby declared he needed to hit the road.

Stirling swallowed as Toby spun two laps of the fountain then headed down the drive with a wave. Lisette left in her own car soon after, leaving Darcy and Stirling holding hands on the verandah.

'I need to get going too,' said Darcy. 'I promised Shiloh I'd help clean the house. She and Dad don't have time and Mum's been fretting over it and trying to do too much.'

'Is she getting better?'

'She is. It's slow though, and she tires easily. Speaking of which, we'll have you up for dinner soon. Mum wants to meet you and I know Dad would appreciate the male company.'

He nodded. It was past time he met Darcy's mum and one brief introduction to her father wasn't enough either. 'You'll come back tonight?'

'Of course.' She nestled closer and fiddled with the buttons on his shirt. 'I can't have my investment getting lonely.'

But lonely was exactly how Stirling felt after she'd gone and he was left in an echoing, empty mansion, devoid of warmth, with secrets crouched in every corner.

He killed a bit of time stripping the bed in Toby's room and tossing the sheets over the end of the stairwell to watch them float like ghosts to the ground. The towels went on top. He descended the stairs, collected the washing and carried it into the laundry for tomorrow. The weather was forecast to be fine again and though it'd easier to use the dryer, Stirling had always loved the smell of line-dried sheets.

He began tidying the remains of their party off the kitchen table—biscuit containers to the pantry, unopened wine to a shelf, a copy of the local *Grassmoor Gazette* that Darcy had brought in her basket.

It was only when he went to plug his phone into the power point above the sideboard that Stirling realised the nursing centre plans weren't where he'd tossed them.

Had they fallen on the floor and slid underneath the sideboard? Except, grunting down on his knees to check, he found nothing on the floor but dust and crumbs. Neither was it caught between the sideboard and the wall.

'Odd,' he muttered.

Too odd.

He stood, clenching and unclenching his fists as he tried to visualise where he'd last seen the plans. They'd definitely been on the sideboard when he'd spoken to Philippa Tan because he remembered staring at them. After that, Stirling didn't know.

His search became purposeful. He turned over everything in the kitchen. Then, thinking perhaps one of the girls had found the plans and moved them elsewhere, he checked the kindling baskets in the kitchen and lounge. Once, then twice. He checked the bins, inside the house and out.

The mudroom followed, then the library. Then every room in Westwind.

The plans were gone. Either accidentally burned—which Stirling doubted—or they'd been taken.

The question was by whom.

Chapter Thirty

'Well, hello, Mistress Lissy,' said Darcy, smiling at Lisette as she waltzed through Darcy's front door with bags of what was no doubt naughtiness. 'To what do I owe this pleasure?'

'Someone has to make sure you don't work all night.' Lisette peered down her nose. 'Don't you look at me like that, Princess. I know you.'

Despite no more advertising, VaVoom's continued abundance of orders had begun to give Darcy mild anxiety. Before Stirling, she simply would have worked in the evenings to keep on top. Now she willingly gave that time to him. But Darcy had a business to run and while she didn't regret a second of her heavenly nights at Westwind, she would not let VaVoom slide for anyone, even the man she adored.

'Besides,' said Lisette, 'I have gossip. Well, not really gossip. More something ... creepy.' She headed for the kitchen, talking over her shoulder. 'Frozen chicken Kievs and a packet salad, in case you're interested.'

Darcy was always interested in a chicken Kiev. 'Thanks. You're a darling.'

'I know.'

Darcy laughed and headed back to her cutting board where she was laying out fabric for five pairs of delightfully summery, pink and white stretch gingham capri pants with a sweet broderie anglaise trim edging the pockets and cuffs. Three size fourteens, one size eight, and a sixteen and eighteen. It thrilled her no end that her designs appealed to such a wide range of women.

Lisette knew where everything was and the sooner Darcy got back to work, the earlier she could finish. If business kept up at this pace, the Janome 1200D overlocker she so coveted would soon no longer be a fancied desire but a reality.

'What's this gossip then?' asked Darcy when Lisette returned from the kitchen with two glasses of chardonnay.

They toasted one another and sipped, then Lisette settled onto a stool. 'Dearest Frances came in after you left this afternoon. She bought a box of Christmas cards, can you believe?'

'I find it harder to accept the idea that you already have them in stock. It's only October.'

'I know, I know.' Lisette waved a hand. 'We are but flotsam in the sea of our postal service's whims.'

Darcy grinned at the extravagant metaphor and returned to pattern-matching the side seams of the first pair of capris.

'Anyway, she ever-so-sweetly asked if we enjoyed our sleepover at Westwind on Saturday night.'

Darcy looked up. 'How did she know we were there?' Her stomach lurched as Lisette's specific words hit home. 'More importantly, how did she know we stayed over?'

'Exactly.'

'Did you ask?'

Lisette nodded and sipped some wine, her legs swinging against the stool rail. 'She just looked at me as though I was mad and said that everyone was aware of our,' she used her fingers to put air quotes around her next words, '"recent shenanigans".'

'That's ...' Darcy hunted for the word to describe how she felt. While the women at Friday night's doe's party knew about Darcy's relationship with Stirling because she hadn't denied it when the subject was raised, the news that she and Lisette were at Westwind again on Saturday night and stayed over was specific. Too specific.

'Creepy?' filled in Lisette. 'Not as creepy as Katrina Hettich coming in five minutes later warning me to be careful who I make friends with.'

'*Pardon?*'

'Uh huh,' said Lisette, nodding. 'She absolutely did.'

Darcy opened her mouth to voice her outrage and found she was at a complete loss for words. Frances's nastiness was a given and Katrina could snipe like a champion when the mood took her, but this was another level.

'What did you say?' Darcy managed finally.

'I played innocent and acted all offended and said that I'd known you since I was a baby, and it was far too late for being careful with my friendship. She went all spluttery and said that she didn't mean you, but your new ...' Lisette made air quotes again and rolled her eyes, '... "boyfriend". So I said, what's wrong with Stirling? And she made this snorty noise and said that we shouldn't take him at face value, then she did this weird puppet-head nod like she knew something no one else did. It was seriously creepy. Which is saying something because, let's face it, Katrina can be bloody weird at the best of times.'

'That's just ...' Darcy was too stunned to finish.

'Creepy.' Lisette slugged a mouthful of wine as though the thought needed washing away.

Darcy leaned on her palms and regarded her friend with angled brows. 'Is someone spying on us?'

'I wondered the same, but surely not. I mean, why would they? Anyway, it's no secret you and Stirling have a thing going. People are going to guess you stay over. Frances is a bitch who gets her thrills winding you up while Katrina's probably still knicker-twisting over what Dougal did to Jayden and needs to take it out on someone.'

'Katrina and Frances I'm used to. It's the thought of someone keeping tabs on us that's disturbing.' A sick realisation curdled in Darcy's stomach. 'Unless it's not us that's the target.'

'You mean Stirling?'

'Yes. But that begs the same question as before. Why?'

'Maybe,' said Lisette, cocking her head, 'that's something you should ask him.'

'I,' said Darcy, rising out of her Mini and kissing Stirling on the mouth, 'come bearing gifts.'

Amusement lit his eyes. 'Is that right?'

'It is indeed.' Darcy was ripe with smugness. Not only had she made a solid dent in her order overflow these last two days, she'd snuck time in on Stirling's shirt. She poked him playfully in the chest. 'You just wait.' He laughed and stood aside as she retrieved a basket from the boot. 'I also brought dessert.'

Arms circled her waist from behind. Stirling's lips pressed against the soft skin of her neck, his nuzzles shooting electricity straight to her lady parts. 'There I was, hoping you were dessert.'

That made her smile. 'I'm more the chocolate on top.'

'On top? I like the sound of that.'

She twirled in his arms to face him. 'You like the sound of anything like that.'

'And you don't?'

'Like it? Oh, goodness no.' She smiled and tapped his nose. 'I love it.'

They kissed, long and slow and sexy and loaded with promise. Then, hand in hand, headed into the warmth of the kitchen. Though spring had well and truly made itself felt, the evenings still cooled rapidly, especially on the shadowy eastern side of the house. Too cold for Darcy and her sapphire cap-sleeved wiggle dress with deep V-neckline and contrasting ruby tunic collar and kick pleat. A flattering dress designed to remind Stirling what he'd missed these last two nights.

'Potato bake,' said Stirling when Darcy's nose twitched at the delicious aromas of the kitchen. 'There's also lamb cutlets and vegetables. Hope that's okay.'

'Sounds beautiful.' She bumped his shoulder. 'We girls do love a domesticated man.'

He was too. The kitchen was tidy, the dishes done and clean tea towels folded over the rails. Stirling's laptop was open on the end of the table, his phone and a notebook alongside.

'Working on something?' she asked, setting her basket on the bench.

'Nothing much. Just a few notes.' He crossed to the laptop and closed the lid, then set the notebook on top and placed the lot onto the sideboard. Darcy frowned. She had the distinct feeling Stirling was hiding something but when he turned to face her there was nothing but warmth. 'How was your day? That's a sexy dress, by the way.'

Her heart gave a little skip that he'd noticed. Darcy ran her hands down her hips. 'Thank you. It's a favourite. Not quite as favourite as a certain, now sadly demised, wiggle dress, but ...' She held out her palms and brought them together prayer-like. 'It was sacrificed for the greater good. To answer your question, flat out. Every time I think I'm in front, another rush of orders comes in. Although I did manage to finish one important task.' She reached into the basket and withdrew a glossy red box. 'For you.'

Stirling took the box, looked at it and then at her with one eyebrow raised.

'Open it.'

A layer of red tissue paper lay underneath the lid, the wrapping sealed with one of her VaVoom stickers. He lifted the package out, his dimple hollowing as if he found the perfect presentation amusing.

Carefully, he split the sticker and peeled back the paper to expose the contents: a beautifully folded and pressed work shirt in an olive-green drill cotton to match his eyes, with a half-placket buttoned front, two chest pockets with button-down flaps, and *Westwind* embroidered on the right breast in pale gold.

The dimple disappeared. For a long moment, Stirling stared, then he traced a finger over the embroidery and looked at her as if to check it was really his.

She nodded, her hands wringing at his expression—a kind of awe mixed with gratitude and something intense yet soft. Something she desperately hoped was more than gratitude. 'Try it on.'

Stirling stripped off his jumper and polo. Unlike his scarred legs, he had no self-consciousness about his chest. With good reason. It was an excellent chest. Smooth, muscled and with just enough smattering of hair to be masculine and sexy.

He pulled the shirt from the box, fluffed it to open the ends, and shoved his head inside.

Darcy laughed as Stirling quickly became stuck. 'Not like that!' Truly, what was it with men and their impatience? She unbuttoned the collar and did the same with the cuffs. 'There. Now you can pull it on.'

Seconds later, he had the shirt on properly and was admiring himself as Darcy fussed around, double-checking the finish. Not bad after a single fitting, but she'd learned a lot about his body these past few weeks. It would have been galling to get it wrong.

'What do you think?' she said, standing back. She'd been right about the colour. It made his dark-lashed eyes pop even more.

'It's great. Really great. Thank you.' He fingered the half placket. 'I like this. Fewer buttons to worry about.'

'There's a reason they're designed that way. It means you don't have shirttails to get caught in machinery or on fences.'

He nodded his approval. 'Clever.'

'I'll make you some more now I know the fit is right. One for every day of the week.'

'Darcy …'

She held up her palm. 'No arguing. I want to.'

'I know you do but you have a business to run. There are probably more like this in Dougal's cupboards.'

No doubt there were. None had been made by Darcy though. None had her love and hope infused in every stitch.

She lifted her chin. 'You can't stop me.'

'No, I can't.' He stepped closer and cupped her cheek, his voice low. 'You know what?'

'What?'

'I don't think I want to either.'

'Then you and I will get on just fine.'

'Funny,' he leaned nearer until his breath caressed her lips, 'I thought we already were. I can turn the oven off.'

Darcy's head nod was like her heartbeat, rapid and barely controlled. 'You do that.'

It wasn't until much later, when Darcy was helping to dry the dinner dishes, that she remembered his question from Sunday night.

'Did you ever find that paperwork you were looking for?'

His hands stilled in the sink for a moment before resuming their scrubbing. 'No.'

'Oh.' Though he hadn't said what it was, she'd had the impression it was important. 'I could ask Lisette again, if you like.'

He shook his head. 'Don't worry about it. I suspect it's long gone.'

She'd dried two saucepans before she spoke again, and even then her voice was hesitant. 'You don't think someone could have come in and taken it?'

Stirling jerked around. 'What makes you ask that?'

'Oh, nothing.' She set down the ceramic baking dish and sighed. 'Actually, that's not true. I wasn't going to mention it, but the truth is I'm a bit bothered.'

'About what?'

She rested her hip against the bench and twisted the tea towel. 'There's been a bit of gossip. About how Lisette and I stopped over on Saturday night.'

'How would anyone know that?'

'Exactly our thoughts. I can understand the assumption that I stayed over—you and I are hardly a secret—but how would anyone know about Lisette? She hasn't said anything and neither have I. And Toby couldn't have let it slip. He left on Sunday. It's very strange.'

'Yes.' Stirling's narrowed gaze switched to the darkness outside the window, his hands once more still in the suds and his voice slow and distant. 'It is.'

'Stirling,' Darcy kept her voice careful, 'is it possible someone's spying on Westwind?'

She'd expected an immediate denial, or at least an indulgent smile at her silliness. Instead his face was shuttered, rigid, his body the same, as though he was concentrating on something far away. Darcy glanced at the window and saw nothing but an impenetrable black night behind the reflection of kitchen lights.

She eyed him worriedly. Gone was the soft greeny-hazel gaze. His eyes now were pure steel, his facial muscles iron hard.

'Stirling?'

Suddenly the sponge was swishing through the water and he was back to normal. 'Sorry. Zoned out for a moment. Someone spying on Westwind?' He smiled. 'I suppose anything's possible but I wouldn't think so. Nothing here to spy on.'

But the falseness in his voice had her wondering.

Chapter Thirty-One

Stirling clenched his teeth against the ache in his legs as he made his way up the slope from the creek paddock. He wasn't thrilled with the heaviness of his breathing either. There was a time when a short hill like this would barely change his heartbeat, but that was before, when he was fit and unbroken.

He shook the thought away. He wasn't broken. Scarred, yes. Out of condition too. Still healing. But broken? No. He understood that now. Darcy had given him that, with her words and whispers and admiration and encouragement. She'd looked at his scars and despite their ugliness, accepted them as part of him. Sometimes, when he was feeling slushy and sweet with love, like a half-melted ice cream, he wondered if her gentle touch had helped heal them faster.

Which made him snort. Darcy was many things, but a saint she wasn't. Thank god.

He was definitely improving. While still painful, the ache in his legs and across his hips were nowhere near as severe as they once were and his fitness he would work on. It took nothing but a laid-out towel and some grunt to do a core workout and the sheds were crammed with heavy objects he could use as substitute weights. If push came to shove, he'd order himself a home gym. Someone might even have one for sale locally. One of the spare rooms upstairs could be converted into a workout space easily enough or he could move the Ducati and set up under the porch. Which might be the better option given the coming summer. Westwind had no air conditioning.

Stirling smiled to himself. He seemed to be making a lot of plans lately.

Darcy again.

He pushed open the door to the mudroom and sat on the bench to remove his boots. His gaze met the laundry and Stirling reminded himself he'd need to do some washing tomorrow morning. The weather was fine and forecast to stay that way for the next four or five days. He hoped so. Helmut had applied the first of the graffiti treatments yesterday. Now the front facade was covered in poultices, giving it the unfortunate countenance of a teenager after a bad shave with a blunt razor.

According to Helmut, temperature could impact the efficacy of the solvent. It was like Goldilocks, needing it just right. Even then results could vary and Stirling wasn't to get his hopes too high. Stirling had accepted Helmut's warnings with equanimity. Anything had to be better than its current ugliness.

He set the boots under the bench and wandered into the kitchen. The room was warm from the sun streaming through the window over the sink and the range, turned low during daytimes now they were milder. He picked up a glass from the drainer, filled it from the tap and contemplated the garden. That would be his next project, for no other reason than it would give him something else to look at. Something that grew and changed. It'd also impress Darcy's grandmother, who was not only a gun seamstress but also, he'd learned during dinner at Roseneath on Friday four nights ago, a handy gardener and the architect of much of Roseneath's impressive landscaping.

It'd impress Darcy too. He might even impress himself.

Dinner had been an experience. Big family dinners hadn't been on the agenda when he was growing up. With his mother an only child and her remaining relatives scattered all over the country, family was in short supply. There'd been celebrations with his grandparents and parties with his mum's friends when Stirling was a small boy, but not everyday family dinners. The closest he'd come had been during weekend and holiday trips to the country homes of boarding school mates, and those dinners had nothing on the harmony and warmth of the Sloanes. They were a family who loved and looked out for one another, and with their gentle quizzing of Stirling about his life, they were clearly, albeit subtly, looking out for Darcy.

Stirling hadn't minded. He'd expected a grilling and had girded himself for it. Darcy's mum had been the wariest. Not rude, but not warm either. It could have been fatigue from her illness, yet Stirling's gut told him it was suspicion. He'd done his best to allay Rachel's fears and her smile by evening's end, along with a return invitation and happy beams from Darcy, made him think he'd succeeded.

He guzzled the rest of the water, set the glass back on the drainer and headed to the end of the table where he'd left his laptop open in preparation for a chat with his mum. Assuming she could get satellite access.

He stopped and stared. The screen was lit and displaying its login page. Stirling frowned. The laptop should have been asleep. The only way to trigger the computer out of hibernation was to press a key or touch the mousepad.

An itch formed along the base of his neck and crawled down his back. He surveyed the room. It was as he'd left it—neat and clean with no papers lying about. He'd been careful of that since the plans had disappeared. What he hadn't been careful about was locking the doors. He did whenever he left Westwind but not while he was on the property.

Finding nothing amiss, he stepped into the hall.

'Darcy?'

Except it wouldn't be her. Darcy had too much work on and unless she'd left something behind, there was no reason for her to be here.

The itch worsened. Stirling glanced again at the kitchen. Nothing but the screen aglow with blue warning. His eyes narrowed. Fists clenched, he forced his breath slow and measured. Treading carefully, Stirling stalked the hall, reconnoitring rooms as he passed.

His head snapped up as a creak sounded above the main stairwell. He remained frozen, ears tuned for any further movement, gaze running back and forth along the ceiling. It could be something. It could be nothing. Quiet noise was a Westwind constant, especially in the wind. The day, though, was calm. Stirling listened several seconds longer and moved on.

With all the downstairs rooms cleared, he moved upward.

One room, then the next. He took extra time in his—Dougal's— room, checking every surface from the bedside table to the bathroom for anything out of place, even sniffing the air for a trace of unfamiliar aftershave. All he could smell was his sandalwood bodywash.

By the time he stood outside the main bathroom, Stirling was feeling more than a bit stupid. Still, he was upstairs and only a few more rooms remained. He may as well finish the job.

When both were cleared, he returned to the landing and scraped his hand over his head. No one was here and most probably no one had been. Darcy's question about being spied on had him jumping at shadows. It'd be laughable if it weren't so worrying. This wasn't a warzone, and he wasn't a soldier. He hadn't been one of those for a long time. Old habits though.

He strode for the stairs. He needed to get his shit together. Get healthy enough to secure his medical clearance to fly again. A bit of research had revealed there was offshore work, flying workers out to gas platforms. Aeromedical jobs too, although he wasn't so keen on those.

Stirling had one leg stretched out to take the first step when he heard the quiet click of a door closing. The mudroom. Had to be. Not trusting his leg or hip to a headlong rush down the stairs, he slid down the banister on his belly and belted up the hall to the kitchen, skidding on his socks as he took the corner.

The kitchen was empty. His laptop screen had returned to hibernation. Not a single sign that anyone had been there. Except Stirling had heard that sound. This wasn't paranoia.

He stumbled for the courtyard, knocking over a chair and crashing the door into the wall when he flung it open. His leg burning, he limped to the end of the paving and stood in the drive scanning the tracks to the shed and creek paddock, then the road to the other sheds. Finding nothing and ignoring the stones digging into the soles of his bootless feet, he hobbled to the front of the house. The carriageway was empty. With a growl, Stirling made his way more slowly to the side of the house and to the garden, then circled.

Westwind was an old property, flush with sheds, farm machinery, thick-trunked trees and dense shrubs. There were a hundred places to hide.

'I know you're here!'

For a few seconds, the countryside held its breath, then noise started again. Birds and insects and animals and trees and breeze. The rustles and bustles of nature turning its back on the madness of man.

Not a hint of human sound.

Yet Stirling could still feel laughter.

Chapter Thirty-Two

Stirling locked the back door and pocketed the key.

Gavin shot him a grin. 'Hard to get out of those city bloke habits, eh?'

'Something like that,' he said, although his security consciousness had nothing to do with habit and locking up was only one of a few protections he'd enforced. Not that he'd be telling Gavin about those. He hadn't even told Darcy.

What good it would do, Stirling wasn't convinced. The house had been locked the morning he and Toby had gone grocery shopping in Hamilton, and still the nursing centre drawing had gone missing. If Mal had a key, which was entirely possible given his close relationship with Dougal, the only way to keep him out would be to change the locks.

He scanned his surrounds as had become his habit over the past week. There'd been no repeat of last Tuesday's intrusion but that didn't mean his trespasser wasn't out there.

'Everything all right?' asked Gavin, eyeing him sideways as they walked to the shed where they planned to spend a few mindful hours cleaning Indian parts, assessing what they could recondition and what they'd need to find replacements for.

'Fine,' said Stirling.

Gavin said nothing for several steps. 'You seem a bit on edge.'

Darcy had said the same only the day before. Stirling needed to work on his acting skills.

Stirling shrugged. 'Just figuring out what I'm doing with myself.'

Gavin stopped. 'You're thinking about staying on then? Good on you, lad.' He patted Stirling's shoulder. 'Good on you.' He resumed his pace. 'That Darcy, eh? She's a woman to make any man want to settle down. Lucky bastard.'

Stirling shook his head and tried not to laugh. Gavin hadn't allowed Stirling any time to protest his assumption. Besides, he was right. The plan was to stay, make a home, a peaceful life. Once he'd sorted a job and got this threat out of the way.

If it was a threat.

Stirling maintained his vigilance as they continued to the shed, although he hoped with more subtlety. Maybe no one had been in the house. Maybe no one had touched his laptop or clicked the door closed. Maybe he'd been made paranoid by the layers of inconsistencies surrounding Dougal's death, when that's all they were, inconsistencies. Not proof. Not fact. Just anomalies that might never be explained. After all, strange coincidences occurred daily around the world in everyday life. Why not at Westwind too?

Gavin proved to be the perfect panacea for his worries. The man was full of stories, from his rideshare-driving adventures to his glory days racing motocross. He was interested in Stirling's life too, asking all sorts of questions about his career and experiences. Stirling didn't mind. Gavin was easy to talk to and he appreciated the distraction, so it was with some disappointment that he farewelled his new-found friend around eleven. Gavin's business was most active in the afternoons and evenings, Hamilton was a forty-five-minute drive away, and a man had to earn his keep.

Stirling fiddled with the Indian a while longer but the joy had gone from the task. The hunched pose as he'd used a toothbrush to scrub the carburettor had taken a toll. Stirling's back and hips ached, and he needed a stretch. A walk before lunch would set him up for the rest of the day and, if the aches weren't too bad, he'd take the Ducati for a test run. Maybe ride into Grassmoor and surprise Darcy.

The thought made him smile.

Stirling was three-quarters of the way down the hill heading towards the creek when he noticed movement at Xavier's monument. He paused and watched for a moment, the corner of his lip lifting as he confirmed his visitor's identity.

'Stirling,' said Mal when he arrived at the edge of the glade. The clearing resounded with birdsong and the soft gurgle of the creek. Happy tunes at odds with the tension thickening the air. 'Good to see you.'

'Mal.'

After a quick shake of hands, Mal eyed him up and down. 'Still a bit of a limp there.'

The comment irritated, though Stirling didn't show it. He'd been at pains to keep his gait steady, determined not to show weakness, but Mal had been observing Stirling as closely as he'd been observing Mal. 'It's getting better.'

'Of course. The young heal easier than old men like me.' Mal glanced at the memorial, pain corrugating his brow and deepening the crow's feet around his eyes. 'Not all, though.' He looked at Stirling and grimaced. 'Sorry. It still hurts, even after all this time.'

Stirling nodded. That Mal had adored Xavier wasn't in question. Unlike the crocodile tears he shed for Dougal, his grief for his son was real.

Mal rested a hand on the angel's foot and stroked the toe with his thumb. 'I didn't mean to disturb you. Xavier always enjoyed spring. And summer.' He gestured at the vast dome of clear sky above them. 'It seemed an appropriate day to visit.'

'No need to apologise and it's me disturbing you. I was out for a walk and saw you here.'

'Checking that Shiloh's looking after your land?'

Interesting how much Mal knew about Westwind. Then again, anyone could have mentioned Shiloh's lease to him, and any news about Stirling or Westwind was bound to be gossiped about.

'Just exercise. Shiloh knows more about looking after stock and land than I ever will.'

'More than likely. She's a clever girl. They both are.'

Stirling had no intention of discussing Darcy with this man. He lapsed into silence and let nature fill the void. Mal's dark green four-wheel drive stood across the other side of the creek, partly hidden by the trees. There must be a bridge or causeway where Mal could cross. Stirling made a mental note to check that out later— and the road leading to the parking area. That both were hidden from the house made his scalp prickle.

'I had a call from Phillipa Tan a few days ago,' said Mal. His tone was conversational but there was an iciness in his eyes that had Stirling's prickles biting deeper. 'Do you know her?'

Stirling said nothing.

'She's the officer in charge of Dougal's fraud case. I missed the call unfortunately. I can't imagine why she'd need to contact me.'

Stirling shrugged as if it was obvious. 'You're Dougal's solicitor.'

Mal gave a tight smile. 'Was.'

Stirling kept watch, studying Mal's every move. The man was hunting as much as he was hunted. Hunting for a sign that Phillipa's inquiry was because of Stirling. Feeling hunted from her renewed interest and the suspicion Stirling had him in his sights. Good. Stirling wanted him uneasy. An uneasy man was more likely to make mistakes.

Mal rocked on his heels, his mouth pursed as he regarded Stirling. 'It made me wonder if they're taking another look at Dougal's case.'

'I hope they are. That money went somewhere, and I'm still not convinced he had the skill to pull off that kind of sophisticated scheme.'

'Not that sophisticated.'

Stirling blinked. He sounded almost amused, almost braggardly. And how did Mal know it wasn't sophisticated?

Mal looked up towards the house. 'Maybe she'd be better off talking to you? Dougal left you Westwind. That's quite an inheritance.'

'Nothing to do with me, and I can't see how that has any bearing on the fraud he committed. I never knew anything about Dougal except that he and my mother had a brief affair and I was the result.' He let that sink in. 'This Phillipa is probably as curious as I am about the reasons why a man of Dougal's standing committed fraud. It's the one question that really puzzles me. It must you too.' He let a heartbeat pass before adding, 'Being his close friend.'

'Of course. But I've also learned, to my distress, that Dougal had his secrets.' Something flashed behind Mal's eyes. 'You being one of them.' He straightened. 'It's good that you're trying to get to know him. He'd be proud of that.'

'Only natural. He was my father, and I guess he must have wanted it if he left me this place.' It was something Stirling hadn't considered before but now it seemed obvious.

'Yes, perhaps that's why he did it.' Mal curved his hand again over the angel's foot. 'It's a special bond between a father and son.'

Stirling didn't have a reply for that. He wasn't sure it was true in his case. His need to know about Dougal was driven by a need to understand himself and where he now stood in the world. That, and his hatred for injustice—and if his gut was right, Dougal had suffered the worst of injustices.

But it seemed Dougal had wanted that bond. He'd reached out, after all. Sent a letter. A letter Stirling had rejected in his teenage ignorance and stupidity.

Sudden regret stabbed deep into his heart. Who was he to judge Dougal, to dismiss him from his life for all those years as a man not up to standard? Dougal had had an affair while married—two affairs that Stirling knew of. Men did it all the time, and while Stirling would never behave that way himself, he wasn't the one walking in Dougal's shoes. Besides, it took two to horizontal tango.

Mal tipped his head back and gazed up at the weeping angel, her stained stony face cupped in rigid hands. 'It's a terrible thing when something happens to a loved one. The pain ...' He shook his head.

Stirling went cold. Mal's tone had the gravity of a man remembering his loss, but there was a slyness beneath the words.

'Believe me,' said Mal. 'It's not something you'd wish on your worst enemy.'

'No.'

'Ah, of course,' said Mal when Stirling added nothing further. 'I forgot. You've already experienced loss.'

Stirling clenched his jaw. This had better not be going where he thought it was.

'Your crew, wasn't it? When you were flying for *Medizin in Krise*.' He shook his head, tutting faintly. 'That poor girl. To die like that.'

Stirling had no intention of responding; he was having enough trouble controlling the urge to punch him. Mal digging into his background wasn't a huge surprise—Stirling had half-expected it. That he'd singled out Alina indicated a different kind of knowledge—a knowledge of Stirling's personal life—and that was a whole new trespass.

'Ah,' said Mal, smiling grimly. 'Not something you talk about. My apologies.'

Stirling's jaw was like granite now. Fury was driving red hot pokers through his brain.

Mal regarded the angel again. 'I can't imagine that's something you'd want to go through again.'

It took all Stirling's strength to keep his voice even. 'I'm not planning on flying into a warzone any time soon.'

'Still …' He smiled and indicated Stirling's leg. 'You need to take care. You've already had a taste of the dangers around here. Imagine how Darcy would feel if something happened to you?'

'Are you threatening me?'

Mal's eyes widened then he slapped a hand to his chest and laughed. 'Threatening you? Why would I threaten you? I'm your father's best friend.' The laughter broke off and was replaced with concern. 'I think perhaps Westwind is getting to you, Stirling. I mean, it's understandable—strange house, strange place. It can get lonely out here. Dougal said as much himself after Brigitte left, and for someone not used to it …'

'I can look after myself.'

'No doubt. I'm sure you're very capable. You're like your father in that way. He was a strong man too. Unfortunately that doesn't always mean immunity from our inner demons, as Dougal sadly proved. You've suffered severe trauma and loss. Perhaps it would pay to talk to someone. PTSD is a real illness, as I'm sure a man of your background is aware.'

So was psychopathy, Stirling thought.

Mal sighed, kissed his fingers and patted them on top of the angel's foot. 'I must get going, let you carry on with your walk.' He turned, took two strides, then stopped to regard Stirling from over his shoulder. His lips parted as though ready to say something, only for Stirling's icy stare to change his mind. With a grimace, he trudged on.

Stirling stood his ground, his gaze never straying from Mal as he stepped across the creek, nor from the four-wheel drive as it zigzagged up the steep hill and disappeared over the other side, leaving the glade once more filled with birdsong and burbles and the inner roar of his own doubts.

Chapter Thirty-Three

Darcy looked up at the throaty growl of a motorbike coming to rest out the front of her atelier. She breathed out. Of course Stirling had come. It wasn't in his nature to let her down.

She hurried for the door, her black heels click-clacking on the polished concrete floor and her strides short, thanks to her curve-hugging black and white floral dress.

Stirling had parked the Ducati at an angle and was in the process of shutting down when Darcy stepped alongside.

He pulled off his helmet, his gaze lingering on her sculpted figure before returning to her eyes. 'You look amazing.'

'And you're looking deliciously handsome.' Astride his bike in thigh-hugging jeans and a biker jacket, he looked more than handsome—thrillingly sexy was a better description. She leaned in for a kiss. 'How about I open the roller door so you can park in the garage? There's plenty of room behind the Mini.'

He jerked back, his eyes darting across the road. 'Why? Has something happened in the street?'

'No, not at all.' Darcy hid her worry with a smile. Stirling had been on edge for several days now but whenever she probed, he responded that he was tired or had a few things on his mind, none of which he'd disclose. The thought that his mood might have something to do with her had Darcy feeling ill. Stirling had come to mean too much for her to lose him now. 'I was simply thinking of your bottom.'

'My bottom?'

'Yes. And Grassmoor's fickle weather. I wouldn't want that luscious bottom of yours getting wet from your bike seat in the morning.'

His alarm eased to wry amusement, calming Darcy's thumping heart. 'I'm staying the night, am I?'

'I should hope so.' She peered closer and tugged on the heavy collar of his bike jacket. 'Unless you're scared of what I might do to you once I have you trapped in my boudoir?'

'Scared? Never. You're all pleasure, Miss Sloane.'

'Glad to hear it.' She patted his collar back into place. 'I'll open the garage.'

Darcy slipped back inside and pressed the button for the roller door, then leaned against the wall and took several deep slow breaths. Something was definitely out of kilter. What, she had no idea.

Whatever it was, Darcy refused to let it spoil their evening. This was to be their first proper date. Not the most glamorous of outings, to be fair, but a real one. One that would show off the everyday side of Grassmoor. The *good* side. Thursday night raffles at the town's one and only pub, followed by dinner in the bistro, a saunter back home and whatever happened thereafter.

A whole lot of loving, if Darcy had anything to do with it.

Cardigan in hand, she studied Stirling as he turned the pages of the sketchbook she'd left open on her workstation. Stripped of his bike jacket in jumper and jeans, shaven and clean, he could have been any handsome country bloke headed for dinner at the pub. Except the tension he'd arrived with still hadn't eased. Even a prolonged kiss in the kitchen hadn't budged it.

'These are great,' he said, smiling at her as she crossed to him. 'For next winter?'

'Yes.' She flipped a page to reveal a canary-yellow and deep pink floral wraparound dress with a plunging neckline and cascade of flounces. 'Although this one I might put back to next spring for the racing season. I've had an idea about creating a range of headwear. With the right fascinator, or even a pillbox hat, I think this would look marvellous.'

'You can make hats?'

She glanced at him from under her lashes. 'Not yet.'

Stirling laughed as he wrapped an arm around her shoulders and kissed her cheek. 'Amazing, gorgeous girl.'

'I am, rather.' She nudged him. 'And you're not too shabby yourself, hot pilot man.'

The cute crinkles that had formed around his eyes disappeared and he refocused on the sketchbook. Darcy let her question die in her head. Tomorrow she would ask what troubled him, what she could do to ease his worry. Tonight was for fun.

Leaving him skimming through the remaining pages, Darcy touched up her kissed-off lippy, draped her cardi around her shoulders, hooked a black patent mini bowler bag over her forearm and declared it time to go.

It was one of those exquisite spring evenings where the air was sweet and cool but not yet cold, the dying sun rimming the trees and the floral planter boxes in gold.

Darcy breathed out softly when Stirling took her hand, hoping it was a sign that he was relaxing, but as they passed the front of Mal

McKenzie's office, his grip tightened. She studied him sideways. His mouth was rigid, his eyes hard.

What was that about?

He glanced at her and smiled, but it wasn't strong or genuine enough to dispel the crease between his brows.

She smiled back and leaned in closer until their shoulders were touching. 'I hope your luck's in—and I'm not referring to later tonight. I'd quite like to win a meat tray.'

'Special, are they?'

'They are. From the butcher in Emu Springs, who happens to make excellent sausages.'

'I'm surprised they're not from Moody's.'

'They were, once. Then Moody's put up their prices and the Hoppers decided to go elsewhere. Charlie Shanahan's second cousin, who owns the butcher, gave them the kind of mate's rates they couldn't refuse. It caused a bit of a scandal.'

'Grassmoor seems to like a scandal.'

'Every town does. It gives locals something to talk about other than wool prices.'

They paused on the main corner for a small cattle truck to rumble past. Diagonally opposite stood the Rangeview Hotel, an art deco delight from the 1920s. It was crumbling a little now, the white rendered brick in need of a paint and its dark timber doors and window frames weather-beaten. Its charm remained though, its raggedy appearance eased by a low decorative hedge and potted Monterey pines guarding the entrance steps.

Behind the windows, people milled about or stood chatting, drinks in hand. The Hoppers would be pleased. Raffle nights were an important part of the club's off-season fundraising.

It wasn't quite the silencing of a Wild West bar when Darcy walked in, but it was close. Heads turned. The hubbub of chatter slowed and sobered. All eyes were directed past Darcy to the man behind her. Some were curious, a couple even offered welcoming smiles; the Byrnes saluted from their table near the bistro entrance, but the overall vibe was reproach.

What on god's green earth was going on? It was as though Dougal Kildare had walked into the room instead of his son.

Darcy hid her dismay with a wide smile and a cheery wave to everyone she knew—which was most of the room—then clasped Stirling's hand firmly in hers and strutted to the bar with all the confidence of a supermodel.

'I'll get it,' murmured Stirling, sliding his wallet on the bar when Darcy went to pay.

'No, you won't,' said Darcy, elbowing him out of the way. 'This is my date, remember?'

His expression clouded but he said nothing further.

Chatter had resumed but the looks kept coming like darts. Darcy wanted to yell at them all for their pettiness. Surely Grassmoor had moved on from gossiping about Stirling by now? He'd been here two months. More telling, he was on Darcy's arm. She was a born and bred local, well liked, and a smart, successful businesswoman. Her trust and favour had to be worth something.

Stirling carried their drinks to a tall table near a window overlooking the main street, Darcy sashaying behind him like she'd not a care in the world.

After a toast, Stirling sipped his beer and cast his gaze around the room, his expression tight. 'Is it always like this?'

Darcy chose to deliberately misunderstand. 'This busy? For Thursday night raffles, yes.'

'I meant this watchful.'

'They're just curious.'

'Then why does it feel like half the place wants to string me up?'

'I suspect they're jealous.' She sipped her chardonnay, twinkling at him from over the rim. She would *not* let this night be ruined by other people's small-mindedness. She leaned closer. 'You are with me, you know.'

That at least earned her a laugh. 'Yeah. Luckiest guy in the world.'

'I'm counting on it. I really would like to win a meat tray.'

There were four Hoppers players selling tickets. Darcy grinned as Charlie Shanahan did his best to avoid her, always finding someone in the opposite direction in need of a ticket whenever he ventured too close to their table. Darcy considered sheep-dogging him into a corner for the sport of it, but her spirit was too dashed for games.

The draw began at six thirty and despite having bought ten dollars worth of tickets, neither Darcy's nor Stirling's numbers came up.

'That was a disappointment,' said Darcy with a sigh, then brightened. 'But I still have you and that makes me a winner.' She pointed to Stirling's empty glass. 'Another?'

He stood. 'My shout.'

Darcy stood too. 'My date.' But Stirling was already heading for the bar.

She sighed and slid back onto her seat and checked her phone. It was rude, checking for orders while on a date, but they'd been coming in so regularly she needed to stay on top, mentally at least. Many were special orders too, from Olympia and her friends. The young teen had emailed Darcy via her website a few weeks ago, ostensibly to inquire about a dress but really to talk about Stirling. No way was Darcy going to let a friend of Stirling's down, and Olympia was sweet, if a bit spoiled, and utterly adored Stirling.

'Darcy.'

She turned to find Leo smiling cautiously at her, as if he wasn't sure of his welcome. Silly man. 'Leo, how wonderful to see you.'

She hugged and kissed him and was warmed to find he returned her brief hug with feeling. 'How are you?'

He shrugged. 'You know.'

'Is my rotten sister still being difficult?'

Leo shook his head in a 'you have no idea' way. 'We've talked, but …'

'Ah.' Shiloh wasn't a talker at the best of times, let alone when it came to her feelings. 'Give her time.'

He let out a tired sigh. 'Been a long time already.'

'It has but you know what she's like. Shiloh thinks too much with her head and not enough with her heart. And her heart belongs,' Darcy poked the centre of his chest for emphasis, 'to you.'

Leo's laugh was pure bitterness. 'Yeah, right.'

Poor Leo. How could Shiloh do this to him? Darcy mentally scowled. Her big sister had better brace herself. Shiloh would be in for an ear-chewing when Darcy got her alone tomorrow.

'You're here with Stirling,' he said.

'I am. We're on a date.' She glanced at the bar. Stirling's back was rigid, his demeanour disengaged from the patrons around him. She couldn't blame him. 'Though I have the feeling I would have been better off cooking at home. I had hoped to show off Grassmoor's friendly side, but everyone keeps looking at him like he's some sort of axe murderer.' She looked back at Leo. 'What is it with that? It's embarrassing—for me and for this town. And don't get me started on how Stirling must feel.'

Leo shuffled and slurped his beer.

Darcy's tone turned schoolmarmish. 'Spit it out, Leo.'

His shoulders dropped. 'There's a story going around.'

This did not sound promising.

'Oh, yes?'

He sighed. 'They're saying Stirling killed a girl.'

'I did.'

Leo jumped so violently he slopped beer over his hand. 'Shit.' His cheeks and neck flushed with colour. 'Sorry, mate.'

Stirling shrugged and passed Darcy her glass of wine. Resignation cut channels across his face, as if he'd expected something like this. Darcy wanted to cry for the poor man.

'What else are they saying?' he asked.

'Nothing. Just gossip.'

Stirling waited. Darcy followed his lead, until the uncomfortable silence had Leo squirming.

'That you flew a chopper into foreign country without authorisation and crashed.'

Stirling laughed. 'MiZ is never authorised to go anywhere. That's the whole point of it.'

Leo glanced from Stirling to Darcy and back again.

Stirling sipped a mouthful of beer and set his glass down. He looked squarely at Leo. 'We'd received intelligence about a group of refugees hiding out in a valley in need of urgent medical help. Word was it was a relatively safe zone but you can never be certain. Turns out a small band of rebels had dug in at one end. The end we flew into. They took us down. One of my crew was killed on impact. The two medics survived. I was badly banged up. Alina crawled to the cockpit to help me and was shot.'

Leo gaped.

Stirling shrugged again. 'It's a risky business.'

'Right. Yeah.' Leo cleared his throat. 'Sorry.'

'Don't be. Alina and Günter knew the risks. We all did.'

For several awkward moments no one spoke. Leo widened his eyes at Darcy as though looking for help but she was distracted, thinking about who could have known the story. She couldn't imagine Stirling telling anyone and he'd only recently shared it with her. Unless Toby had. Or Lisette.

Leo cleared his throat. 'This business …'

'*Medizin in Krise*. It's an aid organisation a bit like *Médecins sans Frontières* except it operates as a guerrilla force. We drop in, do what we can, then get the hell out.'

'This is like … in war zones?'

'War zones, natural disasters. It varies.'

'This is what you did, before here? Piloted for them?'

'Yeah.' Stirling fingered his beer glass, looking like he wanted to down the lot. 'Until the crash stopped me flying.'

'Right.' Leo cast another pleading look at Darcy.

'Stirling's a true hero,' she said, linking her arm through his and smiling at him with pride, though her stomach sloshed with wine and worry.

'I'm no hero.' There was an edge to his voice that warned her not to say it again. 'I just fly. The medics are the true heroes.'

'How the hell did you get out of—' Leo tipped his head. 'Where did you say it was?'

'I didn't.' It was obvious from Stirling's tone that he wasn't going to either. 'Another team was working the top of the valley. They got us out.' He turned his face to the window, his voice barren. 'Took a while.'

'Well,' said Darcy, not wanting to even imagine what Stirling had been through. 'Now we've clarified that misunderstanding, we can get on with enjoying our evening.'

Stirling snorted. 'Just out of curiosity, Leo, where did you hear that from?'

Darcy bet it was that rotten Frances Green. She'd spotted the nasty gossip in the bistro on arrival. Except how would she know about Stirling's past?

Another flush bloomed over Leo's cheeks. 'Couldn't say for sure. The story's going around though.'

Stirling nodded and again shifted his gaze to the window. Night had come, and the streetlights bathed the asphalt in bug-laced circles. Not that Darcy thought he was registering the scene. From his distant expression, whatever Stirling was seeing, it wasn't Grassmoor.

'I'd, er, better move on. Good to, er,' Leo cleared his throat, 'see you again.' With a raise of his glass, he hurried away.

'I'm sorry,' said Darcy, wishing she could do more than offer condolences. Wishing she could cuddle this lovely man's sore heart and heal it with the tenderness of her own.

'Don't be.' Stirling glanced at his watch. 'Should we head in for dinner?'

Darcy was sure dinner was the last thing Stirling wanted, but if he was valiant enough to act as though the previous awkwardness hadn't happened and maintain a stiff upper lip, then she could too.

She hooked her arm through his. 'An excellent idea. This lady needs to fuel up.' She nudged him. 'You'll need your strength too, for later.'

His chuckle lacked real amusement. Still, it was there, and he was trying and that was some comfort. Heads up and straight spined, they sauntered into the bistro while the thinning crowd got the message and kept their whispers to themselves.

⚶

Darcy rolled over, stretched her hand to where a warm body should have lain, and found cold sheet. She stretched further, only to encounter more cold.

Frowning, she listened to the night, expecting noise from the bathroom, but there was nothing except the low-grade thrum of her rousing anxiety. Not wanting to alarm Stirling by calling out, she slid from the bed and draped herself in the silky peignoir she'd earlier discarded on the floor.

She crept on bare feet into the kitchen and paused. A figure stood at the front window, immobile. A statue peering blindly at the night. His jeans were slung low, his chest bare. The shutters had been tilted slightly ajar and slats of moonlight shot through the gaps. They striped Stirling's face and body like prison bars.

Darcy held her hand against her chest and breathed in and out as her heart fluttered. He was a lonely figure, sad. And so, so still. A man lost in his thoughts. Perhaps in himself.

He wasn't lost. Not yet. Not when he had her.

She padded to his side, her voice a whisper. 'Are you okay?'

Stirling remained quiet for several breaths. 'You know, I never really had a home.'

Darcy stared up at his face and waited.

He glanced at her and smiled briefly then looked back out on the street. 'Apart from primary school, I spent most of my upbringing in boarding school. Then there was the army. Then …' He made a sweeping gesture with his hand. 'Everywhere I lived was temporary. It was good. It suited me, my life. No responsibilities, hardly any belongings to worry about. I could move whenever I liked. Go wherever I wanted.'

'Except home.'

He nodded. 'Yeah, except home.' His mouth tightened in one corner. 'Hard to miss something you've never had though.'

Except it was obvious he did. Even if Stirling hadn't experienced home in the way Darcy had, with all its comfort and memory and warmth and love, the idea of it existed in his mind. And he wanted it. He wanted to try for it.

If the world, and his own fears, would let him.

'It's not too late to find one.' She slipped her hand into his. His skin was cool. Too cool. As though more than the night tempered his skin. 'You could make a home here. In Grassmoor.'

His mouth twitched into a wan smile as Darcy's unsaid 'with me' echoed in the air between them. She watched his eyes, his mouth, her breath held.

The smile turned soft. Stirling leaned close and kissed her sex-and-sleep-mussed hair. 'It's too cold for you down here. Let's go back to bed.'

Darcy's heart sank at the dismissal, and at the awful thought that her beloved town could be destroying the simple dreams of the man she loved.

Chapter Thirty-Four

Somehow, Stirling managed to hold himself together in Darcy's presence, though it wasn't easy when his mind was half-cloaked in a red fog and fury bubbled hot and ugly in the deep cavities of his chest. Even after their stroll home from the pub, Stirling's fists remained clenched so tight they felt glued together, but Darcy had the answer. Darcy always had the answer. In the glimmering light of her bedroom, shed of her clothes, skin glowing, she eased his fingers apart and pressed his hands to her waist and smiled at him with promise.

Morning brought filtered golden light that touched Darcy's pale skin and made it as luminous as an angel's. He reached for her, and their lovemaking began slow and sweet before turning hungry and desperate. Afterwards, Stirling cradled her against his chest, savouring her warmth, her breath, the beauty and strength of her, until he could no longer put off starting the day.

He began to pull away, only for Darcy to drag him back.

She stared into his face, a tiny arrowhead of worry between her brows. 'Are you okay, Stirling? Truly okay, I mean.'

'Yeah.' When he was held by her, it felt like the truth.

She continued to scrutinise his face, the arrowhead deepening and a shine of concern in her eyes. When her mouth parted, Stirling silenced it with a kiss, except Darcy wasn't easily fobbed off.

'Hey,' he said, when she went to question him again. 'Shh. I'm fine.'

'I care about you.' She rolled her kiss-plumped lips together. 'A great deal.'

'I know. But I'm all right.' He pressed his forehead to hers, forcing his mouth into a smile, and used one her favourite words back at her. 'Truly.'

She plucked at a few strands of hair on his chest, searching his eyes. 'You'd tell me if you weren't, if there was something wrong?'

'Of course.'

Stirling saw the hint of sadness as Darcy realised he wouldn't be backing away from the lie and his heart ached. He wrapped her even closer, hating himself for hurting her, for his need to hide the soft belly of his soul and the secret fears that lurked there.

He left after breakfast, chuckling at her 'Later, hunky-boy' and feigning normality. Though short, the ride to Westwind helped clear his head. He took the turns at speed, letting the power of the engine rumble through his veins, feeding on the rush, the gyroscopic balance between road and bike.

Stirling might have felt better for it, but not so much that he had an answer for how to handle Mal's latest attack. Because that's exactly what it was—an attack. Leo might not have known where the rumour began, but Stirling did. Mal had already proven in private his willingness to weaponise Stirling's past. Now he'd taken it public.

The question that bothered him most was why. Because if it was for the reason Stirling thought, then he wasn't dealing with a personality clash, turf war or plain resentment. Something that could be dealt with via a man-to-man.

He was potentially dealing with a killer.

Westwind was quiet when Stirling coasted into the drive. He took it slowly, alert to anything out of place, his gaze restless as it swivelled between the house, the gardens, the distant paddocks. He circled the fountain once then followed the road to scout the sheds.

The property appeared the same as when he'd left, but Stirling wasn't about to put much stock in a brief ride-by. Nothing had appeared out of place the other times he suspected Mal had trespassed. Still, apart from clearing each shed individually, it was the best he could do. The urge lingered though, and the irrationality of it only added to his anxiety. Stirling knew enough about PTSD to know excessive fear and worry could be symptoms, along with poor sleep. He buried the thoughts. That was just Mal's mind games. Keeping his eyes peeled, he idled back to the house and parked the Ducati under the porch.

The small twigs he'd inserted at the bottom of the door to appear as though they'd blown in were still in position. Stirling tugged them free and unlocked the door.

He paused inside, listening, breathing in the air, searching for lingering scents, and encountered only the mudroom's usual aroma of old oilskin and leather, and the slight mustiness that emanated permanently from the laundry.

Leaving on his boots and jacket, Stirling stalked into the kitchen, his gaze immediately narrowing on his laptop. He'd deliberately left it in its usual position with the lid open but when he walked around the end of the table, the screen was blank. The weight that had been pressing on his chest eased a little.

He checked the front door. The rubber wedges he'd jammed in its base hadn't moved. It was obvious no one had been here and it would be stupid to search the whole house when the twigs had been in place. Except awareness that something was stupid didn't give peace of mind. With a quiet exhale, Stirling went to reconnoitre.

Minutes later, he was slumped at the kitchen table, boots and jacket stripped off, rubbing his hands down his face. The house was untouched, as he knew it would be, and his anxiety should have eased by now. Instead it had grown worse.

Could he have PTSD? Christ knew he'd been through enough trauma. And symptoms didn't always manifest in the immediate aftermath. Often it was progressive, creeping along like a thief, slowly stealing a person's wellbeing, making their world feel unsafe. Making them paranoid.

And Stirling was showing the signs.

He let out a moan. This had to stop. He wasn't paranoid. He was fine. It was Mal. It had to be.

What he needed to do was rationalise. Decide his next move. Determine if he should make *any* move. Because what could be proven about Mal and his involvement in Dougal's death? Not a damn thing.

Gut feeling, no matter how strong, wasn't evidence.

He dragged his palms down his face a last time and stood. Grumping about on his bum didn't achieve anything and Stirling was too wired and his brain too clouded to think straight. He needed to expend some energy.

Changed into an old pair of trackpants of his father's and a t-shirt, Stirling headed for the bedroom he'd transformed into a makeshift workout area. He started with stretches before moving onto core exercises. The effort had him grunting and grimacing from the pain in his leg, hips and back. He paused, his arms draped across his knees, and chest heaving as sweat threaded his spine.

When his breath returned, he settled onto his back and began leg-raises. Tomorrow he would pay. Today he needed this.

Twenty-five minutes later, his t-shirt sodden and his body pumping endorphins, Stirling felt better, even if his abdominals protested otherwise. Deciding a walk would help him cool down and give him open-air thinking time, he threw on a light jumper and headed out, using a couple of half-dried leaves to mark the door after he'd locked up.

The day was bright, the air fresh and scented with the lemony fragrance of what Stirling could only guess was a distant flowering gum. Though he'd planned to follow the shallow trail that threaded past the creek, his feet had other ideas and he was soon lumbering down the slope to Xavier's memorial.

Bar the chattering birds and industrious insects, the glade was empty today. Stirling was unsurprised. He didn't expect to see Mal, not after their previous encounter. This was also his first time visiting the memorial alone and he experienced a strong need to give Xavier a quiet moment.

He stared at the eternally weeping angel, then at the memorial inscription for a little boy taken too early. The lost son of two men. And who, he was certain, was his half-brother.

Was that what Mal's hostility was about? Not that Stirling was too close to discovering the depth of Mal's involvement in Dougal's fraud and death, but simple jealousy that Stirling was alive when Xavier was dead?

Even beyond the grave, Dougal had something more than Mal. A precious thing. A living son. While Mal, best friend and cuckold, had been left with nothing, just a stone memorial that he didn't erect on land he didn't own. But Xavier could have owned the land one day, had he lived and Dougal let the truth out. And why not?

Dougal had wanted to name the nursing centre after Xavier. Why wouldn't he have wanted to claim the boy as his when the time felt right? Especially with his other son seemingly lost to him.

Stirling sighed and turned his attention to the creek. As he suspected, a small causeway had been laid across the waterway, constructed from a layer of heavy stones and bordered on one side with a series of higher, uneven stepping stones.

Stirling scouted for a branch strong enough to use as a walking stick and found nothing suitable. He eyed the stones and the depth of the creek, then gritted his teeth and stepped out. To his surprise, his overworked leg held up and Stirling soon found himself in a patch of cleared worn land that formed a natural parking bay.

A track led out of the clearing and up a slope. From the ruts and compacted soil, the road had been in use a long time, and remained so. Mal, of course, but why use this semi-secret approach when the memorial was more easily accessed from the house?

What could Stirling do about it? Rip up the causeway? Destroy the stepping stones? He sniffed at the idea. The way his leg and hip were throbbing, he'd be lucky to make it back to the house let alone start ripping up rocks. Besides, he'd promised Mal he could visit Xavier's memorial whenever he pleased, without specifying how. Enemies or not, Stirling would not go back on his word.

He scanned the skyline and frowned at the bruised and swollen clouds bunching over the ranges. The birds and bugs had hushed too, as though braced for thunder. Stirling hadn't considered the weather when he'd set out and now he was in trouble. Though tempted to race the rain, Stirling kept his gait slow and careful as he made his way back across the creek. He didn't need a fall to add to his issues. He paused again at the memorial and set his hand on the angel's foot as Mal had done. The stone was cool and smooth, worn from the grief and heavy rubs of a devastated father.

Stirling shook his head. And with a last pat for his half-brother, he plodded wearily towards the house, no wiser as to how to handle the situation. If Mal's purpose was to discredit Stirling in the eyes of the community so much that he'd be forced to leave, then he'd underestimated his foe. Stirling had faced worse than this. Besides, the only approval Stirling really cared about was Darcy's.

He'd built up another sweat by the time he neared the sheds, and Stirling mused that he should probably take a run into Hamilton for supplies, maybe shout Gavin a pub lunch as thanks for all his help.

He trudged on, his mind on a much-needed shower, gaze roaming between track and house, the menacing sky and shed.

Until suddenly, his gaze locked.

Stirling froze. He blinked, the hairs on his arms, neck and back spiking in a slow horrible wave.

An icy drop of rain hit his shoulder. Another followed. Fat splotches, sparse but building. Stirling barely noticed, his attention too anchored on the four-wheel drive.

Slowly, he took a step forward, then another, and stopped.

Etched into the dust of the car's rear window, like a crude child's game, was a hangman.

Stirling gave a bitter laugh. So Mal wanted him dead? Well, at least he now had confirmation they were at war.

But as he studied the drawing more closely, a chill shuddered through his body, and it wasn't from the breeze or the rain or his drying sweat. The hangman wasn't a man.

It was a woman.

Chapter Thirty-Five

It was closing in on one o'clock when the bell to Darcy's atelier rang. She looked up from her overlocker and frowned at the interruption, then smiled when she realised it could be Stirling come to surprise her with a visit.

She set down the dress she was meticulously blind-hemming—another overseas order from one of Olympia's friends; the girl was quite the referee—and hurried to the door, only for her steps to slow when Darcy caught a glimpse of her caller through the shutters. She paused to smooth her pencil skirt before assuming a welcoming expression.

'Mal,' she said, not opening the door fully. This was a working day and Mal didn't have an appointment. She wasn't about to change her rules for him. 'How nice to see you.'

'And you, Darcy. You're looking as chic as always.' He tried to peer over her shoulder. 'I'm not disturbing you, am I?'

'A little. What can I do for you?'

His smile was forced. 'It's a delicate matter.' He pursed his lips as he again tried to see into the room. 'May I come in?'

A delicate matter? That didn't bode well.

Darcy rapped her finger against the edge of the door before stepping back and sweeping a hand in invitation. She glanced at the street as he passed. The forecast rain had arrived and though not yet heavy, the street and footpath were sleek with it.

She closed the door and stood with her back to it as Mal moved to the centre of the atelier. What his purpose was she had no idea. Apart from their business relationship—he had drawn up her will and an enduring power of attorney after she'd bought the building—Darcy only knew Mal via her family and their connection with Westwind. He had never visited the atelier, professionally or otherwise.

He surveyed the room now, his gaze lingering on the entrance to her living quarters before it skipped to her workspace. 'This is quite a space.'

'It is, but then it has to be. VaVoom is a significant business these days.'

He stood with his hands in the pockets of his jeans, looking every inch the country gent with his shiny brown boots and blue and white checked shirt. He seemed in no hurry to speak, which was annoying. Darcy wanted to finish her dress so she could hurry it to the post office, then travel to Roseneath to pick up her mum for her Friday physio session. The rain and slippery roads would slow her trip enough without Mal making her late.

She headed for her sewing, the clack of her heels a metronome of impatience, picked up the dress then set it down again. It wouldn't pay to try and sew while she was annoyed. 'You mentioned a delicate matter?'

He contemplated the floor for a moment before looking at her. 'Yes. It's rather awkward. I don't want you to think I'm being an interfering old man.'

Darcy's smile tightened. Men who introduced topics with the caveat of not wanting to be thought of as an interfering old man usually were.

He studied her face, then sighed. 'It's Stirling.'

She folded her arms and raised both eyebrows. She would not make this easy for Mal. Patronising men who thought they understood life better than women were her least favourite, and Stirling had been persecuted enough.

'I'm worried about him.'

'Oh, yes?'

Mal grimaced. Clearly this was not progressing how he'd expected. 'He's been behaving oddly.'

Darcy's senses went on alert. 'In what way?'

'Anxious. Jittery. I hate to say it, but the last time I ran into him at Westwind he sounded paranoid. I was at Xavier's memorial, and he came at me. Accused me of threatening him when all I'd suggested was that he needed to take care around the farm. He's already had one accident.' He huffed out a breath. 'Maybe it came across as condescending, I don't know. Even if it was, his reaction was completely out of proportion. Aggressive, even.'

Darcy frowned. Aggressive? Stirling?

He'd been tense lately, yes. Probably even anxious, but aggressive? That wasn't Stirling at all. Yet there was clearly something wrong. He'd been broody, secretive, sad. Even a little jumpy.

'I know you and he are ...'

'Lovers?'

Mal cleared his throat. 'Seeing each other. And normally I'd mind my own business, but I'm worried for you both.'

'I can assure you I'm perfectly fine.'

'Yes, but I'm not certain the same can be said for Stirling. You know about the crash, of course.'

Darcy nodded, her teeth gritted. Truly, this town was testing her patience. People needed to stick to their own knitting.

'I appreciate Stirling is a strong man, a brave one too, but that must have been an incredibly traumatic experience and even the strongest can suffer from PTSD. You only need to look at the current Royal Commission into Defence and Veteran Suicide to know that.'

'You think he has PTSD?'

Mal opened his hands. 'After the other day, I did some research and it seemed to fit. The anxiety and paranoia ...' He shook his head. 'If he does have PTSD, he needs help.' He held her gaze. 'And you need to be careful. Sufferers can do as much harm to others as they do to themselves.'

Darcy rubbed her arms. Though it wasn't cold, the idea of Stirling hurting himself shot icy dread across her skin. 'Stirling would never hurt me.' Nor could she believe he would hurt himself, but neither could she discount Stirling's recent behaviour.

'He might not mean to, but who knows what he's capable off in the throes of delusion? Look, Darcy, I know it's none of my business, and I can't tell you how uncomfortable I feel even bringing it up, but Dougal was my oldest and dearest friend. If his son is ill—and I honestly believe he might be—he'd want me to do all I could to save Stirling from himself.'

Still chafing her arms, Darcy crossed to her cutting table and stacked her fabric weights into a pyramid. She didn't believe Stirling was suffering PTSD. Some anxiety, perhaps, but she'd spent many nights in his bed and his sleep was usually solid. There was no waking up shouting or sweating, like she'd seen in films. The exception had been last night when she'd found him at the window, and after his embarrassing treatment at the pub, she couldn't blame him.

On the other hand, what would she know? She had zero experience of this. One thing was certain, if Stirling was ill, Darcy would do whatever it took to help him to recovery.

'What do you propose?' she said.

'I don't know. Talk to him? Mention his behaviour, that you're worried about him? Encourage him to seek professional help? Unlike me, he'll listen to you.'

Darcy contemplated the fabric weights for a long moment. Finally she looked at Mal. 'I'll consider it.'

Darcy couldn't hide her relief when she spotted Shiloh, Lucy at her heels, walking the track that led from Roseneath's shearing shed to the house. She hurried towards her. It had been a long troublesome day and the sooner she spoke to her sister, the sooner she could get to Westwind.

Shiloh stopped and regarded her with alarm. 'Is it Mum?'

'No. Sorry. Mum's fine. Tired after her physio but otherwise good.'

'What's got your frilly knickers in a twist then?' said Shiloh, continuing her long strides, full-length oilskin coat flapping around her legs. Though the rain had stopped, the sky remained ominous with slate-coloured clouds. According to the bureau, the wintry conditions were set to last several more days.

'Two things.' Darcy started with the easiest topic, although when it came to her sister and her ex-fiancé, nothing was easy. 'First, Leo.'

'What about Leo?'

'I saw in him the 'View last night. Truly, Shiloh, the man's in a terrible state. How much longer is it going to be before you realise you made a mistake and apologise?'

Shiloh flapped her arms. 'I don't know. It's not that easy, you know.' She slowed. 'What if he won't forgive me?' Her voice dropped even further as her step stuttered then stalled like a jammed needle. 'Or forget.'

Darcy only just stopped herself from rolling her eyes. Her sister was scared, and being sarcastic wouldn't help. 'He loves you, Loh. You'll work it out.' She tucked her arm around Shiloh's. 'In a few years time you'll be laughing at yourselves for your silliness.'

Shiloh shook her head.

'You will. All you have to do is talk.'

She marched on. 'What's the other thing?'

Darcy pursed her lips at the change of subject but didn't push it. Shiloh could sometimes be guided but never pushed. 'I had a strange visitor early this afternoon.'

Shiloh raised an eyebrow.

'Mal McKenzie called in.'

'What did he want?'

'He's worried about Stirling.'

Both of Shiloh's eyebrows shot up. 'What does he care?'

'As Dougal's best friend, he feels obliged to keep an eye on him.'

'Huh. Fair, I suppose. A bit weird, but fair.' Shiloh paused at the gate to the back garden. 'Okay, so why's Mal worried?'

'He seems to think Stirling has PTSD.'

'Big call.'

'Just a little.'

Shiloh rubbed her chin. 'What do you think?'

A barbed lump formed in Darcy's throat. She swallowed it away, but the scratch lingered, turning her voice husky. 'I don't know. I don't know anything about PTSD.' She scraped her teeth over her bottom lip. 'But given what he went through with the crash, it's not inconceivable. And there's no question that he's been different lately, but I thought that was because of the gossip.'

'What gossip?'

Darcy almost laughed. She'd momentarily forgotten her sister's ability to always be out of the loop. If it wasn't related to the farm, Shiloh wasn't interested. 'That Stirling had flown illegally into a hot zone and Alina was killed because of his recklessness.'

'Didn't you say it was an intel failure or something?'

'It was. Unfortunately, a few of our smaller-minded locals are choosing to believe otherwise.'

'Huh. Morons.'

Darcy couldn't agree more.

Shiloh draped her arms over the top of the gate and stared into the garden. The hydrangea was in bloom, its frothy display of rain-dappled purple-blue flowers glorious even in the drab light. 'Mal can be a bit of a flog but he might have a point about the PTSD.'

Darcy sighed. She leaned alongside her sister and rested her chin on her forearms, the damp seeping through her cardigan sleeves. 'He might.'

Shiloh eyed her from under the brim of her hat. 'There's a big "but" in that tone. What's up?'

'I can't help feeling there's something else going on.'

'Like what?'

Darcy shook her head. 'I wish I knew, but he's definitely keeping something from me.'

Shiloh slapped the gate rail and reached for the latch. 'Then I guess it's time to take your own advice.'

'Which is?' asked Darcy, straightening away from the gate.

Her sister grinned. 'You'll figure it out.'

This time, when Darcy passed through Westwind's beautifully wrought gates, the flutters in her chest weren't caused by excitement but by trepidation.

Shiloh had been right. Darcy needed to take the same advice she'd been giving Shiloh about Leo and talk to Stirling. Really talk. Except how on earth was a person meant to broach another's mental health status? She was not one to pry, but this was Stirling, the man she loved, and when it came to his wellbeing, how could she not?

The easy way would be to mention Mal's visit, except she doubted that would be received well. Though Darcy could not believe Mal's assertion that Stirling had been hostile and aggressive at Xavier's memorial, it was clear an issue existed between the two men. Even passing Mal's office had made him tense. Mentioning that Mal had discussed Stirling's welfare with her would put him completely on the back foot.

Darcy rolled her damp hands around the steering wheel as she negotiated the driveaway. First and foremost, she would listen and observe. If an opening appeared, she would take it. If Stirling was his usual self, then she'd leave it for another time. Cowardly perhaps, but instinct told her caution was the wise approach.

Stirling trusted her. More importantly, she suspected he loved her, and Darcy would not risk either for anyone.

A rising wind was gusting leaves and debris across the driveway when Darcy swept around the final curve. Distracted by her thoughts and the potholed drive, she didn't immediately spot Stirling sitting on the stone steps until he began to rise, but the sight of him had her already tight stomach clenching further.

Sitting on the step waiting for her? This was not normal. Not normal at all.

Worse was his expression—bleak and haggard, and a very different man to the one who had laughed and kissed her lovingly goodbye only that morning.

He waved her to a stop. For a wild moment, Darcy wanted to ignore him and speed to the rear of the house and her usual parking space and pretend that whatever was wrong wasn't happening. As quickly as it struck her, it passed. She would face the situation with fortitude. That was her way.

Darcy pushed open the door. 'For goodness' sake, Stirling, what are you doing out here in the cold?'

'Waiting for you.'

She eyed him saucily, although she felt anything but. 'Aren't you the eager beaver?'

His chest expanded as he hauled in a deep breath. 'Look, Darcy ...' He dragged his hand over his head. 'I've been thinking, and this thing between us ... it's not working.'

For a horrid moment Darcy thought she'd heard the beginnings of a breakup speech, then she laughed, although even to her ears it sounded high and forced. 'Goodness,' she said, spreading her palm over her chest. 'For a moment there I thought you said something about our relationship not working.'

'I did.'

'I beg your pardon?'

Stirling closed his eyes. When he opened them again, his gaze had lost all its softness, all its sweet, loving Stirling-ness. In its place was granite flecked with ice. 'I'm sorry. I know you had expectations about us.'

'Expectations? Stirling, we've been lovers for weeks. We've ...' Darcy stumbled, too shocked to go on. Of all the things she'd feared for the evening, this was not it.

He looked away, his Adam's apple bobbing. 'It's for the best.'

For the best? The words rose to a shriek in her head. *For the best?*

Who was this man? Her Stirling would never be so patronising. Or so cold.

With gargantuan effort, Darcy calmed the shriek, though her voice remained unnaturally high and tremulous. 'Are you telling me we're *over*?'

He hesitated but only for a breath. When his answer came, it was emphatic.

'Yes.'

Chapter Thirty-Six

Stirling had more than a few things in his life that he wasn't proud of, but hurting Darcy ranked up with the worst.

That single 'yes' had left her frozen with shock and disbelief. Her eyes were round, her beautiful mouth the same. The hand she'd flattened over her chest had slid to her stomach, clutching at it as though she'd been punched. For a long moment she did nothing but stare. Then she rallied. Her hand dropped, her shoulders went back, and all Stirling could think in that moment was how much he loved her, his brave, bright, indefatigable Darcy.

Her chin went up. 'I don't believe you.'

Stirling kept his voice frigid, when all he wanted to do was fold her against him and promise he didn't mean it, that they would be all right, that he'd find some other way through this crisis. 'You need to.'

She had no idea how much. The hangman hadn't left his mind's eye since he'd encountered it that afternoon. It was branded there—a crude caricature of a woman with shoulder-length hair and funny-looking spiked feet imitating high heels. A likeness that

ignited fury and fear in equal measure and raised the memory of
Mal's words at Xavier's memorial.

It's a terrible thing when something happens to a loved one. The
pain …

Stirling had thought Mal was describing the loss of Xavier, but
the words had been directed at him.

And with that came war.

A threat against Stirling was one matter. A threat against Darcy
changed the world. Mal might be clever but he'd made a major tactical
miscalculation if he thought a counterstrike like that would make
Stirling retreat. When it came to Darcy, he would sacrifice anything
and everything to keep her safe, no matter what the cost to himself.

'This isn't you,' said Darcy, moving closer. 'Something's wrong.
Tell me. Let me help.'

Stirling stepped out of reach. He didn't know if he'd have the
strength to stay firm if she touched him. Those distress-filled eyes
were undermining his resolve as it was.

'Nothing's wrong. I've just been thinking things over and realised
it's better we end this now before we both get in any deeper.'

'No.'

The crack in her voice tore at his willpower. He closed his eyes for
a second and visualised the hangman, its simple menace. Safe, he
had to keep her safe. 'Look, Darcy, you're a great girl, a wonderful
girl, but you deserve someone who can give you a full life. I can't.
Not here.'

'But you can. You do.'

He looked away. Taking advantage, she slipped closer. He couldn't
bring himself to step away. Her hand fell lightly on his arm.

'This is about last night, isn't it? At the 'View.'

'No.' Stirling gently held her hand for what might be the last
time. Her skin was soft and silky and warm. He wished he could

kiss her palm and close her hand over it. 'It's about what's good for the both of us. Your future is here, in the place you love, surrounded by people who love you as much as you love them.' He dragged in a breath. 'Mine isn't.'

She smiled, still hopeful, still convinced she could change his mind. 'It could be. If you want it badly enough.'

God, he adored her fortitude. But that wouldn't keep her safe from Mal.

His chest throbbed with the pain of his next words. Words that were lies. 'That's what I've come to realise. I don't.'

Darcy's cheeks paled.

'I'm sorry.'

'You don't mean that, I know you don't. Something's happened. You were fine this morning. We were ...' Her voice caught on a sob. 'We were in love this morning.'

The pain in Stirling's chest shifted from a throb to a sharp vicious stab. He braced against it. Whatever it took, he reminded himself. 'Maybe for you. Not for me.'

Another 'sorry' quivered on his tongue. Stirling slammed his mouth over it. He needed to stay strong, even a bit cruel. Darcy had to accept his words and leave, preferably in anger, for Lisette's or to Shiloh and indulge in whatever comforting behaviours women got up to at times like this. Lisette would be better. Once in her hands, the news would spread around Grassmoor to Mal, who would learn that not only were Darcy and Stirling no longer together, but that the break was unpleasant and irrevocable.

A far from perfect plan, yet what else was he to do? Never let Darcy out his sight? She'd never tolerate it for starters and would eventually coax the reason from him. And where would that leave them? Darcy forever wondering if he had a screw loose while Stirling festered with unprovable suspicion.

He could leave town. Run away. Forget Darcy and Westwind and Dougal and his dream of finding his purpose, and let injustice prevail. Maybe another man could do it but not Stirling. Mal had engineered Dougal's death. The hangman had cemented it. He didn't know how Mal had managed it, or why, but one way or another, Stirling would find the truth.

'Look, Stirling,' she said. 'I know it's hard, this situation. Being here, learning about your dad. You've been through a lot of trauma and upheaval. It's bound to have an effect.'

Stirling stared at her, fear tightening his guts.

Darcy softened her expression. 'Even the toughest men need help sometimes.'

'What are you talking about?' But he knew.

She fidgeted with the bow at her neck. 'Mal came to see me.'

'When?' The words snapped out, his heartbeat accelerating with them.

'Earlier today, at the atelier.' Her tone softened even further. 'He's worried about you, Stirling.'

Oh yeah, Mal was worried all right, but not for the reason Darcy thought. His fingernails dug into his palms. Mal had dared to go near Darcy. Stepped into her home, infected it with his gaslighting poison.

'He thought … he thought perhaps you should see someone.'

'Let me guess, PTSD.'

Darcy nodded.

It took all Stirling's strength not to roar. Instead, he forced himself colder, crueller, hating every agonising moment. 'I'm fine. I don't have PTSD or any other issue. And you need to leave.'

'Stirling, please.'

'We're done, Darcy.' He crossed his arms and widened his stance, his posture deliberately intimidating. 'I mean it.'

For several long seconds she stared at his face, gaze flicking around his features, assessing his body language. Stirling tipped his head a little to the side, his mouth a flat line, a man at the edge of his patience.

'Fine,' she said and his relief at her angry tone almost had him slumping. Her eyes narrowed a little and he tensed again, but Darcy said nothing. She looked him up and down, gave a Shiloh-like *hmph*, and sauntered to the Mini, straight-spined and hips swinging.

Undefeated. Magnificent. And no longer his.

⁂

Stirling wished he could get drunk, anything to wipe the memory of Darcy's hurt from his mind. Except getting drunk wouldn't help. It was also dangerous. He needed to stay strong for her. Drunkenness was weakness, and an opportunity for Mal.

And that arsehole deserved nothing.

He wandered the rooms, his fingers trailing the walls, touching the living history of a house whose soul had been torn out. He and Westwind had been strangers before, but they were kin now.

Each time Stirling ended back in the kitchen, he'd pick up his phone and stare at the screen, hoping for … what? A message of forgiveness? A miraculous solution to the mess he was in?

He needed to think, and he needed to act, but right now his brain was too fogged.

Finally, when his aching body forced him to surrender, he returned to the lounge, where a lifetime ago he'd woken to find Darcy smiling down at him. Though the house wasn't yet cold, Stirling meticulously laid out paper and kindling, then lit the fire.

He slid backward along the rug until he hit the couch and slumped against it. He stared again at the fire, the bright colours reminding him of Darcy in the glow of the firepit, a night when they were happy and full of hope, and high on the intensity of their attraction.

He buried his face in his palms.

All he wanted was to keep her safe. Take Grassmoor's rampant gossip network and set it to work for him for once. But so much could go wrong. Darcy might not say a word to anyone, or discuss their breakup only with her sister, who might tell her dog, if she was in a chatty mood. Darcy could ignore his order to stay away, keep calling into Westwind demanding an explanation, determined to wear Stirling down.

She could even turn to Mal—trustworthy local solicitor and Dougal's deeply concerned best friend—for help.

The thought had Stirling sitting up. He needed this over and the only way to do it was to act. He'd done the worst part, now he needed to get on with the rest.

He checked his watch and calculated. Though he hated asking, it was time to call in a favour.

Chapter Thirty-Seven

Darcy let pure anger drive her home. Anger and incredulity were better than giving over to heartbreak. The grief of it would only blur her vision and loosen her grip on the wheel, and she needed to get home in one piece and plan her next move.

That cold man was not the Stirling she loved. The man she loved was sensitive and compassionate, decent and good. He *helped* people, fought selflessly for them. Why then had he behaved so callously towards her, a woman he cared for deeply? It was as baffling as it was hurtful.

She parked in the garage and entered through the side door. The vast room felt cold and lonely. Even the wall of colourful fabric failed to lift her spirits. Darcy's bones ached with loss. Her heart felt crushed. Her head was restless with worry and confusion.

She wandered her workshop, hugging herself, mouth firmly closed against the sobs that threatened to collapse her to the couch, and attempted to unravel Stirling's rejection.

Could someone have warned him off her? Who would do that? It wasn't as if she was in another relationship when Stirling arrived or even had the prospect of one. Darcy had been single for a couple of years and had made it clear her energies were dedicated to VaVoom.

Dearest Frances? The woman had never been a fan, far from it, but other than out of sheer malevolence, why would she want to break up Darcy and Stirling? It seemed ridiculous. And what could she have revealed to cause Stirling's sudden about-turn?

Could Mal have warned him off? She supposed it was possible if he truly thought Stirling had PTSD and was a potential danger to Darcy. Except what business was it of Mal's and why would he care?

Darcy paused at her cutting table and contemplated her pattern weights. The little heavy bean bags were made of scraps from her favourite childhood clothes, each a comforting memory of carefree days filled with love and laughter. She rearranged them into two lines of three. What else could have made Stirling behave so out of character?

Fear? Except fear of what?

Not for himself. Stirling had risked his life daily for years, all in the service of helping others. It had to be fear for someone else. Someone who truly mattered to him.

Stirling loved his mother and he clearly adored Olympia, but both were overseas and, she imagined, untouchable. She pushed a yellow-gold weight made from an old school skivvy out of line and followed it with its neighbouring green weight.

Toby? From what she knew of their friendship, if either were under threat the pair were more likely to gang up on the culprit. And again, to what end? She shifted a blue weight to the right.

His father? His half-sister Melody?

One was dead, the other settled in America, and Stirling had mentioned Melody's hostility. They were not and probably never would be close. Two more weights joined the others, leaving only one. A flowery pink weight made from a beloved pair of flannelette pyjamas. She fingered the soft fabric. Was it possible?

Darcy frowned. He was protecting *her*? What a ridiculous notion. What protection could Darcy possibly need? She was perfectly capable of looking after herself, as Stirling well knew. Except right now, it was the only thing that made sense in her muddled mind.

Unless his fear was that he might hurt her. That his mental health might put her in danger.

Possible, but then why not say so?

She rubbed a brow. She was too upset and too tired to puzzle this out. What she needed was wine and a good cry, and tomorrow, when she was more herself and could handle it, the advice of people she trusted.

❧

'Just quiche,' said Darcy when Shiloh arrived at lunchtime the next day sniffing the air. 'A frozen one from Moody's. I wasn't in the mood for baking.'

Shiloh peeled off her rain-splattered coat. For once, she wasn't wearing farm clothes and she smelled of soap and shampoo rather than lanolin and sheep poo. In fact, compared to her usual standards, she was looking suspiciously done up. Though her hair was held back with a plastic claw, it had been washed and blow-dried, making her natural highlights shine. Her jeans were clean, and she'd teamed them with a burgundy and white striped long-sleeved shirt and matching puffer vest.

Darcy's eyes narrowed. Shiloh only ever fussed over her appearance for special occasions, and Leo. She would have pried had Lisette not bounded through the door with a bottle of white wine in one hand, a box of Cornetto ice creams in the other, and her chunky bear-eared beanie sparkling with raindrops. A punky black skull jeered from the corner of her nose, making Darcy wonder if Lisette had guessed this wasn't to be a happy lunch, but her friend was as chipper as always.

'Princess! I hope you didn't make anything for dessert because I brought it.' She waved the Cornetto box. 'Blueberry, so we can kid ourselves it's summer. Hi, Shiloh.' Lisette skidded to a halt and gave Shiloh a once-over. 'You're looking glam. What's up?'

'I think that's more a question for Darcy.' Shiloh turned her shrewd gaze onto her sister, neatly avoiding the question. 'What's the big occasion?'

'All in good time,' said Darcy as cheerfully as she could manage, except there was no fooling Shiloh. Her gaze raked Darcy's face, her frown deepening with every sweep, and making Darcy want to pad under her eyes to check if her concealer was doing its job.

Shiloh slapped a hand down. 'I bloody told you.'

Darcy held in a sigh. *Here they go.*

Lisette's gaze ping-ponged between them as she cracked the top of the wine bottle and began to pour. 'Told her what?'

'Spit it out,' Shiloh ordered when Darcy didn't immediately answer.

Lisette slid a brimming glass across the table. Darcy gripped the stem, eyes stinging as tears she'd thought had reached drought status threatened to spill again. She sniffed then swallowed a mouthful of wine. Sufficiently girded, she outlined the events of the previous night.

'How can you be so sure he didn't mean it?' asked Lisette, already one glass down and pouring herself another. Shock tended to do that to Lisette.

'He didn't sound or act right. It was if he was reading off a script. All stiff and …' She gave a frustrated growl. 'It's hard to explain. All I know is that it wasn't him. Not the Stirling I know.' Darcy glared as her sister rolled her eyes. 'It wasn't. There's something wrong and ...' She breathed in. 'I think it's something to do with me.'

'Bullshit,' snapped Shiloh at the same time Lisette let out a vehement 'No way!'

Shiloh stabbed a finger in Darcy's direction. 'Do not go blaming yourself for some man's screw-ups.'

Darcy held up her palms. 'Hear me out before you get too high on your horses. I spent all night mulling this over and there's only one reason I can think of that would make Stirling act this way, and that's if he felt he needed to push me away to protect me.'

'From his PTSD?' Shiloh's tone remained as fierce as her gaze.

Lisette blinked rapidly. 'Stirling has PTSD?'

Darcy sucked on her bottom lip. 'I don't know. He swears he doesn't and I want to believe him, but ...'

'He behaves like he does,' filled in Shiloh.

'Maybe. He's been acting strange, and I know I'm no psychologist but I'm not convinced it's PTSD. I can't help feeling it's something else. Specifically, someone else.'

Lisette leaned forward. 'What do you mean, "someone"?'

'As in someone threatening him?' Shiloh pondered the idea. 'I guess it's possible someone might want to take Dougal's crimes out on Stirling. Bit of a stretch though.'

Darcy hadn't considered that and it opened up a whole new list of suspects. Her idea it might be Mal flew out the window. All she had was Stirling's tension when they'd walked past Mal's office on Thursday night and his reaction when Darcy revealed Mal had visited her. Besides, why would she be in danger from Mal? He was a country solicitor, for goodness' sake. And as far as she knew, Mal hadn't been affected by Dougal's fraud. Not monetarily.

Shiloh directed her next words at Darcy, doubt clear in her voice. 'Is that what you were thinking?'

'I don't know.' She groaned and rested her head on her arms. 'I'm just trying to understand.'

A hand patted her shoulder as though she was an upset dog. Shiloh, doing her best imitation of empathy. Darcy sniffed and lifted her head. Lack of sleep had it feeling as sand-filled as her pattern weights. Lisette and Shiloh both stared at her with concern.

'He didn't mean it.' She straightened and held her hand over her heart. 'I know that man intimately and he would never hurt me.'

'Yet he did,' said Lisette.

'For a reason. And I need to know why.'

'You could try talking to him,' said Shiloh with a wry smile.

Darcy returned fire with a blistering look. 'What do you think I did last night?'

'So try again.'

She breathed in as she remembered Stirling's stiffness, the clenched fists. The hurt he'd inflicted.

'You're the one who said they needed to know why,' said Shiloh. 'Not going to find out unless you ask.'

'All right.' It wasn't as if she had any other options.

'When?' asked Lisette.

'I don't know. After lunch maybe.' Although the fatigue dragging at her body made Darcy wonder if she shouldn't have a nap first.

Lisette mulled this over. 'Why not leave it for tomorrow, when you're looking less …' She winced.

'Haggard,' said Shiloh, earning an elbow to the ribs from Lisette.

'More *princessy*,' Lisette corrected. 'Wear your sexiest outfit. Remind him of what he's missing.'

It was probably good advice. Darcy's concealer clearly wasn't doing a good enough job and she was so tired, muddled and fearful, it was a struggle to keep from breaking down. If she was to wrangle the truth from Stirling she'd need to be at her best. Face him with confidence and a clear head, and not like this, on the cusp of a breakdown or temper tantrum.

'Tomorrow morning then,' she said. Decision made, she breathed in deeply, only to be assaulted by the acrid aroma of burning quiche.

It was definitely an afternoon to spend in bed.

Chapter Thirty-Eight

Alexander was true to his word. The profile Stirling had requested landed in his inbox at six on Sunday morning, a day and a half after he'd asked for help. A day and a half that, without Darcy in his life, seemed to stretch forever.

If you need anything else, read Alexander's note, *call me. PS. Olympia sends a hug and is making noises about being bridesmaid when you marry Darcy. You have been warned.*

Stirling gave a shallow laugh, though it was choked with sadness. Yet another girl he adored who he'd let down. If he had time to wallow, the anguish bearing down on his heart would crush him, but he didn't have time. Not when Mal had his malevolent gaze on Darcy. Burying his pain, Stirling shot a quick thank-you note back to Alexander and opened the file.

Whoever had written the document had done an extraordinary job in the short time available. Stirling hadn't expected anything so comprehensive, but he supposed that when a man like Alexander Maugham asked for something, he got it. The file ran for near forty pages, the contents split into the stages of Mal's life, from birth until now, and included scans of relevant documentation like birth and marriage certificates.

As tempting as it was to skip through to the years in the lead-up to Dougal's death, Stirling settled down to read from the beginning.

Within minutes he was sitting up. He stared straight ahead, a frown on his face, his mind scrambling. There was no mention of the scholarship Mal had proudly claimed to have earned to Dougal's prestigious school. Surely an event that formative would not have been overlooked. And if there was no scholarship, how had his parents afforded the fees? Mal had said the McKenzies were blue-collar workers—his father David a mechanic, his mum Pamela a cleaner. She'd even worked for a while at Westwind.

Stirling straightened even further, his heart thudding. 'You're shitting me,' he said.

Indecision tore at him. He could check the ledgers and confirm his suspicion, or he could read on. Stirling jotted a note and returned to the document. There might be yet more he needed to crosscheck.

Mal's university years yielded nothing other than to reinforce that he was clever and one of the more sought-after graduates. Oddly, despite offers from several major firms, Mal chose a modest but prosperous practice in Geelong that specialised in financial and tax law for small- and medium-sized businesses. It seemed a lesser choice for a man who had so much opportunity and potential. Then again, perhaps his decision was simply because Geelong was that much closer to Grassmoor and his family.

His time with Hannigan and Partners appeared to be happy and successful. Right up until the firm was caught up in the Serious Financial Crimes Taskforce's Operation Teasdale.

There was no evidence of Mal's involvement in the partnership's extensive money-laundering operations. According to the report, he'd been a respected member of the business but junior and not party to the senior partners' malpractice. Or at least had kept his nose clean enough that no involvement could be proved. Stirling had no doubt that the associated taint would have been lasting, which partially answered why such a talented man chose to retreat to Grassmoor and quiet country practice. He was licking his wounds.

Stirling sat back and tapped his pen against his bottom lip. Mal may not have been involved but he was a smart man. He would have noticed there was more to Hannigan's prosperity than good management. He would have watched the players, and he would have learned.

All the while gathering the expertise he'd need to later manipulate Dougal into fraud.

Or maybe he did none of those things. Stirling's gut instinct wasn't evidence. Nor did it answer why Dougal died and why Stirling—and Darcy—were under threat.

When he finished the report, he made a cup of tea. He sipped for a while, re-reading the parts he felt offered most insight into Mal. Then, when he could put it off no longer, he dragged his weary heart and legs to the library.

Stirling plucked free the tiny piece of carpet fluff he'd set into the door frame and pocketed it. With the weather so foul, he'd been leaving unused rooms closed to confine warmth to the main part of the house, and though he knew it was overkill—even paranoid— caution had him enforcing his surveillance system inside as well as out.

The chill hit him the moment he opened the door. Yet another squall was splattering rain against the window, making the room dingy. Stirling scanned the ledger shelves. He would need to find three dates: the final year of Mal's mother's employment, the year of Mal's birth, and the year he went to boarding school. The first he could guess from Mal's birthday. The latter two he knew from the report.

He struck lucky. The dates of his mother's end of employment and Mal's birth fell across a single financial year. Stirling hadn't relished carting three of the weighty tomes back to the kitchen.

He dumped the ledgers on the table and took a minute to warm himself by the range, putting off the moment when he'd open the pages and prove his suspicions correct. Stirling was certain what he'd find and the thought made his stomach contract. Like his predecessors, Benjamin had been meticulous with his records, safe in the knowledge that the secrets contained within would only be seen by himself, or men like him.

Finally Stirling took his seat and began scanning the pages.

He found Mal's mother's regular remuneration easily. It was listed each month, along with the names of other staff. He followed the trail until in September, he found it—a payout of three times her yearly wage. He skipped forward five months, then six. Another payment in April, the month following Mal's birth. The figure was the same as Pamela's pregnancy payout, as if she'd received a bonus or reward for a live birth.

Or hush money.

The thought curdled in Stirling's head. That his grandfather was an adulterer he could process. He could even accept that Benjamin most likely abused his power to convince Pamela to sleep with him. But that he was something worse? That Stirling shared genes with a potential rapist made his stomach roil.

He wondered how Pamela explained the extra cash. Saying Benjamin was a generous ex-boss wouldn't cut it. Three times a yearly wage, paid twice, had to be suspect. Or maybe Mal's father chose to ignore the meaning behind it and bring up the child as his own. Perhaps he thought there'd be more money in the future.

Using his phone, Stirling photographed the relevant pages, set the first ledger aside and opened the next. As expected, at the start of the school year, under Dougal's name and his school fees, was a line that read 'Scholarship Child' and an equivalent amount in the column alongside.

Stirling photographed the page and shoved the ledger away in disgust, then rose to stare out the window, his fingers clenched tightly around the edges of the bench.

What a tangled mess. No wonder neither party encouraged the two boys' friendship. No wonder Stirling nearly mistook Mal for his dead father when he first came to visit in hospital. No wonder Xavier looked uncannily like Stirling as a boy.

Mal and Dougal were brothers.

Bitterness filled his mouth as he made the next leap—Mal, the man he loathed and feared, was also Stirling's uncle.

Chapter Thirty-Nine

It was just before ten o'clock on Sunday morning when Darcy passed through Westwind's ornate gates. She took the drive slowly, her stomach fluttering with nerves and the fear that this morning might not go her way.

It had to. She wasn't ready to let Stirling leave her life, not after they'd shared so much. Nor was she ready to forsake him. If there was something wrong—and there clearly was—Darcy wanted to be there for him. That's what love meant—being there, warts and all.

A cane basket sat on the passenger seat. Inside, wrapped in a clean checked tea towel, was a batch of freshly made scones. Tucked beside them were tubs of strawberry jam and whipped cream. The kind of gift that was hard to say no to. As were, she prayed, her off-the-shoulder sapphire-blue wiggle dress, sheer stockings and patent heels.

The squally weather had left the ground soft and muddy. Though clear for the moment, more rain was forecast and the distant sky was thick with scudding slate-coloured clouds chased on by a fierce westerly. Weather this miserable should have seen light glowing behind the front windows, but the house was as dull as the day, as though it too wallowed in sorrow.

Except Darcy wasn't sorrowful. She was scared and churning with nerves. But what kept her pressing on the accelerator was faith. Faith in Stirling, in herself, in what they shared. And a whole heartful of determination.

They loved each other and Darcy had zero intention of letting anything or anyone stand in their way, least of all Stirling's misguided sense of honour.

She parked in the courtyard and regarded the house. It remained still and quiet, with only wind-tossed detritus skittering around its foundations. No smiling Stirling striding out to meet her. No welcome, no warmth. Shuttered and hollow. Either he wasn't home, or he had gone for good.

Darcy closed her eyes and took a deep breath. No matter the circumstances, she couldn't stay sitting here.

Movement near the edge of the courtyard snagged her attention as she reached for the basket. A figure approached from the trail to the garden and firepit. A man, felt hat lowered against the wind and coat flapping around his thighs. For a breath her heart somersaulted, then she realised her mistake. Though similar from a distance, this man was no Stirling.

She frowned. After their previous conversation, the last person she expected to find at Westwind was Mal. Stirling certainly wouldn't welcome him.

Whatever the reason for his appearance, she hoped he wasn't planning on hanging around. Darcy had a man to seduce.

Basket in hand, she forced a cheerful demeanour and pushed open the door. 'Mal, what are you doing here?'

'Probably the same as you.'

Darcy doubted that very much.

He indicated back down the hill. 'I was visiting Xavier's memorial when I noticed how dark Westwind was. Started me worrying. I thought I'd better do a welfare check. No response though. I was on my way back down the hill when I saw you arrive.'

Of course. After all, it was Mal who'd raised the spectre of PTSD and his need to keep an eye on Stirling for Dougal's sake. Although it was a truly awful day for visiting the memorial and the way back was in the opposite direction to the garden.

'I tried the door but it's locked.' He indicated the little patio. 'His bike's gone too.'

'Stirling's bike?' Her head jerked towards where the Ducati should have been. Darcy had been too distracted by Mal's arrival to notice it missing. Her free hand went to her suddenly churning stomach. No. He could not have left already. He could not.

She swallowed. 'He's probably gone for a ride.'

Mal checked the sky. 'Bit dangerous in this weather.' He switched focus to the back door and frowned. 'I think we should check. Like you said, he's probably gone for a ride, but the way he's been behaving ...' Mal shook his head and regarded her from under his shadowed brow.

Darcy wasn't sure what that look meant. She was more fearful about what a locked house and a missing bike indicated. Her throat thickened. She should have come yesterday, like she'd proposed at lunch. Now it might be too late.

'Did you try calling?' she asked, hating the hoarseness of her voice. The despair.

Mal nodded. 'No answer.'

She looked at the door, torn between respecting Stirling's privacy and the pain in her heart, then glanced at the patio eaves and the recess where the not-very-secret spare key dangled on its hook. A key, she realised, she'd completely forgotten to tell Stirling about.

'I really think we should check,' said Mal, and Darcy could hear her own tension reflected in his voice. 'If he's taken the bike out in bad weather ...' He made a helpless gesture with his hands.

Though she didn't believe for one moment Stirling might be suicidal, Mal's words were enough. 'I'll get the key.'

The kitchen was empty though warm. Wherever Stirling was, they had only just missed him. Everything was scrupulously neat—the sink and drainer clear of dishes, his favourite chair at the end of the kitchen table pushed in, the space in front clear. No laptop, no notepaper, no empty coffee cup. The only out of place item was a tattered Grassmoor district phone directory on top of the sideboard.

He'd gone.

'No,' she whispered, and dumping the basket, shot out of the room and bolted up the stairs as fast as her heels would allow.

Darcy was panting when she flung open the door to Stirling's bedroom, only for her breath to hitch when she saw the meticulously made bed. She moaned, deep and pained, and with leaden legs crossed to it, blinking at the memory of the intimate moments they had shared beneath its covers.

How could he walk out on that love? They'd been special together. Magical. They had been from the moment she'd found him bleeding his life out into the ground and had stripped off her dress.

A sob threatened to erupt. Darcy forced it down. She would not crack, not with Mal in the house. Her grief over her broken relationship with Stirling was private and his patronising sympathy would only make it worse. Or cause her to do something she might regret.

She walked to the ensuite and let go a single sob, but it was one of relief. Lined up like little soldiers on the sink were Stirling's toiletries.

Hand over her mouth, Darcy sagged against the doorjamb. He hadn't left.

It was pathetic, but the need to feel him overcame sensibility. She traced fingers over his things, unscrewed the lid off his body wash and breathed in the comfort of its sandalwood scent. Remembering. Loving. Still fearing for their future.

But he was here. She still had a chance.

Mal's sodden hat on the kitchen table was the only sign of the man when Darcy returned. She listened, and though the house was solid and well sealed, the rush of wind outside was such that she couldn't pick where he might be.

She went to call for him then closed her mouth as the hairs on the back of her neck rose. She'd been too distracted to realise the strangeness of Mal's arrival. Now she had the headspace to think, it was difficult to imagine anyone visiting a memorial on a day this foul, even a beloved son's. It was also clear Stirling was out, yet Mal had pushed hard to come inside.

Treading as softly as her heels would allow, Darcy ventured back up the hall, peering in rooms as she went.

She found Mal in the library, crouched over a large open book covered in fine, faded writing. He was staring at it with what she could only describe as fury. Fury that vanished the moment he sensed her presence.

He closed the book and patted it. 'Westwind's old ledgers. Fascinating. Benjamin seems to have recorded everything. How did you go?'

Darcy didn't answer for a moment. She was suddenly aware that she was alone on an isolated property with a man she didn't trust. And who, more tellingly, Stirling didn't trust.

'His things are still there. We were worrying about nothing. He's probably gone for a ride, as I suggested.' She edged away from the library door. 'We should leave. I'd hate for Stirling to arrive home and find us trespassing.'

'Yes, I guess you're right.' Mal glanced around before his gaze settled back on the ledger. His lip curled then swiftly straightened. He set the book on top of the others, tapping the edges to ensure they were all aligned, and headed to the door. He paused in front of her. 'I'm glad we checked though. Sufferers of PTSD ...' He sucked air in through his teeth. 'You can never be too careful.'

'No,' said Darcy, her voice soft but her pulse loud in her ears. 'You can't.'

Chapter Forty

Stirling's fists flexed as searched with the torch on his phone for the leaves and twigs he'd used to mark Westwind's back door. None remained. Someone had trespassed.

He scanned the yard for movement, but it was pointless. Dusk was falling fast and yet another filthy rain shower was dumping its load. He could barely hear himself think over the rattle of raindrops and wind. He was soaked as it was, and in a mood after his journey into Grassmoor followed by an afternoon of trying to sort his head out.

He hadn't planned to be this late, but a combination of weather and a deep need to remind himself of who he'd once been had kept him on the road. It had taken several hours and a late pub lunch at a tiny town on the flat plains to the north, until finally, somewhere in the sweeping bends, he vanquished his fear and regained control. His genes might be part Kildare but he was his own man, and a good one.

Except to Darcy.

Shoving the thought aside, Stirling braced himself and opened the door, locking it again behind him. He stood in the mudroom, dripping water and listening as he planned his search. If Mal was hiding inside, he wouldn't escape a second time.

He checked the kitchen and pantry and the tiny markers he'd laid in the cellar trapdoor. Satisfied they were clear, he combed the remainder of the house, before returning to the library where earlier he'd discovered his little pieces of fluff dislodged.

Mal had been here. He could feel it in the air, in his gut. Stirling stared at the ledgers. He'd positioned them just so, the top ledger slightly off centre. Not by much, a few millimetres at most. Enough that the stack appeared square at first glance. Whoever had touched them had fallen for his ruse and realigned the books when they'd finished.

Stirling grimaced. He'd expected another intrusion. Mal would be desperate to know how much Stirling had figured out.

Had Mal learned anything he didn't already know? Perhaps. Jayne Bucknell had said she imagined Mal must be aware of his parentage but wasn't certain. They'd discussed it over shortbread biscuits and tea, after Stirling had phoned her early that morning asking if she was free for a chat.

'For what purpose?' she'd replied.

'I want to know about Benjamin.'

There'd been a long pause, and Stirling couldn't help feeling that she knew exactly what he was after and was deciding whether to share.

'I'll see you at nine thirty,' she'd said, before following with directions.

Stirling hadn't needed them. Jayne's address was listed right alongside her phone number in the Grassmoor directory he'd

found in the kitchen sideboard, and a quick google had laid out the
route. She'd hung up as though Stirling were nothing more than a
bothersome telemarketer.

Jayne had treated him with more politeness on arrival, although
had not been impressed by Stirling turning up on his Ducati.
Stirling wasn't impressed with his own stupidity either. The ride
had been slippery, the wind savage, and the ute would have been
safer and kept him dry. Instead, he'd wriggled on full leathers and
taken the bike, like some sort of avenging hero. A mistake, but at
least the blast of cold had helped clear his head.

Only for Jayne's revelations to muddy it again.

Benjamin might have been a wealthy respected man but, as Jayne
had remarked, his feet were made of clay. A particularly crumbly
version, in Benjamin's case. His healthy sense of *noblesse* had little
of the *oblige* that went with it.

'It was quite unsavoury,' Jayne had commented. 'An aunt warned
me to be careful around him, but he never touched me, or any of
my friends.' She smiled and Stirling noted its spiteful edge. 'Wrong
class.'

The shortbread Stirling had eaten to be polite had churned in his
stomach.

'Right.' He fingered the delicate handle of his teacup, wondering
how the hell he could phrase the next question without giving too
much away. 'Were there ever any ...' He hesitated.

Jayne smiled. 'Ah, so you noticed. I wondered if you would.'

Apparently Mal's parentage was a local secret. Everyone knew,
but no one said a word. The question remained though: Did Mal?

If he'd gone through the ledgers, then he did now.

Stirling stalked back to the kitchen and headed for the
mudroom. He'd hidden his laptop in a laundry cupboard inside a

tatty cardboard box and surrounded it with rags and other cleaning paraphernalia.

He set up the computer in its usual position at the end of the table and placed a notepad and pen alongside. Then, when he'd stoked the range into life, Stirling sat, stared at the brightening screen and gave a long exhale.

For several minutes he did nothing, too busy sorting his thoughts. Too worried he might be proving Mal right. That Phillipa Tan would dismiss his report as the ravings of a paranoid ex-soldier who spied conspiracy around every corner.

Then he remembered the hangwoman etched into the dusty rear screen of the car. He remembered Shiloh's dismay at Dougal shooting his dogs, Gavin's questioning of Dougal's suicide, and Dougal's sudden change of will. Finally he remembered Mal's warning about the pain of losing a loved one, and his heart steeled.

The report took Stirling a good chunk of the night. Following the threads and connecting them to the little evidence he had was trickier than he'd expected. Nor did it help that he was physically exhausted and emotionally drained. Sometime around midnight he made a cup of sweet tea and raided the fridge for sandwich ingredients. The sustenance fuelled the following hours, but by the time three thirty arrived he was completely done-in. So was the report.

He scanned through the pages one last time. So much of it was extrapolation, scenarios comprised almost entirely of 'ifs'. *If* Mal knew Dougal was Xavier's father. *If* he blamed Dougal for his son's death. *If* he suspected Benjamin might have raped his mother.

How much would a man crave revenge? How would he go about it?

And if his scheme was discovered, would he be scared enough to resort to murder to cover it up?

As satisfied as he could be with what he'd written, Stirling composed a carefully worded email to Phillipa Tan, asking her to look deeper into what he'd discovered. He hesitated over the send button. Did he really want to do this? Did he really want to put himself at risk of ridicule like this?

He rubbed his mouth, mulling over the consequences if he did and if he didn't. If he had proof, he wouldn't hesitate, but …

Stirling slid the curser away. He opened a new email, addressing it to Toby and asking him to safeguard the attached file. He offered no further explanation, other than he hoped Toby would respect his privacy and not open it unless necessary.

If anything happened to Stirling, Toby would know to read the file and pass it on to the police.

This time, he hit send.

⚬

Stirling glanced up from the cup of tea he was stirring and frowned as he tried to place the sound. There was so much of it—pelting rain whenever a squall came through, the howl of wind-assaulted trees, Westwind's endless creaks and groans as it braced against the elements.

The sound he'd heard wasn't any of those. It was more a hard crash. Like something heavy had slammed into the ground, and not far from the back of the house either.

Stirling checked out the kitchen window. The rain had stopped for the moment but the churning sky indicated it was only a matter of time before the next squall hit. It had been like this since dawn, when lightning cracks had wrenched him awake, his heart racing as he'd tried to orient himself, then unable to return to sleep when his mind turned to Darcy and his pain and regret. Then to the file he'd sent to Toby—another misgiving.

It was now 9 am and Stirling still hadn't let either go.

He dropped the spoon and trudged to the mudroom. Better to check than worry for the rest of the morning.

Stirling pulled on a waterproof coat and boots. He considered one of Dougal's felt hats for a moment and moved on. It'd only blow off and be lost to the wilds, and while his feelings about Dougal remained conflicted, he didn't want to lose any more of the man. Even a hat.

The wind punched him in the face and chest the moment he opened the door. Stirling staggered a little and swore as he grappled with the door and his flapping coat. Turning his back, he zipped the coat to his neck and faced the weather again.

Then he saw it.

'Shit,' he said and marched straight out, yanking the door shut behind him.

The Ducati was on its flank, its side mirror smashed and pannier buckled, its beautiful deco scratched and scarred.

He swore again. The bike weighed over two hundred kilograms. A year ago, he would have had the power to lever it upright. Not now. Stirling stared at it with slumped shoulders. It'd have to stay where it was until he could get Gav or Shiloh to help. Assuming she would. After what he'd done to Darcy, Shiloh would be more likely to sic her dog on to him.

He continued to stare at the Ducati. How the hell had it fallen over in the first place? The centre stand was designed for extra parking stability, especially when travelling with loaded panniers, and yeah, the wind was strong, but strong enough to tip over a bike? The gusts weren't as severe here either, thanks to the low wall protecting the far side of the porch.

A scrape sounded behind him. Not a stick or pine cone tumbling across the courtyard. Something else. Something that shot a cold thread up Stirling's spine and whooshed adrenaline through his veins.

Slowly, his hands flexing, he turned around and grimaced. 'Mal.'

Chapter Forty-One

Mal stood four metres away, a rifle gripped in front of his body, its barrel angled towards Stirling. Not a full shooting stance but it would only take an instant to swing up the gun and fire. A full-length oilskin coat, dark from wet, flapped around Mal's braced legs, giving him the look of a dastardly comic book villain. If the situation wasn't so dangerous, Stirling might have laughed. There was nothing comical about Mal's expression though. His smug mouth was curled upward. Hatred blazed deep and hot in his eyes.

'Hello, Stirling.'

He nodded slowly, not at Mal but at the acceptance of his own foolishness. He should have realised it would come to this.

'Good move,' he said. 'Drawing me out of the house like that. Unarmed.' He tipped his head to the side. 'Is that what you did with Dougal? Lured him out then held him at gunpoint? Forced him to the shed?'

Mal made a chuffing noise that could have been a laugh or bitter disdain but didn't answer.

Stirling opened his palms and shrugged. 'What's the plan now? Make me hang myself like you did him?'

Mal shook his head. 'Dougal took his own life.'

'Maybe he did. Maybe he even did it willingly. But you helped him along. You're the one who destroyed him with shame.'

Mal's lip twitched.

Realisation prickled down Stirling's spine. He'd been only guessing before, but Mal's reaction flung his mind into a spin. 'That was it, wasn't it? You wanted to shame him in front of the very people who admired and respected him. Show them who he really was. So you set him up. What did you promise him? Some sort of get-rich-quick scheme to fund the nursing centre? A nursing centre Dougal planned to name after *his son*.'

'Xavier was mine.'

'But he wasn't, was he? He was Dougal's.' Stirling smiled but it was as cold as the frigid day. 'You shouldn't have shot the dogs, Mal.'

Mal gave another of those laughs. 'You're telling me we got to this point because of the dogs?'

'No. We're at this point because of you and what you did to Dougal and to this district.'

'See, Stirling? That's where you've got it all wrong. I didn't do anything. Dougal did it all.'

'Only because you played him.'

'The only player around here was your father.' Mal's upper lip curled back. 'He had everything, every privilege, yet it was never enough. He always had to have more. The whole rotten family always wanted more.'

'More, like your wife? Like Benjamin wanted your mother? You know about that, don't you? You figured it out from the ledgers, just like I did. The payout. Your fake scholarship.'

Mal shook his head. 'There you go, getting it wrong again.' He smirked. 'I already knew. Mum told me just before she died. You know what that bastard did?'

Stirling's gut sank with dread. He wanted to cover his ears like a little boy, not hear the truth. Yet it was coming, whether he wanted to hear it or not.

'Benjamin raped her. Drunk one night. That was his excuse but it was always going to happen. He'd been eyeing Mum off from the day she started. Your grandfather.' He sneered. 'The rapist.'

Stirling swallowed his shame at his grandfather's actions. He couldn't afford shame. He couldn't afford anything but to hang onto his wits.

Stirling returned Mal's sneer in full. 'Your father, the rapist.'

For a moment, Stirling thought Mal was going to charge him, then he calmed and smiled, as though he'd seen through Stirling's effort to wind him up, force him into a mistake. He jerked the gun to the right. 'Move.'

Stirling stayed put, legs apart, arms loose, every inch of him tingling with hyperawareness. Hunting, praying, for a weakness in his enemy. All he needed was an opening. 'If I say no?'

'Then I'll shoot you like I did the dogs.' Mal gave a crocodile smile. 'Only I might not do it in the head.'

'Fair enough,' said Stirling as though he'd expected as much. 'I don't like your chances of making that look like suicide though.'

Mal didn't sound fazed. 'Maybe you'll just go missing. Another veteran casualty who couldn't cope with his PTSD and took himself off somewhere to kill himself. Maybe the ranges.' He jerked his chin towards the north. 'Plenty of places to hide a body there. And it's not like you don't have form. Everyone knows you have issues. All that terrible *guilt*.'

Another chill ran through Stirling. From what he'd learned, the ranges were thick with stringybark and abandoned gravel and sandstone quarries. As Mal said, an easy place to hide a body. Perhaps not forever but long enough to make identity and cause of death difficult, especially if it was a stomach wound. If Stirling wanted to survive this day, he'd have to fight. Somehow.

'It'll be nicer if you hang yourself,' said Mal, as if he were talking about matching haircuts. 'Like father, like son. Symmetry.'

It was the way he said 'son' that had Stirling's mind racing. 'Is this what this is about? Nothing to do with me knowing too much but some sort of eye for an eye revenge.' His tone rose as anger and disbelief bubbled through. 'You blame Benjamin for your mother and Dougal for Xavier and now you're going to take it out on me?'

'He took him away. My boy.' For a moment, Mal's voice cracked, then it turned savage. 'For once in my life I had more than he ever would, and he took him away. And then, *you*.' The gun barrel jerked dangerously. 'You, who should never have existed, turn up, looking just like him, acting just like him. Taking over Westwind like you belong. Like he'd won.'

'Won? You think Dougal was laughing at you from the grave because he had a son and you'd lost yours? You're a lunatic.'

The rifle flew up. 'Move.'

Stirling's mouth compressed. He needed to keep his gob shut and use his brain. Provoking a man this unhinged would only get him shot. And he wasn't ready to die. Not when he had so much to live for. Not if there was a chance to make a life with Darcy.

If she'd forgive him.

Mal swung the rifle to the right, an order to move out. Stirling didn't. He held Mal's gaze, arms and legs akimbo, using the power pose to prime himself and, maybe, give his enemy pause to think about who he was dealing with. An ex-soldier who'd seen more action than Mal could dream of.

Not a Kildare of Westwind. Himself. Stirling Hawley. A man of integrity. Of conviction.

A man of courage.

'You don't know, do you?' he said, mockery in his voice. Needling might infuriate Mal further, but he had to take the chance. He was running out of time.

Mal's eyes narrowed. 'Know what?'

'Dougal was going to leave you Westwind.'

For the first time, Mal appeared uncertain. He lowered the gun slightly. 'What are you talking about?'

'The will Dougal made through William the week before he died wasn't the first. There was another, made seven months earlier. In it, he left you Westwind.'

'Bullshit.'

'It's the truth. Ask William.'

Mal said nothing for a moment. His jaw worked as though chewing the news over. The wind gusts grew stronger, bringing spits of frigid rain. 'Why would he do that? I never cared about the house. Why do you think I smashed the stonework and painted that graffiti?'

So it was Mal who had vandalised Westwind. Stirling should have guessed. What a cunning trick to make Dougal appear to be driven to suicide. It made Stirling wonder if Mal wasn't responsible for the 'hell' brick too.

Stirling raised his voice as the noise grew. 'I think he felt he owed you.'

Mal laughed. 'A Kildare? Owing someone?' He shook his head, as though the only genetics he shared were with his mother. 'They only know how to take.'

'It's the logical explanation. I think Dougal discovered the truth the same way I did, by chance, and it shocked him to the core. Not just what Benjamin had done to your mother, but that he'd betrayed his own brother. What could he do to make up for it? Leave you the most precious thing he had.' Stirling lowered his voice. 'He left you Xavier, Mal. The memorial. The place where he died. The essence of him.'

Mal's head swung in rapid shuddery oscillations. 'No.'

The rain thickened. Fat drops splattered over Mal's head and pinged off the rifle's barrel. It welted the porch roof like thrown stones and pocked the deepening puddles. The trees whipped, sodden leaves bashing in a rage of sound like a million cymbals crashed together.

'Except things started to go wrong, didn't they? It was all right at the start. You kept enough money coming back to make Dougal think the scheme could work. To keep trusting you. Then what happened? Did he get suspicious when the money slowed? Start to question you? Demand proof of your investments?'

Mal said nothing.

'He realised you were playing him, didn't he? That you weren't driven by a common goal but some sort of sick revenge. So he changed his will again. Then he tried to gather information, desperate to fix things. But you had your scam wrapped up so tight he was left with nothing but his guilt.' Stirling's voice lowered, his anger projecting like a missile at this man who was his uncle. 'And you killed him, you prick. Your own brother. My father.'

The fault-filled good man.

Mal didn't want to hear. 'Dougal killed himself. He put that noose around his own neck and stepped off the drum. I didn't do anything.'

'You talk about bullshit? You forced him, just like you're trying to force me.'

A savage gust rattled the house. The trees shook like they were shattering. The rain was pelting now, sharp wind-driven drops razoring the air.

'He was your best friend.' It was Stirling's turn to choke up. So many wrongs performed in the name of what? Pride? Jealousy? Pathetic, unworthy emotions. 'He was your brother.'

Mal's gaze went dead. 'He was never my brother. Dougal was a cheat who didn't care about anyone but himself. Enough talk. Move.'

Stirling thought about telling Mal to shove it and decided against it. This wasn't over. Stirling might not be the man he once was, but he was still a soldier at heart. He'd go out fighting. All he needed was the right opportunity.

'I said move!'

Stirling stepped from under the porch. The rain struck his head like needles. 'Where?'

'Shed.' Mal bared his teeth. 'Where else?' He indicated the direction with the rifle.

Stirling trod slowly, emphasising his limp, hoping to make himself appear weak so Mal might lower his guard. The yard was slick with puddles and debris. Could he use that to his advantage?

With every step he considered a plan of action only to discard it. Mal was keeping well back, too distant to surprise with a rush attack. Stirling could feign a trip and tumble but to what end? Mal wouldn't help him up and it risked injury, weakening his position even further. Could he kick water in Mal's face? Again, it was too far.

What he needed was a weapon. Something to knock the rifle or distract Mal and give Stirling time to charge. Stirling scanned the yard. They'd almost reached the end of the bricked area. Between there and the shed was nothing but track.

Despair rose like bile. This could not be how he died. He refused to go out this way, defeated. Without fight or courage. He had to think.

Yet every step yielded nothing.

By the time they neared the shed, the squall had scudded eastward and the rain had abated to a few intermittent splatters. Stirling's legs were soaked, his hair plastered to his head. He scraped water from around his eyes to clear his vision and dropped his hand. When he looked up again, his feet refused to move.

From one of the forward beams hung a noose. Below it sat a bright yellow plastic drench drum. His destiny.

Like hell.

He faced Mal. 'You've been busy.'

'Keep moving.'

'You don't want to do this.'

'That's where you're wrong. I do.'

'And then what?' Stirling took a step forward. 'Huh? Then what?'

Mal lifted the rifle to his shoulder.

Stirling looked down the black cylinder that was aimed at his chest. His heart raced, the pound of it thundering in his ears. Every tendon was taut.

'Kill me and you really will have nothing.'

'I said move.'

Stirling was out of options. Mal still wasn't close enough. Stirling would be dead before he reached the end of the rifle.

The barrel jerked. 'Go on.'

Stirling clenched and unclenched his fists and slowly turned, his focus now on the rope and drum. The two potential weapons he could reach. The rope was secured to the rafter and useless. The drum though ...

He stalked towards it, his ears on Mal's movements. The rain returned, rattling against the shed's corrugated iron roof and sides in a cannonade of noise. Stirling stepped behind the drum, his face towards Mal but his focus on his right foot as he pressed his toe against the plastic. At first there was no movement, then, with a little more pressure, the drum slid.

Near empty but with enough contents to aid momentum. Perfect.

He risked a glance down. The drum had a handle moulded into the top. Legs braced, Stirling breathed in deeply through his nose. He flexed his fingers and forced them open. It was now down to timing and manipulation.

'Get on it,' said Mal.

Stirling curled his lip and hoicked his chin like a thug urging an upstart to have a go. 'Make me.'

For a lurching moment, Stirling thought Mal wouldn't take the bait, then Mal took two steps closer, his expression drawn like a snarling animal.

'I said, get on the drum.'

Stirling's heart began to gallop. A lunge, followed by a lift and swing, then the hardest tackle of his life. That's all it would take. 'You know what, *Uncle Mal?* I don't think I—'

'Stirling!'

He whirled towards the voice, dragging Mal's aim with him.

Breath evaporated from his lungs as a figure ran awkwardly towards them through the pummelling rain.

'No,' he said, the words quiet with horror. 'No, no, no.'

It was Darcy.

Chapter Forty-Two

Stirling thrust up his palm. 'Stay back!'

But Darcy kept coming, tiptoeing rapidly down the track on her ridiculous heels, arms out for balance, her flared orange and white polka dot raincoat swinging above her knees.

The sight of her sent terror rising and his heart soaring at the same time.

Stirling cast a panicked look at Mal. The man's eyes were narrowed. Worse, he'd taken two steps back and returned aim at Stirling's chest. There was no way he could charge now. Mal would shoot him and then …

Darcy, please not Darcy.

The words rumbled out of his chest. 'If you hurt her …'

Mal sneered. 'You'll do what?'

Stirling's fists clenched. He turned back to Darcy. She was closing in fast. A gust of wind caught the fur-rimmed hood of her coat and blew it back from her face. Her cheeks were pale. Worry carved her brow. Her scarlet mouth though was determined.

'Darcy, get back!'

'I will not.'

Stirling wanted to roar. Instead, he forced himself to use the same tone as he had when he'd cast her from Westwind. Cold. Mean. A snapped order, as though he were talking to an underling instead of the woman he adored. 'For god's sake, just do as you're told!'

'No.' Her steps slowed. A smile formed. Through the rain, through the wind. A love-laden lighthouse smile beaming at him through the storm of danger.

Stirling lost his breath. Darcy. Brave, beautiful Darcy. Christ, he loved her.

'Mal won't shoot me, will you, Mal?'

Mal said nothing. Left-right-left-right, his eyes flicked between them.

At a loss, Stirling tried a different tack. 'Darcy, please, you need to get out of here.'

'I don't think so.' She cocked a hand on her hip. 'Truly, Mal, what is this nonsense?'

Mal took another step back, the gun wavered. Stirling swallowed. He could see Mal's uncertainty in the frantic movement of his eyes and disliked it more than the deadness. An uncertain man was an unpredictable man.

He needed Darcy to leave. Now.

Stirling tried again. 'Please go. I'm begging you.'

'And leave you alone? Not a chance.' Darcy walked to Stirling's side and took his hand. 'I told you from the start, I'm invested.' She faced Mal. 'Now, are you going to drop that?'

'He'd better.'

Stirling whirled right. Shiloh stood in the middle of the track, feet apart, arms loose at her sides, a brown kelpie crouched at her heel. Mud smothered her from chest to feet.

'Sorry I took so long,' she said in her matter-of-fact Shiloh way. 'Bogged sheep.'

'What the hell are you doing here?' asked Stirling.

Shiloh gestured at Mal. 'Saw his car near the memorial. Thought I'd wander over and say hello. Spotted the gun case and cartridge box on the seat, and seeing as it looked like he hadn't blown his own head off, I figured maybe he wanted to blow off yours.' She shrugged. 'So here I am.'

Stirling looked back at Mal. His cheeks were puffed and blotched with colour. A hint of a pulse throbbed at his temple.

As Stirling was about to ask what he planned to do now, an old model Corolla with its wipers on flat out careened around the side of the house. It skidded to a halt several metres away, spraying mud and stones in its wake. The driver's side door flung open. First, a phone appeared, then Lisette's head.

She propped an elbow on the top of the door and kept the phone pointed at them. 'Smile, everyone, you're on camera!'

'What are you doing here?' asked Darcy.

'Toby called. Said I needed to get my arse pronto to Westwind to check on Stirling.' Lisette grimaced at him. 'Toby says sorry, not sorry, but he read your report thing. Bloody lucky he did, by the looks. Keep smiling for the camera, Mal.'

'Jesus wept,' muttered Stirling, caught somewhere between farce and dread.

'What's next, Mal?' said Shiloh, folding her arms. 'You going to shoot all of us?'

Four pairs of eyes zeroed in on him.

'Which also begs the question,' she continued, 'what the hell's this about anyway?'

'Mal worked out that I knew he killed Dougal,' said Stirling. 'So I needed to hang myself, too. Symmetry, wasn't it, Mal?'

The replies came in a chorus. 'What? Why? But Dougal ...'

Stirling held up a palm. 'Dougal found out Mal was scamming him. He was using the trust money to try and create capital for a bush nursing centre, but Mal was secretly siphoning it into a chain of offshore funds.'

The women broke into chatter.

'Quiet!' Mal arced the rifle between Shiloh and Lisette, before levelling it on Darcy.

Stirling immediately shoved in front of her. Darcy squawked but stayed behind. He locked eyes with Mal. Even through the cold, Stirling felt the burning hatred of the other man's stare. His own was just as savage. And loaded with warning—touch Darcy and die.

'You ...' Mal's nostrils flared as his breath hardened. His finger curled closer to the trigger.

Stirling's stomach lurched. Every sense was trained on Mal. Any twitch, any tremble, and he'd shove Darcy to the ground and charge. Gun be damned.

Mal's finger hovered.

'I wouldn't,' said Shiloh. 'Lucy here ...' She tipped her head. The dog's head was down, her hackles up, hindquarters hunched. 'Is still very upset over the murder of her sister. So am I, you pathetic shit.'

His finger remained curled, then the rifle barrel swung down. 'I've no idea what you're on about, Shiloh.'

'The dogs, Mal. I always thought it was weird for Dougal to shoot the dogs. Especially Rascal. He adored that dog.' Disgust filled her voice. 'But it was you. Innocent, defenceless animals who'd only ever shown love and loyalty, and you shot them.' She looked down at Lucy, still at her heel awaiting orders. Sensing her mistress's attention, the dog glanced up. 'Want to go him, Luce? Yeah, I bet you do. He's a bad, bad man.'

Mal shook his head. 'You've all got this wrong. I arrived here and found Stirling here about to do something terrible.' He waved at the noose. 'You can see for yourself. I was trying to stop him.'

'With a *gun?*' said Darcy.

Mal remained calm in the face her incredulity. 'To shoot the rope.' His mouth crumpled. 'After what happened to Dougal …'

'Oh for crying out loud,' said Shiloh, eyes to the sky. The rain had at least stopped. The wind gusts though, remained ferocious. 'I always thought you were a bit of a flog, Mal. But this has really proved it.'

Stirling's adrenaline rush was abating and with it, cold began to seep in. He couldn't afford to ease off. This was far from over.

'No one's going to believe you, Mal,' Lisette called from behind the car door. She lifted her phone and gave it a little waggle. 'Got it all on video. Sound and everything.'

Stirling had had enough. He took a step forward. 'Time for you to go.'

'Or shoot yourself,' said Shiloh. 'That'd be helpful. Save a lot of hassle for everyone.'

'Loh!' Darcy regarded her sister with horror. 'Don't be awful.'

'Awful?' Shiloh thrust a finger towards Mal. 'He's the—'

'That'll do,' said Stirling. 'Westwind doesn't need any more bloodshed.'

Shiloh's bottom lip dropped. 'Turd deserves it for shooting the dogs.'

'I did not—' Mal hauled in a breath. 'I can see there's no point trying to explain. You've made up your minds that I'm the villain.'

'Because you are,' said Shiloh, boggling her eyes like a teenager going *duh*.

Loathing contorted Mal's features.

'Shiloh,' Stirling warned. Mal still held the rifle. And though he felt Mal's next move would be to walk away, there was nothing stopping him from shooting at least one of them. Most likely him, but potentially Shiloh if she didn't shut up. Stirling focused on Mal. 'Why don't you put the gun down and walk away.'

Darcy stepped to his side and leaned towards his ear as though to whisper, but her voice was loud enough for everyone to hear. 'Shouldn't we hold him here until the police arrive?'

'Hold him how?'

'I could sool Lucy onto him,' said Shiloh.

'I could run him over,' called Lisette, sounding far too excited at the prospect for Stirling's liking.

Stirling held up a hand. God, these women. 'No one's going to do anything. Mal's going to leave and no one's going to get hurt.'

'But ...' Darcy made a helpless gesture.

Stirling grabbed her hand and squeezed it. 'It's okay.' He was confident that whatever freedom Mal managed would be short-lived. Right now, he just wanted him gone, away from Darcy and those she loved. He raised his eyebrows at Mal. 'Well?'

'You're making a terrible mistake. I've done nothing wrong.'

Stirling kept his gaze steely. 'Maybe. Maybe not. I guess we'll find out. Put the gun down. Now.'

'I don't think so.' Mal cast them a final look, turned his back and began walking stiffly down the track towards Shiloh, the rifle pointed downward.

'Watch out, Shiloh,' said Darcy, forcing Stirling to yank her back when she made to step forward.

If Shiloh feared the armed man advancing her way, she didn't show it. She stepped aside with a short mocking bow, like a Regency gentleman giving way to a lady he loathed. Lucy was less polite. She remained hunched, sharp teeth drawn, a low growl vibrating her ribs.

Mal paused as though contemplating whether to have the last word, then gave a martyred sigh and walked on.

His hand still gripping Darcy's, Stirling followed to stand alongside Shiloh. From behind came the sound of a slamming door and jogged steps as Lisette caught up. Together they watched Mal navigate the track until he veered off to the left and was lost beyond the steep slope.

'Do you think he'll shoot himself?' asked Shiloh, sounding hopeful.

'No.' Stirling was sure of that. 'He still thinks he can get away with it. He'll run though. Speaking of which, Lisette, do you have your phone?'

'Sure do.' Without further instruction, Lisette began dialling. 'Police,' she said, then waited. 'I'd like to report an attempted murder. Yes, that's right. A big fat attempted murder. Actually, scrap that. There was a murder, but that happened a year or so ago.' She wandered away. 'Apparently it's a long story …'

Stirling left her to it. Lisette could take care of the drama for the moment. He had another to fix. They were all in for a drawn-out day and it could be hours before he got another chance.

He faced Darcy. 'I'm sorry.'

She regarded him with a frown. 'What for? Mal was the one with the gun.'

'Not for that, although I'd rather you hadn't gone through that either.' He cupped his palm around her face. Her mascara had run a little and her hair was a windblown mess. Completely un-Darcy-like, but to Stirling she looked adorable. 'For hurting you.'

'Silly boy,' she said, placing her fingers over his chest. 'You don't have to apologise. I knew you didn't mean it. You were trying to protect me.'

'Not very well.' He stroked his thumb over her cheek, amazed by her easy forgiveness. By her unique, precious Darcy-ness. 'How did you know?'

'Because, my handsome man,' she patted his chest, 'being cruel is not you. Your makeup is to save people, not harm them. Especially those you care about. Your behaviour was so out of character I knew something was terribly wrong. The only thing that made sense was that you were pushing me away because you were scared for me.'

He swallowed, aware of how lucky he was to have found her. 'I wanted to keep you safe.'

'You did.'

'Not like I should have.' Stirling's throat thickened as he remembered how close she'd come to harm. 'Why didn't you stop when I told you to?' He huffed a breath and shook her a little. 'You could have been killed.'

'But I wasn't, and neither were you. And for that,' she slung her arms around his neck, their jackets squelching as she pushed closer, 'I am extremely grateful. Now, if you don't mind, I've had a trying few days and require a very long, very soothing kiss.'

Chapter Forty-Three

Darcy couldn't stop holding Stirling's hand. Not just holding but gripping it so that every centimetre of her skin fused with his. She and Stirling were huddled at the kitchen table, cups of tea close by and the fresh batch of seduction scones she'd brought going to waste on a plate in the middle. No one was hungry. Shock, she supposed, and anxiety over what lay ahead.

After an initial flurry of conversation and explanation from Stirling of what he'd learned and been through, they'd eased into quiet disbelief. Shiloh was by the sink, half an eye on the room, half an eye on outside, as though any moment she expected Mal to come marching through the overgrown garden and throw himself at the window like a vampire risen from the grave.

Shiloh had no qualms agreeing with Stirling that Mal was a murderer. After shooting a pair of loving dogs, forcing Dougal to put a noose around his neck would hardly pose a challenge. Darcy, however, was still struggling to reconcile Mal's actions with the man she knew. How could he kill his best friend and brother? Yes, Dougal had behaved appallingly, his father even worse, but that didn't mean Dougal needed to die, and Stirling most certainly did not.

And to think Darcy had been alone at Westwind with Mal. It was enough to give a girl the heebie-jeebies. Something she didn't need on top of the shock she'd already suffered.

Lisette was just as antsy. If she wasn't messaging on her phone, she was jerking her head to the mudroom door at even the most minor of creaks, of which there were plenty. Though the rain squalls were easing, the wind remained turbulent, bashing the walls and roof and causing the house to moan and groan in protest.

A pop from the range fire had everyone jumping.

Lisette was the first to laugh, hand dancing around her throat. 'God, my nerves are shot, and there I was thinking how awesome I'd been.'

'Same here,' Shiloh admitted, surprising Darcy. Until now, her sister had appeared to take the drama in her stride.

Darcy supposed she'd been putting on the same unflappable front herself. She may have acted brave, but every second of her audacity had been faked. From the moment she'd spotted Mal with the gun, terror had overtaken her body. Even now she still quivered in the aftermath. Part of it was fear at what could have been, part was exhaustion. It seemed adrenaline combined with pure outrage could steal a lot from a girl.

Both reactions may have left her drained but Darcy had a lot to thank for their rush. Without them, she might have succumbed to panic. Witnessing Stirling at Mal's mercy had made her belly rise so fast it felt like it was trying to crash through her chest and out her throat, dragging her airless lungs with it. Yet she'd marched on, powered by fury that this man—this weak, pathetic excuse of a human—could even think of stealing from her the person she loved. Stirling mattered more than her fear. And she had heart enough for them both.

Besides, she was confident Mal didn't have the guts to shoot her. People like him were cowards.

'I think we're all a bit on edge,' she replied.

'It's normal,' said Stirling, addressing Lisette and then Shiloh. 'You've been through a trauma. There's always going to be an aftershock. The police should have counsellors that can help. I'll ask for you.' He looked at Darcy. 'You'll need to talk to someone too.'

'We all will,' she said, tapping a finger on Stirling's nose.

Lisette shoved her phone on the table and crossed her arms. 'I just wish they'd hurry up.'

So did Darcy. It felt like ages since Lisette had called the police. She let out a sigh. Stirling squeezed her hand and smiled, encouragement and more in his gaze. Darcy's heart gave a long slow somersault. He truly was the loveliest of men. That Mal could have so easily ripped Stirling from her life forever made Darcy want to wrap herself around him and cover every inch of his precious body in her protective adoring embrace. Perhaps later she'd do that, but for now she needed to be strong. For Stirling. For Lisette and Shiloh. For herself. They still had a lot to get through.

As if summoned, a new noise began to undermine the wind—the rev of engines and tyres on gravel.

Shiloh left her post and strode for the front room, returning seconds later. 'They're here.'

Darcy's pent-up body slumped but not in relaxation. Stirling had warned them they'd be in for a long day of interviews and questions. The ordeal of reliving that awful period at the shed was about to begin and she didn't relish the idea one bit.

'You'll be fine,' said Stirling, as though reading her mind.

He was smiling but fatigue and something more visceral etched his face. She thought it might be guilt. For what, she couldn't fathom, unless it was for letting Mal escape, but he'd had the gun. What else could they have done?

'I was just going to say the same thing to you.' Darcy forced her own smile. 'Will you be all right?'

He shrugged. 'I imagine so. Can't see it being any worse than a normal debriefing.'

Which didn't sound fun to Darcy but she supposed Stirling was used to that kind of thing. She lifted her chin. It was time for fortitude. 'Best get on with it then. After another kiss, of course.'

With a chuckle and a murmured 'of course' in reply, Stirling bent to oblige.

As predicted, after an initial spurt of activity, the remainder of the day dragged. Apart from their interviews, there was little to do except watch, make cups of tea and speculate on Mal's motives, means and whereabouts. In deference to Stirling, none of the girls touched the subject of Benjamin's reprehensible behaviour and Dougal's was brought up rarely. His ancestors hovered though, unmentionable ghosts curdling the air. Darcy prayed that Stirling didn't feel their stigma. He was nothing like them. Nothing.

Lisette was excused first, her nerves settled thanks to the police presence and her usual bouncy self back on show. Shiloh stomped off at lunchtime, two scones in her hand and Lucy at her heels, mutterings about neglected sheep trailing in her wake. Darcy had no doubt there were sheep to attend but she'd also overheard her sister answering a call from a desperate-sounding Leo. Shiloh's softening voice had left her feeling thrilled that at least something good might come from this horrid situation.

As for Darcy's own phone, it had been buzzing nonstop, making her regret she hadn't left it in the car. But she'd had to ring her mum to tell her they were fine and not to fret, and that she would be unable to ferry her to her physio appointment that afternoon. From the moment she'd hung up, the screen seemed to flash every few minutes until, finally, Darcy lost patience and turned the rotten thing off. News of Mal's crimes would spread soon enough without her input.

Though Stirling had said she may as well go home and rest, Darcy demurred. Home would only put her at the mercy of the town, and she refused to leave Stirling. He'd been with the police for ages, going over some sort of report he'd compiled on Mal. Someone had to watch out for him.

When the officer in charge requested a visit to Xavier's memorial, Darcy swapped her heels for the scarlet rubber boots she kept in the Mini for emergencies and insisted on joining them. Just as well. Stirling's weariness began to manifest in full on the trek back. His eyes hollowed even further and his limp became more pronounced, and she agonised over how much sleep he'd been getting over the last few days. Likely far less than her, which was saying something. As soon as they'd returned to the kitchen Darcy handed him water and two painkillers and stood over him until he swallowed both.

To make matters worse, there had been no news on Mal, and with every passing hour, Darcy's fear that he might get away intensified. For Stirling's sake, that couldn't be allowed to happen. Without Mal's capture, he would never know peace.

Close to four o'clock, just as Darcy's hopes were rising that Stirling would be free, a woman called Phillipa Tan turned up, and he was commandeered for yet another interview.

To everyone's relief, the weather was at last showing signs of clearing. Needing air, Darcy donned her red rubber boots again, rugged herself up in one of Stirling's coats and took a turn around the front garden. Westwind was messy with small branches, pine cones and needles brought down in the wind. Windrows of detritus mounded the front steps and clogged the empty fountain.

She was pulling random branches from its basin when a motorbike revved up the drive, another vehicle coasting behind. Not recognising either, she ignored them and continued with her task. Police were manning the gate, keeping sightseers at bay, and she doubted Shiloh or Lisette were making a return.

Except neither vehicle veered towards the other police cars. Instead, they pulled up alongside the fountain.

Gavin was first out of his car, Toby not far behind, dragging off his helmet and ruffling his flat hair.

Darcy let out a choked 'Oh', her eyes prickling at the wonderfulness of friends. Stirling had met with trouble and they'd come to the rescue without hesitation. That he could attract such loyalty was yet another sign of Stirling's decency.

'I am so glad you're here,' she said, opening her arms. 'It's been awful.'

The group hug was as heartfelt and warm as she expected. Darcy pulled away, wiping under her eyes. 'Oh, look at me, all weepy. How silly.'

'Hey,' said Toby slinging an arm around her shoulders and jiggling her. 'You've had a shit day. It's allowed.'

Perhaps it was, but surrendering to weepiness was not a part of Darcy's makeup and she needed to stay strong for Stirling. She sniffed and straightened her shoulders.

'Thank you so much for coming. How on earth did you get through?'

'Charm.' At Darcy's look, Toby laughed. 'I made them ring. Took three bloody goes before he answered. I thought they were going to strip-search Gav here but that's what you get for looking dodgy.'

'Oi,' said Gav, pulling on the hems of his tatty shirt to smooth it over his paunch. 'It was my day off. I didn't know some maniac was planning to attack Stirling.'

Toby's laughter faded as he regarded the house. 'How is he?'

'Tired,' said Darcy. 'Stoic. Being far more patient and polite than they deserve.'

Toby rubbed at his sweaty hair. 'I should have believed him. He kept telling me something was off with Dougal's death. Then when he started on about Mal, I thought the house was getting to him, you know? That he was spending too much time alone with his thoughts. I told him he should talk to someone.' His voice turned gravelly. 'I should have believed in him. I should have stayed and helped.'

Darcy touched Toby's arm, understanding his guilt. She'd done similar, letting Mal sneak the PTSD idea into her head. Poor Stirling. How alone he must have felt. 'You're not to blame.'

'No one is, except that maniac solicitor,' said Gavin, anger in his voice. 'If I get my hands on that bastard …' He shook his head as if he couldn't believe what he'd be capable of.

'You and me both, man,' said Toby. 'Any news on that front?'

Darcy shook her head and twisted her hands.

'Crap,' said Toby, looking again at Westwind. The front of the house was alight with the lowering sun, highlighting its poultice pimple and broken finials. What had once been pretty was now ugly. He let out a long sigh. 'Poor bugger. As if he hasn't been through enough.' He jerked his head. 'Come on. Time to break up the party, and Gav here's probably hanging out for a beer. I know I am. I'd bet my left testicle Felix is too.'

Darcy let the men go ahead to give them a moment alone. She wandered around the fountain and stared at the ranges, rubbing her arms. What a truly horrid day. Yet it, like every day before it and to come, would pass soon enough and life would resume.

She just hoped it would be the right life.

By the time Darcy reached the courtyard, Stirling, Toby and Gav were engaged in a hearty, back-thumping group love-in. Stirling's fierce hugs revealed his joy and relief at seeing his friends. He held them both with his eyes closed and his mouth and brow screwed tight. Gone was the controlled lionheart. In its place was a vulnerable man who needed his mates just like any other.

Stirling's eyes sprang open at the soft clomp of Darcy's boots on the paving. He smiled, gaze glistening with gratitude. She smiled back, blinking as her own tear ducts responded to the depth of his emotion.

With a manly clearing of throats, Gav and Toby released Stirling. Darcy took her cue to head for the door. There were beers and food to set out.

Phillipa was in the mudroom, her phone loose in her hand, observing the reunion.

'Any news?' asked Darcy.

Phillipa's attention remained on the men. 'Not yet.'

Darcy would have walked on but the intensity in the other woman's expression gave her pause. Her hackles rose.

'Is there a problem?' she asked, barely able to keep the snap from her voice. As far as Darcy was concerned, this woman's involvement with Stirling was over for the day.

Phillipa seemed to startle. She looked at Darcy and her expression mellowed. 'Only that we haven't caught Mal yet.'

'You will though?'

'We will.' Phillipa returned her attention to the chattering men. 'Your boyfriend's an extraordinary man.'

Darcy followed her line of sight, her chest swelling with pride. 'He is.' She swallowed back yet another lump of emotion. 'He truly is.'

Best of all, he was hers.

Chapter Forty-Four

Each step felt like a mini mountain as Stirling slowly climbed Westwind's grand staircase. Darcy was at his side, her silky hand in his and her steps as tired. It had been a never-ending day, and though Stirling's tread was weary, his mind still chafed with thoughts of Mal and how close today had come to disaster.

Gavin had left just before dark, promising he was a call away should they need anything, anything at all. Lisette had phoned at five thirty to announce she would bring out dinner—a casserole pinched from her mum's freezer—and if Darcy could whip up some mashed potatoes they'd be set. Now Lisette and Toby were downstairs, ostensibly watching television while they polished off a bottle of merlot, but Stirling knew it was their way of giving Stirling and Darcy space and peace.

He closed the door and stood with his back to it until Darcy turned around. 'You saved my life today.'

She opened her mouth as if to speak then seemed to lose her words and shook her head instead.

Stirling knew the feeling. He was struggling to find the right words too. She was the second woman he'd loved who'd risked her life for him. God, he hoped he was worth it.

'I don't know what else to say except thank you.'

Her tender smile made his heart contract. 'I don't need anything else. You being here, being safe, being with me,' she touched her heart, 'is all I care about.'

Darcy stepped towards him. Her clothes were rumpled, her hair still dishevelled despite her efforts to tidy it, and her makeup badly smudged by fatigue and tears, yet she was as gorgeous as he'd ever seen her. More so, because she was lit inside by something more beautiful than her clothes, hair or makeup could ever be.

She regarded him with her head slightly tilted and a finger to her chin. 'What did I say from the start, hmm?'

She was easing the moment by being sexy and funny and Stirling loved her even more for it. 'I don't know. Something about being invested.'

'Correct. And there's one thing you need to know—I'm a girl who takes great care of her investments.' She cupped both hands around his jaw and drew her face close so he could catch every bright sparkle in her gaze. 'Now, my handsome man, it's been a very long, very horrible day, and I think you need some taking care of. By me. The woman who loves you.'

The woman who loves you. His heart throbbed. He did not deserve this, but he'd take it. Because he loved her in return.

'What did you have in mind?'

'Well,' she said, her voice husky, 'I was thinking maybe a long … hot …' her mouth was so close to Stirling's her breath feathered his lips, '… shower to begin with.'

His hands fitted her waist. 'Followed by?'

She brought her lips to the very edge of his. 'The tenderest of cuddles, before, finally …' She drew out the words on a whisper. 'An even longer, even more delicious … sleep.'

Stirling laughed and kissed her with all the energy his exhausted body could muster. Finally, he pulled back and pressed his forehead against hers, his heart floating so high it had to be visible in his eyes. 'I love you, gorgeous girl.'

'I should hope so.' She tightened her arms around her neck. 'And you can tell me that often, if you like. I can assure you I won't get sick of it.'

Stirling wouldn't either.

❧

News came with the sunrise. Stirling had set his phone to silent with the vibrate on and he wouldn't have woken if not for its frantic buzzing on the side table.

He kissed Darcy's shoulder, rolled over and snatched it up. Phillipa. Immediately his pulse began to quicken.

'We got him,' she said after minimal preamble.

'Where?' asked Stirling, putting his hand out to Darcy as she stirred and began to sit up.

'South coast of New South Wales. He was getting ready to meet a yacht that was heading to Sydney. Not sure of their connection but we'll find out.'

Stirling had no doubt she would. After a few more words, he hung up and rolled to face Darcy.

'Well?' she asked, but he could tell from her expression she'd already guessed.

'Mal's been caught. You're safe. We're all safe.'

For a long pause she said nothing, then she blew out a whistling breath before letting a slow, delighted smile spread over her face. 'Now that's what I call a good start to the day.'

Stirling crept his hand under the quilt and traced it over her hip. 'Do you now?'

She caught on immediately, performing a hand-creep of her own that had Stirling's lust rousing like a lion. 'Hmm. I suppose it could be improved on.'

'You think?'

'I know.' She curled her leg over his. 'Come hither, handsome man. This lady feels a great need to tend to her investment.'

Chapter Forty-Five

Stirling took the long way around Grassmoor. He didn't want attention today, and even though almost a fortnight had passed since the showdown with Mal at Westwind, he remained a subject of great interest.

It seemed everyone wanted a piece of him. The sins of his father had been forgiven and so, apparently, had he. Even Joanne at the cafe had waved to him the other day when he'd ridden past to visit Darcy in her workshop. Though it gave him some satisfaction, the rawness of all he'd been through remained.

Toby had promised Eva would help him deal with his issues. Stirling knew it was the right thing to do, the *necessary* thing, but it was hard to shake that feeling of weakness.

He'd do it though. For Darcy.

It was a good day for a ride. Spring was flourishing in earnest and the sky was a magnificent blue. The rain from two weeks ago had left the paddocks lush, and the glossy, contented stock were nose down, making the most of the pickings. Engine noise from the Ducati drew none from their grazing.

Stirling eased down the throttle and turned onto the cemetery road. He parked outside—he didn't want to disturb any mourners and the walk would give him time to think about what he wanted to say.

He grabbed the tools he'd stashed in the panniers and, using Benjamin's ostentatious monument as his guide, wound a trail to Dougal's grave.

From the moment he entered the row, Stirling could see something was off. That someone had been fiddling with Dougal's resting place. With every tread his gut clenched tighter until finally he stopped at the foot of the grave, his throat closing over in disbelief and then gratitude. And ever so slowly, the coil inside him began to unwind.

There were flowers. Some wilted, some still fresh-looking. Someone had even left a potted rose. But the most startling change was in the polished, sparkling granite. Where previously an ugly brick had desecrated the inscription, now Dougal's epitaph ended as it should: Rest in Peace.

Stirling lifted his head to the sky and blinked. Grassmoor had come around. Maybe not everyone, but enough. Locals who'd recognised how badly done by Dougal had been and wanted to correct the error. Who had thought that a son, even an unknown, unacknowledged one, deserved better for his father's grave.

Dougal had been far from a saint but from what Stirling had discovered, he was a decent man at heart. A man Stirling would have liked to have known. Who he *should* have known, had Stirling been less judgemental himself.

He set the now unneeded tools down and sat alongside them, facing the grave.

'We both had our failings, hey, Dad?'

Dad. The word felt weird in his mouth but calling him Dougal didn't feel right either. Dougal was no longer a stranger, a man who

Stirling knew only via his own genetics. The weeks at Westwind had shown him as a person. A man who liked old head-banger music and comfortable rural clothes. Who'd dreamed of doing something good for the community. Who was well liked, respected and admired. Who had loved his dogs. Who had felt remorse and shame for his wrongdoings. Who had tried to put them right.

Because of him, Stirling knew who he was now too. A good man, maybe even a courageous one. A man lucky enough to have a second chance at love and happiness, and who'd defend both with his life. A man who might never fly again but who had the resolve to forge a new path. A man who could and would find help to deal with his demons, because he wasn't weak anymore. He was strong. Strong with Darcy's love and faith.

A man who'd found his way out of uncertainty to a future full of light and hope.

Stirling ran his fingers over the engraved letters of his father's name and thought again of all he'd wanted to say. Except that none of it mattered anymore. Mal had been caught, his scheme unravelled. Dougal had been avenged. None of that would bring his father back.

Stirling gathered the tools and stood with his head bent for a moment. Then he smiled wryly as he realised the few words he did need to say.

'Rest in peace, Dad. Rest in peace.'

And with his duty done, Stirling walked away.

Epilogue

Stirling stood at the edge of the fountain fiddling with his father's watch, his gaze locked on Westwind's grand front entrance. The ugly poultices that had once pimpled the facade were long gone and only faint traces of the screaming, blood-like graffiti remained. Now the pink sandstone glowed in the late afternoon sun, peaceful and pretty.

There were still splashes of red, but they were from the pots of red and white flowers cascading along the verandah and down the stairs—Darcy's chosen wedding colours.

He fingered the red and white boutonnière attached to the lapel of his jacket and earned a swat from Toby.

'You know the rules,' grouched his best man. 'No touching.'

Stirling sighed and rolled his father's watch back and forth on his wrist. Its worn brown band didn't match his charcoal suit but Darcy had convinced him to wear it, to carry a little piece of Dougal with him today. Now that he was standing here waiting for his bride, Stirling was glad he had. He'd finally googled the Latin inscription on the back and learned *Meliora sequimur* meant 'towards better things'. Towards better things was where he was going. Where they were both going. It fitted.

He glanced at the wedding guests, perched on rows of white chairs in a semicircle surrounding the tinkling fountain and facing Westwind. Beyond them, down the track where he'd almost lost his life—again—stood a large marquee where the reception would be held. More pots of red and white flowers decorated its entrance.

Darcy. She'd saved him in so many ways. From bleeding out when he'd stupidly ripped his leg open exploring a property he knew nothing about. From being shot in the chest by Mal when Stirling's only option left was to charge the man. From his heartache and misdirection when he didn't know who he was anymore.

He owed her so much. And today he was going to marry her. The thought made him want to beat his chest like a gorilla.

His mother twinkled a wave at him from the front row. Stirling grinned back at her, still thrilled she'd made the journey. Amanda had arrived two weeks ago and had been enjoying herself since, getting to know her future daughter-in-law and family, and Stirling's new friends. She sat alongside Darcy's mum, who was much healthier and happier these days, and proudly nursing her grandson on her knee. Little baby Jason had brought joy to everyone. Though neither Shiloh nor Leo would confirm nor deny it, Darcy remained convinced Jason had been conceived the night of Mal's escape. After all, the primal need for sex after a life-threatening situation wasn't unusual. Certainly, it had been a hastily arranged wedding and Jason's birth date timed out to the day.

They may have had a shaky start, but Stirling counted Leo as a friend these days. In fact, Stirling had made more friends than he expected. Work helped. The small team of men and women he worked with running scenic helicopter flights along the dramatic south-western Victorian coastline and Gariwerd and the Grampians

National Park were decent sorts, and he enjoyed the job. Mostly. Some tourists could be idiots but the majority were thrilled to be up in the air and the scenery was stunning. The only downer was the travel and nights away from Darcy, though he'd cut back when she got pregnant. Which he hoped would be soon. God knows they'd been doing it enough.

He checked his watch. Five minutes late. Not too bad by wedding standards, he supposed. Shiloh had been fifteen minutes late to her own ceremony, thanks to morning sickness combined with nerves. Fortunately, the clouds of yesterday had drifted east and today Westwind was bathed in glorious sunshine. Soft music piped from speakers along the verandah and mingled with birdsong and the chatter of the surrounding guests.

Gav grabbed his shoulder. 'Hang in there, mate. She'll turn up.'

Stirling huffed a laugh. 'Yeah, she will. She has a new dress to show off.'

When Stirling had asked him to be groomsman, Gavin had waved him off, saying he was too old, but Stirling had insisted. Their unlikely friendship had been cemented in the many hours they'd spent restoring the Indian, and these days, when time permitted, the Buick. It was also Gav who'd unwittingly sown the seeds of Stirling's doubt over his father's death, leading eventually to justice for Dougal and a hefty jail term for Mal. Like wearing his father's watch, having Gav by his side at Westwind felt important and right.

Shiloh was the first to poke her head around the front door. She grinned and gave Stirling a thumbs up before ducking back inside.

'Looks like we're on,' said Toby. He slapped Stirling on the back. 'Good luck.'

The music changed. The gathered guests cocked their heads towards the speakers, frowns appearing on their faces before breaking into wry smiles, chuckles and nods as they recognised Darcy's choice of wedding march: Elvis Presley's 'Can't Help Falling in Love'.

Stirling laughed as he, Toby, Gav and Leo shuffled into position—he should have known she'd choose vintage music.

His laughter faded as the door opened fully and Olympia stepped out, radiant in a scarlet fit and flare dress that made her look frighteningly mature. Stirling glanced at Alexander. His back was straight, his chest out, chin up. The man had every right to be proud. Olympia was growing into a lovely young woman.

Alexander and Olympia had flown in only two days ago and apart from dinner on the night of their arrival, Stirling had barely spent time with either of them. Olympia had dress fittings and wedding preparations, while Alexander was in heavy negotiations with local authorities about the Grassmoor bush nursing centre project he was helping to fund.

The district was abuzz with the news, with none more thrilled than the Sloanes, who understood only too well how much benefit a centre would bring. No longer would locals like Darcy's mum and family have to endure long drives for care, and the community would have another hub around which to rally. Alexander was even demanding a bus as part of the deal.

A small mean part of Stirling wished he could be a fly on the wall when Mal learned Dougal's legacy was being granted, but the trial had been ordeal enough. He wasn't going to waste any more time on his uncle. The man deserved nothing, especially after his behaviour in court.

Mal could have pleaded guilty, saved them a lot of stress and heartache, but he'd denied all wrongdoing, despite the evidence against him. It was as Gavin had said in the beginning, fraudsters never lost faith in their ability to get away with their crimes. And Mal was as narcissistic as they came.

At first, Stirling had been furious at the man for putting Darcy and himself through such an ordeal. Worse were the sly smirks Stirling's way when Mal thought no one could see. The superiority made his blood boil. As for Mal's assertion that Stirling's PTSD was to blame for his paranoid fantasies … that had bitten hard.

It had taken a while, but thanks to Darcy's compassion and Eva's counselling, he learned to let it go. What mattered was justice. Though the money had yet to be recovered, and—according to Phillipa—was unlikely ever to be, Mal's conviction and long penalty had given them the closure they needed. Stirling hoped jail was the hell to which Mal had tried to sentence his father.

Lisette was next onto the verandah, dressed also in scarlet and a large red stone dotting her nose. She gave a vigorous wave to everyone before joining Olympia.

Toby let out a low whistle. 'Bow chicka wow-wow.'

Gav snorted and tried to cover his laughter with a cough. Stirling smiled and shook his head at Toby. For a couple who continued to insist their relationship was nothing more than friends with benefits, Toby and Lisette sure didn't act like it.

Finally, Shiloh stepped out. She smoothed her dress, clearly self-conscious and wary of her high heels, and lined up alongside the others. With a glance from Lisette, they headed down the steps as a group and paused at the bottom.

Stirling swallowed. It was time. Any second Darcy would appear on her father's arm. His soon-to-be wife and the woman he adored.

He squinted, trying to see into the shadowed doorway. He caught a flash from the photographer's camera and suddenly Darcy was at the top of the steps, lit bright and gorgeous and beaming and beautiful.

Gasps and oohs and ahhs rippled from the guests.

Her gaze found his and locked, her big brave heart shining in her eyes. Stirling's chest tightened even further. How lucky he was. How blessed. If not for a twist of fate, his and Darcy's paths might never have crossed. Now here they were, about to promise themselves to each other and embark upon another phase in their lives.

Her father murmured something and Darcy nodded. Slowly the bridal party made their way to the fountain.

Towards him and their future together.

'You look amazing,' said Stirling when she was close enough, unable to stop feasting on her.

Like her choice of music, her dress was pure Darcy—a glorious rockabilly-inspired creation comprising a knee-length full tulle skirt that made her look like a fairy princess, and a boned halter-neck bodice that showed off her beautiful shoulders, silken skin and Marilyn Monroe figure. Her hair was up in a loose pile with a few teased strands framing her face. Her mouth, as always, was a luscious, very kissable red.

His gorgeous girl.

'You're looking rather handsome yourself,' she said, bumping his shoulder. 'But you always look handsome to me.' She smiled at the celebrant. 'Shall we do this?'

'If you're ready.' The celebrant raised an inquiring eyebrow at Stirling.

'Never been readier,' he said.

'Then let's go.' Darcy took Stirling's hand and smiled up at him as 'Can't Stop Falling in Love' faded out and only birdsong and the ruffle of trees remained.

Though his heart was on the amazing woman beside him, Stirling couldn't resist a final glance at Westwind. The sun had lowered further, tinting the sandstone with shades of apricot and peach and rimming the cast-iron lacework balconies of the upper floors in gold.

He remembered the strange feelings he'd experienced those first few times he visited. The way his body had thrilled with the sight of that glowing stone and romantic architecture. The pride and ownership he'd felt for a place he never knew existed.

How he'd thought he heard words whispered on the wind as he'd stared in disbelief and wonder at the villa's uniquely coloured walls. And how he'd imagined the words as 'welcome home' when he didn't know what home was and doubted very much that Westwind would be it.

Funny how life could turn out.

His gaze returned to Darcy. She smiled back at him, her expression loaded with adoration, and his heart throbbed with the intensity of his love for her and the anticipation of their life ahead.

Westwind might be beautiful, but he understood now that true belonging rested with Darcy.

Acknowledgements

The Grazier's Son would never have been completed without the help and encouragement of some very dear friends.

It all started well. I'd been nursing this idea for a few years and was ridiculously excited about it. *The Grazier's Son* had everything I love — a great hero, a beautiful setting, a mystery and a love story. Unfortunately, it didn't have a heroine, and it took some time for Darcy to come along. Once she did, I knew I had the makings of a really good book. All I had to do was get the words down.

Unfortunately, life had other plans. Illness stole my creative brain and between remissions and relapses it took quite a long time to come back. Some days I managed words. Some days all I could do was sit at my computer and sob. Progress came at a snail's pace. There were more times than I can count when I truly thought I should give writing away.

Step in some special people. Namely author buddies Michelle Douglas, Annie West, Monique McDonell, Anna Campbell, Jennie Jones and Janette Paul (Jaye Ford), along with my Newcastle Romance Writers group (especially the Thursday morning Zoom sprint ladies) and the Hunter Romance Writers. It was their support, advice and encouragement that bolstered my flagging belief and kept me going, even when I wanted to chuck it all in. I cannot thank them enough. They are brilliant friends and the best of people.

Also thanks to my agent Clare Forster of Curtis Brown Australia. Clare was the first person to read *The Grazier's Son* and her enthusiasm for the manuscript did wonders for my confidence. After all that time, it was amazing to hear that the book had legs.

Thank you also to the team at Harlequin Australia, including publisher Rachael Donovan and senior editor Laurie Ormond. And a huge thanks to Di Blacklock, who I was thrilled to work with again. Di is an incredible editor who might make me work hard but seriously knows her stuff. She cut my sprawling manuscript down to size and transformed it into the page-turner I'd hoped for. Painful, yes, but oh so worth it.

And the cover design team. Wowsers, did you excel yourselves this time with *The Grazier's Son*'s cover. It is my best yet. Thank you.

Most of all, thank you to my personal hero, Jim. Sorry for putting you through so much worry and icky bits. You were my rock through all the awfulness, but we got there. Phew!